PRIVATE CUMMINGS

a Novel

PETE McGINTY

GRANDVIEW
PRESS

AUTHOR NOTE

In the pages that follow, you will find a narrative that harkens back to a different time and place, one rich in history and culture, yet tainted by the regrettable biases and language of its time. I believed it was necessary to authentically convey the spirit and nuances of that historical period, even if they may fall short of the values we uphold today. It is my hope that you will journey through these pages with an open heart, recognizing that we can only truly move forward when we understand where we've been.

PROLOGUE

September 24, 2003

THIS WILL BE MY FINAL JOURNAL ENTRY. I feel fortunate leaving on my own terms, having lived a full life with no regrets. It's time. What a gift it has been to spend my final days with Jonathon, whose company stirred a sensory imagination that was quite unexpected. I was a forty-seven-year-old recluse when we met in 1973. He was a wide-eyed thirteen-year-old boy. In recalling that visit some thirty years ago, he was effusive in describing my impact on him, having helped him cross from innocence to purpose. His impact on me wasn't fully realized until this week. For he has helped me move in the opposite direction, providing me a bridge to travel back in time, to my own days of innocence when I was a young boy, whose only purpose was to be joyful, push limits, and stay out of trouble.

It's the best way to die, I think, calmed by the sense of innocence, the feeling that nothing in life is serious enough to worry about when the good Lord takes you. No one wants to die young, of course, but how precious to die with the goodness and purity youth provides. In a few hours it will be morning and he will relieve Nathan and take his turn dropping morphine under my tongue, putting a fresh, cool washcloth on my forehead, and holding the straw to my lips so I can sip my ginger ale with a lemon twist. I'm looking forward to what likely will be our last conversation while I'm still able to convey my thoughts with clarity.

I've got a lot to say.

HANK

CHAPTER

1

I SQUINTED AT THE DARK, olive-drab, gabardine wool coat adorned with medals, and pressed slacks that Margaret hung on the back of the closet door. I began dreading the discomfort I was sure to experience, the rough wool grating against my tender skin, as temperatures were expected to reach over ninety degrees. The humidity from the dew on the lawn glistened and steamed like a sauna. As the parade route traveled south down Route 1, the rising sun from the east was sure to heat the day quickly. I would be sitting in the back seat of the convertible Buick Roadmaster, on the left side of the car so I could wave to the gawking crowd with my good hand.

The 1945 Memorial Day Parade was my first public appearance since returning home from a four-month convalescence in the burn center at Brooke Army Medical Center in Fort Sam Houston, Texas. The Grayson town folk were curious, wanting to be the first to witness their hometown hero on display. They'd all surely seen pictures of me in the *Grayson Gazette*, and some had likely seen my thirty-second profile in the WWII Home Front newsreel, *America's Call to Arms*.

As I peered at the medals and ribbons that hung from my coat, I reminisced about when I was a young boy on top of my daddy's shoulders on the corner of Route 1 and Main, straining against the sun to see the marching soldiers who served in WWI. The crippled ones—as they were called—were perched in chairs or on beds of wagons pulled by trucks or horses. I recalled seeing the local Confederate Civil War hero Major Bernard Johnson, who valiantly fought the north in the Battle of Aiken in 1865, walking alone, supported only by a cane. He must have been ninety years old, which meant I was only three or four. But the memory is clear as day.

"It's time to get ready, my darling," Margaret said as she cracked the bedroom door open. "The general is here, and your car is waiting."

General Thomas Mackey, a war hero himself from WWI, represented the Kentucky Department of Veterans Affairs, and was the man responsible for anointing me the grand marshal. It was reportedly quite a feather in his cap to lure me to the honor. And, I'll admit, I didn't make it easy on him. All the reasons I resisted when he first approached me were surfacing again, and I began to feel sick to my stomach. It wasn't the discomfort of heat that distressed me; it was being put on display like a poor deformed soul at a freak show in a traveling circus. Mackey, Margaret, my parents, my sister, and the rest could say all day long that the people were eager to honor me with praise and love to show their deepest gratitude for the sacrifice I made on their behalf. Is that why I had stared at the old veterans, unable to walk, some unable to see, propped up on wagon beds as they made the southerly turn from Main to Route 1? Not if my memory serves me correctly. I leered at them because of the dreadful condition they were in.

"Come on, dear," Margaret patiently said. "The general is waiting." She helped me up and assisted in pulling off my undershirt, which was stuck to the gauze that covered the still-oozing wound on my back. She changed the bandage and helped me into fresh undergarments. I still couldn't pull my boxers up because of the lack of grip on the only two fingers and thumb that remained on my left hand. My right hand was now a stump. Nor could I yet straighten my left arm due to the tightness of scar tissue. I couldn't hold myself to go the bathroom, or even wipe. She held out my crisp shirt and gingerly threaded my arms through the sleeves. I rested on her shoulders for balance as she guided my legs into the slacks. She buttoned the shirt and buckled my belt. She pulled the compression socks over what was left of my feet and slipped them into my new shoes with custom made orthotic contraptions that filled the space where my toes used to be. She draped me into my wool coat and guided the ribbons and medals to hang neatly against the fabric. She secured my sunglasses with a rubber band around the back of my head, as I had no ear cartilage to steady them. The left lens of my glasses was prescription strength which afforded me limited sight. The right lens was blackened, which didn't matter anyway since it covered my eye patch. She placed an army cap on my bald head.

"Private Cummings," the general said, "You look like the finest soldier I've ever laid eyes on. Margaret, he is still one handsome fellow."

"I married well, didn't I General Mackey?" Margaret responded.

"And, by the way Private Cummings," the general said, "You didn't do too bad yourself."

This much was true, for as scarred and whittled away as I was, Margaret had been my savior. We were only married three months before I shipped off. When she first saw me in the hospital in Fort Sam Houston, I thought she might never visit again. And when she did, I tried to convince her not to. But she kept coming back, acting no different than if I was in for just a bruised ego. Where she got the strength, I'll never know, but it was not something I took for granted. I thanked the good Lord that it was me who was so badly injured facing an unseemly future, for I believed she was dealt a worse hand. And now I found myself totally dependent on her for the simplest of needs.

She was every bit as pretty as the day we met. She had deep brown eyes, accentuated by her matching brown hair that she wore long, sometimes in a ponytail. I used to love the feeling when she'd dangle it across my face, something I could no longer feel due to my scars. Her body was shapely and strong. She was raised on a farm and had the sinew to prove it.

"I don't suppose there is any turning back now is there, General?" I said only half joking.

"Turning back?" the general responded incredulously. "Why would you want to turn back? You are the star of the show. The main event for Christ's sake. Now get your ass in that car and sit up tall and straight, soldier."

It was still difficult to balance on my stubbed feet, the phantom pain in my toes causing me to grimace as the stumps forced against the plastic inserts. I leaned on my cane as Margaret and the general supported me under my arms and helped me down the steps, across the yard, and into the back seat of the convertible.

Margaret nestled in beside me. The general sat proudly in the passenger seat, his displaced pride gushing. The driver never turned to see me, but I saw him gaze at my tormented face in the mirror as we made our way to the front of the parade line. Margaret kept whispering in my ear, "It'll be okay. It'll be okay."

I glanced at the back of the general's thick neck and bulbous head as I felt the stares of people who had come to this carnival to see me for the first time. I could hear them over the ambient sounds of people scurrying around. "There he is, that's him, there's Hank." And then shouting out my name in hopes I would acknowledge them. "Hank, Hank, HANK! Over here!" I breathed deeply, sucking in as much air as my lungs would hold, trying not to hyperventilate.

The car made its way to the front of the line and stopped to wait for the bands, floats, and the rest of the dignitaries to form behind. When the clock struck ten o'clock, the gun salute went off, the Grayson High School band broke into "The Battle Hymn of the Republic," and we lurched forward to a deluge of applause. It wasn't unlike the dozen or so previous parades I'd seen, except I now had a front row seat. For whatever reason, our driver was intent on blasting the Buick's horn incessantly as we guided the cluster of participants behind us. As if they don't see me, I thought. The general handed out tiny American flags and tossed candy to the kids, waving like the grand marshal he patterned himself to be.

"Wonderful, wonderful," he shouted back to me. "Isn't this wonderful?"

A plump lady ran at me and handed me a jar of pickles that Margaret reached over me to secure. "Enjoy them, Hank," she yelled. "Jarred 'em myself with love. Just for you."

As we proceeded, more ladies did the same. Within the first fifteen minutes of the route, I accumulated several jars of pickles at my feet. Margaret reminded me that one of the *Grayson Gazette*'s articles referenced my love for pickles, something that wasn't even true, but so be it. Creative writing. Maybe I would acquire a taste.

Eventually, I became brave enough to raise my hand in a back-and-forth wave like the arm of a metronome, and glance directly at the throngs on either side of the car. They meant well, I was sure. The kids couldn't have known the difference between me and a sideshow at the county fair, but I figured it was something I would need to get used to. "Look at him. Look at that man. What's wrong with him? He doesn't have any fingers. What happened to his nose? Can he still hear without any ears? Hey mister ..."

The sun began to shine directly in my eyes as we turned east onto Main Street, temporarily blinding me. But I was certain I saw him. As I adjusted to the brightness, his image became clearer. He was two or three deep behind a group of kids, not wearing his army fatigues, but sharply dressed in a white shirt and red, white, and blue tie, no jacket. We weren't but twenty feet from each other. He leaned forward and began to raise his hand as if to salute but stopped, instead cupping his hand over his mouth. I could sense him gasp. I strained back to see him as we made the turn, the sun temporarily piercing through the top of my sunglasses. When my eye adjusted, he was gone. As the car moved farther away from the corner, I twisted backward to try to find him.

"Did you see someone?" Margaret asked. "Who was that? Who did you see?"

"No one," I said. "It was no one."

CHAPTER
2

"HAVE YOU THOUGHT ABOUT your future, Private?" the general asked as we gathered in the front room after the parade. He was gracious enough to let me skip the honorary luncheon that followed. Nor did he attend himself. Instead, he joined me, Margaret, my mother and father, and sister in our home to have a chat. He was carrying a message from the Pentagon, he said. It was their hope that I would make the army my career and serve in some yet to be defined ambassador role. "Full salary, benefits, a lifelong post," he declared. "We take care of our own, right? No man left behind."

It was a lot to take in. For the last five months I could only take one day at a time, simply to survive, to make progress, to take one more step, to straighten my limbs one more inch.

"So gracious of the Pentagon," Margaret exclaimed. "Hank, we do need to think about what we're going to do now."

"Something to think about," my father said. "But the offer still stands for the two of you to move in with us. We have an extra bedroom, and we can make do. Think about it, Margaret. It will help lighten your load."

My mind went numb as I listened to them banter about what to do with me, as if I was a helpless infant. What did I want? I wanted to stroll barefoot in the Kentucky meadows, ride horses, fish, hunt, and play pickup ball with my old high school teammates. That's what I wanted. God bless them, though.

"If you'll all forgive me," I said. "I'd like to get some rest. It's been quite a day so far."

"Of course, darling," Margaret said as they all leapt to their feet to help me to my room.

"Please, please," I appealed. "I'm fine. Let me try." I steadied myself on the cane and limped forward to the back room that Margaret had turned into a makeshift bedroom. As I lay down, I could hear the hum of the discussion from the front room but couldn't make out their words. I closed my eyes to try to sleep but saw only the image of him standing on the corner, wondering where he went, wondering if he was still in Grayson. He could have easily blended into the crowd and peered through the mass without being detected. But he didn't. He made himself quite visible. Maybe he was going to salute me. Or give me some signal that he would be back. But he disappeared like a speck of sand through an hourglass. Maybe he panicked at the sight of me.

Eliza gently pushed my door open and peeked in. "Awake?" she whispered. She sat next to me on the bed and said in song, "Henry Juuuunior," causing me to smile. Since we were young, whenever she wanted to show affection for whatever reason—maybe to cajole me into giving her a bite of my candy bar or to persuade me to cover for her when she was late coming home from a date—she would rhythmically sing, stretching it out, 'Henry Juuuuuniorrrr.' My sister had always looked after me as though it was her duty. She was just five years older than me, but she had a wise way about her, an old soul. She had intuition. She would have made a great soldier, I thought.

"Something's bothering you," she said. "The parade was a lot. Too much, wasn't it?"

I simply nodded.

"Why don't you think about Daddy's offer?" Eliza asked. "It's so peaceful up there in the woods. Nobody to bother us. Maybe even if you just come up until you get your health back."

My parents and sister had recently moved to Ohio to find work in the steel mills that were flourishing making the metal for the tanks and jeeps to fulfill the needs of the war. My father was falsely accused of stealing from the cash register at Burton's Lumberyard, where he'd worked for twenty years. The actual thief, who pointed his finger at my father, was the owner's son. Everybody knew the truth, except his daddy. I, too, worked at the yard before I shipped off. Mr. Burton had made a glancing gesture that I could return in some capacity, 'Maybe customer service,' he said.

My father held no mortgage on the family home and fifty-acre property in Grayson, where three generations of Cummings were raised. Though he sold it for far less than market value, he was able to buy a four-acre wooded lot and well-built Amish home in Mansfield, Ohio, for cash. He and Eliza found good work in the mills.

"What about Margaret?" I said. "Her life is here. She'll never leave this place, you know that."

"I ain't thinkin' about what's best for her. It's you I'm thinkin' of."

"I can't sort all this out right now. I'm going to need some time."

"Of course you are," she said. "But it ain't like you don't have options."

"If I stay in the army, maybe there is some job where I could write," I said. "Maybe as a reporter or something. Writing's the only thing I'm good at besides hauling lumber, and I'm not going to be doing that anymore. I can still punch the keys of a typewriter with my finger."

"That's the spirit," she responded. "I just want what's best for you. That's what everybody wants."

"Not General Mackey, I fear. He wants me as his trophy. Grayson's own Medal of Honor recipient. His very own. Do you see the way he gloats over me? It's all about him."

"He's a pompous fat ass," Eliza said, causing me to audibly laugh.

"What's so funny?" my father asked as he and the general poked their heads into my room finding us both trying to suppress our laughter.

"Private," the general began. "I've got to ship out now and get back to Louisville. Think about what I said. There is no rush. We can talk about it in a few weeks if that suits you. Work out the details then. Remember, I'm a phone call away if you need anything. Anything at all."

"Thank you, General," I said, reaching my left hand out to him, a gesture he ignored as he raised his right hand in a firm salute. I responded the best I could, straining to lift my right arm to bring my stump to my forehead.

CHAPTER

3

MANY BOYS QUICKLY ENLISTED in the military after Pearl Harbor, believing it was their duty to defend our country. I wasn't one of them. I was terrified and I don't mind admitting it. This put me at some odds with my father who served in WWI and was as patriotic as they come. But he also saw firsthand the grave results war could produce, even among those lucky enough to return home. We compromised that I would not enlist, but if drafted, would serve accordingly.

I'd met Margaret Hitchcock in high school. She was the only girl I ever dated. The only girl I'd ever kissed. She was two years older than me, but equally naive. Believing my armed service was imminent, we married at the Grayson County Courthouse, followed by a small reception at my parents' house, where we would live for the next three months. Consummating the marriage was awkward, both of us nervous with my parents on the other side of a paper-thin wall.

In June 1944, I received my papers. I did my basic training in Fort Benning, Georgia. It was there that I met Sam Boswell. He was a painter, a Renaissance man, from Knoxville, Tennessee. Only a year older than me, he had lived in Brussels studying under the hand of the great Belgian expressionist, Louis Van Lint. Sam was the only man in our barracks of forty soon-to-be soldiers who seemed more out of place than me. He immediately fascinated me. Quirky, funny, witty.

We met the first day of camp. "What's ya name soldier?" he asked me as we lined up for a drill.

"Cummings," I said. "Hank. You?"

"Boswell, Sam," he said. "How the hell tall are ya, anyway?"

"Six-foot-four," I answered.

"Jeez Louise," he said. "Basketball player, right? You get asked that all the time, I imagine."

"I was, and I do," I said.

"Never good at that game, but I was a decent tennis player in high school."

"Not me," I said. "Have never even picked up a racket."

"I could teach ya. You'd be good with your long arms."

Orders to drop to do push-ups interrupted our conversation. But every spare minute we had, he'd find me.

"Is that a wedding ring?" he asked.

"Yes."

"Must be a sweetheart."

"She is," I said.

"Lucky man," Sam said. "Lucky woman too."

Sam spoke with a certain style that drew me toward him. When he finished a sentence, he would dip his head to one side, give a slight smile with his lips and a subtle squint of his eyes. I found it hard to look away. Strikingly handsome, strong, angular, yet soft facial features. Blond hair, though tightly cropped now, once long and wavy in the picture he showed me. Tall and lanky, but not thin. Lean and defined. I pictured him to be European, yet he still spoke with a charmingly slow Tennessee accent.

"What do you mean, you paint with oal?" I teased him.

"What I said, what don't you understand? Oal's a type of paint," he responded.

"How do you spell it?" I asked, egging him on.

"O I L, oal. Someone needs to light a vocabulary far under your ass," he said.

"Far under my ass?"

"Yes, far, F I R E."

It's not like Kentuckians didn't have our own way of saying things but I never picked up the bluegrass drawl. I couldn't help but tease him. His accent was endearing. We both agreed that Tommy Sensibaugh from Brooklyn had the real accent.

And so it went for days—at breakfast, between drills, at lunch, at dinner, in the barracks. It was good to make a friend. I was painfully shy and timid about meeting new people. Anxious how I might blend in with such a cross section of characters. I was now surrounded by boys and men from every nook and cranny of the country. Big guys, small guys, tough and meek, loud and quiet. I was an introvert. Sam was an extrovert. GIs seemed to quickly find commonalities and form cliques. The East Coast guys hung together. The high school jocks found their place. The negros were segregated in separate barracks. Sam and I stayed close to each other. In time, Calvin Netter and Robert Muncie migrated toward us. A bit later, Bob Lavidge and Tony Wildman found us. Other GIs referred to us as the 'intellects,' because we talked about books, music, and art.

Sam regaled us with stories from Europe, a land that once seemed so far away. Sam was different from the rest of the guys. Smart, worldly, intellectual. He was comfortable in his own skin, no pretense, no concern for what others thought of him. Confident and sure of himself. A bit cocky.

All six of the boys in our clique had things in common that weren't evident in other GIs. We moved with a different rhythm, lighter, more airy, a sway of the arms. There was an elegance to us. We'd be teased, called sissies, fairies, light in the loafers. Our group was referred to as 'fruit salad' who hung out at the 'fruit stand.'

Being surrounded by young men with no women around for twelve weeks brought unexpected behaviors. Lots of GIs got erections in the shower. It wasn't unusual to feel a penis against your buttocks or thigh. Many lost their inhibitions about masturbating and did so in full view of others. In the middle of the night, you could hear bedsprings squeaking. Even the most macho guys would show affection for others. Nude wrestling became a favorite sport, for participants and spectators alike.

The army did their best to screen for homosexuals to prevent them from serving, but with the massive need for troops, they couldn't afford to be overly choosy. Nonetheless, officers kept a close watch over GIs and didn't hesitate to pull someone aside and have them go through a more thorough evaluation.

Lavidge and Wildman both got pulled for further testing. Neither of them returned. One morning, Sam was pulled from the barracks and taken away from camp to be evaluated by a psychologist. He was interrogated, tested, poked, and prodded in an attempt to confirm his sexual orientation. He convinced them he was fervently attracted to women, telling them stories about his European conquests, and showing him a picture he carried with him of a young lady he said was his girl back home. She was actually his sister.

The close relationship Sam and I had developed was obvious to others in the barracks. It wasn't long before I was hauled away for the same evaluation, which didn't last long.

"Do you like girls?" the psychologist asked.

"Of course I do," I answered. "I married one."

"Well, you ought to stay away from that Boswell boy," he said. "He's a little bit funny."

Sam said he sought me out because he knew I was 'like him.' I was drawn to him, his intellect, his creativity, the way he sparked mine. We read the same books. Talked the same language. I believed I had met my best friend, someone who would remain so for the rest of my life.

About eight weeks into camp, we were on a bivouac deep into the woods for four nights. Sam and I buddied up and slept together in a pup tent. The temperatures dropped into the forties. The standard way to keep warm was to lay side-by-side and wrap arms and legs around the other. Bare skin on bare skin produced the warmest body temperatures, so we stripped down to just our boxers and doubled up our sleeping bags into one thick blanket. During our first night, as I lay on my side, Sam cozied up behind me with his groin next to my buttocks. Our legs were intertwined. His arm wrapped around my body. His face close to my neck. I felt his erection and remained still as he slowly rubbed it against me. I didn't respond. He asked if I was okay, and I said I was. I was surprised when I became erect. I was excited in a way I'd never felt before. I didn't stop him. I remained still as he continued to thrust himself more aggressively up and down my buttocks until he orgasmed.

"I'm sorry, I couldn't help it," he said. "Are you sure you're good?"

"I'm good," I said.

"Did you like it?" he asked.

"I don't know," I said.

"I'll help you like it. Just feel me holding you," he said. "We can fall asleep together." We never discussed it. We made love to each other the next three nights.

The concept of a man intimately loving another seemed so foreign to me before I'd met Sam. The unfamiliar chemistry that drew us to each other was unsettling, yet inescapable. Before our nights together in the tent, I could only sense that things between us felt funny. Not natural. I pretended the sexual urges I was feeling were fleeting. But they weren't. By the time Sam rubbed his erection against me in the tent, any resistance had melted away. I was a willing participant, surrendering my most vulnerable being to Sam's touch. I trusted him to show me the way. He did.

A few days after the bivouac, one of our drill instructors, Sergeant Owens, pulled me aside. "Private Cummings," he began. "You need to be careful."

"Yes, sir," I said at attention.

"Do you know what I'm referring to?" he asked.

"No, sir."

"Do you like men?"

"I don't know what you mean, sir."

"Are you attracted to men?"

"No, sir," I said. "I'm married, sir."

"Be careful, Private," he said. "That's an order."

"Yes, sir," I said as I saluted him.

While most GIs had the backs of their fellow men, there was a fair amount of gossip and chatter throughout the barracks. Even so, it was considered unseemly for a GI to report an incident or suspicion of inappropriate behavior to an officer. We were expected to handle any differences or concerns within the group.

When I told Sam about my encounter with Sergeant Owens, he immediately pointed a finger at Elroy Jones, a big country boy from Tuscaloosa, Alabama.

"He put his fist in my chest when we were breaking down the bivouac," Sam said. "He said to me, 'You and Cummings play a little game of hide-and-seek last night?' I told him to get out of my face. He asked me, 'How'd that Kentucky sausage taste?' I told him to mind his own business. He pushed me away and said, 'We don't want your type in the army. You make me sick.'"

"Why didn't you tell me?" I asked him.

"Didn't want you to worry about it," he said.

"Well, now I am," I said. "We can't be doing this anymore."

"What do you mean, *doing this*? Doing *what*?" he asked. "Loving each other?"

"You want to get kicked out? Court-martialed? Like Bobby and Tony?"

"That's not going to happen," Sam said.

"If we get caught, it is," I said. "We can't let that happen, Sam."

"We can be careful, sure," Sam said. "But they can't stop me from loving you."

"Loving me? You really love me?"

"Yes, I really love you," he said. "You don't love me?"

"Sam," I said. "Please."

"Please what?" Sam said exasperatedly.

"You act like this is perfectly natural, like you expected it to happen," I said.

"It *is* natural," he said. "But no. I didn't expect it to happen. That ain't how love works. But you can't tell me you don't feel what I feel. You can't deny that. Go ahead. Try to."

I looked into his blue eyes and gave a faint smile of surrender. He was right. I couldn't deny it.

As camp came to an end, we each got our orders that we knew would separate us. Sam was fortunate to have been chosen to use his artistic talent as a camoufleur, creating designs for uniforms, vehicles, and buildings. He was off to Virginia.

I was chosen for gunnery training in Clovis, New Mexico, and would soon ship off to Guam.

Close friendships were formed throughout camp. As GIs received their orders to ship out around the world, goodbyes were difficult. Handshakes were often followed by hugs and firm slaps on each other's backs. My goodbye with Sam was grueling, our hug an embrace that was hard to break away from. He slipped a letter into my pocket and told me to read it on the plane after liftoff. I'd never felt such sorrow. I thought about Margaret and was heartbroken to grasp the reality that our goodbye lacked anything close to this sentiment. I said goodbye to her as a friend. I said goodbye to Sam Boswell as my lover.

CHAPTER

4

MY FIRST LOOK INSIDE AN AIRPLANE was when I climbed the steps of the C-47 transport that would carry me to New Mexico. The quarters were close with soldiers shoulder to shoulder as I reached into my pocket to find Sam's letter. I held it close to my face and cupped my hands around it.

Sept 15, 1944

Dearest Hank,

By now you are miles away, a distance that strains my heart. May we never forget the feeling of warmth which resonates between us. It is impossible to predict how this will unfold. But know that I will always keep you in my heart no matter where this war takes us. Maybe, just maybe, it will bring us back together again, whether in this lifetime or another.

Fondly,
Sam

"From your girl?" the soldier next to me asked as he saw tears swell in my eyes.

"Excuse me?" I said.

"The letter," he continued. "From your girl back home?"

I nodded without looking at him.

Upon our arrival at the base, I was thrown into an intense six-week gunnery training course. I scored 935 out of a possible 1,000 on my qualifications testing, earning me the mark of Superior Qualification. I was chosen to be a tail gunner on the new Boeing B-29 Superfortress bomber. With a range of over 3,000 miles, the bomber was the first that could fly the 16-hour round trip from Guam to Japan and back, allowing us to attack deep inside the country.

The six weeks went by in the blink of an eye and afforded rare moments of free time to think about anything other than my training. I received eight letters from Sam, twice as many as from Margaret. Sam put the photo he had shown me in camp—the one from Europe with his blond hair, long and wind-blown—in his last letter to me. Inscribed on the back, he wrote. *Don't forget me.*

Before I knew it, I was in Guam flying training missions over the Pacific in a B-29. The tail gunner's position was the loneliest. Situated in the most rear section of the plane, behind the rear wings and under the plane's rudder, I crunched my gangly frame into a tiny, pressurized capsule, facing backward, protecting the back end of the bomber from tail attacks. At my fingertips were two 50mm machine guns and a 20mm cannon.

We had a lot of down time at the base. Too much, which gave me ample time to think about Sam and Margaret. I fruitlessly tried to convince myself that my relationship with Sam was a fling and that I would regain my footing as a husband. But my identity had been stripped. My very being turned inside out. So lonely. So afraid.

Sam taught me what a kindred spirit was. More than taught. He showed me. Through his eyes I saw the wide, wild, world. He fascinated me. He demonstrated a purpose. He had ambitions bigger than this world could hold. He stretched my imagination and stamped his mark on my soul. My ruptured heart ached more as the days passed. I loved him. I couldn't convince myself otherwise.

On November 2, 1944, I flew my first mission to Japan on the bird, the Sassy Susan, under control of Captain Dick Kline and copilot Staff Sergeant Ernie Thompson. I had gotten to know them well during training, along with the rest of the crew. They were fine men, and I was proud to be among them. My partners were the other gunners—waste-gunners Bruce Mabee and Gerald Robinson, and top-gunner Dick Henderson. John Able was the radio operator. We were all in the same training class from start to finish, but this was my rookie flight. We sat together before I had to escape the cabin to my turret capsule by way of a plank flanked by ammo, bombs, controls, and wires. Once there, my sole job was to protect the bird from Japanese fighters. The mission was a success, and fortunately noneventful from my view.

Once back on the ground in Guam, the fellows dumped a bucket of cold water over my head to commemorate my first flight. The next day, we would make another round trip from the base to Japan. Upon settling into my capsule, as we neared Japan, enemy fighters approached us and I saw my first action, shooting down three fighters. All told, our guys shot down over a dozen and we successfully accomplished the mission and returned home to base without so much as a scratch. The adrenaline of seeing the enemy approach made my heart beat out of my chest. It was the first time I ever feared for my life, and I instinctively acted on my training as I swung the turret back and forth while pulling the triggers on the guns. Seeing the planes fall from the sky was surreal. It wasn't until I was safely back in the cabin that I felt an enormity of sorrow that I had killed other men, a feeling I was told would go away over time. It never has.

I would fly sixteen more missions before my last.

On December 15, 1944, the Sassy Susan was one of two hundred bombers that took off from the airfields of Guam. On board were the crew from my rookie flight six weeks earlier, plus Private Harold Addison, Private Pancho King, and Flight Engineer Louis Bales, each making their first flight on the bird. The mission was a moderate success, as we reported that 25 percent of the 500-pound bombs hit their intended targets. Less than one hour into our return trip, we were ambushed by enemy fire from both sides and the rear. I whipped the turret from side to side and up and down to try to knock the hostile fighters out of the sky. Our plane was hit several times, 20mm cannon rounds shearing through the aluminum skin. I saw four bombers in our formation fall, their crew either killed or bailing out into the Philippine Sea below. Over the interphone, I heard pure chaos and reports of carnage. A voice, hard to distinguish in the noise and confusion, yelled out in pain, "I'm hit. I'm hit!"

A second later I felt a searing pain in my upper arm. I'd been hit as well. I couldn't take my flight jacket off because of the tight quarters and limited use of my arm, so I couldn't apply a tourniquet. All I could do was stuff a bandage down my suit and apply pressure, and lean my weight into the capsule's side to quell the bleeding. I'd have to wait until it was safe to abandon the turret before leaving the capsule for help.

It was difficult to decipher words over the interphone due to the commotion, but I could make out that Bales, King, and Thompson were wounded.

The enemy fire ripped holes through the skin of the plane causing the cabin pressure to drop. The temperature inside the fuselage dropped below zero. Captain Kline, unharmed, dove the bird down from 30,000 feet to 5,000 in less than two minutes to make it easier for us to breathe and to find warmer air. Once we were out of range of the enemy fighters, I opened my hatch and made my way forward. Mabee and Robinson were unhurt and had pulled Dick Henderson down from his top-gunner position. He was convulsing in pain, blood seeping from his chest, staining the leather of his flight jacket dark red. He had no chance. They helped me remove my jacket and applied a tourniquet under my right shoulder, an inch above where a 20mm round had shattered my arm. Robinson stayed with me and helped me back into my jacket, or I'd have frozen to death. Copilot Ernie Thompson was gravely wounded. Kline reported the plane was in good shape, fuel load not in jeopardy, all wing hydraulics operable. He believed the landing gear had failed to deploy, but he couldn't be sure. We were still three hours away from base.

The last thing I remember was hearing the screams of, "BELLY LANDING, BELLY LANDING, BELLY LANDING! Everything that happened between that moment and waking up six days later in the hospital in Guam was relayed to me later, or I learned through written reports.

CHAPTER

5

I HEARD A VOICE and saw a blurred light through the thin layer of gauze over my eyes.

"Private Cummings, can you hear me?" a voice asked. "Private Cummings?"

A throbbing pain pulsated through my feet and hands. My face felt like my skin had been ripped away. I sensed pressure against my body as if smothered in cloth. I tried to speak but could barely produce a moan. My chest ached when I tried to breathe, and I felt a raspy rumble in my lungs. I didn't know where I was.

"Private Cummings, if you can hear me, try to give me a sign," the voice said.

I pushed out a moan and raised my arm a few inches.

"Private Cummings, you have been in an accident. You are in the United States Naval Hospital in Guam. Do you understand, sir? Give me a sign."

I was able to nod and moan again.

"You've suffered severe burns and other injuries, but you're in the best hands here, sir. We've kept you pretty sleepy, but we're bringing you out of it now. Understand? We need you to come back to us now."

It may have been minutes, or perhaps hours, as I became more aware of the condition I was in. I felt the gentle presence of a nurse next to me, her voice soothing and comforting. As I continued to wake, the throbbing pain in my limbs turned into a searing pain that felt like someone was stabbing my hands and feet with a knife. The nurse called for morphine and within minutes I relaxed into a numb daze. This cycle would continue over and over for the days and weeks to follow. I couldn't get enough drugs to settle the incessant pain. There would only be fleeting moments of being of sound enough mind to understand what the doctors and nurses were telling me. My memory was not to be trusted as reality stirred with confusion.

Delusion turned to hallucinations in a haunting but enchanting way. At times nightmarish. At times fantasy. Dreams are different, for you know the difference between the dream state and the conscious state. Any distinction between the daze and consciousness was measured by my level of pain. In the depths of illusion and deception, I believed I was dead and could feel a sense of peace. The returning pain was the stark reminder that I was alive.

I was wheeled back and forth many times from my ward to an operating room where people in white gowns would remove the soaked dressings from my face, hands, and feet, and slice away dead tissue that had scabbed over the open wounds. Despite being pumped up with morphine, as soon as this procedure of debridement began, I would scream in agony. Whenever I would hear the screams of others, I knew what was happening to them. Their howls were haunting.

Hours, days, weeks, I had little sense of time.

In addition to debridement, there were skin grafts and surgeries. I looked at my hands after a procedure. My right hand was gone. Nothing but an oozing stump wrapped in gauze. My toes were gone. I didn't know what my face looked like. The inside of my mouth was wilted and dried. I was fed through a tube.

A nurse came to my bed with bags of red gook. "You're getting new plasma today, Private," she said.

A speech specialist would sit next to me, helping turn my moans into words. The biggest problem was getting enough force from my lungs to push sounds out. They had been damaged by the smoke and flames. A pulmonary therapist helped me with breathing exercises.

After one procedure, I woke in my bed and there was no covering over my left eye, but my vision was blurry, colors blending together, shapes morphing into each other. I was able to match faces and voices I'd become familiar with.

Nurse Nancy was my favorite. Her voice was soft and, though she wouldn't touch it, I would feel her energy as she hovered her hands over my wrapped face.

"You know, Private, you are my darling," she would say. I learned a lot about the shape I was in from her. She had a way of delivering traumatic news in a lighthearted way. "And I'm going to make sure you get out of here, even if you're not in one piece anymore." Then she would laugh. "You are left-handed now, Private. And you still have your middle finger so you can tell people where to go," she'd chuckle. "My daddy had to have a nose job too. He was a boxer, so they had more to work with, but they didn't do a very good job. You'll have a better nose than him. They will be starting from scratch," she'd laugh again.

Once I was able to speak, I told her I wanted to die. "Oh, darling, that's the medicine talking," she said. But she knew better. It wasn't the morphine. I did want to die. She knew it. The thought would sweep through me in waves. I wanted the pain to stop, and I was beginning to understand that my recovery was going to be long and grueling. I was going to be crippled. A grotesque monster without fingers, toes, ears or a nose, nearly blind. Dependent on others for essential needs.

There was a photo of me taped to my bed frame to remind people that there was an actual human being underneath the bandages. Nurse Nancy would say, "My, aren't you a handsome man. Your wife must be a lucky woman." My wedding ring was salvaged, removed before they took my ring finger. She looped yarn through it and hung it from my bed frame. On Christmas morning, she taped Christmas lights on the wall above my headboard.

I was desperate to understand what had happened, but the hospital staff offered no details other than reporting the extent of my injuries. I had suffered third-degree burns on both hands, feet, face, and torso. They saved what they could. My nose and ears burned away, little cartilage remained. My right eye was destroyed. My left eye damaged, with limited vision. The humorous bone in my right arm was shattered, little muscle remained. The doctors worked to save it.

Realizing I often returned from the surgical ward with less than I entered with, I told Nurse Nancy with all seriousness, "Be sure to have them save at least one finger so I can type." She was overjoyed when it looked like I had the last amputation behind me. To humor me, she said, "Not only did I make them save one finger, but two, plus your thumb. You can thank me later." I never knew going into an operation whether I'd return with my right arm.

In time I was able to recall being in the wounded B-29 and remembering the cries of 'belly landing,' so it became evident that we had crashed, causing the fire. That's as far as I could get.

One morning I stirred to find two blurry figures in army dress on one side of my bed, a doctor and nurse on the other, and I learned why people kept calling me a hero.

"Private Cummings," one of them began. "I'm Colonel Roberts. This is Sergeant Timms."

I acknowledged them with a nod.

"Is he awake and alert enough to understand us?" the colonel asked the doctor.

"Why don't you ask him?" the doctor responded.

The colonel returned. "Private Cummings, how are you feeling? Are you awake enough to hear us?"

I nodded my bandaged head.

"Can he speak?" the colonel asked the doctor, who didn't seem to respond.

"Can you speak?" he directed at me.

"I try," I whispered.

"Good. Glad to hear," he continued. "Private Cummings, we are here to tell you the details of your actions and bravery that you displayed on December 15, 1944. Do you recall anything?"

"No," I shook my head. I took the deepest breath I could and braced myself.

"On December 15, 1944, during a mission over Japan, your plane, the Sassy Susan, under the control of Captain Richard Kline, encountered a fleet of Japanese fighters and sustained dozens of rounds of fire, killing and injuring several crew members. The craft suffered severe damage. The landing gear hydraulic lines were severed. Captain Kline fought against the odds to bring the craft back to base and valiantly attempted to land safely. Kline had radioed to base to prepare for a belly landing because he feared the landing gear was not functional. He dumped as much fuel as possible in anticipation of a crash. According to witnesses on the ground, the nose landing gear never deployed, causing the fuselage to slam to the ground, severing fuel lines and causing the remaining fuel to ignite, enveloping the plane.

"Private Cummings, the details I'm going to share with you that happened subsequent to the plane coming to rest have been verified by surviving crew members and the ground rescue team. Though your right arm was rendered useless, and you were in extreme pain, after you escaped the burning craft, discovering that several crew remained inside, you re-entered the burning plane and are credited with saving the lives of Harold Addison, Louis Bales, and Pancho King. You repeatedly returned to the burning fuselage, despite attempts by others who tried to restrain you. Once those three men were safely being attended to on the ground, you returned one final time in an attempt to help others in trying to rescue Captain Kline, whose legs were trapped. You finally relented and were pulled away. By then you had suffered severe burns."

"Captain Kline?" I whispered. "Did he make it?"

"No sir, he did not," Sergeant Timms said. "I'm sorry. Copilot Thompson, Dick Henderson, and Bruce Mabee all perished in the crash."

Small bits of my memory were being stimulated as I listened. I remembered flames. I heard screams. I felt confusion. But all of this was happening as though I was suspended above the scene as it played out beneath me.

"Private Cummings," the colonel interrupted my thoughts. "This must be a lot to comprehend, but you do understand the nature of your heroics?"

I thought of Kline and Thompson. And Henderson and Mabee, two of my best friends. Did I not try to save them? I remembered seeing Dick Henderson on the floor of the fuselage, his bloodstained flight jacket, the look in his eyes. Yes, I remember that. How the hell did I save anybody? I remembered now, my arm hanging limp from my body, and pain. The pain.

CHAPTER
6

"WE HAVE A MESSAGE from the desk of President Roosevelt we'd like to read to you. I assume that would be all right?" the colonel said.

I nodded in disbelief. I now could feel the presence of several more people at the foot of my bed.

The President of the United States of America, authorized by Act of Congress, July 12, 1862, has awarded in the name of Congress the Medal of Honor to:

PRIVATE HENRY EARL CUMMINGS JUNIOR
UNITED STATES ARMY

December 29, 1944

For conspicuous gallantry and intrepidity in action at the risk of his life above and beyond the call of duty.

Citation: On December 15, 1944, returning to the Guam base from a successful mission over Japan, the B-29 flying fortress, the Sassy Susan, sustained damage from an attack of a fleet of Japanese fighter planes. Despite being seriously wounded during this battle, Private Cummings continued his duty as the rear tail gunner, disabling twelve Japanese aircraft. After the attack, he assisted to wounded crewmen, providing first aid and comfort. Due to disabled landing gear, the plane crashed upon landing, causing the fuel to ignite. Private Cummings was the first to escape the burning plane, and before the ground rescue and fire team could reach the plane, he re-entered the fuselage and found Flight Engineer Louis Bales struggling to unfasten his safety harness. Cummings was able to free Bales, who safely fled the plane with minor injuries. Cummings remained in the burning fuselage and found Private Harold Addison, who was disoriented, unable to find his way from the plane. Cummings pulled him from his knees and guided him to safety. He then returned to the fuselage and found Private Pancho King, who had sustained fractures to both legs, and began pulling him through an opening. The rescue team arrived at this moment and completed bringing King to safety and escorted Cummings away from the flames. In addition to his damaged arm, he had now suffered visible severe burns to his hands and face. Yet aware of the extreme danger, he returned once more to the cockpit where he discovered rescue members attempting to extradite Captain Richard Kline from his seat. Upon entering, he stepped into a river of burning octane fuel which ignited his boots. Rescue crewman Ralph Treadway pulled Cummings from the plane and began to attend to him. Private Cummings' profound concern for his fellow crewmen, at the risk of his own life, went above and beyond the call of duty, among the highest traditions of the United States Army and the Armed Forces of this country.

Signed by President Franklin D. Roosevelt
The White House

"Congratulations, Private," Sergeant Timms said. "Well deserved." He apologized for not being able to present the actual medal but assured me it would be presented to me in a formal ceremony soon.

It didn't dawn on me the weight of the honor that was bestowed on me. My pain was intensifying to the point where I could wait no longer for my next course of morphine, which the nurse wasted little time injecting into my IV. I likely didn't react in accordance with the magnitude of the moment.

But I did manage so say, "I'm honored." Though I couldn't comprehend that I'd deserved anything considering the state I was in.

"Thank you, Colonel," the doctor said. "It's been a grand occasion, but I believe Private Cummings is due for some rest now."

"Yes, of course." The colonel's voice tapered off as I drifted into my dream state.

I later learned that the reason the medal was awarded so quickly was because it was believed that I would die, and the army wanted to showcase an American hero to lift the spirits of those back home. "To show people what heroes are made of," Colonel Roberts said.

The actual medal was awarded a week later in a ceremony featuring the colonel, sergeant, and the crew members I was credited with saving. An army photographer captured the ceremony of Colonel Roberts gingerly laying the medal upon my chest. I was also awarded the Purple Heart, the Army Distinguished Service Cross, the Silver Star, the Army Commendation Medal, and the Army Presidential Unit Citation, all sprawled across my chest next to the Medal of Honor in perfect order. The sudden flash of the camera bulb startled me and burned my eye. An army communications specialist was on hand to interview everyone, including me, but I left the storytelling to others. An article including the photo was distributed and printed in newspapers across the nation, including the *Grayson Gazette*. It was the first time that Margaret, my family, or anyone else outside of the Guam hospital, saw my physical condition. The article also went into more detail about my injuries than previously shared, including why the medal ceremony was so rushed.

Margaret and my parents had been notified I was injured and being cared for in a hospital, but weren't aware of the severity, and the information they received was random and sketchy at best. Shot in the arm. Suffered burns. Wrapped and bandaged, I was unrecognizable in the photo. My mother was in denial, refusing to believe it was me. It led to the first of her many nervous breakdowns.

"That's not Hank. They made a mistake. That's not my son," my father later told me she said.

Other men from my unit came for the occasion, including First Lieutenant William Radcliffe, Captain Marshal McPeek, and Colonel Ralph Skinner. Nothing, however, including the medals and ribbons, compared to the bittersweet moment hearing the voices and seeing the blurry faces of Louis Bales, Harold Addison, and Pancho King. Before then, the crash was an abstract event that I couldn't place myself in. It became real seeing those men. Bales was in near perfect condition and would returned to service soon. Harold Addison had been shot in the shoulder but would make a full recovery. Pancho King was in a wheelchair, having suffered shattered legs plus second degree burns on his hands and face. But he was still Pancho, the life of the party. From that moment on, as long as we were both still in the Guam Naval Hospital, Pancho rolled his wheelchair into my room often to lighten both our spirits.

The six weeks I spent in the intensive care burn unit before being moved to the general ward were the most grueling of my life. I fell into a deep sadness, "Just a little melancholy," the staff psychiatrist would say. "You'll get over it. It's a choice." The debridement procedures never stopped. I begged the nurses to kill me instead of torture me. Once again, Nurse Nancy tried to lighten the occasion. "Private Cummings, how many darn times do I have to tell you, we don't commit murder in this hospital!" I begged her to make an exception for me. My thighs were raw from the skin they harvested to graft over the stumps of my hands and feet. I had phantom pain where my fingers and toes once were. I was near death on several occasions because of infections and the trauma my internal organs suffered, given last rights three times.

Nurse Nancy was the first to hold a mirror to my face. For once she was deadly serious with me, trying to warn me about what I would see. It was also the only time I saw her cry, though she must have done so often in her solitude, seeing so much pain every day in the ward.

"My love," she said. "I can't sugarcoat this. You're not a pretty sight." She held the mirror to my face. She was right. I had no preconceived notions that I'd be recognizable as the Hank Jr. that climbed into the tiny turret of the Sassy Susan. But I was alive, and I would survive. I would eventually be reunited with my wife and family. Captain Richard Kline would not be going home to his wife. Staff Sergeant Ernie Thompson wouldn't be going home to his fiancé. Bruce Mabee would never see his children again. Nor would Dick Henderson, whose wife would deliver their only child after his death. Harold Addison, Louis Bales, and Pancho King would all see their families again. Their lives were my reward.

I had fifteen surgeries over my 40-day stay in the intensive care ward. I would have another twelve in the months to follow.

"I hear you're going home, darling!" Nurse Nancy hooted as she surprised me at my bedside. That news hadn't made its way to me yet.

"Home?"

"I saw your discharge papers, had to sign them myself. Along with six other people. My John Hancock will always be there. Am I the first to break the news?"

Two days later I would be on a medical transport plane on my way to the burn unit at the Army Medical Center in Fort Sam Houston, Texas. Several men from my base were able to see me before I shipped back to the States. Pancho was long gone having been sent home weeks earlier. Saying goodbye to the doctors, nurses, staff, and my fellow soldiers was sentimental. Nurse Nancy, teased me, "In another lifetime, you and I ... well darling, I guess we'll never know." I would miss her.

It was comforting to be back in the States, soil I wasn't sure I'd ever see again. The Medical Center facility was far above anything I'd experienced in

Guam. The expertise of the staff, the equipment, the physical therapy department, all first-rate. I now wanted to live.

Margaret and my family came to visit as soon as they were allowed. I was no longer cocooned in gauze. Dressing covered wounds that were still open, spots on my legs and back where skin was freshly harvested for grafting, some areas of my face, and a nasty burn on my torso that was stubborn to heal. Though I was mostly unwrapped, I was far from recognizable, and I was not a pretty sight. I had become accustomed to seeing the scarred and carved up creature I had become. Nothing could prepare others. I was eager to see them, but also felt great trepidation, fearful of their reaction. Oh, how I wished Nurse Nancy could be the one to prep them to lighten the mood. Give perspective as only she could.

The staff psychologist, Dr. Bagley, and I became quite familiar with one another. He was an older man with a gentle bedside manner. He stayed beyond his shift to join the reunion. There was no privacy in the ward. The patient beds were no more than six feet apart without even a curtain in between. Dr. Bagley was able to borrow two mobile partitions from the surgical unit to surround my bed, providing some sense of intimacy, sensitive to the emotional moments that would come.

We argued whether I should wear the medals and ribbons, an argument he won. He convinced me that evidence of my valor would somewhat deflect the inevitable grief and sorrow. I was concerned that I didn't appear as a braggart, which he found hilarious. I was stone serious. He said, "Private, you've just saved me many hours of trying to figure you out." He wrapped the ribbon from the Medal of Honor around my neck and pinned the other accolades on my gown. He propped me up between pillows and the bed frame.

Minutes later, he peeked around the partition. "Ready to see your wife, Private Cummings?" Margaret followed him. She couldn't speak. I sensed her eyes were darting around the room. It's what she did when she was nervous or scared. She approached my bedside, struggling to say something. She tried to remain her stoic self, straining to hold back tears.

"It's okay, Mrs. Cummings," Bagley said. "No one expected this to be easy. Would you like me to leave?"

She shook her head. "I just ..." she began. "Oh, Hank. My dear Hank."

We sat in silence for several minutes before she leaned to embrace me. "For better, for worse," she said. "You're stuck with me." Her ponytail mixed with tears and fell across my face. I raised my arms and rested them on her shoulders and pulled her close with what strength I had. She slowly stroked her fingers over my medals and ribbons. "My hero. Our hero. Our nation's hero."

I hadn't noticed that Dr. Bagley had left. When he returned, he again peeked around the partition. "Private, you've got some other loved ones who are mighty anxious to see you."

I looked around Margaret and saw my parents and sister standing next to the doctor. Eliza was the first to advance toward me, followed by my father. My mother remained standing next to Dr. Bagley.

"Hey good-lookin'," Eliza said. She kissed me gently on my forehead.

My father stood at the foot of my bed and tried to mutter my name. I think he was trying to say, 'I love you,' but could only blubber the words as he began to cry. His shoulders heaved up and down.

"Mr. Cummings," Bagley said, "Let it out. It's okay to cry." Please don't encourage him, I thought.

My mother still hadn't moved and looked downward. I hadn't been able to formulate a constructive thought, torn between my own emotions and watching those unfolding around me. My thoughts darted to Sam Boswell. I wondered how he would react seeing me. Where is he now? Why haven't I heard from him? Did he even know?

I looked back at my mother and noticed she was looking at my bandaged stumps of feet.

"He had such pretty toes," she finally said.

Seeing my family represented a bridge to my new reality. I would be totally dependent on them. The weight of that was obvious on their faces as well. It was comforting to have them near me. I had declined my scheduled morphine because I wanted to be alert during the visit. Sensing my pain, Bagley summoned the nurse who injected a dose into my IV and, within minutes, I drifted off. When I woke, I was alone.

I saw them again the following morning. They stayed in Fort Sam Houston for two weeks in a boarding house the hospital provided for long-term stays and visited several times a day during that time, visits that began to define new dynamics of my relationship with each of them.

Margaret couldn't stop pitying me, which began to frustrate me. Our conversations evolved and deepened in an honest reflection of what we were facing. She assured me she would take care of me. Stand by me no matter what. "For better or worse," she kept saying. "Stop saying, 'or worse,'" I snapped. She didn't have to keep reminding me that she drew the short end of the straw. I felt the need to keep apologizing for the fate I had served her.

"I don't know what to say," she said. "What can I do, Hank?"

"You don't need to do anything, darling," I whispered to her. "Sit with me. That's all I need."

My visits with Eliza lightened my spirits. She acted no different than if we'd been sitting on our front porch over tea, me of whole mind and body. Her matter-of-fact tone grounded me that I would recover and live a full life. "As if you have a choice," she said. It was typical of her. She never cried over spilled milk. Her whole life, she would say, "If you're lucky enough to wake up, you're strong enough to face the cards you're dealt."

My father preferred to visit alone. Our moments together were the most tender. He'd been my best friend, always by my side. He taught me that showing emotion was a strength. He was a hugger. A crier. A kisser. He, not my mother, kissed me goodnight when I was a child. When we said goodbye before I left for boot camp, he hugged the breath out of me and kissed me on my cheek, his tears mixing with mine. As gentle as we was, he was also a rock with an internal strength matched by his physical presence.

He led by example. He never spoke unkindly of my mother, who was withdrawing into sadness and unpredictable behavior. Despite any difficulty she presented, he supported her with kindness. He masked his pain from others. He would never answer the question, 'What's wrong with Mommy?' He would deflect or ignore, with pretense that all was good. Though it wasn't.

When she'd join him on our visits, she often sat in silence. I was unsure if she was sad for me, or herself. Maybe angry. He never left her alone with me. For that I was grateful.

Saying goodbye to them was difficult, but my spirits were buoyed by our time together. The visits left me with a sense that I would be okay. No matter the struggle we faced, we would go forward with strength and dignity.

The remaining weeks in Fort Sam Houston focused on rehabilitation and additional surgeries, morphine, and antibiotics to fight off nagging infections. Skin grafts. More debridement. Reattaching tendons and nerves in my damaged arm. I was fitted with special shoes with prosthetics in their tips. I had to learn to walk again, now with withered leg muscles and tender stumps for feet. Each step shot searing pain through my legs. When I would rest after our sessions, I would feel tingling, throbbing, and sharp piercing pain of pins and needles in my toes that were no longer there. I would have begged the doctors to cut them off if I still had them.

Several surgeries began to reconstruct my melted face, focusing more on function than form. Little cartilage remained of my nose and ears. They widened my nostrils and cleared my nasal passages. In my right eye socket, they implanted a glass eye. They worked to rebuild my lips. Progress was slow and frustrating. Grafts to my face left a field of divots and ruts, rigid and tight.

"We're making progress," the doctors would say.

One morning I received a visit from the parents and wife of Harold Addison. Addison was from Waco, a four-hour drive from the Fort Sam Houston hospital. His wife, Betty, brought a dozen red roses and a box of candy. It was wonderful to see them and talk about Harold. They were effusive with their gratitude. The visit was emotional. They read me a letter that Harold had written them about me.

A reporter from *Life* magazine showed up one afternoon, having flown from New York. He had been dispatched, with a photographer, to do a feature story on me. By then, I was beginning to adjust to whom I had become. The enormity of distinction I'd received helped me regain my sense of confidence and pride. I agreed to the story, not sure if I had much of a say. The reporter made it clear that the army had encouraged it. I wore sunglasses and a green cap with 'ARMY' in yellow above the bill. I couldn't add to the story about the crash. They knew more than I could recall but certainly aggrandized my bravery. I didn't believe I was ever soaked with burning octane fuel from head to toe. I was given last rights six times? Didn't think so. I knew of three, but so be it. They were going to write a story to sell magazines. And they did.

After spending a total of five months in hospitals, they rushed my discharge. The Grayson Memorial Day parade was a week away.

CHAPTER
7

AFTER THE PARADE, when General Mackey finally left our house, I joined the rest of the family in the front room to listen to them banter about what to do with me as if I weren't there.

"How are you goin' to continue your job at the bank and still take care of him?" Eliza asked Margaret.

"My mother is going to check in on him. What are you so worried about?" Margaret responded. "You don't think I'm capable?"

"Of course I'm not suggesting that. I'm just trying to do what's best for everyone. What's best for Hank."

"And you don't think it's best that he stay in his home, near the people he knows? With me and my family? The VA hospital in Lexington is less than two hours away."

"The VA hospital in Columbus is only an hour away from us," Eliza persisted.

"Why don't we ask what Hank thinks? What do you want, son?" my father interjected. "What do you think would be best for you?"

"This is my home. Margaret's home," I said. "My life is here."

"Well, I think that settles it. Let's move on with that plan and see how things go," my father said.

"See how things go?" Margaret snapped. "We're not going to see how things go. This is what we want. You heard him. Our life is here."

"Maybe I move back to Grayson," Eliza said. "You know, to help. Even if just for a bit."

"NO! You do not have to move back to Grayson," Margaret snapped again. "We'll be fine!"

My father approached Margaret and hugged her. "Of course you will, honey." He walked over to Eliza and kissed her on the cheek. "Why don't we go back to the hotel. We can visit again this evening."

My mother was despondent, adding nothing to the discussion. She spent most of her time looking out the window. It wasn't until my father extended his hand to help her stand that she acknowledged our goodbye.

I was tired and needed to lie down and rest my feet. Margaret helped me to my room. The army equipped us with a bed with handrails, a wheelchair, crutches, a cane, three pairs of special orthotic shoes with prosthetic toes, two glass eyes, eye patches, sunglasses, several pairs of glasses with various strengths of magnification, haphazard gloves that were to serve some purpose I couldn't determine, a breathing mechanism, special salves and creams, hats, T-shirts, and a variety of smaller knickknacks. In my closet hung winter wool, summer khaki, dress blue, and work fatigue uniforms. On the floor sat a new pair of boots, without prosthetic toe inserts. On the closet shelf rested a fresh dress cap. A framed American flag graced the wall. The jacket I wore to the parade, adorned with all my medals and ribbons, hung neatly on the back of the closet door. All this, thanks to General Mackey, who stressed he was my go-to guy. Whatever I needed, if the army had it, he would get it. I believed him. He was proud of his accomplishments on my behalf, and not shy to let others know the strings he could pull.

Margaret had placed a little cow bell on the side table in the event I needed to summon her. I didn't have the strength in my voice to carry beyond my room. She had set up a small table with a typewriter and a stack of paper for when the urge to write would strike. I tapped some keys with the index finger of my left hand and was relieved that I could press them with little pain. I used to be able to hammer out one hundred words a minute. Now I would train myself to use the hunt-and-peck method.

From my room, I heard people coming to the door throughout the day. Most of them dropping off food, not wishing to bother me. More pickles. Occasionally, Margaret would crack my door open and ask if I wanted to see someone. My high school basketball coach called on me. So did my old boss at the lumberyard. Some friends and teammates from high school stopped by. I didn't have the strength to see anyone, and often pretended to be asleep so Margaret didn't have to fib. She encouraged them to leave notes and call another time. A constant procession of cars drove past the house honking their horns. Someone planted a sign in our yard, *Hank Cummings Jr., Grayson's American Hero.*

I had become accustomed to taking my recovery day by day. It was difficult to comprehend what this new normal would be. Margaret's income from the bank would not be enough to sustain us. I was still active and receiving my army salary, which was meager, but it was fortunate that I would continue to have the medical care benefits through the VA in Lexington. Mr. Burton left a note that a job was waiting for me at the yard when I was ready. *Something in customer service,* he wrote. I imagined that he'd have me sitting in a rocker by the front door greeting people as they entered and exited, like some propaganda tool, *Come meet Hank Cummings Jr. and get 25% off your next order.* The only viable option, it seemed, was to take General Mackey up on the Pentagon's offer to continue my career in the army. Some kind of 'ambassador role,' he'd said. I didn't figure I'd be a handsome poster boy for a recruitment post. Maybe they'd have me riding in parades the rest of my life. Whatever it might hold, it seemed worth exploring.

Other than her steadfast determination that I would stay in Grayson, Margaret wouldn't discuss how our future might unfold. I couldn't tell if she was in denial or simply choosing to keep her head down focusing one hour, one day at a time. She was pragmatic that way, matter-of-fact. She must have been processing our options, limited as they might have been, but she kept it to herself and wouldn't talk about the subject, not wanting to cause me stress. Whenever I'd breach the topic, she'd deflect and tell me I need not worry, it's too soon to think about. "You need your rest, Hank. That's all you need to do, just rest."

I would never have described our relationship as heated and passionate before the war, but rather tender and warm. We both sought comfort in each other's arms, and we loved each other as we knew how. We relied on one another in a way that provided us each with a sense of security. It was a dependability we both could count on.

Eliza's instinct allowed her to clearly see this dynamic. She would say that we 'settled' for each other. "You don't need another sister," she'd say. "You've got me." She wasn't jealous, she just called it like she saw it. She always carried a bit of a chip on her shoulder toward Margaret, holding her responsible for keeping me from what she considered my full potential. Eliza had many suitors when she was young, but she said, "I ain't settling for any immature country boy. I'll know love when I see it, and I ain't seen it yet." I could never reconcile the greater cross to bear—settling on 'good enough,' or risking never having a steady partner through life. She chose the latter.

Eliza was my protector. She filled the role of my emotionally absentee mother and did so with a strong voice and a tender touch. She was my trustworthy confidant from as long back as I could remember, a source of wisdom and inspiration. She was an old soul. She wasn't book smart, hated school, but was instinctive. "I don't know, I just know it," she'd say when I'd ask her how she knew so much. She's the one who pulled gravel out of my knee after a fall, poured alcohol on a fresh wound, laid a cold cloth on my forehead when I had a fever, fixed me egg sandwiches that were out of this world.

She returned that afternoon without my parents. I heard her and Margaret talking in the front room. Eliza apologized for being pushy about wanting us to come to Ohio. "I know it ain't realistic," she told her. "It would never work. We just want what's best for the two of you." I didn't hear Margaret respond. I could envision her nodding in stoic agreement.

"How's my little brother doing?" She entered my room and closed the door. "You've had a big day. It's all people can talk about." She sat on the edge of my bed and grabbed a tube of salve from my bedside table. She gently began applying it to my scarred face, around my eyes and lips. "Anything you want to talk about?"

"No, nothing in particular. A lot to figure out," I responded.

"I'm thinkin' about moving back here," she said. "I was talkin' with Daddy about it and he thought it might be a good idea. That is, if you'd want me to."

"Not sure about that Lizzy," I said. "Let's give all of this some time to figure itself out."

"Things don't figure themselves out. We've got to figure them out."

"Well, it's just a lot right now," I said. "I've been starting to think more about what I'm going to do. Don't seem to have many options."

"What's this over here?" she asked, pointing to my typewriter. "You're a writer. And a good one. And what the hell's 'xxhhgui' supposed to spell?"

"It's a start," I said forcing a smile to my lips. "Thinking about what the general said about an army career."

"I don't trust that man, Hank. Somethin' about him. Seems to be all about what's good for him."

"You might be right, but he's helped me a lot."

"The damn fool looked like he thought the parade was in his honor this morning. You must not have noticed the big grin on his face and how he waved at folks like he was the decorated one."

"He's a general, Lizzy. He *is* decorated. He's a prideful man. Big personality, yes. But a big heart too, I believe." I paused for some space. "I don't need to rush into anything. We'll figure it out."

"Oh, that's what Daddy keeps sayin'," she said as she laid her head on my chest. "Your lungs sound so much better than when you were in Texas." She wrapped her hand around my fingers that were still too stiff to bend. I grimaced when she rubbed them around the tips where my fingernails used to be.

I heard the floor creak outside my door, and so did Eliza. Though she didn't say anything, she looked down in what I sensed was pity. Not pity for my decrepit state as much as her concern being left with Margaret. She looked up and gave a slight shake of her head, as if to say, 'You poor soul. What am I going to do with you?'

Margaret, too, had good instincts. After Eliza had left, she quizzed me on what the two of us discussed. "She has an agenda, Hank," she said, "You do know that, right?"

"Just wants what's best, Marg," I said.

"Wants what's best for her is more like it," she returned. "Thinks she has all the answers."

"I'm tired, Marg, please, let's not talk about it."

"We have to talk about it, Hank. I can't live looking over my shoulder being judged about how I'm going to take care of you, like I'm a bug under a microscope."

"Of course you can't. But cut her some slack. My family just wants what's ..."

"Dammit, Hank! *I'm* your family. You think this is easy on me? You think I'm not scared? You think I haven't suffered? You think I'm not wondering how we're going to make it through this? You just got home and we haven't had a moment's peace to ourselves. Before I knew it, your family was on our doorstep. The general won't leave you alone. Cars up and down our street. People knocking on the door. More tuna and chicken casseroles than we'll ever be able to eat. And the pickles. What's with the pickles? We have enough pickles we could open a pickle store. When did you say you liked pickles? For the love of Jesus. Pickles."

She began to laugh, which proved the best medicine for us both. A big belly laugh that turned to tears. The first time she'd allowed herself to cry in front of me. Vulnerable. Real. Human. Warm.

I remained in the house in the days that followed. My family returned to Ohio pledging they would visit again soon. Eliza gave up on the notion of moving back to Grayson. Margaret and I settled into the routine of my daily care and needs. Bathing, getting dressed, eating, doing my physical and respiratory therapy. She was a good caretaker. A good partner for helping me through the days.

I woke one morning to the delivery of an army chest full of personal belongings, which I'd been anticipating. Margaret untied the ropes that held it together and opened the lid. I was taken by the familiar musty smell of my footlocker. She began taking the items out, opening small boxes that contained personal artifacts. My toothbrush, razor, shaving cream, hair tonic, comb, and the like. There was a package of clothing—shirts, slacks, socks, and some boots. A carefully packaged box contained photos, including a framed photo of her. She was moved to learn I always kept it next to my bunk, no matter where I was. A few photos of my parents and Eliza that they had sent, as well as some photos of me. One box contained my dog tags and a cross necklace. She pulled out a thick manilla envelope that had been taped together and began to open it. She acquiesced when I stopped her. "Leave it be," I told her. "I'll take a look at it later. Be a doll and put it on the table in my room."

When I retired for bed at the end of the long day, I sat on my bed and slid a letter opener across the top of the stuffed envelope, breaking the tape away, and emptied the contents out before me. It contained what I had anticipated. Letters. Some tucked back in their envelopes, some strewn throughout the bunch. I rifled through the clutter to find letters from Margaret, Eliza, and my father. Some were from buddies from home. My heart began to race. There were letters that were missing. The ones from Sam Boswell.

CHAPTER

8

GENERAL MACKEY typically made the trip from his home in Louisville once a week—noon on Fridays—during the first few months I was home. He had arranged a driver to escort me and Margaret three times to the University Hospital in Lexington for a progression of reconstructive surgeries to begin rebuilding some semblance of a face, but there was a long way to go. Though Margaret had learned to drive while I was gone, she couldn't manage driving far beyond the comfort of Grayson. Sure, Mackey had an ego and relished acting as my handler, but I was comforted by his presence. Margaret and Eliza shared their suspicion of the man, one thing they had in common, along with their stubbornness.

Other than those hospital visits, I remained mostly in the house, occasionally venturing out to the front porch to greet people who had stopped by. Margaret tried to coerce me to begin assimilating back into the public, but I found it unsettling—the stares, the pointing, the gawking. I refused to have my picture taken anymore, though several newspapers and magazines approached us hoping to do stories. I couldn't escape a request by the army that the hospital took frequent photos to document the progress of surgeries.

The general would always confirm his visits. "See you next Friday as usual," he'd say upon leaving. "I'll have sandwiches and potato salad ready for you," Margaret would always say. She found it convenient that he loved pickles.

It was out of character for him to call to tell us he was going to visit us on the morning of July 16, a Monday, and would be joined by a couple other officers. He wanted to make sure we would be home. Margaret said he sounded 'different, just different that's all,' on the phone and he wouldn't divulge the nature of the visit. "We'll talk about it when we see you," he said. "We'll be there at 08:00."

I had not yet risen when I heard three heavy raps on the front door. Margaret welcomed them in. The general introduced her to the two men who joined him, Agent Mairs and Agent Carpenter. Margaret offered them coffee and asked them to have a seat in the front room. "May we sit at a table?" a voice unfamiliar to me asked her.

She came back to my room to help me get dressed. "Something doesn't feel right, Hank," she said. "The general barely said hello to me, wouldn't look me in the eye. What could this be about? The two men ... they are 'agents,' what does that mean?" I said I didn't know and asked her to help me with my uniform. It would be the first time wearing it since the parade. She obliged and made sure the medals and ribbons lay flush above the left breast pocket of the olive wool coat. "What's going on, Hank?" I ignored her.

The three men stood when Margaret and I entered the dining room. We exchanged a salute. "Mrs. Cummings," the general, who never referred to her so formally, said, "May we speak with your husband alone, please?"

"Certainly," she said, giving me a suspicious look while retreating to her room in the back of the house.

"Mrs. Cummings," Mackey stopped her. "We need to ask for absolute privacy for at least an hour. Are you able to grant us the house to ourselves with Private Cummings for that period of time?"

She nodded as she grabbed her purse and left.

The weight in the air was palpable as the general introduced me to Mairs and Carpenter.

Mairs began, "Private Cummings, Agent Carpenter and I represent the Army Investigation Unit, based in Arlington, Virginia. We are here to discuss an important issue and we ask for your candid participation. Am I clear?"

"Yes, sir," I said.

He pinched his thumbs against the clips of his briefcase, popped it open with a loud snap, and pulled out two olive green folders and set them on the table.

"Private Cummings," Carpenter began. "First, I speak for the United States Army and the whole of the country in thanking you for your bravery and unselfish service. That being said, we have a serious issue to discuss with you regarding your conduct while in service. We need to ask you some questions and, as Agent Mairs stated, we hope we can trust you will be forthright with your answers. Are you ready to begin?"

"Yes, sir," I answered.

"Are you familiar with a Private Samuel James Boswell?"

"Yes, sir."

"You know him personally?"

"Yes, sir."

"When and where did you meet Private Boswell?"

"We met in boot camp, Fort Benning. That would have been summer of '44."

"What was the nature of your relationship with Private Boswell?"

"We were friends."

"Friends."

"Yes, sir."

"When you say, you were friends. What kind of friends were you? Describe your friendship."

"Close friends. We had a lot in common. We spent time together."

"What exactly did you have in common, Private Cummings?"

"Well," I paused and stumbled. "He was, is, an artist. I was a writer. So, we had a sort of creative expression in common."

"What else? Is that all?"

"Yes, well, I don't know. Yes, I suppose that's all."

Carpenter opened the folder to reveal a stack of letters and pushed them forward, across the table, in my direction. They were the letters that were missing from the chest of my belongings. The letters from Sam.

"Private Cummings," Carpenter said as he spread a number of letters out in front of me. "Are you familiar with these letters?"

I nodded.

"These are all letters to you from Private Samuel Boswell, correct?"

I nodded.

"And you are familiar with the contents of the letters?"

I nodded.

"Would you agree that the sentiments expressed to you from Private Boswell are affectionate and intimate in nature?"

'Yes, sir,' I whispered.

He pulled another letter from his briefcase. "Private Cummings, are you familiar with this letter, from you to Private Boswell?"

I nodded.

"You would agree that in this letter, you use descriptions of affection and intimacy?"

I nodded, "Yes, sir."

With each word Carpenter spoke, I became more despondent. I pulled a pair of sunglasses from my breast coat pocket and balanced them on my face. Having the letter I wrote Sam meant that they had seized his personal belongings too.

"Private Cummings," he continued. "Do you want to reconsider? Maybe expand on your answer. Your relationship with Private Boswell?"

I shook my head and stayed silent.

"Very well then. Private Cummings, let me cut to the chase. Have you and Private Boswell ever engaged in homosexual behavior?"

"Do you find Private Boswell to be an attractive man?"

"Are you in love with him?"

"Is he in love with you?"

"Did you ever have sexual relations with Private Boswell or any other man?"

"Have you ever committed sodomy with Private Boswell or any other man?"

"Have you ever been sexually attracted to another man?"

"Are you physically stimulated by the sight of a naked man?"

"Private Cummings, as we stated, you may choose to remain silent. However, in declining to answer, it leads us into making our own conclusions. Do you understand?"

"Private Cummings, have you ever kissed Private Boswell? Have you ever intimately touched Private Boswell? Has Private Boswell ever touched or kissed you? Have you ever touched Private Boswell's genitals? Has Private Boswell ever touched your genitals?"

The questioning went on for an excruciating sixty minutes before General Mackey stopped it. Addressing the two agents, Mackey asked, "May I ask the two of you to step outside for a bit?"

The general pulled his chair next to mine.

"Private, let's go totally off the record, man to man, you and me. I assume you understand the gravity of this issue."

I nodded.

"You understand you are under a formal investigation for homosexual behavior and/or activity. The agents have significant evidence as you can see, more than they showed this morning. I can't stop this from going forward. I'm speaking to you as a friend now, not as a general. I don't see a way out of this for you, Hank. It breaks my heart, but as you know, the army has zero tolerance for homosexual behavior. Are you? Are you a homosexual?"

I wanted to hide beneath my scars. My heart, my soul, shredded during the moment.

"Are you, Hank?" he continued. "You can't hide from this. Tell me what in the hell is going on with you. What the hell happened with Boswell?"

I ignored his question and asked, "What now?" speaking for the first time in over an hour.

"Tell me what the hell happened," Mackey shot at me with an angry tone. "You're going to have to answer for this. And if you have no answers, the army will have the answers for you. You'll be out, Hank. Blue ticketed. Discharged. Do you understand the magnitude of what you're facing?"

"And Sam Boswell?"

"Sam Boswell! You're worried about Sam Boswell? You'd better be worried about yourself!"

"Tell me. Is he being investigated too?"

"Jesus Christ, Cummings. Yes. He's done. Just like you're going to be if you don't have any better answers for this."

"They met with him?"

"Yes, goddammit, they met with him."

The general had regained a sense of calm. "Hank, do you understand the consequences if you are blue ticketed? You'll be stripped of everything. Stripped of your benefits. Medical care. GI Bill. Your medals, Hank. Your Medal of Honor, Hank. Your fucking Medal of Honor!"

Carpenter came back into the house. "General Mackey …"

"A minute, Carpenter," Mackey snapped. "Give us a minute."

"Yes, sir."

"What now?" I asked him again.

"I'm not sure. It's now going before the medical board. They are the ones who make the final determination. No trial. No judge. No jury. You likely won't be court-martialed, thank God. It won't be a dishonorable discharge, but it's the next closest thing. Probably a blue discharge for undesirable behavior. A blue discharge is noted as 'other than honorable.' And it means you'll be out. Out, as if you never served. I've been through these before. They don't mess around. And I fear they may want to make an example out of you. I don't know. But that's what I fear. They won't want a homosexual to be recognized and awarded with such distinction as you have been. May want to hold you up as an example that no soldier is above the law."

The military used all their might to screen for homosexuals to prevent them from entering because officials believed they made poor soldiers, thought their presence in units would threaten morale and discipline, and believed they would corrupt others. Tens of thousands made it through the screening and were forced to conceal their sexuality or keep their behavior as inconspicuous as possible. Until 1943, soldiers caught having homosexual relations were court-martialed, imprisoned, and dishonorably discharged, all in a very public manner having a grave impact on their future. He said I was lucky since, after 1943, homosexuals no longer faced the threat of imprisonment or dishonorable discharge, but were still discharged for undesirable behavior. This is what we were up against.

"Can I fight it? Appeal it?"

"No, Hank. There is no appeal process. This is the army. They are the law. They have the evidence. The letters. Witnesses. Interviews they've conducted with others. Boswell."

"Sam? What did he say?"

"I have not seen all their evidence. I don't know."

"Witnesses?" I asked incredulously. "There were no witnesses to anything."

"They have witnesses," the general said. "I can't tell you anymore."

"This can't be happening," I said. "What about my surgeries? My health care needs?"

"All benefits will be terminated," he said. "Listen. I am trying to fight this. I am on your side. But the odds aren't in your favor."

"What's the process? How long does this take?"

"They've already been working on your case for several months. It's in the hands of the medical board. I don't know how backed up they are."

"My wife," I stumbled out.

"Yes, Hank," Mackey said. "I suppose you're going to have to figure that out. Along with a lot of other things. I'm sorry. But this is the way it is."

"Awarded for killing Japs and saving the lives of American soldiers. Punished for loving someone," I said in disbelief.

CHAPTER
9

"WHAT WAS THAT all about, Hank?" Margaret asked. "What's going on? General Mackey was deadly serious, not like him. Agents? From the Army Investigation Unit? I saw that on their briefcases. What's being investigated? You're in trouble. Tell me, Hank."

"It was a confidential matter. I'm not at liberty to discuss it with anyone," I said.

"I don't believe you. There was something about the general's tone. He wasn't himself. When has he ever called me, 'Mrs. Cummings?' Not since we first met. He's always been so warm to me. He was so different today."

"Yes. I know. It's a serious issue. But I can't discuss it. I'm sorry."

"You're lying," she said. "Are you in some sort of trouble? Tell me now, Hank. At least tell me you're okay, that you're not in trouble. Surely you can tell me that."

She sat across the table and crossed her arms. Her piercing gaze was focused on me and she wasn't going to back down. I wanted out of my uniform that now felt scratchy and unfamiliar, no longer agreeable to me. I removed the

Medal of Honor from around my neck and pinched it between my index finger and thumb. I didn't have enough sensation to feel the raised symbols and letters on its front. Above the medal's five-pointed star was a bar with the raised letters of the word 'VALOR.' The bar acted as a ledge upon which rested a gold eagle. I placed the medal on the table.

"I am in trouble," I finally said.

She sat silent and motionless. Without looking up, I could still feel the intensity of her glare.

My fate was inevitably sealed. "I'm being investigated for having an inappropriate relationship with another soldier," I said.

"What do you mean?" she curtly asked.

"Inappropriate," I repeated.

"As in what?" she said. "What do you mean, inappropriate? Like criminal?"

I couldn't look at her.

"Did you steal something? What did you do?" she shouted.

"Another man," I said. "A relationship with another man."

"What are you talking about?" she screamed. "Like, physical? Like a romantic thing?"

"That's what they are inferring."

"Inferring?" she shrieked. "What's that supposed to mean? Inferring? Don't play games with me, Hank. Tell me."

"In boot camp, I met a man. We became friends. We had a lot in common with each other, and not much in common with anyone else in camp. So, we became friends. Close friends."

"Continue."

"The army got it wrong, Marg. They misinterpreted our relationship. As, as being ... more than just friends."

"More than just friends? As in homosexuals?"

"That's their interpretation. But they got it wrong."

"What, they made it up? Is that what you're saying? They made it up out of thin air?"

"Well, no, not out of thin air. Sam and I wrote to each other a lot after camp ..."

"Sam? His name is Sam. Sam what?"

"It's not important."

"To me it is. What the hell is his name?"

"Sam Boswell. He's from Tennessee. Like I said, we wrote letters to each other. The army found them when they were gathering my belongings. They went through them, and they found the letters."

"And they were love letters?"

"No. It's not like that. But they were ... affectionate. We expressed private thoughts to each other. The army misinterpreted them."

"Sex? Did you have sex with him?"

"It's not like that," I said.

"Oh, really, Hank," she said. "Then what's it like?"

"It was stupid. We made a mistake."

"Did you have sex with him?" she repeated.

"Margaret ..."

"Answer the damn question, Hank."

I looked up to find Margaret holding her face in her hands. I looked back down. We sat in silence for several minutes. I'd already stripped Margaret from having a normal life. Now it was on the edge of ruins and I didn't know how to recover.

She remained stoic. "What now, Hank? Did they kick you out?"

"They might," I said. "Probably will."

"How could you do this?"

"I know," I said. "I mean, I don't know."

"You don't know?" she said sarcastically. "I'll bet you don't."

"I realize there is nothing I can say that would make sense out of this," I said. "I can't explain it. I'm so sorry. I'm just so sorry."

"Now you're sorry. I'll bet you are. What else?"

"Nothing else," I whispered.

After several more minutes of silence, she rose, grabbed her purse and car keys, and left without speaking. There was nothing else I could do. The physical pain of my burns paled in comparison to the emotional torment I'd caused us both. She didn't return before nightfall.

After a restless night's sleep, I woke to Margaret standing beside my bed smoking a cigarette, holding a cup of coffee. I don't know how long she'd been there but, based on the length of ash, I figured it had been several minutes.

"What now, Hank?" she asked. "Are you awake yet? Enough to talk?"

I nodded yes.

"So what's next? What are we going to do?"

"I don't know."

"Well, here is what I propose," she coolly said. "I am your wife. I'll do the best I can. And even if I can't love you, well, I'll try. Not sure I can, but I'll try. Last night I wanted to throw you out. My mother convinced me that's not the Christian thing to do. Try as I may to disagree, I cannot. I know this won't be easy, but, well, it is what it is."

Without waiting for my response, she set the cup of coffee on the bedside table and left the room. I felt a sense of relief if not exactly gratitude.

Over the next several weeks, my days became brutally routine. Margaret's relationship with me turned businesslike. She did the essentials. Attended to my medical needs, helped with physical therapy, prepared my meals, did my laundry.

In August, with benefits still intact, we made two more trips to Lexington for reconstructive surgeries. She braved the long drive since General Mackey could no longer assist us. There was nothing more that could be done for my hand and feet. I learned to be grateful that I had good use of my left thumb, index and middle fingers. They had fitted me with a prosthetic which consisted of a sheath of rubber that I would pull over my stump. Where my fingers had been was a hook. I detested it but it was functional, allowing me to scoop things up, pull up my slacks, pull open doors, even scratch an itch. Most of the work still needed was to reconstruct some semblance of a nose, ears, and lips, and loosen the grafted skin around my eyes. Nothing more could be done for my right eye, leaving me with the choice of either using a glass eye, or wearing an eye patch, or both, for the rest of my life. The cornea in my left eye was damaged by the fire. I was lucky to have limited sight, which was expected to improve over time, allowing me to do simple tasks, including reading and writing. I was labeled legally blind.

On November 1, 1945, I received a phone call from General Mackey. "Hank, I've exhausted all my efforts. The medical board has ruled to blue discharge you. You'll be notified via letter soon." He promised to stay in touch, but he would no longer be able to serve me in any formal capacity. "I'm sorry, Hank, but …" his voice tapering off not wanting to complete the sentence, "You've brought this on yourself."

On November 15, my twentieth birthday, mail carrier Smithers delivered the verdict in a simple brown army envelope.

It read:

Undesirable Discharge from the Armed Forces of the United States of America.

This is to certify that Private First Class Henry Earl Cummings Jr. was discharged from the United States Army on the first day of November 1945 as "undesirable." As such, all government benefits for his service have been terminated and he has been stripped of any and all Military Awards, Decorations, and Commendations.

Signed T. H. Jameson, By the direction of the Commandent, Eleventh District, United States Army

I handed the letter to Margaret.

"So, now it's official," is all she said as she handed it back to me without emotion.

I gathered myself at the typewriter and wrote Eliza, asking her to come with my parents for a visit as soon as it was convenient. I assume Margaret read it before she mailed it, but so be it.

The following Saturday, my parents and Eliza arrived around noon. They didn't know why they had been summoned, but tension was evident by Margaret's tone upon greeting them.

After uncomfortable pleasantries over tea and coffee, Margaret began. "Are you ready, Hank? To tell them? Or shall I?"

I started to stumble over my words, not able to articulate anything of meaning or value.

I gave my father the blue ticket letter.

"Undesirable?" my father balked. "What the hell does that mean? Undesirable. A Medal of Honor hero ... undesirable? I don't think so. What is this?"

"What?" my sister asked. "Let me see that." My father passed her the letter, which she then passed to my mother.

Margaret found the words I couldn't manage and stated clearly, "He had a homosexual relationship with a man in boot camp, and the army kicked him out. He's considered undesirable."

"No!" my mother yelped. "No he's not."

"Oh yes," Margaret responded. "Yes, he is. They investigated him. Two men sat right there, at the kitchen table, and laid it all out for him. He had a boyfriend ..."

"Stop it!" my mother screamed. "I can't ... just stop it."

Eliza came and sat next to me and put her hand on my shoulder. She gazed at the floor.

After several awkward minutes, my father said, "Is it true, Hank?"

Before I could respond, Margaret said, "Oh, it's true."

"I'm asking my son," my father said sternly.

At last I responded. "It's true I've been discharged. It's true that I became close to a man. We cared for each other very much. We made some mistakes.

But to categorize me as a homosexual is ... well, it's a lot of speculation on the army's part. That part isn't true. I am not a homosexual."

"Well then," my father said. "We'll fight it. We won't stand for this. You're a national treasure. A goddamn hero. They can't do this to you."

"Yes, they can," Margaret said. "They can and they did."

"Hogwash," my father said. "We'll get a lawyer. We are not sitting still for this. They can't do this."

My mother removed herself from the conflict and went to the kitchen. Eliza scooted closer to me and whispered that she loved me no matter what. My thoughts drifted to Sam.

CHAPTER

10

I WROTE TO THE GENERAL and asked if he would visit.

"I got your letter," General Mackey began. "Hank, it wouldn't be appropriate for me to visit you in any official capacity. But I'd be able to visit in a noncommissioned manner. As a friend."

"I couldn't ask for more," was my response.

It was a snowy Monday afternoon when the general made the drive to Grayson. I was amused to see him in non-military garb—khaki slacks, flannel shirt, unmarked jacket, and a John Deere cap on his head, looking more like a Kentucky farmer than an esteemed general.

Margaret was at work, which put our visit at greater ease. I hadn't shared precisely when the general would visit, only to tell her that he would be stopping by when it was convenient. I needed time with him alone, without her interjecting her agenda into our conversation.

I told him that my father had been contacting attorneys but that none of them would take the case. They found it a futile fight. The general shared that there was some momentum within the military to reform how homosexuals were being treated. Much of this, he said, was due to the massive strain on the need for troops—not because of newfound empathy or acceptance—which was lessening the intense weeding out process. Cases of gray areas, individuals who were deemed unfit to fight, could perhaps be assigned to other duties not as demanding or physically grueling, ironically such as writing or art.

"I don't imagine this can change anytime soon," Mackey said. "But there may be a day when it does. For now, I recommend you try to go on with your life the best you can. And do so with no expectations. If I can think of another route for you, I'll let you know. And I'll keep my ear to the ground on this. I promise. I'm on your side, Hank. But to be clear, we didn't have this conversation. I'm here as Tom Mackey, not General Mackey. Do I have your word on that?"

"Yes, sir," I said. "A question, though. What about the upcoming surgeries? I don't want to look like this for the rest of my life."

"The benefits have been cut off, no grace period. I'm sorry. I'll still fight for you, but no promises. Understand?"

"Yes, sir."

"It's, yes, Tom," he responded. "Now say it."

"Yes, Tom. Thank you."

As we said our goodbyes, Margaret pulled into the drive. They greeted each other on the sidewalk.

"You did not see me here, Margaret," Mackey said. "If you think you did, you'd be mistaken. God bless." He turned and left.

Several months later on an April afternoon, I was in my room, pecking away thoughts on my typewriter when I heard a knock at the door. Thinking nothing of it, I put my head back down to the keys.

I heard Margaret greet the visitor. "Yes, he's home. But we were not expecting company," she said.

"Well, you see, I was just driving through town and thought I'd take a chance," a familiar voice said.

"Would you mind waiting for a moment? Let me see if he's presentable," Margaret said.

"Not at all, ma'am."

I was frozen as she entered my room.

"There is a man here to see you. A Sam Black. He said he's a friend of yours from the army."

"I don't know that name," I said.

"Well, he's waiting on the porch. Do you want to come see? Maybe you'll recognize him. Or should I tell him to leave?"

"I don't know," I said as I limped into the living room where I could peek through the curtains. Sam Boswell was standing ten feet away, separated by a lace curtain blowing in the breeze.

I paused for a moment and said, "I don't know him. Tell him to leave." I paused to hear their exchange before returning to my room.

"I'm sorry," Margaret said. "He's not able to see anyone at the moment. Maybe some other time."

"Yes, ma'am," I understand. Please tell him I called on him and give him my best."

I began to close my door after entering my room, only to feel Margaret push against it.

"Who was that man, Hank?" Margaret asked.

"I told you I don't know."

"I don't believe you." She turned back toward the front door, as if meaning to confront the man, but as she did, the car accelerated away.

Reentering my room, "It was him, wasn't it? He had a Tennessee accent." I nodded.

"That was the last time you'll ever lie to me," she said. "Understand?" I nodded.

The next day, Margaret left a Holy Bible on my bedroom table next to my typewriter. It was opened to St. John, Chapter 8. She had written on a clipped piece of paper with an arrow drawn on it, pointing to Verse 32.

I needed the strongest of my magnified glasses to read the small print:
And ye shall know the truth, and the truth shall make you free.

CHAPTER

11

"IT'S *Life* MAGAZINE," Margaret said as she held out the phone for me. "Mr. McMillan, who wrote the article."

"Please understand, Mr. McMillan," I said. "I'm trying to live a low-key life. I don't want any spotlight on me."

"Oh, but the spotlight shines brightly on you, Private Cummings," McMillan said. "Once a hero, always a hero. The country is interested."

"I beg of you, please. There are lots of other heroes you can write about, I'm sure."

"None like you, Private."

"I'm sorry, I must go," I said as I hung up the phone relieved that he wasn't calling about my discharge

The call came nearly two years since I was discharged. I never took for granted how fortunate I was that it had not been revealed yet. I felt like the shoe was going to drop at some point—it would be a miracle if it stayed out of the public's eye forever.

It was understood that the army would only release my records if formally requested to do so. To our knowledge, the only people who knew were Margaret's mother and my family, and they each felt an obligation to protect me. The call from *Life* felt threatening.

As the seasons of time passed I sought comfort in the solitude of my room. Fueled by my imagination, my typewriter and books provided the means to create my own world, protected from the one outside that seemed so cruel.

I journaled my deepest thoughts. I wrote poetry. I wrote letters to my father and Eliza. I began dabbling in historical fiction, from the point of view of a soldier. I created Private Murphy, a ball tail gunner on a B-29, stationed in Guam. I took care to avoid autobiographical references. When I typed, I lost myself in Private Murphy's world of make-believe realism, and in a matter of weeks had written nine short stories that I believed were of substance. I shared them with Margaret. She read them all without looking up. Upon finishing the last one she placed the pages on the couch next to her. When she rose to look at me, her eyes were moist.

"Hank," she began. "These are remarkable. You've created something here. You really have." She picked up the stack and began shuffling through the pages stopping to reference and read back to me various lines that stood out to her.

It was her idea to submit them to *Reader's Digest*, but I wanted nothing to do with any recognition. "Submit them under an alias," she said. Let's make up a name for you. No one has to know it's you. I'll help you. We can do it together."

Something stirred in me. I felt it in my stomach, in my chest, in my heart. A burden was lifted. Even a hint of joy, an unfamiliar emotion. Margaret was by my side as a partner again. For at least a fleeting moment, I felt hopeful, a sense of renewed faith restored.

"These are the kinds of stories they publish," she continued. "We've got nothing to lose. Let's do it." She giggled at the thought. "You're writing again, Hank. You're really writing."

All I needed to do was write. She would do the rest. She created the alias Captain John Sterns, a former marine. To further distance us from my identity, she secured a post office box in Ashland, Kentucky, some twenty miles away from Grayson. Our submissions would be postmarked from Ashland, and any correspondence in return would come there as well.

Within a month of submitting the first three stories, we received a letter from the magazine's publisher:

September 17, 1947

Captain Sterns,

Thank you for submitting your stories, titled <u>Through the Eyes of a Private</u>. On behalf of our editorial staff, we found them insightful and delightful, and intend on publishing them in upcoming issues. Since you've labeled each story as one, two, and three, might we presume you have additional stories, or intend to develop such? We would be interested in securing them and developing an ongoing series, and are prepared to provide compensation of $4.50 per story. Please correspond in return if this sort of arrangement is agreeable with you. Enclosed, please find our check for $13.50 for the rights to publish the ones you've submitted.

Most sincerely,
B.H. Kizer
Publisher
Reader's Digest

This proved the beginning of more than just an escape, but a path of fulfillment and contribution that I had deemed unreachable. One of my greatest fears since the war was that I would never be able to or contribute financially, but for a small monthly stipend my father sent us.

The arrangement with *Reader's Digest* was informal. There was no contract. They could choose to discontinue the series at any time. Nor was $4.50 a month a significant contribution. But it was a start. With Margaret's support and prodding, I dedicated myself to writing substance with the goal of publishing on a grander scale. Once I had written my twentieth short story of Private Murphy, I had enough content to recraft into the form of a novel.

Reader's Digest was founded by a man named DeWitt Wallace while he was recovering from wounds he received in WWl. I learned it was he who took a liking to my work because of his interest in our country's military history. I befriended the editor, Donald Perkins, who encouraged me to turn the work into long-form. He was optimistic that through his connections with Manhattan publishers, I might have a future. The trick was to not reveal my identity, which proved challenging when he wrote that he needed my physical address so he could send me a box of previously published war-related articles and stories—fact and fiction—about the experiences of soldiers serving our country. He would not be able to send the package to a post office box. Luckily, Margaret had a friend in Ashland and was able to use her address as our base.

Margaret opened the box to find a letter from Perkins on top of several magazines and separate articles and stories.

October 16, 1947

Dear Captain Sterns,

It is a delight that I share these pieces with you as I believe you'll find them of great interest. Specifically, you must be aware of a Private Henry Cummings, who suffered horrific injuries in a plane crash in Guam, and subsequently was awarded the Medal of Honor. As luck may have it, he is from Grayson, Kentucky, which is a short trip from your home in Ashland. You'll find in our July 1947 issue a reference of him in a longer piece about the travails of our fine soldiers. I am aware that you served in the Marine Corps but must inquire if you have ever met Private Cummings. Perhaps you could find him? I know it would be a divergence

from your normal series, but how interesting it might be for you to write
a piece on him. Mr. Wallace personally asked me to reach out to you. As
you know, he suffered terrible injuries in the Great War and continues
to marvel at others through this kindred connection.

Sincerely,
Donald Perkins
Editor
Reader's Digest

With trepidation, Margaret found the article that included me. It was short, no more than three paragraphs in a longer piece, compiled from secondary information that had already been published elsewhere. We were able to find humor in a photo they published of me during the parade. Included in the frame was a young boy rushing toward me with a jar of pickles, including the caption, *The Pickle Man.*

I responded that I was aware of Private Cummings, as the entire country surely was, but had not met him and was not sure whether I could connect with him. But at the request of Mr. Wallace, I would try. My attempts, of course, proved futile. No one seemed to know where he currently lived and what little information I could gather was that he wanted to be left alone.

Within months I'd submitted thirty-six stories to the magazine, three years' worth, which I thought would be more than they would accommodate. Then, I focused on a long-form novel of historical fiction about the journey of Private Murphy as he fought the Japanese. The WWII soldier was a popular genre with publishers during this time, which made the market cluttered for a new author to gain traction. Nonetheless, with the help of Donald Perkins, we submitted the manuscript to several houses. We received back eight rejection letters, but at last, the publishing house Barter & Lloyd showed interest and they assigned an editor to help me smooth out the rough edges. In 1949, my first novel, *The Darkness Over the Pacific*, was published. I received a check for

$1,500 and a contract with royalties based upon sales moving forward. They wanted more.

I feverishly pecked away, the sounds of the keystrokes offering soothing company. Margaret provided for my needs and managed her own work and social life outside the house. It was the deal we made.

I had yet to find success with a second book. Two manuscripts had gone nowhere, rejected without the offer to help. 'Unfixable' is what the editor wrote. Yet, I was a writer and it became my focus with zeal.

My enthusiasm ended when I received another call from *Life* magazine. A different reporter. He said the magazine had remained committed to running another piece on me and that through a public records request, they had learned of my discharge.

"We're going to run a story whether you cooperate or not," the reporter said. "This is an opportunity for you to manage the conversation. What does 'undesirable discharge' mean? What could a Medal of Honor awardee have done to be called undesirable?"

I declined to participate.

Three months later Margaret and I woke to a sign that had been planted in our yard. *Sodomizer.*

I hadn't told her about the call from *Life*. She was not prepared for the public display and attacks that would sweep through our lives. Her only target for her disgust and embarrassment was me. "Remember when I told you you've ruined our lives, Hank?" she asked. She slammed the door so hard the wood around the hinge cracked. The phone rang endlessly. The doorbell rang. Cars paraded by our house. The spectacle I had tried to escape from was now in full view, even if I wasn't. Margaret burned the signs that continued to be planted in the yard.

She turned away interview requests, denying everything. "They got it wrong," she told everyone, "No comment."

Margaret threw the *Life* magazine that had been tossed on the porch across the room at me. It was a two-page piece including three photos: my army portrait, one from my hospital bed being awarded the Medal of Honor, and the army portrait of Private Sam Boswell.

The headline read, *Honor No More.*

CHAPTER

12

THE NEXT SEVERAL YEARS were the most difficult. Margaret and I barely spoke. We were business partners and roommates. Nothing more. I had accepted that this is how I would live out my years. It's how I imagined I would feel in my old age, not in my thirties. My writing was my respite and afforded me moments of security and comfort. Away from the sounds of the typewriter keystrokes, the distance between Margaret and me was deafening.

In 1955, she legally changed her name back to her maiden name, Margaret Hitchcock. She found a job at a bank in Lexington, Kentucky. We sold our house and moved to Frankfort, just north of Lexington. "You can come if you want," she told me. "But don't expect much from me."

With this move I felt even more isolated. On the rare occasions when I left the house, I would wear a hat and sunglasses, hide my face with a bandana, and wear gloves that I'd stuffed with tissue paper to resemble fingers. The house was secluded on an acre of land surrounded by trees.

I called General Mackey to tell him that we were now in Frankfort and asked if he could make the hour drive for a visit, which he did. His tone was warm and understanding. He told me he had not given up on reversing the discharge. By now, numerous lawsuits had been filed against the military requesting the release of those who had been incarcerated. The topic was unsavory, however, with little to no public empathy for those involved. He felt it better to stay quiet, 'under the radar,' he said. "Let's let some other things play out, maybe set a precedent, and then perhaps you'll have a stronger legal case if you choose."

I felt the door was open to ask him a most private question. "Do you know where Sam Boswell is? Can you find him?" He looked down without responding. "I'm asking you as a friend, Tom."

"I'll try," he said.

A week later, he called. "Write this down. 326 Paramount Lane, Knoxville, Tennessee, 37901." He hung up.

I had written Sam dozens of letters over the years, none of which I sent. The writing was therapeutic and a way to keep him alive in my thoughts. I fantasized what his responses might be if we could communicate openly with each other. I wondered if he did the same. I must be alive with him as well. Otherwise, he wouldn't have come to the parade. He wouldn't have taken the chance to visit me at my house. Had he made any other attempts to see me or contact me? Did he know I didn't live in the little house in Grayson anymore? I wondered about the fallout from his name being published as my lover in *Life*.

I held the torn piece of paper with his address in my hand. It felt like a key to a forbidden land. I could barely read my own scribbles as I had not become adept at holding a pencil. I wrote the address out again, slowly, ensuring that I had it right.

I sat at the typewriter and wrote.

June 7, 1956

Dearest Sam,

I miss you. I long to see you, to touch you, to talk with you. I pray you are well. Please forgive me if I am intruding. I saw you at the parade and also on my porch when you came to my house in Grayson. My heart melted each time. There is so much I want to say. Mostly that I am sorry. Sorry for any pain I've caused you. I've tried desperately to let go. But I'm unable. I would understand if you never want to hear from me again. If I don't hear back from you, I'll take that as the sign. If you want to write back, do so as follows: Address it to Attn.: Captain John Sterns, c/o Reader's Digest, 480 North Bedford Road, Chappaqua, NY. Captain Sterns is an alias I use for writing. I've published several stories, some enclosed for fun. Also know that any correspondence may be read by another.

If you choose not to write back, I'll understand and still forever hold you dearly in my heart.

Affectionately yours,
Hank

Our mailbox stood on a post at the end of our drive, one hundred feet from our front door. I walked down the drive and waited for the mail carrier, who typically came around noon on Fridays. I sat on a stump nearby until I heard his truck approach. I rose to greet him and handed him the letter. He drove away without uttering a word.

Margaret made weekly visits to the post office to fetch whatever correspondence I may have received. I often received a package from *Reader's Digest* with letters from admirers or others wanting to reach me for some reason. Many of them were from soldiers sharing their stories.

A month after I'd written Sam, Margaret dropped a bundle from the publisher on my desk.

In it was a letter from Sam.

July 9, 1956

Dear Captain Sterns,

I hope this letter finds you well. I trust my reaching out to you is not an intrusion. I am writing to commend you on your stories in Reader's Digest. I have a story that you might find of interest. Please let me know if you'd like to hear it and perhaps we could arrange a meeting. You may remember me from Fort Benning. I will never forget the games we played together.

Most sincerely,
Norm Edwards

We'd both become creatures of routine and I could count on Margaret's schedule like clockwork. She rose precisely at six in the morning to do work on whatever puzzle she had spread across the dining room table. At seven she'd prepare breakfast, usually consisting of eggs, toast, and perhaps a serving of fruit if it were in season. We typically ate together at the small kitchen table. The cold, yet polite conversation was something we'd both adapted to, strictly business. By 8:15, she was dressed and out the door to her job at the bank. I would then retreat to my room and typewriter for the day. Not on this day. Instead, I sat on the couch in the front room with a view of our drive, waiting for Sam Boswell.

The car approached and stopped near our front walk. He sat there for several minutes before he got out and made his way to the door. He looked good. Trim, fit, his hair, still blond but with wisps of gray, now long and pulled behind his ears. He looked every bit the artist that he was.

I stood inside the front door and opened it before he could ring the bell.

"Samuel," I sighed.

"Oh my dear," he responded.

I balanced my weight against my cane and backed away to give him room to step inside. He reached for me and put his hands on my shoulders before tenderly stroking my face with the back of his hand. I fell into his arms and broke down. He pulled me against him and tightly wrapped his arms around my back. I dropped my cane and did the same. My chest was heaving as he patted and rubbed my back. I have no recollection of how long we stood there. When our tears slowed and we could catch our breath, I pulled back from him.

"Let's sit," I said.

"May I? May I see your face?" he asked as he gestured toward my sunglasses. I nodded. He pulled them from my face. "I need to see you," he said. "All of you. Don't be afraid."

"I'm sorry," I said as I broke into tears again. "I'm so sorry."

He reached for my hand, my remaining fingers. "Is this okay?" he asked as he began to hold them. I nodded. With his handkerchief he dabbed at my tears. "You have nothing to be sorry for."

"You look so good to me," I said. "I can't believe you're here."

"I can't believe I am either," he smiled. "It's so good to see you."

"Where do we start?" I said. "How do we do this?"

As I tried to summarize the past ten years, I thought how incredible it was to see him, to be with him. I rushed through the important things for fear of running out of time. I couldn't look into his eyes enough. They were bluer than I remembered. And it may have been the morning light, but they sparkled. He looked strong and healthy and had specks of acrylic paint under his fingernails as an artist would. I wanted to run my fingers through his hair. I wanted to kiss his lips. While I marveled at how attractive I still found him, I thought how grotesque I must seem in return. If so, he never gave so much as a hint.

"Your turn," I said.

He told me he had left the army before my discharge, therefore was never formally blue ticketed, but did lose his benefits. He moved to San Francisco after serving, where he tried to establish himself as an artist. After several years, he moved to Manhattan and had success with galleries and dealers. In 1954 he returned to Knoxville to help care for his aging parents but was planning on moving back to San Fransisco soon. He wasn't even aware of the *Life* magazine article, living in New York when the issue came out. "Besides," he said laughing. "Who reads *Life* magazine? Plus, everybody already knows I'm a fag!"

"Do you have someone in your life?" I asked.

"I do, Hank," he replied. "I've been with Steven for three years."

"Are you happy? The two of you?"

"We are. Yes."

"I'm happy for you," I said.

For four hours we talked. About the past, present, and future. We talked painting, literature, philosophy. I was transported back to the moments we shared at Fort Benning. We held each other before our goodbye. I would likely never see him again, though we promised to stay in touch and always let each other know where our lives took us.

"I love you," I said.

"Ditto," he responded. "I do. I promise."

Chapter

13

MY RETREAT INWARD in the weeks and months after Sam's visit was obvious. As more seasons and years passed, the distance between Margaret and me continued to widen. I had accepted my reality. No wonder she began to rebel against hers. She said it was becoming unbearable living in a home with such a negative, depressing aura. She complained I never talked to her. I returned that I felt barely acknowledged. For two decades my days became nearly identical. I wrote and read. I didn't leave the house except for nighttime walks under the safety of darkness.

Margaret lived a life outside the house. She had her work. She had friends and a social life that didn't include me. She spent most of her time away from me, acting only as a caretaker, meeting the obligations demanded of her by my condition. She eventually stopped trying to coax me outside. I was stuck. She wasn't.

On a chilly October morning in 1971, she approached me. "I think it's time you moved to Ohio," she began. "This isn't working for either of us. You know it and I know it. I've tried. But I can't do it anymore." She waited for a response I did not grant her. "Well?"

Eliza and I had talked often about this. But my mother's mental illness was taking too much of a toll on her, and she worried it would be too difficult for everyone, especially me. As bad as it might be in Frankfort for me, she feared it would be worse in Ohio. She said Momma was crazier than ever since daddy died. That it wouldn't be good for me to be around her.

"I can't," I responded to Margaret. "They can't have me. They just can't."

"Well, where else would you go?"

"What do you mean, where else would I go? What are you saying?"

"I'm just saying."

"You're just saying *what*?"

"I can't stay with you, Hank. I'm leaving. Leaving you. Leaving this house. This is not a home for me anymore. I can't stay here. If you can't move to Ohio, you can stay here. We'll find someone to come in and care for you. It's your house. You can do as you please."

"What else do you need to tell me, Margaret? Tell me the rest of the story."

"I don't know what you mean."

"The truth shall make you free," I said. "Go ahead. If there is more to it, tell me now. Don't think you're protecting me. You can't hurt me."

She told me. Everything. She'd been carrying on an affair for over ten years with a man from Grayson, a former coworker named Glen Burkholder. I'd met him. He used to make deliveries to the house. I remember he'd sometimes linger around, and they'd have tea on the porch together. She said they had been in love for many years. She never imagined leaving me until his wife died, paving a way to uncomplicate their relationship. Tragic as it was, she said. She saw her future with him. She needed to be set free. She was sorry.

I wasn't hurt. I wasn't confused. I was relieved. In setting her free, it would also set me free.

"I understand," I said. "I love you for all you've done for me. I wouldn't be alive without you. I'm only sorry I couldn't have been someone else for you."

"I'm sorry too. This is best for you, Hank. You've got to find a life outside of these walls. You can't hide behind your typewriter the rest of your life. I'll find someone who can help you. I shouldn't be that hard to replace."

This caused me to laugh. We talked longer than we'd talked in years. We both shared things we'd kept from each other for decades. I wondered if we could have dealt with other things in our marriage the way we were dealing with the end, perhaps it could have led to a different outcome. The tone was warm and intimate. I held no grudges. No hard feelings. I knew in my heart she was a good soul who was dealt an awful hand. Perhaps, I wondered out loud, if I wasn't blue ticketed, still had my honor, if I could have assimilated into society without shame of showing my ugly face.

"Perhaps," she said.

I did love her for the commitment she showed me for nearly three decades caring for me. To see the joy drained from her face and the weathering around her eyes becoming more pronounced through the years saddened me. She had aged. The kindest thing I could do as her husband was to let her go.

She intended to move to an apartment in Grayson that Burkholder had found for her. But she said she wouldn't leave our house until finding a suitable caretaker for me. "I'm not going to leave you high and dry, Hank."

The first call I made was to Eliza. "Momma's a handful," she said. "If this is what you need, we'll find a way to manage. But I'd be lyin' if I said it's gonna be easy."

I hadn't seen my mother since my father's funeral seven years before. We never spoke on the phone. I occasionally wrote her. She didn't write me. She had found some peace through abandoning my existence. I couldn't comprehend how either of us would adjust to being under the same roof together. Stress triggered both of us in negative ways. And the burden on Eliza, I feared, would be too much. We agreed the timing wasn't right as long as Momma was still alive.

Margaret reached out to agencies who provided in-home health care services. For weeks, people came to the house to meet me and evaluate my situation. They usually said my needs were outside the scope they could provide.

"What you need is a maid and a butler," one of them said. She was right. Margaret changed the direction of her search. Instead of looking for a health care provider, she placed an ad in the paper.

Looking for able-bodied individual to do basic household functions such as cleaning, shopping, cooking, and provide companionship for disabled WWII veteran.

Dozens of people responded to the ad and for several weeks paraded in and out of the house. Many were younger women, students at the University of Kentucky. Meeting me proved uncomfortable. Most were polite but anxious to get on their way.

We finally found Sally Bamberger, a fifty-five-year-old widow and grandma to three, whose husband was buried in Normandy. She seemed competent, understanding, kind, eager to take the job, and lived ten minutes away. The arrangement would be for her to come to the house every weekday morning at seven-thirty to prepare my breakfast. She would do whatever shopping or household chores necessary, go to the post office and bank, come home and prepare my lunch and dinner. She would leave by two o'clock but call me at seven o'clock each evening to check in. On weekends, she would call me at seven o'clock each morning and evening to touch base. The three of us decided to try it.

It was a dreary Saturday morning when Glen Burkholder backed a pickup into our driveway to help Margaret gather her belongings and move them with her to her new apartment. I stayed in my room. She came to say goodbye, sat on my bed and cried. I told her nothing more needed to be said. "I owe you happiness," I said. "I sincerely hope you find it."

She said she was just a phone call away and wouldn't abandon me. She told me everything was in order with the divorce papers and it would take three months before it was final. I asked her how long she planned to live in the apartment. "Three months," she said.

CHAPTER
14

SALLY WAS A GODSEND. She treated me with dignity and respect that I hadn't experienced since the war. She was punctual and responsible. She provided good company and managed to make me laugh and smile on every visit. She was an excellent cook. No longer was I fed eggs and toast for breakfast. There were now pancakes and waffles on the table. Omelets and ham. I ordered lunches and dinners off a menu she created. I would make my choices for an entire week, making it easier for her to shop and prepare the meals. Every Sunday, I religiously chose her pot roast. She would surprise me with treats, candy, and ice cream. And pickles. We made a separate arrangement for her to act as my ad hoc business manager, providing a check and balance on my finances, even doing basic editing on my writing.

I couldn't have hoped for a better arrangement. It also eased Margaret's concern and allowed her to transition into her new life with little guilt. She would visit me two times a month, every other Saturday morning. I told her it wasn't necessary. She said she was doing it more for her than me.

I was able to write to Sam, now living in San Francisco, without fear or guilt to tell him of my new circumstances. He wrote back that he was relieved for me. He was still with Steven, and still happy. Upon my request, he sent recent pictures of himself and his paintings. I pinned them to the wall above my writing table.

It was Christmas Day, 1971. I woke to the beauty of several inches of fresh snow, causing the limbs of the pines to droop. I looked out my window at the birds pecking through the powder on the bird feeder in search of seeds. Sally was due to arrive at noon after spending Christmas morning with her grandchildren.

She never arrived. I called her house but there was no answer. I phoned Margaret. Again no answer. Did I misunderstand? Get the time wrong? No. I was certain. I kept calling both numbers throughout the day, but to no avail. At five o'clock, I called the operator and asked for the number of Glen Burkholder, Grayson, Kentucky.

"Hello, Merry Christmas," a man said.

"Glen?" I asked.

"Yes, who is this?"

"Glen, I'm sorry to bother you. It's Hank Cummings."

"Oh, Hank. It's no bother. What's the purpose of the call?"

"Is Margaret there? May I speak with her?"

"Hank?" Margaret asked upon picking up the phone.

"I'm sorry to bother you, but Sally was supposed to visit today at noon, and she didn't show up. I've been calling her all day but there is no answer. This isn't like her. Something's wrong."

"I'll see if I can find out something," she said. "I'll call you back soon."

An hour later, she phoned. "I couldn't find her, Hank," she said. "We called the police and Lexington area hospitals, and they have nothing to report. It must have been a misunderstanding. It's Sunday. She doesn't visit on Sunday, does she? Doesn't she have a son out of town? Maybe she is there?"

I continued to phone her house, but still no answer. Finally, I retired to bed and a restless night. Per our routine, Sally would be here at seven-thirty in the morning, a Monday.

I was sitting in the front room when a car pulled into the drive. It was Margaret.

"Sally's dead, Hank," she said. "The police found her car late last night around midnight, overturned, down the embankment in the ravine on Washburn Road. Based on the tire tracks and the snowfall, they figured she'd been there all night."

Stunned, I said, "That ravine is not even a mile away. Washburn Road. She was on her way to see me."

In her car, the police found two wrapped presents for me, a scattering of groceries including fresh meat and vegetables, all the ingredients for a pot roast, and a container of Neapolitan ice cream.

She was going to make me Christmas dinner.

I was a wretched mess. Margaret stayed with me through the day. She shopped for groceries and prepared some meals for me, enough to get me through the week. She said we'd find another Sally. I doubted that.

She returned on Tuesday afternoon, accompanied by a man. He was Sally's son, Peter.

"My mom loved you, Private Cummings," Peter said. "She talked about you all the time. You have no idea how much purpose you gave her. How much joy. My wife, son, and I spent Christmas Eve at my sister's house here in Lexington. My mom came over early Christmas morning for breakfast and to open presents with the grandkids. She left at exactly 11:45. I'll never forget it. She said, 'Hank will be waiting and I'm never even a minute late.' We all hugged her goodbye."

"I loved her too," I said. "She was an angel to me."

"Private Cummings," Peter said. "On behalf of our family, I have a request. Her funeral is Friday. We want you to speak. To say a few words. Maybe a reading."

"Oh, Peter, I don't know, I ..."

"She would want that. We all want that."

Margaret gave me a slight smile.

"Before you say no," Peter continued. "Let me tell you a little more about my mom. My sister and I were just two and three years old when my dad was killed in the war. Neither of us have any memory of him. My mom raised us by herself. Never remarried. She spent her life volunteering, helping those in need. Her heart remained warm and open, yet she was a tough cookie. A stiff upper lip type. The past few years, something changed in her. She became sad and withdrawn. She blamed it on menopause. Who knows. We were worried about her. Then she met you. And she began to shine again. Do you know what she did with the salary you paid her? She gave it to the church in your name. So whether you knew it or not, you were feeding the poor. She said you reminded her of our dad. 'He has your dad's soul,' she said. She was protective of you. We all wanted to meet you. She said, in time. 'I'm working on it,' she told us."

"She spoke of you often, and the grandchildren," I said.

He paused. Margaret sat closer to me on the couch and put her arm around me. "Hank," she simply said.

"Okay," I said softly. "I'll do it. I'd be honored."

"Thank you," Peter said. "One more thing. We know you are a hero. We ask that you wear your army service uniform, badges and all."

Margaret was at the house promptly at eight o'clock on Friday morning to help me get dressed. I had not worn the uniform since the interrogation at my dining room table. She had long ago wrapped it in plastic to protect it. I was technically prohibited from wearing it due to my discharge. The same held for my medals. I didn't care.

We arrived at the church well in advance, in time to meet the rest of the family and Reverend Sipes, who would conduct the service. We exchanged stories and tears. The reverend told me how Sally's contributions helped keep the food bank open. He presented me with a plaque of acknowledgment, of which a duplicate would forever hang in the front foyer of the church.

The family insisted Margaret and I walked into the chapel with them.

Wearing my army dress blues adorned with my medals and ribbons, including the Medal of Honor ribboned around my neck, made me feel like a hero again. Not only to the country. Not only to Sally and her family. To me as well. Everything else melted away. If even just for that moment.

It became my turn to speak. I rose and steadied myself with my cane, then proceeded to the lectern. I reached into my breast pocket, pulled out my reading, which Margaret had arranged to be printed in large type, and put on my reading glasses. One could hear a pin drop.

> *The LORD is my shepherd, I shall not want.*
> *He makes me lie down in green pastures;*
> *he leads me beside still waters;*
> *he restores my soul.*
> *He leads me in right paths*
> *for his name's sake.*
> *Even though I walk through the darkest valley,*
> *I fear no evil;*
> *for you are with me;*
> *your rod and your staff—*
> *they comfort me.*
> *You prepare a table before me*
> *in the presence of my enemies;*
> *you anoint my head with oil;*
> *my cup overflows.*
> *Surely goodness and mercy shall follow me*
> *all the days of my life,*
> *and I shall dwell in the house of the LORD*
> *my whole life long.*

After the service, I declined the invitation to join the family at Sally's daughter's house. Instead, Margaret took me home. She came inside with me to talk about what to do next. I told her I thought it was time to move to Ohio.

After she left, I called Eliza. "Does the offer still stand?" I asked. "Of course," she responded.

CHAPTER

15

MARGARET HELPED ME pack my possessions. I didn't have much. Didn't need much. With Burkholder's help, she would oversee the sale of the house and auction off furniture, dishes, and other household items that neither of us wanted.

Everything was in order when Eliza made the ten-hour round trip in her pickup truck to fetch me on an unseasonably warm March morning. Sally's daughter, son, and grandchildren came to meet her and say goodbye. We shared a pot roast made from Sally's recipe. It was as good as ever.

I was apprehensive at the prospect of these new beginnings, especially with the anticipation of how my mother would respond to my presence. She'd conveniently erased me. Now she'd be forced to come face-to-face with her denial. Eliza tried to temper my anxiety by working to convince me that she barely knew night from day and spent all her time in one of her many rockers throughout the house with her nose buried in a book, often reading the same one multiple times before moving to another.

How I would navigate around the woman who gave birth to me and tolerate her behavior was something I couldn't predict. I hadn't spoken to her or seen her since my father's funeral. Even then, attempts at kindness were rebuffed. When I tried to hug her goodbye, she turned from me. I had long ago reconciled the sadness of losing her. My allegiance for many years was solely with my father and Eliza, and I felt sorrow for the burden my mother placed on them. My father always reasoned that it wasn't her fault, that she was sick with an illness that turned her into a different person, oblivious to her behavior and its effects on others. He never stopped loving her, even doting on her when she didn't deserve it. Eliza was much more pragmatic, focusing her attention and care strictly on my father. She said it was her job to help support him in his efforts to remain of strong mind and body despite the constant wear of caring for my mother.

When my father died, Eliza became her sole caretaker, much like Margaret had been for me, out of obligation and necessity. This gave me empathy for Eliza, Margaret, and even my mother, as I could relate to the role of helplessness and the need to rely on others for so much.

"How much does Momma know?" I asked as Eliza began to guide the truck north.

"Not much," she said. "She knows you're coming home with me, but she doesn't know it's forever. She said, 'Oh really,' when I told her. I'm not sure it registered."

Mother was seventy-seven years old and other than her deteriorated mental state was fit as a fiddle.

"You know," Eliza continued. "This might be good for her. To have you home. It's goin' to be up to you. She doesn't initiate any conversation. She usually just rocks and reads. She likes to wander around the woods. She loves the birds. She keeps their feeders full and shoos away the squirrels and chipmunks that try to poke their snouts inside the holes to get to the seeds and corn. The same birds come back every spring. She recognizes them and calls them by the names she's given them."

"I'm looking forward to wandering the woods myself," I said. "It will be nice to have the freedom to roam without worry of being seen. Does anyone besides Momma know I'm coming?"

"Only Ed. Ed Klein. He owns the market where I do my shopping. He's a good man. A good friend. Loved Daddy and looks in on us to make sure we're okay. He knows all about you. Daddy wasn't shy about talking about his son. 'A national treasure,' he called you. But Ed is also well aware of your desire for privacy. He'll help protect that for you, I'm certain. But I want you to meet him. Wait, didn't you meet him at Daddy's funeral?"

"I don't remember meeting anyone," I said. "Does anyone know? You know."

"Your discharge? Not that I'm aware. Daddy never discussed it with anyone as far as I know. We never even talked about it."

"That's why I don't want anyone to know I'm here. They'll start digging around. Curiosity, you know? Other than the *Life* magazine thing, it's been kept under wraps. I owe a lot of that to General Mackey."

"How so?"

"He said he made my file go away. Not sure now if anyone could even find a record of it."

"Well then, no one has to know, do they? No one will know. I'll make sure of it."

Eliza lit the last cigarette of the pack. "Shit," she said. "Gonna have to stop and get me some more."

"I'm worried about how much you smoke," I said. "Plus you've got a really nasty cough."

"Don't you worry 'bout me," she said. "My cough's nothin' more than allergies."

"Doesn't sound like an allergy cough," I said.

"Smokin's treated me fine so far," she said. "Ain't gonna stop now. Besides, you sound like Ed."

"Well, maybe he's right," I said.

"Na," she said. "I should go back to filtered, though. That'll be my compromise."

The sun and breeze through the window soothed my face. This was my favorite time of year. Spring brought new growth, leaves, buds, and blossoms. Fitting that my new beginning would coincide with the woods and flowers around the new house coming back to their fullness in just a few weeks. I felt a twinge of that unfamiliar joy as I closed my eyes and drifted into a nap.

I dreamt, as I often did, of scenes from stories not yet told. Perhaps my imagination would flourish in my new surroundings, and I would at last venture beyond the world of Captain Sterns. For years, my agent, Fin Talbot, had been encouraging me to write under the byline H. E. Cummings to detach me from the WWII genre, the popularity of which had passed with the advent of the Korean and Vietnam wars. Book sales had been flat and I had not published since 1965.

I woke as we were crossing the Ohio River, approaching the Cincinnati skyline. "What do you think of H. E. Cummings," I asked Eliza?

"Who?" she asked.

"You know, as an author," I said.

"You mean, E. E. Cummings, the poet," she said.

"No, I mean H. E. Cummings, as in Henry Earl. The novelist."

"Ha! I love him," she said. "Are you going to do it? You know how proud that would have made Daddy? And maybe Momma. Might make you more real to her."

"Maybe it should be H. E. Cummings Jr."

"Yes, perhaps. I like that," she said.

The next time I would sit at my typewriter, I would be writing as the novelist H. E. Cummings Jr. And I would venture beyond the sights, sounds, and smells of WWII.

The rolling hills of the countryside of northeast Ohio felt familiar. A rain cloud moved over us in an otherwise blue sky as dusk approached. A light rain fell, sprouting a rainbow in the distance as Eliza steered the truck down

Yoder Road to the long gravel lane that led to my new home. "See," Eliza said, pointing to the rainbow. "Daddy's callin' you home."

When I was last here after my father died, it was winter. The skies were gray, and the only sound heard was that of the snow crunching beneath our steps. The entire property now glistened with color, birds chirping, creatures scurrying, buds beginning to sprout. I could faintly hear the water cascading over stones in the nearby creek. It was a comforting homecoming.

"This feels right," I told Eliza. "It feels like home."

"It's where you belong," she said. "It's where you've always belonged. Let me go ahead. Maybe you stay put for a sec."

I got out to stretch my legs, leaned against the pickup, and glanced toward the house. My mother was sitting in her rocker. When our eyes met, she rose, turned from me, and walked into the house.

CHAPTER
16

THE SECLUDED HOUSE that sat at the end of a long, private lane on a four-acre lot of overgrown trees had belonged to our family for over thirty years. It was technically in Mansfield, Ohio, but the area was known as 'Little Kentucky.' It was not far from the steel mills that once forged the armor that made tanks, jeeps, ships, and planes during the war years. I always wondered if the skin of the Sassy Susan came from these mills. The black smoke still bellowed from the mill's massive stacks and colored the sky a rich gray on even the sunniest days.

In the early part of the twentieth century an Amish man, Elijah Yoder, sold the 400 acres that his family once lived on and farmed so it could be divided into small plots of land to accommodate the hundreds of men and their families coming to work in the mills, including mine. The overwhelming majority of workers who settled in the area came from across the southern side of the Ohio River, and it wasn't long before the whole district took on an Appalachian Mountain character and was nicknamed Little Kentucky. It wouldn't be uncommon to be greeted by a chicken at the front door and find dirt floors inside. Many homes still had outhouses. Children lacked new clothes and shoes and were often forced to wear ill-fitting, mismatched outfits that came from hand-me-downs, donations, or the Salvation Army. The most cherished commodity was the bicycle, which provided freedom for one to explore as far as he or she could pedal. There was usually just one per household, shared by all family members, making for an interesting array of mismatched sizes of kids and frames.

Yoder Road ran east and west through the middle of the original Yoder property, leaving an equal two hundred acres on either side—north and south. On the south side stood the hundreds of small homes of Little Kentucky. The house my father bought was the only habitable house on the north side. The roughly two hundred acres of land that surrounded the house was owned by a real estate developer from Cleveland who had allowed it to become overgrown with trees and brush. Many offers had been tended to my father and Eliza over the years, but they both stood firm that there would never be one good enough to part with the property.

The house was built in 1894 by Jensen Yoder, son of Elijah. Also on the property once stood a barn and a one-room church which served the Amish community. With the exception of Jensen's house, all the other structures were on the south side of Yoder Road and were razed for the development of the Little Kentucky housing development. The road used to just be a dirt path known as Cattail Lane due to the abundance of cattails all around. During the land transaction, the developer renamed it Yoder Road as a recognition of the Yoder legacy.

Like all the Yoders, Jensen was a simple man. A carpenter by trade, he helped build dozens of homes and barns for the Amish community. The two-story saltbox was well constructed using the finest materials available and tendered with exceptional craftmanship. Built from wood and iron, it was timber framed with post and beam construction. The finished wood floors barely squeaked. The doors were two inches thick, made of oak, and were hung precisely with a perfect fit. The outside walls were finished with wood siding that had been painted several times over the decades, always a rusty or dark red. The roof was shingled with cedar that came to the area via the Himalayas. The house had four bedrooms and one bathroom, fully plumbed with thick iron pipe. Water was provided by a spring well, heat by a woodburning stove in the middle of the main room, the largest room in the house. Toward the back of the first floor was the kitchen and dining area, the staircase, and the bathroom with a tub. Sturdy wooden stairs led down to the roomy cellar with six-foot high ceilings and a tiled floor. Shelves and cabinets lined the walls on all four sides, originally used for storing canned goods. In the middle of the room remained an eight-foot by six-foot oak dining table surrounded by twelve chairs. Jensen built the table as the house was being framed, its size making it a permanent fixture too big to be removed unless cut into pieces. Upstairs were four bedrooms, one in each corner, two windows in each room. The front door rested two steps from the ground in the middle of the house. On either side of the door were two five-foot-high by three-foot-wide windows. Each side featured the same. Two large windows in the back of the house were split by a back door leading out of the kitchen.

It was a standard Amish home, the size and floor plan consistent with most of the other Amish homes in the area, the repetition making them rather easy to assemble. Jensen prided himself on constructing them, including building the oak tables in the basements before all the framing was complete. Amish families ate their meals at the kitchen table, but the basements were used socially for large gatherings.

Ironically, both Jensen and his wife, Anna, died in the basement two years apart; Anna first in 1940, followed by Jensen in 1942, both of heart attacks. They had no children due to a complicated first pregnancy that resulted in a stillborn baby boy followed by several miscarriages.

The Amish population had become smaller during the early part of the twentieth century and those who remained migrated about fifty miles southeast to Holmes County. Jensen and his wife separated themselves from the community and were thus excommunicated. They remained in Mansfield and adopted an English lifestyle. Upon Jensen's death, no will could be found. Nor could the court find any living relatives, so the state of Ohio inherited the estate. The house and the four acres it stood on were sold through an auction in 1943 to my family. The property was the perfect landing spot for them, having sold the fifty-acre plot of wooded land in Grayson, where I'd spent most of my childhood.

Jobs in the Mansfield mills were plentiful in the early forties as the war effort created high demand for the steel the mills produced. My father and Eliza found work in no time, he as a welder, and she as a riveter. They lived in a boarding house near downtown until the Grayson property was sold for a good price, making it possible to buy the property in Little Kentucky for cash.

The house was in good repair when they moved in. It needed a fresh coat of paint and some scrubbing inside, but it was obvious Jensen had given it love till the day he died. The land surrounding the house had been left to nature, overgrown with little or no yard to speak of. Tall pines were scattered among maple and oak trees providing seclusion from anything other than the deer, foxes, raccoons, opossums, and other creatures that inhabited the land. Yoder's Creek ran through the property and was stocked full of turtles, frogs, and crawdads. Largemouth bass and bluegill were plentiful in the nearby pond. Other than the drive and the house, the land fell back to its primitive state, making it the perfect respite for my family who were private people, apprehensive and ill-fitted to acclimate to the northern Ohio culture.

According to Eliza, my mother first showed signs of mental illness after I was born but recovered enough to function until I returned from the war. She would not recover from the trauma of my disfigurement and subsequent discharge. Her condition would be diagnosed as mental stress and melancholy. Her behavior became erratic, and she stayed tethered to the property. When my father and Eliza came home from their shifts, they would often find her in the front room, in her rocker—one of three in the house—staring out the window. Sometimes, even having soiled herself because she hadn't moved for hours. She would vacillate between talking gibberish one moment, to manic intellect the next.

Doctors prescribed heavy doses of psychotic drugs such as chlorpromazine and Thorazine. They made several trips to the Cleveland Clinic where she underwent insulin shock therapy treatments, often putting her in an apathetic and catatonic state. Most of the time, she was incapable of doing even the smallest tasks, such as cooking or cleaning. My father and Eliza cared for her the best they could, staggering their shifts so she would never be left alone. During her manic moments, she was a voracious reader. Her favorite author was Louis Bromfield, who resided ten miles away at his home, Malabar Farm, in the town of Lucas, Ohio. Bromfield was a fiction writer and made his fortune in Hollywood, recrafting many of his books into screenplays that became hit movies. He was also a conservationist whose passion was land, water and soil conservation, and farming techniques. His nonfiction writing focused on the land of north central Ohio, something my father figured mesmerized her as she gazed out the window into the woods. My father never surrendered to her illness and read the Bible to her every evening between dinner and bedtime which seemed to give her peace. She would often wake in the night and go to her bedroom or front-room rocker with a book. My father, waking up to the empty spot next to him, would find her, and lead her back to bed. Sometimes she would go to the basement and sit at the long table and read. There were times when my father put padlocks on the front and back doors so she wouldn't wander off into the woods.

Eliza was not as attentive, but she was devoted, nonetheless. Since my father spent most of his time by her side when he was home, the burden of running the household fell on Eliza, and she began to resent it. She would admit to leaving messes around the house, dishes in the sink, and laundry unfolded. My father imagined this was out of spite and resentment for my mother, but he never challenged her. Voices were never raised in the Cummings' home.

My father stood six-foot-two, lean, with wiry long arms and fingers. His body reflected the wear of one who spent his life doing manual labor. His once blond hair grayed as he aged and was always maintained in a fashionable crew cut. He still trusted my mother to keep it trimmed. He believed all life circumstances were God's way and remained loyal to the Episcopalian faith, attending Grace Episcopal Church downtown every Sunday morning without fail. When they first moved to Mansfield, my mother would occasionally join him, but her visits became less frequent over time. He volunteered in the food pantry every Saturday morning, which provided much needed nutrition for the homeless and poor. He was always polite and approachable, but not outgoing. People often mistook his demeanor and shyness as indifference.

My parents met at a dance in Grayson right before the outbreak of the Great War. My father was five years her senior, just twenty-four when they were married in the courthouse six months after they met. Eliza Jane Cummings was born in 1921, just three years after the end of the Great War.

After I was born my mother suffered severe postpartum depression. Attempts to breastfeed me proved challenging as her milk did not come in for several days. She locked the two of us in the bedroom for an entire day before my father broke the door down. He found her on the floor holding me, blood everywhere. She had sliced her left wrist with a razor, deep enough to nick the radial artery, which clotted to prevent her from bleeding to death. Eliza remembers following him into the room. She said she would never escape the trauma of seeing me, covered in blood, resting on my mother's lap in her red-stained white gown. Her protective instincts for me were immediately codified and she built a wall to protect the two of us from my mother's unpredictable behavior.

Just as my father would never discuss the atrocities he witnessed in France, he would not discuss those which occurred in his own home. He carried his burdens deep within, never revealing them to others.

As I became old enough to sense my mother's instability, I would ask Eliza, "What's wrong with Momma?" When I reached the age where 'nothing' was no longer an acceptable answer, I demanded she tell me what she knew.

"Momma's crazy," she finally confessed. "That's what's wrong with her."

"What do you mean, she's crazy?"

"She's just crazy, that's all."

"How do you know that?"

"She's nutty. Her brain don't work right."

She pledged there were things she couldn't talk about. Would never tell me. But that changed.

On Christmas Eve, when I was seven, I witnessed my mother lunge at my father with a knife in the kitchen. We were all sitting at the tiny dining room table when she started slamming her hands rhythmically on the table. Thud, thud, thud, thud! The milk started sloshing over the sides of the glasses. The knives and forks bounced up and down making a clatter. My father kept telling her calmly to stop it. But she continued until he rose from the table and approached her from behind, attempting to restrain her arms. She wrestled her right arm free and grabbed the knife from the place setting and swung it violently behind her, nicking my father's cheek. Eliza and I both screamed for her to stop, and she began to shake and cry in hysterics until she collapsed forward, her face landing in the bowl of her homemade apple pie. My father whispered over and over, "It's okay, everything is fine," until she slid off her chair to the floor, still in his arms.

We left our apple pies on the table and Eliza took my quivering hand and led me to the bedroom we shared. I pleaded with her. "Why is she crazy? What made her crazy? Why doesn't she love us? Why did she do that?"

"She just is," was her pat response. "Daddy won't talk about it. I don't know why. Quit asking, will you?" But I wouldn't stop asking. So, Eliza started talking. In as graphic detail as her mind allowed, she told me of witnessing our mother throw herself down the basement steps; of the time the doctor made an emergency house call and pumped her stomach after she consumed rat poison; of the time when she saw their father cut her from a leather belt she used in a poor attempt to hang herself in the bedroom closet; and of the time when she watched him break down the bedroom door and found her leaning against the wall in the corner of the room, holding two-day-old me in her arms, both of us covered in blood.

I would never again ask, 'What's wrong with Momma?'

CHAPTER

17

ELIZA SET UP MY BEDROOM in the northeast corner of the house. She thought the cellar, with its long oak table, would provide the perfect writing space. She carried my typewriter and all my business belongings down the stairs before I had a say. She thought it best to create a safe space for me, a place where my mother rarely went anymore for fear it was home to the ghosts of Mr. and Mrs. Yoder. She secured an additional hand railing down the steps to give me more stability. She did the same on the stairway leading up to my bedroom. I didn't have to navigate the stairs much in the Grayson or Frankfort homes, only on occasion to go the basement to fetch something.

The cellar would prove perfect, though I would have to hunch to avoid banging my head on the wooden ceiling beams. The table was nothing short of majestic. Its strength, beauty, and craftsmanship gave off a sense of security and stability. Above it was a simple light that hung from the ceiling, the kind that hangs over billiard tables in pool halls. It did not provide sufficient light for my poor eyesight, so in time, Eliza arranged for an electrician to add additional lighting to the space. Any other cellar would have been damp and musty, but not one that was built by a Yoder. This room was designed to hold gatherings of people, not just canned goods on the shelves. To be sure, Eliza installed a dehumidifier and a humidifier so I could make sure the climate would be agreeable with my damaged lungs.

"What do you think?" she asked me when I followed her down the stairs.

"It's perfect."

"And you'll be out of Momma's hair down here," she said. "More important, she'll be out of yours."

I had no dreams of reconnecting with my mother during these new living arrangements. I kept probing Eliza about how she was responding to her new roommate. She finally told me what I assumed all along. "I haven't told Momma that it's permanent," she confessed. "I told her you were just coming for a visit."

"Well that's not going to work out very well when she discovers otherwise, now is it?"

"She don't need to know how long the visit's goin' to be for."

I heard the front door swing shut and Momma's footsteps in the kitchen above us.

"Dinner!" my mother bellowed. "Dinner!"

"Momma's hungry," Eliza said with a roll of her eyes. "Let's go."

I rose from the cellar to see my mother sitting at the kitchen table staring out the back window. She appeared not to notice me as I walked by.

"Hi Momma," I said. She looked over and gave me a nod. "It's good to see you."

Without turning to face me, she said, "Your daddy is sure to be sorry to have missed ya."

Eliza reached for my arm and led me outside onto the porch. "I don't think it's a good idea for you to start any conversation with her," she said. "Let her do the talkin' when she's ready. And don't take it personally. I stopped talkin' to her about anything but the basics of survival. She don't say a whole lot, and it used to be that the more I tried, the less she would. It only hurt me. Until it didn't, and I gave up on expecting much out of her. Now I just leave her be. That's my advice to you."

"She seems almost catatonic," I said. "The look in her eye. It's familiar. It reminds me of the expression I saw in soldiers' eyes during the war."

"Whatever catawhatever means, I'll take your word for it," she said. "If it were up to me, I'd put her in the mental hospital. A home. But Daddy made me promise, if anything ever happened to him, I would never do that. Not saying it's an impossibility, though."

"DINNER!" the voice rang from the kitchen.

"You sit out here and relax, maybe walk around and get acquainted with the property, if you're able. I'll go get your cane," Eliza said. "Tonight I think it's best that you don't eat at the table with us. Let's give it some time, like I said."

I was a bit wobbly on the uneven ground with no clear paths to wander upon. Nonetheless, it was serene to walk through the woods. I followed the sound of water trickling over the stones in the nearby creek. It was getting dark so I couldn't make out whatever creatures I heard stirring on the banks and plopping themselves into the cool stream. I figured the creek and its banks must be full of frogs, toads, and salamanders. Maybe some crawdads. The ambient sound of crickets and birds made sweet music. I envisioned sleeping with my windows open and drifting off to the sounds of bullfrogs and grasshoppers and waking up to the love calls of robins and cardinals.

Before it got too dark, I found my way back to the house. On the side table on the porch, Eliza had left a ham sandwich and a rich helping of potato salad. Pickles on the side, of course—I'd acquired a liking to them over the years. An iced tea to drink. I sat in the chill of the fresh spring air and enjoyed my first meal since arriving in Mansfield before going inside to the warmth of the house.

My mother had gone upstairs and would not come back down before retiring to bed. She didn't have much to say over dinner, Eliza told me. Not even a question about why I was visiting.

"You'll get used to it," she told me. "Really, it hardly phases me anymore. The less I worry 'bout her, the better. She don't seem to worry 'bout me, so

I stopped worrying 'bout her. She lets me know when she needs something. And as long as I give it to her, she don't make much of a fuss. I make sure she eats, sleeps, has clean clothes, books next to her rockers. Her pills. You know, the basic necessities."

"This thing with Momma's going to be hard to adjust to," I said. "At least I figured we'd find a way to talk to each other. I was so hoping for that. What happens when you go back to work tomorrow?"

"You're used to being alone, right?" she answered. "And so's Momma. I figure the two of you will get along fine. I'll make breakfast and lunch for you both before I leave for work. You can eat it whenever and wherever you want. Just don't complain 'bout bologna and mayonnaise on Wonder Bread."

I went down to the cellar, sat at the table, and wrote a letter to Sam to let him know of my new circumstances. I asked if he would consider visiting me now that I was in Ohio. I didn't write much about my mother. I still had so much to process before I could articulate that dynamic.

As Eliza predicted, I wouldn't see my mother again that night. I sprawled out on my bed that was built eighty years earlier by Jensen Yoder. The box and mattress were new and stiff. Eliza had bought new pillows and bedsheets and made the bed with the precision of a nurse, the sheets tucked in too tight for my liking around my feet, but I had no complaints. I was at peace, further comforted by the surround of the cool breeze and sweet sounds from the woods whisking through my open windows.

My mother was sitting in the rocker in the front room when I came down the stairs the next morning. "You're still here," she said as a statement. Not a question.

"Yes, Momma. I am. I might stay for a bit if that's okay."

"Don't bother me none," she said, retreating back to the book in front of her.

'Don't bother me none either,' I told myself.

Eliza was busy finishing the day's food prep in the kitchen, already running late for her shift. She hastily said goodbye, giving me a kiss on her way out. "You'll be fine," she whispered. "I'll be home by three-thirty."

My mother walked past me on her way to the kitchen to sit down to her breakfast that Eliza prepared. Mine was in the fridge to eat whenever and wherever I wanted. I retreated down to the cellar to unpack some things and get better situated. In many respects the room made for a much more productive space, with shelves, cabinets, and room to spare. Not being much for clutter, Eliza long ago removed all the things left over from Jensen Yoder and my father.

After a bit, when I was sure the kitchen was empty, I went upstairs to eat my scrambled eggs and bacon. My mother had retreated to her bedroom, maybe trying to stay out of my way and keeping me out of hers. If not for endless land, I would have felt largely confined to my bedroom and cellar, taking only necessary trips to the bathroom and kitchen. My mother's space was confined to her rockers. One in her bedroom. One in the front room. And one on the front porch. She ate all her meals at the kitchen table, in the same seat, staring out the same back window at whatever activity nature provided her.

I had to resist the urge to replay my many years of sadness because of her emotional distance. She may have been nuts during my childhood, but she was still attentive to me. She had a proclivity for imagination that I was thankful to have inherited, and she loved regaling me with her wild stories. Regardless of her erratic behavior, I loved her, and she remained a loyal provider and companion all through my teenage years, never missing a basketball game or music event at school. My father never spoke unkindly about her. Even when pushed. How much he suffered silently trying to reconcile her manic moods, I could only guess. He never spoke a bad word about anyone, always seeing the good in a person, even if they had harmed him. Eliza was tougher on her than anyone. As a result, my mother was not as giving to her, and it bred resentment. Eliza was the bad kid. I was the saint. I never blamed Eliza for how she felt, having suffered more trauma than I at my mother's hand. She would say to me, "There are three mommas in this house. One for Daddy. One for you. And one for me. *My* momma ain't the nice one."

My mother wept when I went off to war. She said to me, "You'll never be my little boy again." When we hugged goodbye as I stepped off the porch, she turned to walk back into the house without looking back, and said, "Never again."

She never wrote me during the war, even though I begged to hear from her. Letters from my father and Eliza proved my sister was right about the three mommas. My father's letters lofted praise upon her for her stoicism and strength dealing with having her only son at war, and talked of how well she was caring for the household, raving about the casseroles and roasts she prepared. Eliza only mentioned my mother in passing, even though in all my letters home I asked how Momma was. "Nutty as ever. Mean to Daddy. Intolerant of me. Not the same since you left."

The pain of her emotional absence upon seeing her the in the hospital in Fort Sam Houston broke my heart. My father said it was too painful to see me in such torture. "How hard it must be for her to see her son so wounded," he said. But I imagine her pain grew from something deeper inside her, an inability to cope, that had little to do with me. Watching other mothers heap love on their wounded sons in the hospital ward shown a spotlight on her dysfunction. Eliza said the closest Daddy ever got to raising his voice was when he had to force her to attend the Memorial Day Parade in my honor. She didn't want to be seen and pointed at, 'That'd be Private Cummings' momma 'oer there.'

During my first few months home, she showed hints of softening. "She's doing her best," my father said. "So hard for a mother to see her son in such a condition. She's getting better." He meant well, but it rang hollow.

The point of no return came when they learned the truth about my discharge. "Whatever pain Momma was in before has now turned to shame," Eliza told me matter-of-factly. "She's trying hard," my father would say. "Just give her time."

I rose from the cellar and walked into the kitchen to prepare a cup of tea. My mother was sitting at the table. She spoke directly to me for the first time since we'd been alone together.

"Where's your medal? Did they take your medal with your honor?"

CHAPTER
18

I LEFT THE HOUSE to walk in the woods. I passed my mother, who was sitting in her front porch rocker, without acknowledging her. I grabbed a stool in the event I would find a suitable spot to rest among the critters and brush. I marched through thickets and thorns with a sense of purpose, not leaving anything behind, but moving toward something new. The vision of my mother now was that of a sick, mean old woman, long removed from the nurturer who seeded imaginary thoughts of possibilities in a young boy's head.

To prevent getting lost I followed the stream, which made a 90-degree turn away from the house. It occurred to me it would be good if I knew the exact layout of the four acres of land I could lay claim to. The stream fed a large pond, situated in an open, unkept field. I could sense from the sounds it was well-stocked. What a fishing hole this must be. I put my stool down on the bank, the legs sinking a couple inches into the mud as I sat. I resisted the urge to take out my pad to write, deciding to sit in silence with my thoughts. I flicked them aside as they filtered through my mind, breathed, and tried to relax. Breathing in the beauty of the solitude, breathing out the emotional toil.

Bumble bees hummed around the sunflowers and dandelions. The soft breeze kicked up the fluffy seedheads of the cattails that bordered the pond. A bullfrog leapt into the water with a ribbit. A turtle's shell skimmed along the surface. Dragonflies zoomed around me like fighter pilots, their peacock-feathered colors shimmering in the sunlight, causing me to squint.

I ventured to the other side of the pond where I came upon a rickety, wooden dock protruding into the water. On the bank next to it lay a few home-made fishing polls. There were footprints in the mud. Half the size of my boots, perhaps they belonged to children. I had ventured too far into land that wasn't mine. I found my way back to the stream by circling around the other side of the pond. To my left rose an apple orchard bordered by several tall maples, the leaves in full bud. Wood slats were nailed to the trunk of a tree I passed. I traced them up. They were hastily made stairs leading to a treehouse, balanced between the tree's sprawling branches. Encircling the trunk were names and symbols that had been carved into the bark. In some cases the bark had been chipped away making the smooth surface of the tree's outer ring permanent home to the deep gouges of letters and names.

That evening after dinner Eliza pulled out the deed to the house with the property lines clearly marked. She explained the geography of Little Kentucky relative to downtown Mansfield. What seemed like a secluded respite now felt closer to civilization than I preferred. Nonetheless, the house could not be seen from the property's borders, whether the foliage was in full bloom or had shed its leaves to bare branches during the colder months. "You're safe here," she said. "Just make sure you know where your here is. No one is goin' to bother you."

In following the stream to the fishing hole, I had crossed our property line and ventured into what was known as 'the farm,' which she explained had not just the pond and the treehouse, but also a big fire pit that shot sparks high into the sky and whose smoke would waft over the house if the wind was right, an old broken down church house that Jensen Yoder had built, and an old Amish cemetery where, among others, the Yoders were buried. About this time of year, when the weather would start to break, she told me, the kids from

Little Kentucky often rode their bikes to the farm to create their own kind of mischief. "Been doing it ever since we moved here," she said. "And not once has anyone ever come on to our property that I know of. There's nothin' here for them. All the fun they need's over there," pointing to the farm.

"One time, though, Momma wandered herself over there and the kids spotted her. They shooed her away. Momma claimed they yelled at her to get off their farm. Nothin' else came of it, but that night Ed Klein paid me a visit to tell me it might be good if Momma didn't go back. To my knowledge, the kids spooked her enough where she wouldn't have even without the warnin'."

"How did he know about it?" I asked.

"A woman who works at the market for Ed, Betsy Smith, is the mother of a couple boys from the neighborhood. One of them saw Momma, and it was a topic at their dinner table that night. Betsy felt it best to give off a warnin'. It happened just last summer. I figure it was the older boy, forget his name. He's worse for the wear of the two. The younger boy, Jonny, the kid's a peach from what I hear."

"You said only Ed knows about me?" I asked.

"Well, no, not exactly. I mean a lot of people know about you. Like I told you before, Daddy talked you up all the time, so proud. A lot of people know of you. Know you're a hero. Ed's the only one who knows you're here now."

"Can we keep it that way?" I followed up.

"Well, little brother, I don't know because you know how things get out. We can try. I trust Ed."

"Promise me," I snapped. "Please, we talked about this. I don't need anything outside of this." I drew a big circle with my finger.

"Promise I'll do everything possible," she said. "But, Hank, do you really think you'll be able to ..."

"I don't think," I interrupted her. "I know what I need. It's privacy, Lizzy."

"I told you I want you to meet Ed. He stops over from time-to-time. He wants to meet you. He's good company. I like my privacy too. But I'm no hermit. Can't be. The market is the place people go to talk and gossip.

Everybody and everything goes through the market. Ed will be your fiercest protector. He's like the mayor. Or better yet, the sheriff. His word matters 'round here."

"Is he married?" I asked.

"Widowed," Eliza responded. "Why do you ask?"

"You seem affectionate toward him," I said. "What more do I need to know?"

"Not a damn thing. Mind your own business."

"Kids?"

"Yes," she said.

"How old?"

"Doesn't matter. Grown."

"You're seeing him, aren't you?"

"We're friends, okay? Enough," she said. "I'm not tellin' you any more until you meet him. Judge him for yourself."

I could only smile. Eliza had her share of suitors over the years. That much I'd known. But she was far too tough to be tamed. Wasn't one to waste her time on anyone who didn't have the potential to measure up. She never could find the patience to give anyone a decent chance. She had aged well. She let her long hair turn gray with no thought to giving into the commercial temptation to color it. Her figure remained trim, wiry, like our father's. Her face was angular. She was at home and comfortable in her own skin working predominantly with the men in the mills. One of the boys. Not someone to be messed with. My father told me a story once of a new fellow who began flirting with her in hopes of striking something up. The other men watched with glee as she strung his fragile ego over the rocks, enjoying the prolonged torment, before he came to realize what so many others had—you don't mess with Eliza Cummings.

What men could do and did do with Eliza Cummings, however, was drink Pabst Blue Ribbon and smoke Marlboros, which I would come to learn she did quite often after her shifts. Ashamedly, I must admit she was more of a man's man than I.

The late spring rainy season in north central Ohio made for a fresh, lush, green landscape surrounding our house. Daffodils, tulips, forsythias, magnolias, and rosebuds bloomed. The month of May brought a welcome warmth to my skin.

The serenity that washed over me on a warm spring evening was interrupted by the sound of yelling coming from my mother's room. I couldn't make out what was being said. Both Eliza and my mother fighting to raise their voices to be heard over the other. It didn't last long before Eliza stormed onto the porch and ran to her car.

She turned back toward me and said, "Git in."

"Why? What happened," I asked.

"Need to get the hell out of here. Goin' for a ride. Come on."

She hastily maneuvered the car around to the drive and took off, kicking up dust and gravel in her wake. She turned onto Yoder Road and headed west away from town. I remained quiet. It was several minutes before she spoke.

"Sometimes, Henry," she began. "Sometimes the woman gets the best of me. This is one of those times."

"What happened?" I asked.

"We're supposed to go to Cleveland next week to see her doctor. It's a regular trip, twice a year. It's the only way we can keep her on her meds. Believe me, you don't want to see her off her meds. She told me she won't go. It ain't a choice, I told her. She told me she'd run away tonight. She did that once when Daddy was still with us. Left the house and hid in the woods. Made him go out with a flashlight lookin' for her. He put padlocks on the doors for a month after that. That's what I'm goin' to fuckin' do tonight. I'll lock the bitch in the house so she can't leave."

"Lizzy, slow down, take a breath. Why won't she go?"

"The last time we went they gave her shock treatments, ETC or ECT, something like that, I forget. But they didn't help. They said they won't try it again. I told her that. She thinks I'm lyin' to her. The doctor said he might want to change her medication. Hell, Hank. She's on eight different pills a day, some twice a day. I practically have to shove those down her throat. She has to go. No choice. No goddamn choice."

"Is it me? Because I'm ..."

"No, it ain't 'cause you're home. She's just crazy. Simple as that. I try to keep all this inside, like Daddy did. I don't know how he did it. The man was a saint."

"I'm sorry. I don't know what to do," I said.

"Nothing you can do. Nothing I want you to do. It's a storm we'll ride out."

"This is the only time I've heard even a voice raised since I've been home."

"Don't happen often," Eliza said. "Things operate pretty routinely for the most part. What you've been seein' is pretty much how it is most of the time. But every so often she gets my blood boiling. And, well. It boils over and has to go somewhere."

She turned the car back toward the house but had to make a stop on the way. "I need to pick somethin' up at the market. Won't be long. You can stay in the car. I'll park it in back where no one will see us."

"No, can't you take me home first?"

"I ain't leaving you alone with Momma right now. Just take a second."

She pulled into the EK Market lot and circled around back where a white Cadillac was parked. "Thought you said no one would be back here," I said.

"That's Ed's," she said. "Be right back. Don't worry."

She returned to the car five minutes later with a twelve-pack of Pabst and a case of nonfiltered Marlboros. "Ed says hi," she said as she pulled the tab off a cold can of beer and lit a cigarette.

It was dark by the time we returned home. She pulled down the drive. "That's strange," she said as the house came into view.

"What?"

"No lights on. Momma always turns on the lights. Hates the dark. Somethin' don't feel right."

She grabbed her beer and cigarettes and moved toward the house, calling out on her way with a raised voice, "Momma, Momma?"

As she got to the front door, we heard a loud thud and the sound of breaking glass.

As I was making my way up the porch steps, Eliza was running up the stairs to my mother's room. No sooner had I begun to push open the front screen door did I hear her bloodcurdling scream.

"No! Momma, NO!"

She raced down the stairs yelling, "Hank, come with me. Hurry. COME!"

She ran out the door around to the back of the house, screaming. I followed her as quickly as possible. When I turned the corner from the side, I saw her. She was hanging by a rope, a noose tied around her neck. Her legs violently kicking against the shattered kitchen window on the first floor. Blood splattering in all directions, against the house and on her white nightgown. Gasping for breath. She was still alive.

"Momma! Momma! Momma!" Eliza kept screaming. "What have you done? Why? Momma. Why?"

I steadied myself and bearhugged her, hoisting her up enough for Eliza to remove the noose before the three of us dropped to the ground in a heap. My mother choked and gasped for breath. Blood was seeping from a deep gash on the inside of her thigh. Femoral artery.

"Call an ambulance," I shouted. "Now. Go!" Eliza ran inside to the phone. I removed my shirt and tried to tie a torniquet around her gushing leg, but I couldn't grip the fabric tight enough to make any difference. I screamed for Eliza to hurry back. I watched all the color drain from my mother's face as I waited for Eliza to return. By the time we secured the torniquet it was too late. She'd bled out. I didn't have enough sensitivity in my scarred fingers to feel a pulse. Eliza was panicking and didn't know how to look for it. There was nothing we could do. She died in my arms before the ambulance arrived.

"Oh my God," Eliza said. "Jesus fuckin' Christ. The nightgown. It's the same one she wore when she slit her wrist when you were a baby."

CHAPTER
19

I WENT INSIDE as soon as the ambulance arrived. I looked out upon the scene through the broken, bloodstained window. Feeble attempts by medics to revive her proved fruitless. She was gone. I looked up from where they were covering her body to find Eliza's eyes looking back at me, saddened, yet resolved, as if to say it was always going to end like this.

Previous attempts to kill herself were calls for attention. Otherwise, she would have sliced into her wrist more deeply while she held me in her arms. She would have taken the entire bottle of pills instead of just half while I was away at war. She would have made certain to position herself so her head wouldn't slip out of the gas oven as soon as she began to struggle after she returned from seeing me in the army hospital.

She wasn't hanging long by the time we arrived at the back of the house. Her neck wasn't broken, indicating she didn't fall with her full weight from the second floor. The makeshift noose didn't slice into her throat. It was another selfish act. A need for attention. She didn't count on the jagged glass from the kitchen window slicing her artery. She must have dropped herself as soon as she heard the car pull in the drive, expecting us to rush to her. To save her. To tell her everything was going to be okay. That she was still loved. That she wouldn't have to go to the Cleveland Clinic for shock therapy treatments. *Whatever you want, Momma.*

I met Ed Klein that night.

Before the medical examiner could even arrive to pronounce the official cause of death, Eliza called Ed. I watched her meet him on the porch where they embraced. He stroked her face, dabbed at her tears with a handkerchief, and stroked her hair in a sign of affection I'd never witnessed Eliza receive.

She took him around to the back of the house where the body remained. He knelt and pulled the sheet back to reveal my mother's face. He rested his hand on her forehead and whispered as if in prayer. This man, who I'd yet to meet, was closer to my mother than I. They sat on the ground and waited for the examiner to come and take the body.

Eliza and Ed stepped into the house.

"Hello, Hank," Ed said upon entering. "It's so good to meet you. Sorry to be meeting like this of course."

"Hello, Ed," I said. "As good a time as ever, I suppose."

"Yes. I suppose," he said.

"I'll grab us some pops," Eliza said on her way to the kitchen.

"Wait, Lizzy," I called out remembering the sight of glass and blood splatter on the floor and walls. "It's a mess in there."

"No worse than what I've already seen tonight, Henry. No worse than seeing Momma swinging by a rope."

She returned with four fingers of bourbon straight up for Ed and a Pabst for the two of us. "A toast to Momma," she said.

"To Momma," Ed repeated as we clinked our bottles against his glass. "I'll go clean up the kitchen."

"We're both a bloody mess," Eliza said. "Should get into some fresh clothes."

She yelled out to Ed over the sound of broken glass being swept up that we were going to change and come back down. "Don't you dare go anywhere, Sweet Pea."

My mother's blood soaked through my clothes and ran down my legs into my boots. I drew a bath and looked at my naked body in the mirror. The nightgown, I thought. A nightgown that she'd saved for almost fifty years. I remembered the times I considered killing myself. It always occurred to me—and in fact became a deterrent—how I would be found. I wondered if my mother thought of that. Of course she did. Of course. I lowered my body into the warm bath and sunk my head beneath the surface.

If her intention was to hurt me, she'd have been more successful using words. The lasting effect from when she asked if they took my honor when they took my medal conjured up not just pain, but spite. Selfishly, I was relieved and hoped that as her soul ascended to the heavens it was healed along the way so my father could be reunited with her free of burden.

After my bath, I pulled on some clean clothes and lay down on my bed. Another chapter was now before me. A house without my mother, and a relationship with Ed Klein, however forced. Maybe a friendship.

"Hank," my sister called out. "Git on down here. Come on now, Henry."

"Where do we start?" Ed asked.

"Well, here I am," I said. "Took our mother to bring us together."

"Your momma was ill," Ed said. "I mean mentally. Very ill. You know that, right?"

"Oh yes," I said.

"Nothing anyone could do to help her. Your daddy did everything he could for her. Eliza, too. The doctors. Everyone."

"Oh, I'm well aware," I said. "But that nightgown was a kick in my ass. Hard to feel it wasn't a bullet aimed at my heart."

"What do you mean?" he asked. "About the nightgown."

"Oh, never mind," I said. "Hard to feel she didn't resent the hell out of me."

"She resented everyone," Eliza said as she lit a cigarette. "Hated life."

"A mother's love," I said with a smirk.

"Funny thing ain't it?" Ed said.

"Sure is," I answered rhetorically.

My life would be easier now. Eliza's too. No more timing my visits to and from the cellar to avoid her. No more turning a deaf ear to her sniping comments. No more worrying about finding her on her rocker on my way back from walks.

"What now, Lizzy?" I asked my sister. "Funeral? Celebration of life?"

"Ha, ain't gonna be no funeral," she said. "No one knew her besides us three. She didn't have any friends."

"Did you ever talk with her about what she wanted?" Ed asked.

"Hell no," Eliza said. "She wouldn't have been able to make sense out of that."

"Cremate her," I said. "Sprinkle her around the property. Ashes to ashes."

"Not bury her next to Daddy?" she asked.

"Whatever you want," I said. "Whatever you think is best."

I was comforted by Ed's presence, this man who I had so much more to learn about. Maybe my father's best friend. Certainly, Eliza's. He was gentle and kind. Older than Eliza by ten years at least. I was happy she had found happiness. She must have met her match.

I excused myself to give them some space and get some rest. Told Ed it was nice to meet him, and I hoped to see him again soon. I meant it. He rose when I got up to leave and extended his hand. I couldn't remember the last time I shook a man's hand. Couldn't recall anyone wanting to shake mine. I reached out without thinking and let him wrap his hand around my fingers.

"You and me now, kid," Eliza said as she gave me a hug. "Orphans."

I sat on my bed and looked at the bloody clothes dumped hastily on the floor next to my boots, my favorites. They fit my deformed feet perfectly. The clothes I would dispose of. The boots would need to be cleaned up.

I wrote to Sam. I longed for his voice, but he had never shared a phone number with me. I wrote him in detail about the evening. The sight of my mother swinging as she gasped for air. The blood splattering in all directions.

It was when I wrote about wrapping my arms around the body to raise her enough for Eliza to remove the noose that I broke. My tears flowed thinking that it was her emotionally estranged son who hugged her during her final breaths.

I pulled the letter to Sam out of the typewriter, set it aside, and began to write to someone else.

May 4, 1972
Dear Mother,

CHAPTER

20

I WOKE TO THE SMELL of bacon and scrambled eggs, went downstairs and, for the first time in weeks, sat at the kitchen table and had breakfast with Eliza. I could still feel the presence of my mother and found myself looking over my shoulder several times believing she was lurking behind me. Like a ghost.

"Seems like a good man, this Ed Klein," I said.

"Glad you think so," Eliza said. "He is."

"Would it be fair to say that the two of you are a couple?"

"A couple of what?"

"Don't be a fool."

"Yes, that would be safe to say. But we keep it private. We don't parade it. His wife's only been dead for a few years, and he feels the town folk wouldn't take too kindly to him if they knew he was shackin' up with crazy Eliza. His kids wouldn't either. But, you know, I'm fine with it. I don't need to be out gallivantin' 'round town on someone's arm. I like it the way it is."

"How long?"

"That gets a bit more complicated. Ed bought the market sometime in the early sixties. From an Amish family. They sold produce and fresh meat. We always bought our fruits and vegetables there before Ed bought it and 'course kept shoppin' there. So, we all met him and Jeanie, his wife. She was lovely. Died of cancer. Brain. Wasn't much left of her the last five years or so of her life. Three different brain surgeries, each one takin' more of her life. Just awful watchin' Ed go through it. Anyway, he expanded over the years to the full grocery store it is today. People call it the church of Little Kentucky 'cause that's where everyone hangs out to shoot the shit. He's so respected. Kind of acts as the judge and jury 'round these parts. People call him the sheriff. He's generous as can be. He takes care of people who might be having a hard time. Man loses his job or somethin', he'll put the bill on their tab and won't even ask for it to be repaid. There is a big basement under the market where men play poker and dice, stuff like that. I think Ed takes his cut so he can pay off the debts of others. He'll never fess to it though."

"All fine and well, but you're not answering my question."

"What was your question?"

"How long have you been his girlfriend?"

"Well, Henry. First of all, I ain't nobody's girlfriend. I'm fifty-one years old. How long? Ed and I've always fancied each other. Somethin' 'bout him just draws me to him. I used to say to him, 'If you weren't already caught, I'd throw you some bait.' But he was always loyal to Jeanie, 'course, even when she couldn't even move and didn't know where she was. Poor soul. When she got sick, 'bout ten years ago, Daddy was his rock. When she was in the hospital, he'd come over after seein' her and they'd have some beers. A cigar. They'd often ask me to join them. I'll tell you something I don't think I've told no one. I believe that's when I fell in love with him. Watchin' him sit in Momma's rocker crying 'bout Jeanie. I just wanted to hug him and mend his heart. Daddy died about a year after Jeanie got sick. That's when Ed was *our* rock. To Momma and me. Came over to check on us all the time. He knew Momma was sick in the head even though we never spoke 'bout it and he was always there for us. Whatever we needed. He kept coming over to see us, to check on us. And more often than not, the two of us would end up sittin' on the porch talkin' after Momma went to bed. Just spendin' time together. Jeanie was in a home, a nursing home. We got real close, though nothin' ever happened. Wasn't long after Jeanie died, well, everything changed. And I mean in a hurry."

"You love each other."

"Oh, yes. We do."

"Well, Lizzy. I'm happy for you. You didn't have to hide this from me."

"I didn't expect to hide it forever."

"You deserve to be happy. To be loved. And he doesn't have to be a stranger. So long as he respects my space and privacy, where I am with things."

"Told you before, he not only respects where you are, he'll protect you. I can promise you that."

Eliza oversaw all the arrangements with our mother. No obituary. No announcement. No funeral. We had her cremated and scattered half the ashes around the property and the other half over my father's grave in the Mansfield Cemetery. Ed joined us for our own intimate wake where we told one crazy story about her after another.

Eliza kept telling me not to feel guilty. If I felt guilty about anything it was that I was relieved to have her gone. At peace that she was out of her own misery, assuming she even knew how miserable her life was.

'Did they take your medals with your honor?' my mother asked me. 'Did you have sex with that man in the showers in the barracks? Did you pleasure yourself thinking about him? You like to look at naked men?' She walked behind me and started to slap the sides of my face with a wet towel. I went to reach for her, but my arms were gone. Burned away. Still smoldering at the empty holes in my shoulders where they used to be. My mother laughed. 'How do you pleasure yourself now, son? Now that you have no hands.'

I woke in a cold sweat. The nightmares. My mother. Her spirit invaded my subconscious and came out at night while I slept. For weeks. Every night.

'Why don't you have a nose? Can you still smell my perfume? What

happened to your ears? Can you still hear me when I call for you? When I gave birth to you, you had all ten fingers and toes. Where did they go? What must it feel like to be an invalid? A man who can't even walk properly. What happened to your eye? Can you see me laughing at you? Your father would be ashamed of what you've become. Poor boy who never leaves the house. Can't even tie his own shoes. Can't even see well enough to drive a car. Who's going to care for me when I'm old? You are already more feeble than I. Oh my. What to do with you, Hank Junior? What a fine mess you've created for your mother. Do you even think about what you've done to me? You've ruined my life. Pathetic little man. You were perfect when you came out of my womb. Look what you've done to yourself. You selfish little boy.'

I became afraid of falling asleep knowing that doing so would extend an invite for her to visit. I would stay awake as long as I could, hunched over the typewriter, pecking away, creating nothing but gibberish on the page. My routine of taking a glass of bourbon to bed to induce sleep turned to sipping from the bottle. In restless fidgets I'd grab for it in the middle of the night.

I was a baby with no arms and legs. My mother laid me on the floor. I was hungry. She sat on the edge of the bed wearing a white nightgown stained with fresh blood. 'That will teach you,' she said. 'No arms. No legs. No life. You poor thing. What's a mama to do with such a poor little thing?'

I never believed in ghosts until the nightmares. She may have been gone physically, but her spirit was fully present. I would wake in the middle of the night feeling her hands holding my legs down. Hearing her voice. Feeling cold wind whipping through my room. I regretted scattering her ashes around the property and hoped for some hard rain to wash them down to the creek to float them far away. Knowing they were there, among the flowers and trees, spoiled the beauty of the place, and I couldn't seem to escape feeling I was stepping on her, which must have angered her.

Eliza emptied my mother's room and closet to its bare floors and walls. We kept her bedroom door closed. After one of my nightmares, I woke to use the bathroom. I walked into the hall to find her door and windows open, sending chills down my spine. I went back to my room, closed and locked the door, and urinated in a glass.

CHAPTER
21

THE ONLY WAY I KNEW how to cope with my emotions was to write. To put my head down and slam my finger against the typewriter's keys. When the nightmares became a ritual, if I woke I would get up and write about them. If I didn't wake till morning, I would do it right out of bed. This made them fictional and harmless. I would write about the spirit I felt still lurking around me. The open doors. The cold air. I wrote and wrote until it all became nothing more than a fictional tale and with no warning everything stopped. My mother's door never reopened. I no longer felt the chill of wind or her cold hands on my legs. It seemed as though her spirit had tired. She couldn't hurt me anymore.

Other than journaling and letters, I had not attempted to write anything commercially since moving to Ohio. Through my mother's haunting, she oddly gave me a purpose. The early notes of those eerie encounters with her were nothing more than typed scribbles. As I progressed, my writing became more storylike, and I expected that I would someday share them with at least Eliza. I added descriptive context that wasn't part of the original subconscious torment and wove them into short fictional tales of horror. I was onto something.

My war stories were born from experience. When the WWII genre's time had passed, I struggled to search for familiar subjects to write about. What my mother gave me posthumously was an emotional journey through dread, fear, and terror. It was time to get back to work.

Waking up each day with a purpose helped me adjust to this new life that Eliza called 'the second coming of Hank.' "You're startin' to act like the old Hank," she said. "I've missed you." She used this occasion to lure me out of the house more regularly. I loved our rides in the country. Five miles west was nothing but farmland and open roads. We'd go for what seemed like hours without another soul in sight. On one such ride, we were ten miles from home when she had another one of her coughing bouts. This one was worse than the others. So bad, she had to pull the car over. It lasted for over ten minutes.

"You need to see a doctor," I told her. "This isn't normal."

"It's just the cigarettes," she said. "I need to switch to filtered."

"You need to quit," I said.

"Ain't gonna happen. Tried it. Can't do it. I like to smoke."

"It's going to kill you someday."

"Something's gonna kill all of us someday," she said. "I'd rather go out with a Pabst in one hand and a Marlboro in the other enjoyin' the ride. Besides, Ed's wife, Jeanie, didn't smoke *or* drink and the cancer still got her. Ain't no guarantees either way, it seems."

The next morning, I found traces of blood on the toilet rim, but I figured it must be a woman thing. I wasn't going to embarrass her by asking about it.

Later in the week, Ed came over for a drink after he closed down the market. He noticed what I'd missed. "Did you cut yourself?" he asked.

"No. Why?" she answered.

"You have blood on your shirt," Ed said.

"Oh, that ain't nothin'. Bloody nose," she said.

"Bullshit," he responded.

"I said it ain't nothin'. You got a light?" she asked as she put a cigarette in her mouth. "I hate these filters."

I looked at Ed and shook my head. He hunched his shoulders in a sign of surrender. "Stubborn woman," he said.

I waited until she excused herself to change her shirt. "I'm worried about her. Her cough's getting worse. She's losing weight. I found blood in the toilet earlier this week. She needs to see a doctor."

"I know," he said.

It turned out he didn't need to work hard. The next day her cough became more persistent, and she began to hack up more blood. I convinced her to call Ed and ask him to come over. He took one look at her. "Let's go," he said. "Get in the car." The hospital immediately admitted her. I was able to talk to her on the phone that evening. She was in good spirits. Said they had run some tests, and everything would be fine. "I'll be home tomorrow."

But she didn't come home. It was late in the day when Ed phoned to say he was stopping over on his way home from the hospital. I braced myself for bad news. And that's what Ed delivered. He looked like he hadn't slept. Looked haggard. Dark circles under his eyes.

"It's cancer, Hank. Lung."

I looked down. We sat in silence for several minutes. Ed was emotional, his face in a handkerchief. I didn't know how to comfort him.

"How bad?" I asked.

"Looks bad. X-rays showed a large mass in her right lung."

"What's the ... you know ... like what's next? What can they do?"

"Don't know yet for sure. A biopsy. Surgery. Don't know yet."

"How is she doing?"

"She doesn't know yet. Doc Bartlett is a good friend. I asked him not to tell her yet. Want to make sure I'm with her. You too if you're willing. We'll tell her tomorrow."

"Christ," I said.

"She thinks they're keeping her overnight to run another test in the morning.

She's got to have a sense, but ... I just told her they don't know anything yet."

"Are you willing?" he asked after a pause. "To come with me tomorrow?" I said, of course.

Ed arranged to meet Dr. Bartlett in Eliza's room at nine o'clock the next morning. He would pick me up at eight-thirty. The closest I'd been to being seen in public since moving to Ohio were cars passing by us on our country road drives. My privacy? "We'll do our best," he said.

My fear of Eliza's prognosis was overcome only by my foreboding angst for being seen. By the time Ed left, it was too late to call Eliza. I went upstairs to prepare for bed but only made it as far as the bathroom, where I leaned over the toilet and threw up. I could see more signs of Eliza's blood on the white porcelain inside the bowl.

I would spend my first night in the house alone. I wondered if it would be the first of many. Eliza was alone. Ed was alone. We were all alone. Not the script any of us signed up for.

I didn't sleep. I wrote Sam a letter that I set aside, in the stack of so many others that I hadn't sent him. I wrote to my mother.

The morning brought a deep chill, temperatures dipping well below thirty degrees allowing me to cover up from head to toe. Besides my jacket, I put on a hunter's hat that Eliza had bought for me. The kind with the flaps that I could pull down over my ears. I pulled on the awkward gloves the army issued me when I left the hospital. The fingers were stuffed with cotton to fill them out. Last, I put on my sunglasses.

"If I didn't know better," Ed said when I got in his Cadillac, "I'd think we were going hunting."

When we entered Eliza's room, she burst out in laughter upon seeing me.

"What in God's good name are you doin' here?" she said. "Jesus Christ, you got hands now and everything."

"Good morning to you too," I said as I sat on the chair next to her bed. In the safety of her room, I removed my hat, jacket, and gloves. I figured we might be here awhile.

Dr. Bartlett was a tiny man with a neatly-trimmed white beard matching the color of his hair. I felt in good hands.

Ed sat next to Eliza on her bed as the doctor delivered the news.

"There is no easy way to do this, so I'm just going to throw it all out there," he began. "Eliza, my dear, the X-rays revealed a large mass in your right lung. The biopsy we gathered through the scope confirmed that it's cancer. Advanced. Stage four."

I wrapped my fingers around her left hand. Ed held her right. Eliza stared straight ahead and showed little emotion other than the color that drained from her face.

"I'm sorry," the doctor said.

"So?" she said matter-of-factly. "What's next?"

"We can take it out. Dr. Allen Kramer is a wonderful surgeon. I've already consulted with him. He's recommending a lobectomy, where he would remove the lower lobe of the lung. It's a serious surgery, but common and straightforward. He thinks he can get it. But it's a choice. Your choice. We can try to treat it with other measures, but ..."

"Take the son of a bitch out," Eliza said as the color returned to her face. "Let's do it."

CHAPTER
22

ELIZA AND I SPENT the rest of the day together. I sensed a reflective resolve in her. She may have been putting on a tough front, but I sensed she knew how bad of shape she was in and that this could be the beginning of the end. She cried thinking of Ed going through this again.

"I ain't plannin' on checkin' out just yet," she said. "But if I get hit by a bus on the way home from here you gotta promise me you and Ed will stay close. He's a peach."

"I promise," I said. "He's got nothing to prove. I've seen how he loves you. Seems to care for me. I know he's a good man."

"Let's say that happens," she said. "I get hit by a bus. I need to know you'll be okay."

"First of all, you're not going to get hit by a bus. I haven't yet seen one in Mansfield. Second, I am nothing if not a survivor. And the same goes for you."

"I just worry that you ain't out there. The hell what people think. It's who you are inside that matters. Anyone who knows you sees that in sixty seconds."

"I know it sounds easy," I said.

"I ain't saying it's easy," she said. "I know it's damn hard. I see it in you every day. But was it easy survivin' the fire? All the work you had to do to learn how to walk again. To hold a pencil. To get your lungs workin' again. Was any of that easy? But you did it 'cause you had to. You had no choice. What would happen if you had no choice, Henry? What then?"

"Lizzy, I've got deeper scars inside than outside. Scars no one can see. People can be cruel. You know I did my best to get back out there. And you know what happened. People looked at me like I was a monster. Mothers pulled their kids away from me when they pointed and stared. Whenever I'd make eye contact with someone, they'd look away. I could hear people talking behind my back. I kept trying. Margaret forced me to. It proved too much for her as well. It was like there was a hole in the boat and as hard as we tried to bail the water out, it came in faster, and it sunk us."

"I think you gotta find a way through this," she said.

"Perhaps, but is there anything wrong with the way I live? I am comfortable. I'm an introvert. I like my privacy. My space. It's not like I don't like people, I do. But I don't need anyone around me. I love the house. I love the nature. As long as I have someone to give me a hand with things, I'm good."

"Listen, Hank," she grabbed onto my arm. "This cancer might be the bus that hits me. We've all got to face that. So, it's just a 'what if.'"

"Sure, I know," I said. "I'm not stupid."

"Well, what if?"

"I get it," I said. "Something we need to think about."

"Another thing," she said. "Beyond havin' help with someone doing the shoppin' for you, I worry about how isolated you are. The only people you've ever seen at the house have been me and Ed, not countin' Momma. You only leave the grounds when I can coax you out for a ride. You're by yourself all day. Don't you ever get lonely?"

"No, I don't."

"You might think so, but it can't be good for you."

"How do you know what's good for me?"

"Listen," she said. "I'm just gonna cut to the chase here. Ed has a friend. He's like you. You know."

"What do you mean, like me?" I knew what she meant but she's never said the word.

"Come on, Henry. You know."

"No, I don't know," I smiled at her. "Say it."

"Alrighty," she said. "You want me to say it?"

"Yes, I want you to say it."

"You're sure you want me to say it?"

"I'm sure I want you to say it."

"Okay, I'll say it. He's a homo, like you."

"A homo?" I squealed. "You mean gay like me? GAY?"

"Stop it you gay fool. Yes, he's gay like you. Plus, he's disabled."

"Disabled too?" I screeched. "An exacta! Holy moly. Jackpot! About time you faced the truth," I said laughing.

"Didn't mean to be funny. Ed says he's a nice man. Might be good company if nothin' else. Or are you holdin' out for that painter friend to come back to you?"

"That painter friend?"

"Come on," she said. "We ain't got time for bullshit. It's true. You think about him. You write him. He sends you drawings. But he's in San Francisco and last time I checked you're in Mansfield. I just think you're lovestruck and it ain't gonna go nowhere. Love him all you want. None of my business. But don't you think you deserve to have someone to spend time with if nothin' else? I'm not tryin' to meddle, just tryin' to look after my little brother."

"So, you told Ed about me?"

"Jesus, Henry. I didn't have to tell him. Nothin' goes further with the two of us. Sorry, but we all need someone to talk to. Share things with. Confide in. And you need that too, whether you know it or not."

She was right.

"You ain't got nothin' to lose," she said. "You know Ed well enough that he ain't gonna steer you down the wrong lane. Maybe this fella can come over for a drink some night. What do you say?"

Chapter

23

AFTER SEVEN DAYS in the hospital, Ed brought Eliza home. She'd aged ten years. Her silver hair, unwashed and knotty. Her coat hung on her frame like rags on a scarecrow. Her legs were bare and spindly. On her feet were the slippers the hospital issued her. Had Ed not been with her I'd have thought she escaped under the darkness of night.

But she still had her spunk. "Afternoon, Henry," she said to me in a raspy voice. "Sorry I look like crap." Ed helped her into the house and into her bed that he'd moved into the living room so she wouldn't have to navigate the stairs. She fell fast asleep no sooner than her head hit the pillow.

Ed and I sat at the kitchen table. "We're just buying time, Hank," he said. "Weeks, months, a year. They don't know. Depends on how she responds to treatment."

"Does she know?" I asked.

"No," he said. "Does she need to know?"

"Hasn't she asked?"

"No. Not yet."

"She probably already knows. Or she doesn't want to."

"Maybe," Ed said. "Listen Hank, you're going to need some help. She's not going to be able to take care of things like before. She's going to need help too. I can only do so much."

"Of course," I said. "I don't know what to do."

"I've already made arrangements," he said. "There is a woman, a dear friend. Her name is Mildred Perkins. She took care of Jeanie. Did whatever we needed her to do. A wonderful soul. I talked with her. She's available and willing to come over every day if that's what you need. I've told her everything, Hank. I'm sorry if I've broken your confidence, but she needs to know what the job entails."

"I understand," I said.

"Now you need to know, she's a colored woman. I trust that doesn't bother you."

"Of course not. Why would you even say that?"

"Well, in these parts colored people aren't treated too well."

"I served with negros in the army. They don't bother me at all."

Mildred Perkins was a ray of light. Bright and bubbly with a warm face and sparkling eyes. Her frame was plump. Her voice was booming and inviting. She was quick with a laugh. She worked in the kitchen at the elementary school for thirty years before retiring. She was gracious and giving and spent much of her time doing volunteer work. She worked for Ed for six years helping take care of Jeanie. After Jeanie died, Ed kept her on to clean his house and keep the market tidy.

"Heard lot 'bout you Mr. Hank," she said. "Don't know what Mr. Ed said 'bout me, but half it surely ain't true."

"I'll assume the good stuff is the half that's true," I said, causing Mildred to belly laugh and snort.

Ed and Mildred laid out the plan. She would do whatever shopping we needed, prepare our meals, clean the house, and provide joyful company. She would arrive each weekday at eight o'clock and not leave until the afternoon, after she'd prepared dinner. Beyond that, she'd be on call whenever we needed her.

Eliza told her that we'd only need her for a few weeks. The rest of us knew better.

Mildred proved nothing short of a godsend. She managed all her tasks with ease and provided great friendship, blending in with Eliza and me like we were all family. She'd met my father and mother and knew them both to be exactly who they were. Understood sadness, she told us. Her grandpa was brought over on a slave ship and sold at an auction in Charleston in 1847. He worked on a plantation for a wealthy cotton farmer where he met Mildred's grandma. Her father, uncle, and two aunts were all born on the plantation. "Mr. Roy and his wife were good to them," Mildred said as she recounted the history. "Our family ain't hold no grudge. But we know we was the lucky ones." That all changed after the family moved to Ohio. Her father was killed. Beaten and lynched by the KKK. Her mother never recovered. I found Mildred's joyful spirit miraculous given her history.

"Only through sufferin' does a woman find her strength," she told me. "I wake up every day with a choice. I can be happy or unhappy. I choose happiness."

Mildred proved not only a gift to me, but good medicine for Eliza, whose spirits were lifted each time Mildred arrived. I'd hear her in the morning from my bedroom as she bounded through the front door. "Good morning, Miss Eliza," she'd boom. "You lookin' mighty pretty today as always."

She helped make the house a home. She made sure the fruit bowl was always full of apples, oranges, and bananas. She'd bring flowers every week that she picked herself from the side of a country road on the way. She would bring us books from the library and not return them until we'd read them, never asking us for the fine money.

We paid her fairly. In cash every week. Though he wouldn't admit it, I was sure Ed paid her too. Every time I gave her the envelope with her wages, she'd say, "Love you, Mr. Hank. But you know I'd do this for free if you'd let me." Occasionally, I'd slip some extra money in the envelope. Every time, she'd give me the money back and scold me. "Now if you don't start paying me right," she'd say, "we gonna have a problem."

I could never figure her age. She must have been seventy years old. Maybe seventy-five. Ed didn't know either. Her energy brought our world to life. "Don't you ever get tired?" I'd ask her. "Not when I'm awake," she'd say. "Plenty of time to rest when I'm in the ground. Can't live life sleepin'."

Her husband of over forty years died five years earlier. She had three children and seven grandchildren. Only her daughter, Sylvia, and grandson, James, still lived in Ohio. She always tried to be home by three o'clock because she cared for James after school until his mother got off work. Sylvia never married and couldn't be certain who James' father was. None of the men she bedded with would come forth to claim him. "The apple of my eye," Mildred would say of him.

"Why didn't you tell me?" Eliza snapped at me upon returning with Ed from her follow-up visit with Dr. Kramer. "I'm so damn angry. With both of you."

"What did he say?" I directed toward Ed.

"Our girl is going to start chemotherapy and radiation treatments," he said as he rubbed her back. "We're going to try to lick this thing."

"Oh, fuck," Eliza said. "My hair is going to fall out."

After a pause, she broke the tension. "I'm gonna look like you, Hank. We'll look like brother and sister again."

The little strength she regained after surgery was taken away once she began her chemo treatments. She lost her appetite and became frail. She became nauseous. Her hair began to fall out. She developed headaches. The skin on her chest became raw and painful from the radiation treatments. Nevertheless, she remained stoic and determined. She wouldn't accept what seemed the inevitable fate.

The treatments continued through the winter. Despite her weakness, Eliza insisted that Ed move her bed back to her bedroom upstairs. "If I can't climb the stairs, life ain't gonna be worth livin' anyway," she said. She began wearing one of the many colorful scarves that Mildred had bought to warm her bald head. I took to wearing them too. Ed visited every morning before opening the market and every evening after closing. We played board games. Monopoly and Clue. We played Scrabble. No matter the weather, Mildred would walk with her twice a day to get her moving. If Mildred wore a white dress and a white cap, you'd have thought she was a nurse the way she cared for us. Eliza took to calling her Dr. Perkins, or sometimes Doc.

Friends from work would show up unannounced, causing me to scamper to the cellar. She let me put a sign on the front door asking people to please call first:

If you are here to see me, no disrespect but please flee,
Go home and use the phone, to call to see if I'm home.
And if I don't want to be seen, don't take it that I'm being mean,
Just try another time, a call costs just a dime.
You see I'm often unpresentable, cause this curse was unpreventable.
I promise someday I'll be ready, especially if you bring me some spaghetti.

On March 1, Ed and Mildred showed up with dinner and a cake to celebrate my one-year anniversary in Ohio. Despite the struggles and changes during the previous twelve months, it was a joyous occasion. Eliza had been off chemo and radiation for over two weeks and was beginning to feel better, giving us hope.

The following day, Ed took her to a scheduled follow-up appointment with Dr. Kramer. The report wasn't good. There was now a mass in the remaining upper lobe of her right lung. A small mass appeared in her left lung. The cancer was metastasizing to other organs. The doctor's advice was to make the most out of the time she had left. Nothing more could be done.

Ed moved her bed back downstairs. Her strength that forged her will to fight the disease now helped her face her fate with dignity, resilience, and resolution. She no longer had the strength to take her walks. Her breathing became more labored. Her coughing fits more violent.

I dreaded the discussions we now had to have before it was too late. Making sure everything was in order. Her will. The arrangements. I also needed to know what she would want for me. Before I could broach the issues, she proactively called a meeting with Ed and me. She invited Mildred to join us. There was no debt. The house, car, and old pickup were long paid off. She was up to date on all the bills and taxes. Always was. She wanted to leave all her possessions to me other than some special things she had set aside for Ed. There was some money. She wanted some of it put in a trust to ensure my long-term care. She had made Mildred the beneficiary of her life insurance benefit she had through the mill. Mildred threw a fit. "You ain't got no say in it, Mildred," she said. "But I need something from you. I need you to promise me you'll stay on to help Hank."

"You ain't need no worry 'bout that, Miss Eliza," she said. "I ain't goin' nowhere."

She begged us not to put her back in the hospital, but when her pain became unbearable and she would no longer eat, Ed called for an ambulance.

The sadness of watching my sister leave her home, never to return, was unbearable. Ed followed in his Cadillac. The last ambulance that had left our home carried my dead mother.

JONNY

CHAPTER
24

NOTHING WAS BETTER than the last day of school. The countdown began on May 1, and we could all recite on demand not just how many days were left, but hours. Rick Weiland was good at math. He could recite the minutes right off the top of his head. The final day was always on a Wednesday, making the last three days purely ceremonial, though they'd dock our grades if we skipped them. The teachers had a tough time hiding their glee in ridding themselves of us for the summer.

I was thirteen years old heading into the summer of 1973 without a care in the world. The Vietnam War ruled the news and many TVs were tuned to the *Five O'Clock Follies* each afternoon, the televised press conferences piped into American homes with reports from the frontlines. At six-thirty every evening, most people watched the *CBS Evening News* with Walter Cronkite. Families in the neighborhood had sons who were either in, just out of, or trying to avoid Vietnam. Cecil Turley's (we called him Tubs) brother, Sterling, was killed in action in 1967, when Tubs was seven years old. His mother nearly medicated herself to death as a result. His dad was a violent drunk. And his older brother,

Jarvis, an asshole. How much of it had to do with Sterling, nobody knew. Tubs never talked about Sterling, as if he shoved it deep into the recesses of his brain, so deep it was unretrievable. The older brother of Pete Sullivan (Sully) and his friend hitchhiked to Canada and hadn't been heard from in three years. Jim Radebaugh's (Radish) oldest brother, Kirk, was a grunt marine on the front lines in Nam. His mother lived on a steady diet of sedatives and red wine.

As budding teenagers, we had little concept of what was real and what wasn't. JFK, RFK, and MLK had been assassinated. War and racial protests were everywhere, but when you have no perspective, all of these tragic events blended in with watching *The Waltons* and *Rowan & Martin's Laugh-In* on TV.

Summer would be full of running around Yoder's farm, Little League baseball, and camp at Hidden Hollow. I earned a little money cutting grass, and my mom would pay me two dollars a week for doing all my chores by six o'clock Sunday. I never saved a penny. Spent all of it on model cars that I'd spend hours building, painting, and applying decals on, only to blow them to smithereens with firecrackers that I would glue inside their plastic frames.

Billy Nelson was my running mate. We were inseparable and the default leaders of the Greasy River Gang, so named because during a hard rain, the oil from the neighborhood drives and roads would mix with the rain and wash down the road, in colors of yellows and greens, resembling a greasy river. We weren't really a gang. We were a club. But the name "Greasy River Club" didn't project the right tone. I personally didn't like calling ourselves a gang. The bad kids had gangs, of which there were plenty in the neighborhood. I argued that we could officially be the Greasy River Gang but do business as a 'club.' It was one of the few arguments I lost. We were destined to be a gang.

The oil in the greasy river originated from the undersides of the cars that were in a constant state of repair in the drives of the Little Kentucky neighborhood of Mansfield. No one took their cars to a garage or gas station for repairs. If you didn't know how to fix something, chances are the guy next door did. I loved the smell of grease, oil, and exhaust fumes that always hung in the air. Everybody's dads and brothers old enough worked in the mills or factories that sat a few miles away to the west. The boys who didn't latch on to one of these jobs typically signed up for the army or marines. Nobody went to college. Didn't seem necessary.

The houses were small ranch homes, most with three bedrooms, one bath. Many of the attached garages had been turned into an extra room for the excess kids that came along throughout the years. The lots were all the same size, cookie-cutter style, the streets laid out in a symmetrical grid, with names alphabetically ordered. The roads all ran parallel to Yoder Road. The first road to the south was Amos Road. The next, Burt. Followed by Carey, David, Edward, Franklin, Gregory, and so forth. All the way to Marshall. It was impossible to get lost. The locals skipped the formal names when referring to them and took to calling them by their first letter followed by 'street.' Turn left on B street. They live on G street. Drop this off at the Harris' on F. And so on. I lived on D. Billy on E.

We were aware of the richer neighborhoods on the east side of downtown. On the west stood one even poorer. We all seemed fine with that deal. We didn't long for much. All we needed was a bike and a baseball mitt, both usually hand-me-downs. Balls and bats were shared among all. Most in the gang had their own bike which made it easy for all of us to travel the mile to the farm.

We called it a fort, but it was really a tree house, perched twelve feet up in a sprawling maple tree. The one-inch plywood base was custom cut to lay atop three sturdy branches sprawled out in symmetrical fashion. Half-inch thick, four-foot-high walls, and a roof enclosed the structure. A camouflaged tarp was strung across the top and stapled to the slanted roof to protect us from summer rains. The fort had windows on three sides and the door was hinged and we could lock it from the inside. Even the windows had inside shutters that we could close, making the fort feel impenetrable from intruders of nature or human form. We stapled screens inside the window frames to try to keep out the swarms of mosquitos, flies, and bees that called the farm their home in the summer.

The fort was built about four years earlier by Tub's brother, Jarvis, and his buddies, who still considered it theirs and once in a while would run us off so they could take girls there to do whatever they tried to do with girls. Occasionally they'd leave a condom on the floor to remind us they had squatting rights. Jarvis liked to brag that he took homecoming queen Tina Anderson's virginity in the fort. Though we didn't believe him, the fantasy fed plenty of thrills for us when we were alone under the safety of our bed covers at night. Last year, one of the initiation rites was to admit to the group that you had pleasured yourself to the story. Nobody denied it, except Tubs.

I remembered to take a hammer and some nails with me because every year the steps, which were nothing more than slats of wood, each about a foot long, loosened and became unsteady. Tubs got his nickname because last year he broke two of the steps due to his chubby frame. Truth was, he wasn't any heavier than the rest of us, but it gave us his nickname.

Billy and I raced our bikes down Yoder Road, kicking up dust as we went. We both had Schwinn Sting-Ray chopper style bikes, with banana seats and high handlebars. Both were hand-me-downs from our older brothers. Billy's brother Gerald had welded a three-foot-tall roll bar to the back of the seat when it was his, as though it would protect the rider if the bike ever flipped. He liked to take risks to come across as the cool kid. He gave the Sting-Ray to Billy when he had saved enough money to buy a used dirt bike. He was two years older than Billy. Just fifteen, he already shaved and sprouted muscles of an older kid. He scared us and he knew it.

Gerald ran with Tubs' older brother, Jarvis. They led a different type of club—a real gang—one who harassed the younger kids, chased girls, drank beer and Boone's Farm wine, smoked cigarettes and pot when they could get it. Jarvis had been arrested for stealing his dad's car when he was fourteen. He didn't really steal it. He just borrowed it. But all his dad knew was when he left the mill after his shift, his car was gone so he called the cops to report it. They spotted it, pulled it over, and found Jarvis behind the wheel. If the driver had been anyone but Jarvis, the cops would have probably taken him home and let him off the hook. But Jarvis already had a record for stealing cigarettes from the Red & White convenience store, so they cuffed and booked him. Like

Gerald, he looked two years older than his sixteen years. They both got away with buying cigarettes, beer, and *Playboy* magazines from the five-and-dime downtown, whose old lady cashier couldn't care less about poisoning the minds and bodies of teenagers. We all pooled our money to buy the cigs and magazines from them at a markup. This summer we decided we would try to score some beer and Boone's Farm.

I pounded extra carpenter nails into each step as I went, making sure they were tight and secure. The fort was active pretty much year-round, but only during the summer did our gang call it headquarters. Younger kids didn't have the rights to it and whenever they used it, they did so with caution. Billy brought a hand broom to sweep out some of the crud left over from the older kids. Cigarette butts, candy wrappers, empty beer cans, a condom still in its wrapper. Once we got it in good shape, we hung out at the base of the tree and waited for the rest of the gang. By three-thirty that afternoon everyone had showed. We did rock paper scissors to determine the order of official entry.

It was a mandatory meeting. Be at the fort by three-thirty or you're going to be in trouble. No one expected much work to be done on this afternoon, given the excitement of our newfound freedom. But it gave us a good reason to tell the rest of the gang, 'Be there or else.' "Or else, what?" Tubs asked. "Or else you might get voted out," I said. "Just be there." He was. So was Radish, Sully, Steve (Hickey) Hickman, and Billy, who we named 'Billy Jack' after the lead character from the movie of the same name. Yes, we all had nicknames. Mine was 'Johnny Lightning,' named after the Johnny Lightning Special racecar that won the Indy 500 a couple years earlier. The model I built of the car was the only one I wouldn't destroy. I kept it on a shelf in my bedroom. It was the second one I built. I blew up the first one. This one I wanted to hang on to.

Once we were all inside, we closed the door and the window shutters. "Everybody in," I said, commanding everyone to clasp hands in the middle. "Welcome to the summer of 1973," I began. "The first rule of the gang is that what happens here, stays here. No exceptions. Violate this rule and you're out. The second rule is that we take care of each other. We got each other's backs.

Know what I mean? Someone gets in trouble, needs something, gets in a jam, we come through for each other. Even if that means lying to save someone's hide. One of us gets in trouble, we all do. Got that? Any questions so far?"

"How long we gotta hold hands?" Radish asked.

"Shut up, Radish," Billy said. "This is serious."

"Right," I said. "Are we all clear? We'll figure out the other stuff later. 'Greasy River' on three. Ready? One, two, three, 'GREASY RIVER!'" With that we broke the clasp.

"What's the other stuff?" Sully asked.

"Bylaws," Billy said. "Our rules and regs."

"Did you hear the crazy old lady that lives over there died?" Hickey asked, pointing to the Cummings house a hundred yards or so through the woods.

"No shit," Radish said. "Cummings? Liza Cummings?"

"Eliza," I said. "Not Liza. It's E liza."

"What kind of name is E liza?" Sully asked.

"Doesn't matter," I said. "It's her name. And she wasn't crazy. Just private. Died of cancer."

"How the hell do you know so much?" Tubs asked.

"My mom knew her," I said. "She shopped at the market. My mom saw her all the time."

"I heard Mr. Klein was bonkin' her," Radish said.

"Shut up, Radish," Billy said. "You don't know anything."

"Just tellin' you what my daddy said, is all," Radish replied.

"Well, doesn't matter now, does it?" Billy said.

"The old man, the cripple, lived with her, right?" Sully said.

"He's crippled?" Tubs said.

"More like deformed," Sully said. "Ain't got no legs or arms. Can't see or hear. Bomb blew up on him in the war. Turned him into hamburger."

"He's not hamburger," I said. "He got burned up bad though."

"Anybody seen him?" Radish asked. Everyone shook their head no.

"He's Eliza's brother," I said. "My mom has seen him, but she won't talk

149

much about him. But she knows from Mr. Klein that he got messed up bad. He knows him pretty well, but he don't ever talk about him, according to my mom. Can't really see to get around. Don't know what he's going to do now with his sister being dead and all."

"We should go spy on him," Tubs said. "I want to see what he looks like."

"No," I shouted. "We're not going to spy on him. We're going to leave him be. My mom said he wants to be left alone. He's really private. She said to never, ever, never go cross into his property. We all clear on that? Are we?"

Everyone eventually nodded. "I'm serious," I said. "I'm making this a rule for us. Don't you dare do it. Not screwing around here."

"My daddy told me he'd whoop me if he ever caught me goin' on that property," Sully said. "He said to stay away from that man."

"So did my daddy," said Tubs. "Best to follow Lightning's advice. I don't want nothin' to do with him."

"Does that settle it?" I asked.

"Anyone got any smokes?" Sully asked.

CHAPTER
25

"TELL ME MORE about Eliza's brother," I said to my mom after we sat down for dinner.

"All you need to know is to leave him be," she said. "You and all your friends."

"We will. I made them all promise. I want to know more about him. Why is everything so secret? I know you've seen him. What's he look like?"

"Jonny," my dad said. "Listen to your mother and leave him be."

"I promise we won't bother him," I said. "But why can't I know something about him? Other boys are saying he's a monster. No arms. No legs. Face burnt off him. Is that true?"

"No, that's not true," she said white-lying to me. "He's a war hero. He was in a fire, and he suffered bad burns. He moved in with Eliza a while back. That's all you need to know."

"Is it true he doesn't have any hands?" I asked.

"Stop it," my dad said. "Eat your peas."

"I heard the same thing Jonny heard. He's a monster. Deformed. Grotesque," my older brother, Tommy, said, making ghoulish noises and twisting his face into spasms.

"Gosh darn it," my father said as he banged his hand on the table. "This conversation is over and we ain't going to have it again. Am I clear? I said, am I clear?"

"Yes Pops," Tommy said. "Yes Dad," I added.

I knew my mom wasn't telling me everything she knew, of course. She was a vault when it came to prying something out of her she didn't want out. She'd worked for Mr. Klein at the EK Market as the bookkeeper and part-time cashier. He hired her when his wife got too sick to work. Once in a while she'd open and close the market when Mr. Klein had to take care of other things, like when his wife was sick and dying, and when he was taking care of Eliza Cummings when she was sick. She knew a lot more about the happenings in the Cummings' house than she would ever let on to. And my hunch was that she'd been there more than the one time she told us about.

After I excused myself from the table, I was heading outside to ride my bike when I heard my mom and dad talking, still sitting at the table. When I heard my dad say the name Cummings, I stopped and stood in the hall to eavesdrop.

"What are the arrangements for Eliza?" I heard my dad ask.

"Don't think there are going to be any. She was cremated and Ed told me they spread her ashes around the property like she wanted. I think the boys from the mill were going to have a memorial for her, but not sure what's happening."

"Too bad. She was a nice lady. I'm sure lots of people would like to pay their respects. Private though. Must be where her brother gets it from. Her daddy was a nice man. Too bad his wife was deranged."

"I don't think Hank Jr. is private because he's a natural loner. He just doesn't want to be seen by anyone. Ed told me that when he used to go out in public when he lived in Kentucky, people gawked at him like he was in a circus. Nearly had a nervous breakdown. Since then, won't show his face if he can help it. Ed thinks Eliza didn't want a funeral because she wanted to spare her brother from having to see people."

"What's Hank going to do now?" my dad asked. "Without Eliza?"

"Ed arranged for Mildred Perkins to help Eliza out when she got real sick, you know, the colored lady who helped him with Jeanie. I think she's going to stick around to help Hank from what he told me."

"He's going to stay in the house all by himself?"

"I reckon so," my mom said. "Don't know if he's got anywhere else to go."

"He's blind, right?"

"Legally," my mom said. "So 'course he can't drive or get around on his own. Not that he would leave the house anyway. You know, he's a writer. He's a loner."

"Poor guy," my dad said. "I feel for him. Such a nice man."

"Sure is, just shy. Soft spoken. But polite as can be. Always calls me ma'am. Really is a shame. Ed will be sure to stay in touch with him."

"You know, people at the market ask Ed all the time about the guy, and he tells people to mind their own business. All it does is stir up curiosity. And it leads people to speculate. Say all kinds of things about him."

"Well, Ed's right," my mom said. "People just need to leave him alone. He's not a bother to anyone. Why should they care?"

"Like I said," my dad said. "Curiosity."

"Well, curiosity killed the cat, you know."

I went on about my business, got on my bike and rode to Billy's house. His dad worked the three to eleven shift at General Motors and carpooled to work with his friends from the plant. During the school year, the only time Billy saw him was on the weekends because he'd always left for work by the time Billy got home from school. His mom worked downtown at a hardware store and didn't get home from work until six, so Gerald and Billy had the house to themselves all afternoon. Mr. Nelson scared the bejesus out of all of us. He wore a dirty white T-shirt and greasy jeans. His black hair was always slicked back with Brylcreem. He was a mean drunk, always seemed to have a bottle of something in his hand. Was prone to slapping his wife and sons around on occasion. It wasn't unusual for Billy to be sporting a black eye or bruises on his arm. From what I could tell, Gerald was following in his dad's footsteps.

"You ain't seen nothin'," Gerald said as he stepped out of his dad's car with a twelve-pack of Miller beer. "Or I'll whoop your scrawny asses."

If his dad knew he took the car out, he'd whoop Gerald's ass for sure. Gerald might be able to whoop the whole Greasy River Gang's butts at the same time, but his dad would drop him in a heartbeat. Billy learned the hard way that he best cover for his older brother.

"You boys tryin' to reclaim the fort?" he asked us.

"It's our fort now," Billy answered.

"The fuck it is," Gerald said. "Go ahead and have your little games durin' the day. But best stay away from it at night, you hear?"

We hoped the fort wouldn't have the same allure this summer to older kids as it did in summers' past. But it looked like Gerald had other ideas, sparking the image of finding empty beer bottles and cigarette butts in the morning.

"Why don't you build yourself a new fort? One you can put a mattress in," Billy said.

"We built this one. You go build yourself one," Gerald said.

"The farm is big enough for all of us. Why don't you guys hang out at the church?"

"Place is infested with rats and shit," Gerald said. "Besides, you think I'm goin' to pop a cherry in the house of the Lord?"

I must admit, it was funny. I was sure the reason they stayed away from the old Amish church wasn't because it was a church, nor had we ever seen rats in it. Truth was, it was haunted by Old Man Yoder, and we were all scared to go in it, though it did offer us a great place to play *I dare you*. Certainly, the ghost of the old man wouldn't take too kindly to teenagers drinking, smoking, and trying to round the bases with their girlfriends on his grounds. It was the only thing I imagined Gerald was scared of besides his daddy—the ghost of Old Man Yoder.

Billy and I straddled our Sting-Rays and watched Gerald stuff the twelve-pack in a gym bag and hop on his dirt bike. "Get on with yourselves and mind your own fuckin' business," he said as he rode off.

"What an asshole," Billy said. "Ain't no way he's going to keep us out of the fort after dark."

"How are we going to stop him?" I asked.

"Don't know, but we'll think of something. I have a few secrets saved up. Maybe use them as levers if we need to?"

"You mean leverage," I said.

"Whatever."

Billy and I rode down to Radish's house where we were met by Tubs. The original plan was for us to go to the fort and hang out for a couple hours till nighttime.

"Ain't going to the fort tonight," Billy said.

"Why not?" Radish asked.

"My brother's going to be there."

"Screw that," Tubs said.

"You want your ass kicked, Tubs?" I asked. "Let's just ride down to the hole tonight. We can hang out there."

Some called it the swimming hole, some called it the fishing hole. We called it the hole. No specific group lay claim to it. It was open to all. Old men fished it during the day. Families sometimes picnicked there on Sundays. Once it warmed up, it was great for swimming if you weren't afraid of stepping on a turtle or seeing a garter snake slither by you. It was on Yoder's farm about fifty yards away from the fort. Everyone called the land the farm, but it was part of the original Yoder property that was never farmed, left to grow wild, making it the perfect playground for the neighborhood. Nearby was a fire pit full of burnt up logs surrounded by a couple dozen large stones. Yoder's creek wound throughout the land and wrapped around the hole. The church was a good ride away, a couple of hundred yards. On the other side of the church was the old Amish cemetery where all the Yoders were buried. We all had the image of Old Man Yoder rising out of his grave and going into the church to pray in a pew in the first row, ten feet from the altar. The pew was never dusty and didn't show the wear of the other pews, which were all in some state of poor repair. Someone used it. Figured it must be Old Man Yoder.

We rode down Yoder Road and turned onto the dusty path that led to the hole, passing the fort on our left. "Screw your brother," Tubs said. "Let's go. Come on." He turned and started riding toward the fort.

"I'm with him," said Radish. "Come on you chicken shits."

I looked at Billy, shrugged my shoulders and said, "He said 'at night.' It's technically not night yet, right? Come on." We followed Tubs and Radish.

Once inside the fort, Billy said, "Well, Tubs. Since this was your idea, you be on the lookout."

"Deal," Tubs said.

I pulled a pack of playing cards out of my pocket and separated out a euchre deck. Billy and I were pretty much unbeatable even without cheating, which we were capable of resorting to whenever we fell behind. We had key words to indicate what suits we were each strong in, and we'd hold the cards in our hands with the number of fingers showing how many cards we had in that suit. For example, if I held three fingers on the outside of my hand and said, 'shit,' that meant I had three spades. If I held four, and said, 'damn,' that meant I had four diamonds, and so forth. We didn't consider it cheating because everyone had their own system, so it was all fair game.

I couldn't get my mind off Hank Cummings since overhearing my mom and dad after dinner. I thought how the poor guy can't even hold a hand of cards. I caught myself looking in the direction of the house, wondering what he was doing at that very moment just a few hundred feet away.

"Lightning, look alive," Billy said, jolting me back to the game. "The suit is spades. Your play."

"Sorry," I said laying down a king and taking the trick. "Game."

"Screw you," Tubs said.

"And your mother," Radish added.

Radish lit a cigarette and strained to see out of the window in the dusk of the approaching darkness of night. "You hear that?" he asked. "Sounds like a dirt bike."

"Let's get out of here," Billy said. "Fast! GO!"

We tripped over ourselves scampering down the steps. We hopped on our bikes and headed back toward the hole.

"Fuck," Radish yelled out. "I think I dropped my cigarette in the fort."

"You dumbass," Billy yelled back. "Fuck!"

CHAPTER
26

THE NEXT MORNING, Billy showed up at my house with a fat lip. "What happened to you?" I asked.

"My brother came into my room when he got home last night and smacked me when I was sleeping. Great way to get woke up," Billy answered. "Said, 'I told you to stay out of the fort at night.' He found Radish's cigarette. I'm going to kill that motherfucker."

I knew that wasn't going to happen. Radish was the biggest and strongest of all of us. He was a bully, which worked to our advantage when we needed him. But he was someone you didn't want to piss off and he knew we'd never kick him out of the gang for fear of our lives.

"What an asshole," I said. "There's gotta be a way to share the fort without us getting our butts kicked. Can't you talk to him?"

"He already said we can have it during the day. His buddies and him get it at night. I ain't gonna push it with him no more."

This put a big damper on our summer plans, which included hanging out there at night whenever we could sneak it. It was big enough to sleep four of us at a time. We were already planning how to pull that off with our parents, each of us saying we were staying at someone else's house and heading to the fort with our sleeping bags. We already settled on the first foursome by a competitive rock paper scissors contest, won by me, Tubs, Sully and Radish. We used rock paper scissors because there was no way anyone could cheat. Even though we knew Gerald and his friends weren't going to use the fort every night, Billy said he argued that he never knew when his girl was going to get out of the house. He was essentially 'on call' to jump at any chance of taking her up that tree.

The gang had agreed to meet at the fort at ten o'clock a.m., our first official full day of summer. It was a clear, sunny day, just like every summer day should be. Except for Tubs, everyone was there on time. About half past ten, we heard a commotion outside the fort and looked out the window to find Tubs fast-walking toward us, struggling to catch his breath.

I yelled out the window, "Tubs, what the hell you doin'?"

Between breaths, panting, and putting his hands on his knees, he said, "Sorry ... I just .... my bro ... my brother took my bike. I ran as fast as I could to get here on time."

"Why didn't you call one of us?" Billy asked. "I could have put you on the back of my seat."

"Didn't know he took it till I went out to get it. Would have been too late."

"Git your ass up here," Radish said.

"Am I in trouble?" Tubs asked.

"We'll let it slide this time," I kidded, though with a serious look.

Radish held out a pack of cigarettes and offered them to the group.

"No smoking," Billy said.

"Bullshit, since when?" Radish asked.

"Since my brother busted my lip open for you being a stupid jackass last night, that's when," Billy responded.

"What? You sayin' we can't smoke now?" Sully asked.

"That's what I'm saying," Billy said.

"That's bullshit, when have we ever not been able to smoke up here? Just 'cause Radish fucked up once. Screw it. Light it up Radish. And give me one too."

Billy grabbed for the lighter, but Radish held him back with his outstretched foot to the chest. Billy went back at him but I grabbed him.

"I don't see any harm in smoking up here during the day," I said. "But Radish, you screwed up good last night and Billy's lip is proof of it. You owe him."

"Don't owe him shit," Radish said.

"You want to stay in this gang?" Billy asked.

"You don't make the rules, Billy Jack," Radish said. "Don't threaten me. You ain't got the nuts to try to kick me out."

"I agree with Lightning," Tubs said. "You should say sorry. And quit mouthing off."

"Fuck you guys. Okay. I'm sorry," Radish said. "But this calls for settin' forth some bylaws so we don't got no fuckin' gray areas."

"That's what we're here to do," I said. "It's the first order of business."

This was to be the gang's third summer. The previous two years we had used our first day together to write up the summer's bylaws. We called them rules our first year. None of us knew what bylaws were until Sully went to the mill with his dad one Saturday to retrieve the thermos he'd left in the breakroom. Among the random papers pinned to a bulletin board was a list of breakroom dos and don'ts. At the top was printed in all caps and bold, **BREAKROOM BYLAWS.** Sully ripped the paper from the board and brought it back to us. Ever since, we no longer had rules. We had bylaws. It sounded more serious. Since the Timken Mill had eight bylaws, that's how many we wanted.

"First," I said. Let's review last year's bylaws.

What happens here stays here
We have each others' backs
Scrape the mud off your shoes before entering

Don't leave food or food wrappers
No girls
You can't bring anyone else up here without permission in advance
Disputes will be voted on—majority rules
Always be on time

Hickey was the oldest member of the gang at fourteen and had found himself a girlfriend during the school year. As expected, he took exception to rules five and six.

"Just 'cause none of you have a girl don't mean I should be penalized for it," Hickey said.

"You wouldn't have the balls to bring that little string bean up here anyway, you wet noodle," Tubs said.

"Blow me, Tubs," Hickey said. "You ain't never even felt a boob yet."

"The hell I haven't," Tubs said. "'Sides, she ain't even got no titties yet."

"No cheatin' at cards," Sully said. All you guys cheat at cards."

"That'd be nine bylaws," Hickey said. "We'd have to drop one of the others."

"We're not bound to eight," I said. "We can add to them if we need to. But I would vote no on Sully's proposed amendment."

"Me too," said Billy. "Me three," said Tubs. "Me four," said Radish.

"That's four against already," I said. "Case closed."

With that, the bylaws were voted on to remain with no changes from the previous year other than adding a clause: *Smoking permitted until seven at night.* Our next order of business was to discuss what kind of trouble we were willing to risk getting into. We called them 'trouble makers.'

"I still want to see Missy Botkin naked," Tubs said.

"Who don't?" Hickey said. "How'd that work out for you last year?"

We had it on the list the previous summer. Tubs and Sully camped out under her bedroom window one night waiting for Missy to turn her light on and strip down for bed. As they were huddled behind a shrub, Missy's dog, Lucy, got loose and Mr. Botkin started chasing the pooch around the yard. Lucy sniffed out Tubs and Sully leading Mr. Botkin to find them hunching down outside Missy's room. He told them, "Scamper on home now boys. I'll make sure your daddies are waiting for you." They did, and their daddies were.

"Nothing like that this year," I said. "Nothing that's going to break any laws and screw things up for all of us."

"How 'bout this," Hickey said. "You know her and her friends go to the swimming hole a lot in the summer. Let's do some recon and set ourselves up to do some spying on 'em when they do. Maybe set us up a little hiding place in the thicket over there. Bring some binoculars."

"I like it," Billy said.

"Me too," chimed in Tubs.

"Okay," I said. "We'll put it on the list. Any objections? Approved, then"

"Some of the ones from last year are still good," Billy said. "Read em off, Lightning."

"Okay," I said as I flipped through the pages of the gang notebook that I always carried and kept safe. "Here are some trouble makers that can carry over: who can climb the highest in the fort maple tree, bike race down Yoder Road, who can stay the longest lying down on Old Man Yoder's grave, who can last the longest in the church by themselves sitting on Old Man Yoder's pew, and, of course, who can score the June, July, and August issues of *Playboy*. These all sound good to me. Vote on 'em?"

"What about beer and Boone's Farm?" Radish said.

"Vote on these first," I said. "We can talk about others later. Anyone got any problems with these being set forth? Okay, all approved. Now what else?"

"Beer and Boone's Farm," Radish repeated.

"How so?" Billy asked.

"Didn't we say we're gonna get drunk this summer?" Radish asked. "How 'bout a contest who can score the booze?"

I looked at Billy, who shrugged his shoulders. "I see no harm. Any objections? Okay, added to the list."

"How 'bout one for who can drink the most without puking?" Sully asked.

"One step at a time, Sully," Hickey said. "Ain't even got the booze yet."

"Hickey's right," I said. "If we score the booze, then we can vote on that. What else?"

"I want to see your brother boinking Tina Anderson," Radish said to Tubs.

"Do so at your own risk," Tubs said. "It's your life. Not going there."

"Agreed," I said. "Anything else?"

Everyone looked around at each other waiting for someone to throw something else into the pot. Finally, Radish did.

"I want to see what that old man looks like," he said, pointing in the direction of the Cummings' house.

"Yeah," Tubs said. "Me too."

"Good one," Hickey added.

"Approved," said Sully.

"Come on, Lightnin'," Radish said. "Write it down."

Billy looked at me waiting for a reaction. He knew I'd think this was crossing a line. It seemed too risky.

"Not worth it," I said.

"Grow some nuts, Lightnin'," Radish said. "Don't be a pussy. We ain't said we gonna cross into his property. Just want to git a look at him's all. Who else is in? Already got me, Tubs, Sully and Hickey. That's four."

"Stupid idea," Billy said. "We'll get our butts kicked."

"I ain't suggestin' we break into the man's house," Radish said. "Just sneak up to the line and try to spot him outside or something like that. Ain't breakin' no law or nothin.'"

"Yeah," Tubs said. "What's the big deal? Besides, vote's already four yesses."

"Haven't voted on it yet," I said. "Needs to be formally brought forward."

"Jesus H. Christ, Lightnin'," Radish said. "You can be such a fuckin' pussy. Bring if forth."

I felt sick to my stomach. If my mom and dad knew that this discussion was even happening, they'd ground me for a week. If they found out we approved it, they'd ban me from the fort for the summer. If we ever got caught, I'd be banned for life.

"I don't like it," I said. "Too much risk."

"Like Radish said," Sully added. "Not like we're breakin' no law. Don't see it being no big deal. Let's go. Call the vote, Lightning."

"You pussy," Radish said. "Call the vote. If you ain't got the balls, I'll call it."

It was an unspoken bylaw that, like being trusted with the gang notebook, I was responsible for calling the votes. That's the way it always worked and I wasn't going to let that slide to someone else. I couldn't stop this. I needed to call the vote.

The vote was 4-2. Trying to spot Hank Cummings was added to the list.

CHAPTER
27

"IT'S A BAD IDEA," I said to Billy as we rode our bikes home for lunch. "I don't know about you, but if we get caught spying on Mr. Cummings, I'm screwed."

"You don't have to be a part of it," Billy said. "And you ain't responsible for what those bozos do."

"Kind of am," I said. "Unless one or two of them do it on their own. If it's a gang thing, my mom and dad will know I was a part of it. At least letting it happen."

"But ain't you curious too?"

"Of course, but you gotta respect the man's privacy."

"How they gonna know?"

"They'll know, trust me."

"Ain't there a picture of him anywhere or something? All they said was they want to know what he looks like."

"The man never leaves his house," I said. "Who's going to have a picture of him?"

We got to my house and made bologna sandwiches on Wonder Bread slathered with mayo and mustard. I mixed us up some Plan X, our drink of choice. Everyone in the gang loved Plan X. Only Billy and I knew the recipe. One cup of whole milk per one teaspoon of sugar. Plan XX called for a double helping of sugar. My brother, Tommy, came into the kitchen when I was stirring it up.

"Fix me up a glass of that crud. Make it a double," he said as he made two bologna sandwiches with mayo, peanut butter, and pickles.

"You're gross," Billy said.

"Try it," Tommy said. "You might like it. Tastes like pussy, not like you'd know." He took a big bite of sandwich and washed it down with a swig of Plan XX. "Hey, I heard you got busted in the fort the other night by your brother, Billy. Best stay away after dark."

"I don't see why we can't share it at night," I said. "You know, work something out where we get it once in a while."

"I don't give a shit," Tommy said. "You gotta talk to Gerald about that. He's the one getting his dick wet. I never go there anymore." Ever since Tommy got his license and had the backseat of my parent's car available to him, he had no need for the fort.

"Can't you talk to him?" I asked.

"Hell no, he don't listen to nobody," Tommy said.

Billy and I grabbed our mitts and went out for a catch. Little League tryouts were that afternoon. Hickey's dad was one of the coaches and Hickey was trying to stack the deck to get us all on the same team. The year before, Hickey's dad was pissed at him because he didn't cut the grass on time. Didn't even choose him for his own team and arranged for Hickey to end up on the Cubs, the worst team in the league. Hickey had been on his best behavior the days leading up to the picks.

I was working my way to play pitcher this year. Billy was a natural catcher. We had our fingers crossed. My dad taught me how to throw a curve and a knuckleball, neither of which I could control well. I'd have been the first Little Leaguer in history to throw a knuckle in a game, and I was determined.

"Give it up," Billy said as my knuckle attempt bounced up and hit him in the nuts.

"That was a strike. It just broke late, like it's supposed to," I said. "You gotta learn to catch it."

"Screw it, go back to your fastball," he said. "At least I know where that's going."

"Alright," I said, as I lobbed another knuckleball at him. The ball headed straight down the middle, the seams not moving an inch, and darted down at the last second away from his glove, splitting open the one good lip he had left.

"You asshole," he said as he threw his mitt at me. "Get yourself another catcher. I'm bleeding ain't I? Fuck yes, I'm bleeding."

As upset as I was about popping him in the lip, I was happier that I'd been able to throw two knuckles for strikes that would have been unhittable. He's just gotta catch them.

"When you get a mask and nut-cup on, you'll be okay," I said.

"Fuck off, Lightning," he said as he got on his bike to ride back home. "I ain't catching you no more."

Billy picked up the hothead trait from his old man. He always got over it fast, though, and I knew this would be no exception. I went around to the backyard where my mom was planting flowers.

"Tell me more about Hank Cummings," I said.

"That's 'Mr. Cummings' to you. What's with you anyway?" she said. "Why this sudden curiosity over this man?"

"Just been thinking about him a lot," I said. "Feel real sorry for him since his sister died. All alone over there."

"Well, that's the way he wants it, so let's keep it that way," she said.

"How was he burned? Did a bomb blow up?"

"It was a plane crash."

"Wow, was he a pilot?"

"Nothing cool about war, Jonny. Lots of boys come back from war in bad shape. World War ll, Korea, Vietnam. Look at poor Billy's dad."

"Billy's dad is just a mean drunk," I said.

"Why do you think? Wasn't that way before the war. He was a sweetheart in high school. He came back a changed man. And look what happened to your friend Cecil's brother. Didn't come back at all from Vietnam. Mrs. Turley will never recover."

"You said Mr. Cummings was a writer," I slipped, forgetting that was something I overheard from eavesdropping.

"When did I say that?"

"Oh, maybe I heard it somewhere else," I said. "Is he?"

"Yes, he writes. Not sure what, but I know he does. And I know he's been published. Like you."

It was a bit of a stretch to call getting a couple short stories printed in the Johnny Appleseed Junior High School bulletin being *published*, but I took it like a champ.

"See, we have something in common," I said. "Too bad he's such a loner. Wouldn't it be cool if I could meet him someday?"

"Yes," she said. "I suppose that would be nice, but don't ever get your hopes up."

"You've met him, haven't you?"

"You won't let up, will you?" she said without looking up from scraping dirt aside to make room for some bulbs.

"Come on, Mom, tell me."

"I've met him, yes."

"Is it true ..."

"Enough. That's it. I don't know how many more ways I can say this to you. He is none of anyone's business, and that includes you."

"Okay, but ..."

"Let me ask you a question for a change? What if you had a deep, dark secret that you didn't want anyone to know? But someone knew it. And another person wanted to know it and kept hounding the person to tell them. How would you feel if they told your secret?"

"I get it." Making a broad assumption, I said, "Well, next time you see him, tell him your son is a writer just like him."

"Okay, Jonny," she said. "If I ever get the chance, I'll tell him."

"Or have Mr. Klein tell him."

"Enough young man. Aren't tryouts this afternoon? Best get going now."

I'd made progress—a solid foot in the door—at least more than anyone else in the gang. But I doubted I'd squeeze another drop out of her.

At tryouts that afternoon, it was time for the wanna-be pitchers to show their stuff to the coaches. Coach Strine, the gym teacher and basketball coach from the school, had brought a large portable chalkboard to the park. Across the top, each of the positions were listed. Pitcher, catcher, first base, second base, and so forth. Every kid was to sign up for two positions indicating both their first and second choice. I got to the park early so my name would be at the top of the list. My first choice was pitcher, my second, center field. Billy was one of the last kids to pull up on his bike, riding straight past me without looking up, in his trademark passive- aggressive manner. His lip had swollen to twice its size. I followed him to the board to watch. He picked up the piece of chalk and studied the lists. He turned back to see me lurking over his shoulder, then wrote his name under shortstop (first choice), third base (second choice). He turned back and said, "Say you're sorry, asshole." I said, "You're sorry, asshole." He said, "Let's try this one more time. Say 'I'm sorry. I'm an asshole.'" I said, "I'm sorry. I'm an asshole." With that he turned back and switched his first choice to catcher.

"Pitchers and catchers, mound and home plate," Coach Strine yelled. "Let's go."

Pitcher was the glory position. It's the one the girls watched. The most pressure. No place to hide. Even if a kid could whip strikes in their backyard, doing it in front of a crowd made a lot of them piss their pants.

"Jonny Smith," Strine shouted. "Pick your catcher and take the mound. You got twenty pitches to show your stuff."

Billy and I jogged onto the diamond. He said, "One finger for fastball. Two for a curve. You try to get fancy on me, I'm quitting the gang. You understand me?"

"Yes sir, Billy Jack," I said.

"Fuck off," he said as he took his place behind the plate. He poked one finger down under his mitt. I wound up and threw a heater, right down the middle. Then another, then another. He put two fingers down and I lobbed a curve that would have made Tom Seaver jealous.

Nineteen pitches in, all but three were strikes. All the coaches were laser focused on me and I could hear them chattering to each other. One to go. "Knuckleball coming!" I shouted loud enough for all of them and Billy to clearly hear. Coaches scrambled to stand behind me to see if it would move. Billy's eyes didn't blink. I lobbed it slow and high. It darted right, then left, then right again. Billy didn't flinch. It rose three feet before the plate, then the bottom dropped out as if gravity had had enough and fell right into Billy's mitt, right where he expected it. "Strike three," Billy yelled as he jumped to his feet and pumped his fist in the air.

"You're a lucky fuck," Billy said to me when we met up.

"You're a natural catcher," I said. "I knew you'd catch it."

After tryouts, all the kids waited to find out where they'd been picked. Billy, Hickey, and I were all chosen by Hickey's dad on the Orioles. The rest of our gang were scattered throughout the league. Billy and I had to pony up and buy Hickey a banana split at Dairy Queen on the way home, but it was worth it.

The gang was planning to meet at the fort after dinner. I wasn't able to go because my mom invited my cousins over for a cookout and I had to stick around till they left. It was rare for me to miss a gang meeting, but there were times it was out of my control. This was one of those times. I could never get out of a visit with my cousins. To make up for it, my mom was letting me spend the night at Billy's house. It was near dark by the time they left and no sooner did their rear lights round the corner from D Street before I hightailed it to my bike, swiping some of my mom's homemade chocolate chip cookies along the way.

I pulled into Billy's drive and saw Gerald in the garage working on his dirt bike. "What's up little rat fuck?" he said.

"Hi Gerald," I said. I couldn't help myself and asked, "Are you going to the fort tonight?"

"None of your fuckin' business twerp ass," he said. "Maybe I am, maybe I ain't."

He turned his attention back to his bike as I met Billy coming around from the backyard. He was wiping tears off his cheeks.

"Let's ride," he said as he got on his bike.

"Pussies," Gerald yelled out at us as we rode away, Billy yelling back, "Fuck off, Gerald."

"What's up?" I asked Billy.

"Nothin'," he said.

"Bullshit, you're crying," I said. "What's wrong?"

"Just my old man. It's nothin'. The usual. Drop it. Please."

I knew when not to push things with him. He usually told me everything, but I could sense when to back off.

We rode out to Yoder Road and headed to the farm. I rode behind him in silence. The great thing about us was that we could enjoy being together without having to fill our time with conversation. After about ten minutes, he slowed so I could pull up beside him. His eyes were dry but red.

"Where we going?" I asked.

"Let's just go to the hole and hang out," he said. I ducked back in behind him and stayed in his tracks as he turned onto the path and rode past the fort to the pond. We laid our bikes down among the cattails. He picked up a few stones and started skipping them across the water. The sun had set beyond the pines near the farm's border.

"You guys meet up at the fort after dinner?" I asked.

"Just four of us," he said. "Tubs couldn't come."

"Right," I said. "Anything up?"

"Radish and Sully both showed up with something interesting."

"*Playboys?*"

"I wish," he said. "Binoculars."

"So what?"

"Well, when it was time to break up to head home, they didn't come with us."

"Where did they go?"

"They rode over in the direction of the Cummings house."

"Oh shit," I said.

CHAPTER
28

WE SAT DOWN ON THE BANK of the hole and Billy tuned his transistor radio to the Indians game. His dad had promised to take him to a game over the years, but never came through. This summer my dad had already bought four tickets to a game in late June against the Tigers to take me, Tommy, and Billy. My family wasn't perfect, but compared to the rest of the guys I was lucky. My mom and dad seemed happy, rarely fought, worked their stuff out, didn't beat me, provided three square meals a day, and the kind of structure a kid needed.

Radish's and Hickey's parents had already either split or divorced, no one knew for sure. Just knew that their dads weren't around much. Last summer I was hanging with Radish, having a catch in his front yard on a Sunday afternoon and his dad pulled up and said, "Let's go Jimmy, it's your day with me. Where's your sister?" "She ain't coming," Radish shot back, sparking no reaction from his dad. He coaxed me to stick with him. His dad took us to where he lived, in a boarding house with a bunch of other men. They were all sitting in the front room in their dirty white T-shirts, some still in their boxer shorts, watching a western on a small black and white TV. The room was smokey. Ashes spilled out over the sides of ashtrays scattered around. Radish and I sat on the floor for three hours and watched TV before his dad said, "Let's go, time to go home." Radish didn't act one way or another. Just another day with his dad. I about cried myself to sleep that night thinking about him.

Sully's mom was a nice-looking lady, about forty years old, already divorced twice with three kids. It was no mystery why she had so many suitors. She had a naturally thin and fit body without putting any effort into it. She wore short jeans shorts and a bikini top around the yard in the summer. On hot days we all liked to hang out in his backyard where she would set up a sprinkler and join us running through it, giving us lots to think about when we were alone at night. All she wanted to do was find a guy to settle down with. But all they wanted to do was sleep with her and move on. She had a big heart with a hole that couldn't be filled.

Of the six of us, no one had a better home life than me. It was hard to comprehend the fate that had been cast upon my mates. They didn't choose their parents, brothers, sisters, or homes. Growing up with drunks, abuse, beatings, unfaithfulness, some near poverty. I believed the gang gave some of them more stability than they had in their own homes, and I felt some sense of responsibility to keep it that way.

Radish was the outlier, indifferent to feeling any responsibility for the rest of us. He had a history of creating problems, bending the rules, walking the fine line. So when Billy told me he was already working to spy on Mr. Cummings, it sent a chill up my spine.

"Radish is going to screw things up for us," I said to Billy. "Summer's just getting started and he's already pushing the limits. Nothing good is going to come out of this."

"Not much we can do about it," Billy said. "I tried to stop them. Told them to at least wait until we could all talk about it. Radish said, 'Fuck that.' Just wouldn't listen to me. Couldn't stop him."

"No," I said. "'Course you couldn't."

Billy and I called everyone Saturday morning for a mandatory meeting at two o'clock.

"What the heck guys," I said to Radish and Sully. "What did you do last night?"

"Whatcha mean?" Radish asked.

"The Cummings property," I said. "Did you go there?"

"Fuck yes, we did," Radish said. "Didn't see shit, there weren't no lights on in the house, and Sully was too scared to cross through the pines to get closer. Pussy."

"Shut up," Sully told him. "My daddy told me them pines is the border. We said we ain't crossin' the border."

"You don't know where the fuck the border is," Radish said.

"I think Sully's right about the pines," I said. "I think that's the border too. Best not cross it."

"Well, can't see shit unless we do," Radish said. "Besides, you just sayin' that. You don't know."

"Give it up," I said. "Leave the poor man alone."

"What the fuck you give two cents 'bout that cripple for?" Radish asked.

"Let it be, Radish," I said.

"What, you Momma fuckin' him or somethin'?" Radish said.

"Enough," Billy barked. "Radish, what the hell? Shut your mouth. You can't talk 'bout Lightning's mom like that."

"Fuck off Billy Jack," Radish barked back.

"STOP!" I yelped. "ENOUGH! Stop. Calm down, Radish. Calm the fuck down."

I pulled out a pack of cards and we kicked up a game of gin rummy to settle the tension and move on to other things.

Later that day when Billy, Hickey, and I were having a catch, Hickey said, "You know, Lightning, we all been talkin' and all of us want to see what that guy looks like. You just wastin' your time tryin' to git us not to. What you say to that Billy Jack?"

Billy hunched his shoulders in a noncommittal way. "Come on, Jack Snack," Hickey continued. "You ain't goin' back on your word now. Tell him what you told us. We're goin' tonight."

"I'm curious," Billy said. "I mean, I don't want to get in trouble, you know, cross the line, but you know, if everyone else is going, I don't see no harm in goin.'"

I threw my best knuckleball to him, and he caught it. "Nice try," he said. "Besides, Lightning, you don't have to come."

CHAPTER

29

WE LEFT OUR BIKES near the hole and followed a path away from the fort to avoid Gerald or anyone else. We knew every square inch of the property except when we got closer to the row of pines. We found ourselves struggling through thickets and thorny bushes, stepping over downed trees and upended roots. When we got to a slight clearing, I could see the outline of the Cummings house. It was well guarded by trees and shrubs grown wild, but as we got closer, we found some spots where we had a clear view from about a hundred feet away. We teamed up in threes and spread out a little. Billy and I stayed with Hickey. Tubs went with Radish and Sully. There were lights on in the house, but all the curtains were pulled so you couldn't see inside. The hair on the back of my neck raised at the thought of Mr. Cummings sitting inside by himself with us trying to get a glimpse of him.

After about fifteen minutes we saw the headlights of a car coming down the long drive toward the house. As it got closer, I recognized it. It was Mr. Klein's Cadillac. We crept down lower to avoid the headlights as it circled to a stop. Mr. Klein got out, opened up the trunk, and lifted what appeared to be a folded chair of some kind, which he brought to the passenger side of the car. Someone opened the door from within and Mr. Klein gave the chair a hard downward shake. It popped open. It was a wheelchair.

"I didn't know he was in a wheelchair," Billy whispered to me.

"Shhh," I said with a dirty look.

He helped a man scoot from the car seat into the wheelchair. I could hear the faint whisper of words but couldn't make them out. Mr. Klein rolled the chair to the porch and backed it against the steps positioning the man to face us. He was silhouetted by the porch light, so it was impossible to make out any features. He appeared to be small. And bald. I strained to see if I could spot ears or a nose. Mr. Klein pulled the chair up the steps one at a time, like someone pulling a dolly with a washer up from a basement. With one hand, he pulled at the screen door, swinging it wide open, and pulled the chair into the house. Hickey wouldn't release his grip on the binoculars. All of us remained still, unable to move.

After no more than five minutes, Mr. Klein came out of the house, got in his car and left. We waited several more minutes in silence waiting for some sign of activity in the house. By this time it was around nine-thirty and for those of us with curfews, we were up against the clock. I motioned with my thumb, let's go. Radish shook his head. We had agreed we were going to stick together on this. No lone wolves. I motioned more adamantly and so did Sully, which convinced Radish to back out of the pines to join us. Once we felt we were out of danger of being found out, we compared notes. Most of us thought the man was Mr. Cummings. Sully had the best binoculars of the bunch. He swore he saw hands, fingers, ears, and a nose. All the things we were told Mr. Cummings was missing.

"Had to have been him," Billy said.

"But I saw his hands," Sully said.

"Then who could it be?" Hickey asked. "Thought you said he never sees anyone besides Old Man Klein, Lightning?"

"I didn't think he did," I said. "And my mom says he never leaves the house. So, no clue."

"Had to have been him," Billy said. "Makes no sense for Mr. Klein to drop off a cripple and just leave him there. And we know Cummings is a cripple."

"This ain't the last time we're doing this," Radish said. "Only wet my whistle for more. Even got a funny feelin' down in my shorts."

"Hey man," Tubs said. "My heart's racing like I'm riding a roller coaster. Had the same feeling as when we were peeping into Missy Botkin's bedroom window."

"Yeah," I said. "How'd that work out?"

"We ain't gonna get caught," Sully said. "Ain't no one ever 'round this part of the farm. Just need to be cool about it."

"We'll talk about it later and figure out what we're going do next," I said.

No sooner did I finish my sentence than we all heard Gerald's dirt bike revving down the path off Yoder Road that led to the treehouse. There were a few ways in and out of the farm, some harder than others. The main path was the easiest one and the one that led closest to the treehouse, but we had options.

"Let's book," I said. "Back way, Thomas Lane."

"Pronto," Billy said.

"After you," said Tubs.

They followed me out single file. Once we made it out to Thomas Lane, I slowed down and looked over my shoulder. Even in the dark, I could tell not everyone was with us.

"Who's missing?" I yelled back as I pulled my bike over and stopped.

"Christ," Billy shot back. "Radish and Sully. They ain't here."

CHAPTER
30

MY WORST FEARS didn't materialize. Radish and Sully didn't hang back so they could give the Cummings house another go. They did it to spy on Gerald and his girlfriend, which gave me a much needed sense of relief and humor. Especially when they described to us the scene they witnessed.

"We hunched down in the cattails at the edge of the hole," Radish began. "Needin' to be sure not to be seen and all." Looking at Billy, he said, "Heard your brother pull that piece of crap dirt bike up the base of the tree. When he shut the motor down, all's ya could hear was them gigglin' and shit. Waited till they went up into the fort before we moved in closer."

"One step at a time," Sully added.

"Yeah, inch by fuckin' inch," Radish said. "Anyway, we get close enough to hear 'em. He puts a tape in the player and hits play. You know what tape he put in?"

"Grand Funk Railroad?" said Billy.

"Nope," Radish said.

"Steppenwolf, Magic Carpet Ride," said Tubs.

"Wrong, Tubby. Any other guesses?"

"Hell, I don't know. Hendrix?" I said. "Santana?"

"The fuckin' Carpenters! Then he starts serenadin' her. Starts singing about birds appearing, fallin' in love and shit—Sully and I almost lost our dinner. He's fuckin' singin' to her. Now if that ain't ever a boy tryin' to git in a girl's pants. By now we moved closer figurin' we'd have plenty of warnin' him bein' all preoccupied with gettin' in this little girl's panties."

"Still sounds risky," Tubs said.

"Shut up you tuba," Radish said. "We ain't dumb."

"So then what?" Billy asked.

"Except for the music, it got quiet. Figured they were making out. But here's where it gits good and juicy. You tell this part Sully."

"Why me?" Sully asked.

"Cause I ain't able to say the P word, that's why," Radish says.

"Pussy?" Hickey asked.

"No you pussy," Radish said. "Shut up and listen."

"Okay," Sully starts. "What's Gerald's girl's name, Billy?"

"Linda, I think," Billy said. "If it's the same girl as last week, at least."

"Yeah, that's it. Linda," Sully continued. "So, Linda starts getting all fidgety and squirmy. You could just tell. Starts saying things like, 'What are you doing? Stop it. Wait. Whoa. Easy.' Shit like that."

"Git to it," Radish said. "Here's where it gits good."

"So," Sully continued. "She finally comes right out and asked, 'What exactly do you want me to do?' And Gerald goes, 'I am going to make this as simple for you to understand as possible.' That's exactly what he said, I'll never forget it. Then he says, are you ready for this?"

"Yes, what?" we all said in unison sitting on every word.

"He says, 'I want you to put your lips on my penis.'"

"No way," Billy squelched.

"No shit. 'I want you to put your lips on my penis and suck it.' Fucker didn't even say dick or cock. Came right out with the medical term, penis."

We're howling at this point.

"That's the P word you can't say, Radish?" Hickey howled. "Penis? You can't say penis? Penis. Penis. Penis!"

Even Radish was laughing. Then he says, "It gets a whole lot better. But first of all, I gotta ask, Billy Jack, has this chick ever had Plan X?"

"Maybe," Billy said. "I've made it for Gerald before. Maybe he gave her some, why?"

"Oh," Radish goes. "This is fuckin' great. So, anyway, she goes, 'I ain't gonna touch that thing,' she called it a thing. Even she can't say the P word. She goes, 'I ain't touching that thing with my mouth. Taste like crap.' Gerald goes, 'No it doesn't.' Oh my fucking God, are you boys ready for this?"

"Yes!" we all yelled. "What?"

"He goes, 'Tastes like Plan X.'"

He could barely get the words out he was laughing so hard. I thought he was going to pop a nut. We were all in hysterics. After all the stress of the Cummings' house situation, nothing could have brought us back as one like this story.

"What happened then?" Billy asked.

"It gets even better," Sully said, "She goes, 'I hate Plan X.'"

As if that was the deal-breaker. I admit, I was somewhat annoyed that she said she hated the drink. She'd be the only one ever. But the thought that if Gerald would have said something like, 'Tastes like bubble gum,' she may have said, 'Okay, I like bubble gum,' and done the deed was gut wrenching funny to me.

When we could compose ourselves again, Billy said, "Then?"

"Well," Radish said. "Then we knew he wasn't gonna git no pussy so we left and went home."

"You guys still played with fire," Billy said. "Gerald woulda' kicked your hides."

"Ain't 'fraid of him," Radish said.

"Should be," Billy shot back.

"Ain't," Radish repeated.

"Should be."

The story brought Gerald down to size in our eyes. Big talker leaving condoms around like having sex with Linda was a regular thing. Now we knew better. He could certainly still kick our asses, but knowing he was full of shit was pretty funny. We still needed to stay on his good side because Billy was angling for him to buy us a *Playboy* and some cigarettes.

When I got home that night, I wrote down Radish's story about Gerald in my writing notebook. I had begun to develop a series of short stories that usually had some gross or unexpected twist. This would be the only nonfiction of the bunch so far. No need to even embellish it.

I was anxious and a bit embarrassed to read my stories out loud. Reading to the gang began after Billy was snooping in my notebook. He didn't mean to, I left it open to the page of the story, *Judy's Fine Moment*. Once he read the first few lines, he couldn't put it down. "I'm sorry," he said. "It was just too good. You've got to read it to the guys."

One time I mistakenly brought my writing notebook with me instead of the gang notebook. When I went to record something, I realized the mistake of mixing them up and let out an, "Oh shit."

"What?" Billy asked.

I told him what happened and that's when he egged me on, knowing I had my stories with me.

After arguing a bit, the rest of the guys piled on and I finally acquiesced. "Okay, okay," I said. "This story is called, *Judy's Fine Moment*."

"Wait till you hear this, guys," Billy said.

"Shut up," Hickey said. "Let him read it."

"I will," said Billy. "But when he reads about Judy, just think of Tina Anderson—pretty Miss Perfect. I think that's who it's about."

"Shut up," Sully said. "Read it already."

"*Judy's Fine Moment*," I began. "Here goes."

"*Ben Tailor's sister, Judy, claimed she never farted.*"

"Who is Ben Tailor?" Tubs asked.

"It's a story, dumbshit," Billy said. "He's a made-up dude. It doesn't matter. Shut up and let him read it."

I continued. *"Now anyone who claims they haven't farted loses all credibility with me. But the conviction with which she made this claim was rather convincing. Ben used to try to bait her into it. She'd be taking a nap on the couch and when she woke up, Ben would be there laughing his ass off, saying, 'Ha, ha, Judy cut the cheese,' just hoping to catch her off guard with a response of, 'Oh no, did I really?' He would even sneak into the bathroom and hide a tape recorder behind the toilet before she would go in to use it to see if she would fart while taking a dump. But to no avail. It would have been a little easier to take if she was more accepting of other people's farts. But she thought it was gross when someone farted. Like it was something so unnatural and distasteful. She thought that it was something people ought to be able to control. Of course, she found it incredibly annoying that not only did we fart, but we enjoyed the act immensely. Finally, after a lifetime of frustration, Ben figured it out. He had been a lifelong sufferer from hemorrhoids. He had tried everything short of surgery, when finally a doctor prescribed a special cream that would give him some relief. The problem is, the doctor explained, 'It will create problematic flatulence.' And he was right. It did. A little dab of this stuff on your butthole and about thirty minutes later, you were in for the worst gas you've ever experienced. Now Ben's challenge was how to get this cream on Judy's butthole. It had him stumped until one Saturday morning, a gift fell into his lap. He was walking past the bathroom door and Judy had just gotten out of the shower when he heard the words that would change Judy's life forever. They were in fact, Judy's own words, 'Bingo, why do you always have to stick your nose up my butt when I'm naked?' The rest was easy. The next morning, Ben made sure Bingo was in Judy's room when she woke up. He also made sure that the dog had a nose full of hemorrhoid cream. Further, he made sure the house was full of his friends. About thirty minutes after Judy woke up, she comes into the kitchen for her morning toast. And we joined her. That's when it happened. And it happened again. And again. And again. And again. Before she even had time to move, she had rattled off about ten impressive bullets of gas. As quick as we've ever seen Judy move, she tore upstairs to the bathroom. And with every step came the sweet sound and smell of problematic flatulence coming from Judy's butthole. Now, Judy may never fart again, which would be okay with us. Because for the rest of our lives, we will always be able to cherish what is now referred to as, 'Judy's fine moment.'"*

By the time I was finished, the entire group was snort laughing. Hickey had been drinking a Coke, which was now spraying out of his nostrils. It only made us laugh harder.

"Why have you been keeping this gem from us?" Radish asked. "Now I've got this picture of Tina Anderson throwin' gas junks out of her ass. Fuckin' brilliant."

"He's got more where that came from," Billy said. "Read 'em *Jimmy's Revenge*."

"Not now," I said. "Better pace them out."

"Cards?" Hickey said.

"Break 'em out," said Radish. "Hey, did you guys notice that the curtains on the old man's house don't go all the way to the top? They're the kind that start about a foot or so down from the top of the windows."

"I saw that," Hickey said.

Radish continued, "So, I'm thinking if we can find a tree to climb high enough, we might be able to git an angle, follow?"

"Shit yes," said Sully. "Climb up one them pines. With the glasses, should be able to see in."

"Maybe," Radish said. "There's a big maple round the side of the house too. Easier to climb and you ain't got to worry 'bout gittin sap all over your hands."

"We don't know where the line is on that side of the house, though," I said. "That'd be pushing beyond what we agreed to."

"Hell," Sully said, "Just 'cause we don't know where the line is exactly don't mean the tree's on his land. Could be on the farm."

"Going back again tonight?" Billy asked.

"We are, at least," Radish said, nodding to Sully. "You fuckin' betcha."

"I'm in," said Tubs. "Me too," said Hickey.

"You boys ain't in?" Sully asked me.

"Don't know," I said. "Have to see."

It was noon and the Orioles had their first practice of the season, so we had to go. Radish and Sully stayed behind in the fort, no doubt laying out their plans for the night. Billy was strongly leaning toward joining the rest and started trying his best to coax me.

"Figure it this way," he said. "If we get caught, you're as good as busted too. Might as well not miss out."

"You really know how to motivate a guy, Billy," I returned. "I can just see Tubs falling out of a tree and breaking his leg."

"Think about it," he said as we pulled our bikes into the park.

"If you catch all my knuckles today, I'll come." I said.

"Talk about motivation," he said. "Deal."

He caught all my knuckles.

CHAPTER
31

BY EIGHT O'CLOCK that evening, everyone had arrived at the hole, taking my advice and coming in the back way off Thomas Lane. We had some daylight to kill since the days were getting longer.

"Oh shit," Radish said. "I left the binoculars hangin' in the tree by the fort."

"Need 'em," Sully said. "Let's go."

They took off on their bikes across the field to fetch the glasses, and I felt a sense of dread that the night was already being met with complications. They made it back in one piece.

Though we couldn't see the car, we heard it as it came down the Cummings' drive. We all got quiet as we heard a car door close, then the sound of a trunk being slammed down, after another minute a second car door close. Last, the bang of a screen door closing. We all imagined in our heads the same scene we'd witnessed the night before. It had become dark enough to head toward the line of pines, finding our way through the downed logs and thickets along the way.

The Cadillac was still parked in the drive when we got to the line. We could sense movement inside the house as the light from the lamps cast shadows against the insides of the curtains. The screen door opened and Mr. Klein walked out of the house, stopping just a couple feet from the screen door. An arm extended from inside the house to prop the door open. The arm had no hand. Before our very eyes, inside the door frame, stood Hank Cummings Jr. Clear as day.

Nobody moved a muscle, but we could hear each other's breath, like the sound of gasps one makes when having the shit scared out of them. Hickey surprised me and handed me his binoculars. The men were talking, and though we couldn't make out the words, the tone was friendly. As Mr. Klein took one more step from the house, the full figure of Hank Cummings stepped outside. Hickey grabbed for his binoculars, but I wasn't giving them up, keeping them razor focused on Mr. Cummings. Emotions raced through my body. I was looking at something I wasn't supposed to see, but I couldn't turn away. Hickey again tugged at the strap of the glasses and I released my grip as he took them. I was still staring straight ahead. I realized my jaw had dropped when a fly buzzed in and out of my mouth. As they said goodbye, Mr. Klein put his right hand on Mr. Cummings' back and gave him a couple warm taps. Mr. Cummings reciprocated with his left hand, which, even without the glasses, I could tell was deformed. He went back inside and Mr. Klein drove off down the lane.

"Holy fuck," Radish whispered, "Holy fuckin' fuck."

"It's true," Sully added quietly. "The dude looks like a freak. A monster."

"Okay," I said after a long pause. "We've seen him. Let's get out of here."

"Fuck that," Radish said. "I ain't done lookin'. I'm gonna' find a way to git up and look down over the top of them curtains."

"What else is there to see?" Billy asked.

"Well, he ain't alone, for one," Radish said.

"How do you know that?" I said.

"The wheelchair," he said.

"What about it?" I asked, "Just cause there was ..."

"You ain't see it?" he interrupted me. "It was sittin' just inside the door. And I seen feet on the footrests. Didn't you see? Cummings ain't in there by himself."

"Well, so what?" I said.

"So what?" Radish said. "You ain't even more curious now? This dude that never leaves the house, don't never see no one, now he's got a man in a wheelchair visitin' him every night? That ain't spikin' no curiosity? Bullshit, so what."

"I've seen what I needed to see," I said. "Anyone else ready?"

"I'm done," Tubs said. "Me too," said Billy.

"Don't screw things up, Radish," I said. "We'll be toast."

"No sweat, you noodle," Radish said.

I slowly backed up trying to retrace my steps. Billy and Tubs tagged after me. We didn't talk until we got back to the hole.

"That was fucking wild," Tubs said. "It's true. He doesn't have ears or a nose."

"Or hands," Billy added.

"The poor guy," I said. "Can't even imagine."

"Think about it," Tubs said, "Poor guy can't even whip his own meat around. Must be hornier than a rabbit on a deserted island. Must rub it against something."

"Must admit," Billy said. "I'm still curious. Now I want to see even more."

"Na man," I said. "Best we left like we did."

"Ain't going to be able to sleep tonight," Tubs said. "That's for sure. If I have nightmares, I'm going to come over and crawl through your window, Lightning, and crawl in bed with you."

"Thanks for letting me know," I said. "I'll be sure to keep it locked."

When I got home I went straight to my room, pulled out my writing notebook, and wrote an ode to Mr. Cummings that I titled, *Imagine*.

Imagine looking in the mirror and not recognizing the face before you.
Imagine looking at pictures of yourself when you were once whole.
Imagine waking up in the middle of the night thinking it was all a dream.
Imagine reaching to scratch your nose or earlobe that was no longer there.
Imagine reaching to shake someone's hand forgetting that you had no fingers.

Imagine the skin on your face melted like plastic.
Imagine being afraid to leave your house for fear you'll be laughed at.
Imagine continuing to live.
Imagine wanting to die.

I tossed around in bed, unable to sleep. I wondered if it would have been better to simply let Mr. Cummings live in my imagination. I thought I'd be able to let him go having seen him. But I couldn't. I was more curious now. Not as much with his physical condition, but his emotional. I started feeling guilty knowing we crossed a line. I began thinking of those things that only come with the cover up, not the crime. How were we going to keep this secret? For sure, Radish and Sully would blab it out. Their parents didn't pay enough attention to them to care. About them or Mr. Cummings. Probably the same with Tubs. And when, not if, but when my mom and dad found out, I'd be in a shitload of trouble. I'd done precisely what I promised them I wouldn't do. I wanted to march into their room, wake them up, sit on the floor and sob till snot ran from my nose, playing the sympathetic character begging for forgiveness.

At nine o'clock in the morning, my mom came in my room and woke me up from a deep sleep that I'd finally fallen into a few hours earlier. My first thought was how stupid I was for not coming clean the night before. Would have at least made a bad situation a little less so by now.

"Billy's on the phone for you," she said, causing me to let out a huge sigh of relief that she noticed. "What? Bad dream?"

"You could say that," I said.

"Early for him to be calling, don't you think?" she said. "Hope everything's all right. He sounded out of breath."

"Hey, Billy Jack," I said. "'Sup?"

"Radish called me," he said. "Gotta meet. Now. At the fort."

"What's going on?"

"Don't know," he said. "I gotta call Hickey. You call Tubs."

"Shit," I said. "This can't be good."

"Don't know. Call Tubs. Swing by on your bike and we'll ride together. See you in five."

Tubs agreed, "Something must have got fucked up."

Radish, Sully, and Hickey were already at the fort by the time the three of us rode up, totally gassed.

"Well, if it ain't The Three Musketeers," Radish said. "Sure got here in a hurry, dint ya."

"What's going on, Radish?" I said huffing and puffing.

"Nothin' much," he said. "What's goin' on with you?"

"Cut the shit, Radish," Billy said. "What the hell happened last night you had to call an emergency meeting for?"

"Oh, that," he said. "Well little pussies, shoulda stuck around's all I can say."

"Screw you, Radish," I said. "What?"

He took a long drag off his cigarette, enjoying screwing with us.

"Ah, it's nothin' really, is it Sully?"

"Nah," Sully said. "Ain't no thing, right, Hickey?"

"Right," Hickey said laughing.

"How 'bout some cards?" Radish asked.

"Radish," Billy said. "You're such a cocksucker."

"Alright," Radish started. "You boys missed a show last night after you left. We're huddlin' down there near the pines waitin' for it to git darker, all a sudden he, assume Cummings, puts some music on. It's like old love stuff. Like from old movies. Big band shit. Hell, I don't know. Pretty loud. Anyway, we wait it out a bit knowin' somethin' funny's goin' on. At least feels like it, ya know. But it's kind of loud, so we can start movin' around without worryin' about no one hearin' us. So, I'm up on my feet now and I tell Sully and Hickey I'm gonna look for a tree to git up into to try to see inside the house. Found one looked good. Sully hoists me up enough I could git my foot up onto a decent branch to git goin'. I git up about ten feet and look through the binocs. Could see Cummings' head and face. Clear as fuckin' day. Looked like he's sittin' up on a couch or somethin.' The light's shinin' on his face pretty good. Dude's fucked up. Ain't seen nothin' like it. Anyway, climbed up a few more branches. Pull the binocs to my face again. You ain't even gonna be ready for this. Are they Sully? Ain't gonna be ready, right?"

"Nope," Sully said. "Just hang on to your willies."

"What? Go on," Billy said. "Go!"

"Like I told you last night. He ain't alone. You think the wheelchair guy's sittin' there beside him with a drink in his hand just shootin' the shit? No. Ain't no man sittin' next to him with a drink in his hand. You know what instead? He's layin' there with a face in his lap. The cripple guy, not Cummings, the crip from the wheelchair is laying on the couch face down. And his hands and face planted right smack dab in the old man's crotch. Now, I ain't gonna profess to know what was happenin' down there 'cause I ain't up on all this fag shit, know what I mean? Ain't smart 'nuff to speculate on that. I'm wavin' down at Hickey and Sully tellin' them to git their asses up in a tree to see what I'm seein' in case, you know, maybe I'm hallucinatin' or somethin'. What'd you see, Sully?"

"Sure as your momma," Sully said. "It was kind of hard to make out, but pretty sure I saw the one cripple suckin' the dick of the old guy like they're fuckin' faggots."

"No way," Tubs said.

"Yes, way," Radish said. "Hickey?"

"Yes, fuckin' way," Hickey added. "They are fags clear as day."

"Jesus," Billy said. "That's juice. What next?"

"Ha," Radish said. "What's next is Sully fell his ass out the tree. Branch broke. So we fuckin' booked it back to the lake ain't believin' what we seen."

"You sure about what you saw?" I asked. "I mean, really, a blow job?"

"Hey man," Radish said. "Ain't gonna exaggerate. Don't know for sure. I mean, didn't see the cripple's lips on the old man's ..."

"Penis!" Sully shrieked.

"Cock, you fuckwad. It's cock. C O C K," Radish said through the laughter. "But whatever I seen, it ain't right and you know it. They be fuckin' faggots. Ain't natural what we seen. Noooo way, José with a capital H."

"Jesus H. Christ," Tubs said. "No way. You're right. That ain't natural to be having another man lying in your lap face down, whether you got your pants down around your ankles or not."

"It ain't quite over," Radish said. "We git our asses back to the hole and we hear that Caddy pull down the drive to the house. We hear the car door open and shut, then the screen door bang shut. 'Bout ten minutes later, this is what we hear. Car door close. Trunk slam shut. Another car door closes. The car starts up and goes down the drive to Yoder Road. Old Man Klein brings the cripple over and then comes back and picks him up. He's an accomplicment!"

"Accomplice," I said.

"Whatever," Radish said.

CHAPTER

32

I'D HAD ENOUGH OF RADISH AND SULLY for a while. Spying on Mr. Cummings had taken over the spirit of the gang, and it wasn't fun anymore. Billy and I convinced Tubs and Hickey that, as a gang, we were done with Mr. Cummings. What Radish and Sully did on their own time was their deal, not ours, not approved by us. Even if they blabbed about what they saw, I wasn't there. Sure, I'd caught a glimpse of Mr. Cummings, but I never set a foot onto his property or did anything that bad. Anyone could have been taking a walk along the pines and looked over and saw what I saw. I still had to decide whether or not to admit it to my mom, come clean in case she might find out anyway.

My interest in Mr. Cummings only grew, though, and I was so determined to keep my personal thoughts and feelings under lock and key I wouldn't even give Billy the privilege of peeking inside. To deal with it, I wrote. I didn't know there was a term for the type of writing I started. I learned later that it is called 'historical fiction.' My character, Mr. Cummings, was real. So was his current condition and circumstances. Those things I knew. I knew almost nothing else about the man, other than he was badly injured in the war.

At one point he was a thirteen-year-old kid no different than me, having a catch with his buddies, riding his bike, playing with model cars. Perhaps he was in a club too. Even with his own tree house built high in a maple tree. Maybe it's because I found him so unsafe that I thought of him as a child in many ways. How hard it must be to be so alone. Or perhaps it was precisely the opposite. Perhaps he was a simple enough man to not need anything or anyone else. Who was this mystery man in the wheelchair? Also crippled by something bad. Maybe the war. Maybe an illness. Maybe a car wreck like Roy Campanella.

I guessed Mr. Cummings had no family left after his sister died. Was he the last Cummings? Without anyone to take care of him. Did he wish he died in the war, like Tubs' brother? What does he think about when he looks in the mirror? Is he religious? Does he believe in God and pray? I overheard my mom tell my dad he was a nice man. Mr. Klein looked after him. Arranging for the colored lady to take care of him, shopping, cooking, and such. And bringing the man in the wheelchair to visit.

All these questions and more found their way into my notebook and I started writing about his life mostly through my own imagination.

With the help of Billy and Tubs, I tried to make a pact that the gang would stop snooping around Mr. Cummings' house, and not discuss it outside of the gang.

"I ain't promisin' nothin'," Radish said. "How you expect me to keep that a secret?"

"Because it's one of our bylaws," I said. "What happens in the gang stays in the gang."

"Bylaw says, what happens here stays here," Radish said. "What we seen didn't happen here. It happened over there." He pointed in the direction of the Cummings' house.

"It's context," I said.

"What the fuck is context?" Radish asked.

"It's a technicality," Billy said. "It doesn't only matter about things that happen in the fort. That'd be ridiculous. Sully, knock some sense into him."

"Rad," Sully began. "I think he's right. I think we gotta honor this."

"I think it's bullshit," Radish said.

"Listen Radish," I said. "You either take this gang seriously or you don't. And if you don't that's a problem."

"He's right," Hickey chimed in.

"Now," I said. "Do we need to vote on this or is it understood?"

"Alright," Radish said. "But that ain't stoppin' me from doin' what I want outside of the gang. And you ain't gotta be so fuckin' technical."

"I suppose that's right," I said. "Like if you blew your hand off with one of those M-80s you goof around with. That'd be on you. Nothing to do with the rest of us. And, dammit, be smart about it, okay? We're all going to be walking a tightrope of getting in big trouble. And if that happens, the summer is ruined. It'll be toast."

"Fine," Radish said. "Still can't believe we saw the crip suckin' off the old man."

"That ain't what we saw," Hickey said. "Can't be sure of nothin' like that. Just know his head was down there in the man's lap. Pretty sure he had pants on."

"Like you said, Hickey," Radish said. "Can't be sure of nothin', so we can't be sure he had pants on can we? And in my memory, he ain't wearin' no pants."

"Change gears," Billy said. "Lightning, read us another story."

"Don't have my notebook," I said. Since I'd been writing about Mr. Cummings, I had not taken my writing notebook out of my bedroom, so I wasn't going to make the mistake of bringing it to the fort.

"Since when don't you have your notebook?" Sully asked.

"Just have the gang notebook," I said.

"Come on, man," Billy said. "You know 'em by heart. Rattle one off for us. Give us a good way to change the subject. Give us, *This One Time*."

"Alright, I'll try. It's a short one. It's called, *This One Time. There was this guy, Joey. Funny guy. This one time, him and me and a friend named Maxie went to see the Indians play. We're in the stands drinking beer and yelling and so forth, because we were playing the Yankees. We yell ourselves hoarse and get loaded and have a good time since the Indians beat the crap out of them. So, we're all in a good mood. Maxie says, 'Hey come on over and have some more beers.' So we go to Maxie's place, and we walk in and in the front room is this big dog licking his nuts like there's no tomorrow. Maxie, he's trying to be cute, so he says, 'Man, I wish I could do that,' and Joey, he don't miss a beat, he says, 'Knock yourself out, man. He's your dog.' Fucking guy was a riot."*

"That's a good one, Lightning," Tubs said. "Give us another one."

"One's enough for now," I said.

CHAPTER
33

I WENT TO GRAB THE GANG notebook from my nightstand when I woke up Saturday morning, but it wasn't there. I must have left it at the fort. In it were our bylaws, trouble makers, and fun stuff, like the time Tubs crapped himself trying to squeeze out a fart. The guys trusted me with these secrets, and it was up to me to guard them with my life. In a state of panic, I jumped from bed, put some clothes on, and took off to the farm.

I threw my bike down at the base of the tree and climbed the steps. It was strange that the door was cracked open—it's an unwritten rule that the last one out makes sure the door is shut tight and latched. Even Gerald honors that. When I reached the top step, I pushed it open all the way and saw the notebook tucked inside the door. I let out an audible, "Whew."

As I climbed up the last steps and crawled into the fort, all the hairs on my arms and neck stood up and a chill went through my body from head to toe. I wasn't alone. In the corner was a young colored boy, sitting in a tight ball, his arms gripping his legs against his chest, trying to make himself into the smallest possible shape. His eyes were as big as silver dollars looking straight at me, his mouth open. He was shaking. Both of us were stunned. Frozen.

"Who are you?" I finally said.

He tightened the grip around his legs and pierced his lips.

"Just tell me who you are."

He looked downward and shook his head from side to side.

"It's okay. Talk to me," I said. "I'm not going to hurt you."

I moved inside the fort and leaned against the wall facing him. We sat in silence for what seemed to be several minutes. He was scared shitless. I tried not to stare at him, looking down at my notebook from time to time. Occasionally, he would raise his head to catch me looking at him and then lower it again. As quick as a rabbit, he bounded for the door and jumped from the fort, barely touching a step along the way. I reached for him, but he was too quick. He made his first sound as he landed. "Ahhhh, ahhhh, dangit," he screamed.

I looked out to find him on the ground at the base of the tree on his back. He looked up and attempted to stand but fell again. I hurried down the steps and stood over him.

He looked up and spoke, "I'm sorry, mister."

"It's okay," I said. "Who are you?"

He tried to stand again but couldn't put any weight on his right foot and fell again. He started to cry. "My ankle," he said through his tears. "It hurt bad."

"Okay," I said. "I'll help you. But you gotta tell me your name. I'm not going to hurt you. Don't be scared of me."

"James," he said.

"Good," I said. "That's a start. What are you doing here? Where do you live?"

"I'm sorry, mister. I'm sorry. I don't think I can walk."

"Just stay down. I'll help you. Where'd you come from?"

"Over there," he said, pointing back over his shoulder.

"That house over there?" I said, motioning toward the Cummings house. He nodded.

"What are you doing there?"

"With my grandmomma," he said.

"Does your grandmomma work for Mr. Cummings?"

He nodded excitedly.

"What's her name?"

"Mama Perkins," James said. "Mister, I ain't able to walk."

"First of all, my name is Jonny," I said. "Don't need to call me mister. How old are you, James?"

"Eight," he said. "I'm eight years old."

"Is your grandmomma over at the house now? The Cummings house?" I asked.

He nodded again.

"Do you think you can get up if I help you?" I asked.

"Don't know. I'll try."

James got up on one knee and I reached under his arms to help him up. He yelled out in pain. I wrapped his arm around my shoulder and tried to help him hop on his left leg. Because of the logs, rocks, and brush in our way, it proved impossible to make any progress. "Can't do it, mister," he said through tears, dropping back down to the ground.

"That makes two of us," I said. "Let's sit down here." His ankle was already swelling around the top of his dirty white Chuck Taylor low-top sneakers. I feared it might be broken but was too squeamish to touch it. His left knee had a nice scrape on it and was puffing up. He started to cry hard enough for snot to come out of his nose.

"You're gonna be okay," I said. "Don't cry."

"I'm gonna get in lots of trouble," he said. "Ain't supposed to be over here. Is that your tree house?"

"Kind of," I said.

"I'm sorry. I shouldn't of been up there."

"Don't worry about that, it's no big deal," I said. "I've just got to figure out a way to get you back to the house. Should I go get your grandma?"

"Don't know if that's a good idea," he said. "Mr. Cummings is kind of funny 'bout people."

"Do you know him?"

"Sure, I know him."

"Is he a nice man?"

"Sure is," James said. "Mr. Cummings is real nice. But he ain't much welcome to strangers."

"If I knock on the door, will your grandma answer it or will Mr. Cummings?"

"I reckon my grandmomma, but I don't know."

"Let me think," I said.

"I want my grandmomma," James said, still crying. "Go get her, will ya please, mister?"

"Okay, I'll go," I said. "Wait here and don't move."

"Thank you, mister."

I set off toward the Cummings house. My heart was pumping out of my chest as I got closer. Thumping harder than when I was crouching beneath the pines with binoculars in my hands. Once on the property, I walked as slowly as possible, hoping to be spotted by Mrs. Perkins in the yard before I'd have to knock on the door. I kept creeping closer. Then closer yet until I was a few steps from the porch, when a plump, colored lady wearing an apron wrapped around a flowery dress opened the door.

"Hello, young man," she warmly said.

"Are you Mrs. Perkins?" I asked.

"I am," she said. "And who in God's green earth might you be?"

"My name is Jonny Smith," I said. "Is James your grandkid?"

"He is, why? What kind of trouble has he found? Where is he?"

"He's over there a bit," I said. "I found him in the field. He's hurt and can't walk."

"Oh good heavens," she frantically said. "How hurt? What's wrong?"

"Just a hurt ankle, I think. But he can't walk, so I came to let you know."

"Well, Jonny, I kindly thank you. Can you take me to him?"

"Yes," I said.

"Can you wait just a second? I'll be right back." She went back into the house. I could barely hear a conversation between her and Mr. Cummings. His voice was deep, soft, and he talked slowly. She reappeared, "Lead me to that little troublemaker," she said. "Jonny Smith, is your momma Betsy?"

"Yes ma'am," I said.

"I know your momma," she said. "She's awful sweet."

"Yes, ma'am, she is."

"So, how did you stumble upon my little rug rat?"

"He fell out of a tree," I said.

"Well that figures. He loves to climb trees. Ain't that good at it, though. As if that ain't obvious," she laughed.

"Yes, ma'am," I said. "He's right over here."

We got close enough where I could see James' head above some brush.

"Grandmomma!" he shouted.

"James," she yelled back. "What in God's good name have you gotten yourself into? And watcha doin' way over here?"

"I'm sorry, Grandmomma," he said. "I'm real sorry."

"Let's take a look at you, boy," Mrs. Perkins said kneeling down over him. "Where do you hurt?"

"Right here," he said pointing to his ankle. "And here, here, and here," pointing to his knee, elbow, and chin.

She gently took her hands on either side of James' lower leg and moved them down toward his foot. She got no further than a spot a couple inches above his ankle before he let out a scream that could be heard all over the farm.

"I'm afraid you may have broken your ankle, young man," she said. "Do you think you could crawl up on grandmomma's back?"

James nodded. I stood there in amazement as she bent down on all fours. "Jonny, can you help James up onto my back?" I nodded and gingerly helped

James up on one foot and pulled him from the other side onto his grandma's back. "Jonny, come round front of me, help me to my feet."

Mrs. Perkins stood up carrying the full weight of James on her back. "Now walk alongside us makin' sure I don't fall along the way," she said to me. "Don't need both of us down on our backs."

Step-by-step, with sixty pounds on her back, Mrs. Perkins stepped over rocks, moved around brush, and climbed over downed trees and branches. I walked as close to her side as possible without risking tripping into her, waiting for her to fall into me for support at any second. She never did, making it the entire journey with just a few beads of sweat on her forehead. As soon as she crossed the line of pines, she dropped back down to her knees and James rolled off her back onto the yard.

"Thank you, Jonny," she said. "You can run along now. Please tell your momma I said hi."

"Yes, ma'am," I said. "I'll be sure to."

I looked toward James. We gave each other a nod and wave. I backed away, turned, ran back to my bike and pedaled home.

CHAPTER
34

"YOU'LL NEVER GUESS who I just got a call from," my mom said as I walked into the kitchen. I hunched my shoulders as if to say, who?

"Mr. Cummings called me to thank me for raising such a fine young man. And he told me to be sure to thank you for helping Mrs. Perkin's grandboy."

"I didn't know what to do, Mom," I said. "He fell out of the fort and busted his ankle up. I didn't know whether to come home first or knock on Mr. Cummings' door, but ..."

"You did the right thing," she said. "Sounds like he broke his ankle. Mildred is taking him to the emergency room right now. Mr. Cummings said if it weren't for you, they might have never found him."

"We'd have found him eventually," I said.

"I told Mr. Cummings that you were a writer, just like him," she said. "He said, 'Is that so? Maybe someday you could bring me something he's written.' What do you think about that?"

"I haven't written anything yet," I said. "Nothing good enough to share, at least."

"Well maybe that's something to shoot for," she said. "Write something that I can give to Mr. Cummings to read."

"Maybe," I said. "We'll see."

I went straight to my bedroom and pulled out my writing notebook. In all the excitement I'd forgotten to grab the gang notebook to bring home. Screw it. I sat at my desk and reread some of my writings. I was right, none of them were good enough to leave the comfort of the notebook. I considered whether any of them could be recrafted as a piece I'd be proud enough to share with anyone, let alone, Mr. Cummings.

And what to do about James in the fort and the events that led me to Mr. Cummings' front porch? The gang shared a circle of trust that allowed—even forced—us to share some of our darkest secrets. I hated the thought if Radish or Sully would have found him and I imagined the conversation.

"Hey boy, what the fuck you doin' here? Who the fuck are you? What you doin' on this side of the tracks? Best get the fuck outta here if ya know what's good for ya or we'll whoop your black ass."

I rode to Billy's house, arriving right as his mom was finishing cooking their usual Saturday morning breakfast—blueberry pancakes, bacon, and eggs.

"Billy, grab an extra place setting for Jonny," his mom said. My stomach was tied in knots, but I hadn't eaten anything and there wasn't a breakfast on any diner menu I liked better than Mrs. Nelson's. No sooner had I taken a seat than Mr. Nelson came in from the garage where he'd been working on his car. Same dirty white T-shirt and greasy jeans. Slicked back, Brylcreemed hair. He sat down without acknowledging me, wiped his oil-stained hands on the napkin, threw it back down on the table, and picked up the morning newspaper. Gerald sauntered down the hall from his bedroom, came up from behind me, and smacked me on the back of the head before he sat. For the next twenty minutes, Mrs. Nelson did her best to make strained conversation. She was a devoted wife and mother, even if it wasn't reciprocated by her husband and oldest son. She directed most of her questions to me.

"How's your summer going, Jonny? How's your mother? Are you looking forward to junior high next year? Are you kids having fun at the farm? Are you pitching this afternoon? Not getting in any trouble are you? Do you want more bacon?"

"Fine. She's good. Yes. Yes. Think so. No. Yes, please."

Billy kept kicking me under the table to distract me from the weirdness going on above it. We both scarfed down breakfast as fast as possible. It always made me sad for Billy that his family meals were so awkward. It was important to Billy's mom for them all to sit and eat together. Family time, she described it. For Billy it was torture time. The silence of the unspoken word always hung over the table. Watching Mrs. Nelson try so hard to provide a family atmosphere was painful and I wondered how and why she kept up the facade. 'Keeping up appearances,' is what my mom called it.

We excused ourselves and went back to his bedroom. First, I swore him to secrecy that what I was about to tell him could never go further than the two of us. I proceeded to tell him in full detail about finding James and everything that happened, including the phone call from Mr. Cummings to my mom, and his mention that he'd like my mom to give him something I've written. "No way. No fucking way. No way," he kept saying. "Way," I said. "Way cool," he said.

"Have your mom give him *Judy's Fine Moment*," he said. "He'll love that."

"No way," I said. "I'm not giving him any of that trash. This is serious. He's a serious writer. I've got to come up with something good. Gonna work on it."

"You could always write about Radish and Sully spying on him," he said sarcastically.

"Not funny," I said.

"Do you think he's a homo?" Billy asked.

"No, I don't think he's a homo," I said. "At least I hope he's not. Who knows? And what difference does it make?"

"But what was that crippled guy doing to him?"

"I don't know, but I don't want to think about it."

"It's all I can think about," Billy said. "You're lying to me if you're saying you don't wonder. Tell me the truth."

"Yeah, I wonder," I said. "But it's none of our business. Just worried that Radish is still going to screw everything up for us, you know?"

"Yep," Billy said. "Radish said he wants to see the cripple sucking the old man's wee wee for himself. Wants evidence. Wants to see the boner."

"Ain't it enough that we saw what the man looks like?" I asked. "That was the plan."

"Not for Radish, it ain't."

"Shouldn't have been snooping," I said.

"Well, too late for that now. Cat's outta the bag," Billy said.

Billy's door swung open about six inches. "Yep, cat's outta the bag now." Gerald was standing in the hall looking through the opening between the door and frame.

"You say that old guy is a faggot?" Gerald said. "Huh? That what you said? Suckin' wee wees?"

We didn't answer as he pushed the door open and stepped into Billy's bedroom.

"So, you been spyin' on the dude, huh? That it? Momma's gonna be mighty unhappy 'bout this. And Pop's gonna kick your asses, both ya."

"Fuck you," Billy said. "You don't know shit."

"I know what I heard," Gerald said. "What? You makin' the whole thing up? Then you be spreadin' rumors that the old man's a fag? Hell, that's worse. Pick your poison, boys."

"What are you doing snooping on us?" Billy asked. "You're in violation of us."

"Violation? Ha, that's funny," Gerald said. "I'm violatin' you? I'd say you violatin' that old man. That's what I say."

"You ain't gonna do nothing," Billy said. "It ain't even true. Made the whole thing up. Just for you. Knew you were snooping."

"We'll see 'bout that," Gerald said as he turned and closed the door behind him.

"Fuck," Billy said. "We're fucked."

"How did he hear us?" I asked. "What's he going to do?"

"Who the hell knows?" he said. "This is getting too hairy."

"Right," I said. "We've got to tighten things up with the gang at least. Somehow we need to get Radish to calm down. Whatever Gerald does, he does."

"We'll just say he's lying if he says anything," Billy said.

"Right," I said. "But we've got to get Radish and Sully under control."

Our first baseball game was that afternoon at one o'clock. Normally, Billy and I would have been so excited we'd be peeing our pants, and would have spent a good hour or so having a catch to warm up. Instead, we spent our time going through every possible scenario that could happen between Radish and Sully, and now Gerald.

The game was a disaster. Billy couldn't catch the knuckle and my curve ball hung right over the plate. The batters sat on my fastball. I got yanked and sent to play center field by the fourth inning and we lost 10-5.

We went straight to the fort after the game. I was relieved to find the gang notebook where I left it. In the corner of the room where I'd first seen James cowering, there was a book. Dr. Seuss, *The Cat in the Hat*. James left it there. I hid it in some shrubs near the base of the tree.

"Wait till you hear this," Tubs said, as he poked his head through the door first.

Hickey, Sully, then Radish followed.

"Tell 'em," Tubs blurted. "Go on, tell 'em."

"Okay, okay," Radish began. "First the crip was sittin' on the old man's lap. Just fuckin' sittin' on his lap on the couch. His spindly crippled legs hangin' off the side. The old man's like cradlin' the dude with his arms around him. Hell, ain't got no fuckin' hands. Just these fuckin' stubs of meat wrapped around the crip. Then they started kissin'. The crip's kissin' that deformed gross face. The man ain't even got lips. And the crip's kissin' all over em. Fuckin' gross. Them's dudes are faggots if I've ever seen one."

"Ha," Sully said. "And you ain't even ever seen one."

"Fuck I haven't," Radish said. "I seen 'em now. Juicy mother fuckin' shit's what it is."

"Listen," I said. "Who else saw it? Sully?"

"No," Sully said. "Didn't see shit. I was gittin ready to climb up the tree when that car starts coming down the drive again, so we booked back into the trees."

"Yeah," Radish added. "That Mr. Klein dude came back and picked the crip up and took him away. What a fuckin' game they all playin'."

"Alright, guys," I said. "Listen. We've got to keep all this quiet. Please. We can't let anyone else know about this. I really need you guys to promise. This is gonna come back and bite us in the nuts. We're all gonna be screwed. Have any of you guys said a word to anyone about this?"

"Not yet I ain't," Radish said. "But ..."

"No buts," I interrupted. "We've gotta make this a gang rule."

"I just gonna say, it's hard not to squeal this juice," Radish said.

"Yeah," I said. "I know. But we have always put the gang first. And we've got to do this now. If this gets out to anybody, the gang is through. We're done. Toast. Gotta bring it in on this one guys. If you give a rat's ass about me. If you give a shit about any one of us. Come on, bring it in."

I put my hand out as a gesture for others to follow to stack hands. "Come on. In." First, Billy. Then Tubs. Then Hickey. Finally, Sully and Radish.

"Alright," I said. "Greasy River Gang on three. One. Two. Three."

In unison, "Greasy River Gang."

"Break," I said. "What happens here stays here. I don't want to talk about it anymore. But, whatever you guys need to spill, it stays here. That's the rule. Got it?"

In unison, "Got it."

My faith in the humanity of the gang was restored.

CHAPTER
35

I OPENED MY NOTEBOOK to a blank page staring back at me. The thing I enjoyed about writing was that the only way a story gets told is that it comes from nothing but imagination. Nothing makes it on the page until the pen begins to move. The pen doesn't begin to move until the brain tells it to. To me, a real writer was someone who could create a story so powerful it could change your life, affect how you think. J. D. Salinger did that. I'd read *Catcher in the Rye* three times before I turned twelve. Holden Caulfield was my imaginary friend. F. Scott Fitzgerald. George Orwell. John Steinbeck. I'd read them all and was amazed at how they made me think about things. I didn't know what Mr. Cummings wrote. Only knew he did so. I wondered if his pen was powerful enough to move minds.

The only audience I'd considered writing for when I was thirteen were the goonies I hung out with, never dabbling in anything serious. That's why most of my decent stuff was nothing more than thirteen-year-old gross humor. My historical fiction of the imagined world of Mr. Cummings was for my eyes only. Now, I faced a real assignment—to write something on demand, by request, worthy of having it shared with the man himself. The thought terrified me.

Maybe he was just being polite. I could imagine the conversation: *You know, Mr. Cummings, Jonny wants to be a writer just like you. 'Oh really, perhaps I could see his writings someday.' Or, Jonny writes a lot, perhaps you'd like to see something he's written. 'Sure, but tell him to be a doctor instead.'*

Since I had begun familiarizing myself with how to write historical fiction, I thought it would be good to try it for Mr. Cummings. What better character to memorialize than Jensen Yoder? I broached the idea of writing about Yoder to my mom.

"That's a wonderful idea, Jonny," she said. "In fact, Ed Klein knew the man, and he knows the history of the Yoders like the back of his hand. And, of course, he knows Hank Cummings very well. He'd probably be able to give you some insights on what Hank would like to read. He's a deep well of knowledge, and I'm sure he'd be happy to talk with you."

"Whoa, mom," I said. "That's not exactly what I had in mind. I was thinking I could kind of make up my own story about him. It's called historical fiction."

"Historical fiction? But why do that if you have could have so much information at your fingertips and can write nonfiction?" she asked.

She had a point. But the thought of meeting with Mr. Klein, especially after having witnessed him come and go from Mr. Cummings home fulfilling whatever his duty was with the man in the wheelchair, gave me the willies.

"Maybe I'll try to get a story started first," I said. "Then we can decide whether it would be a good idea to speak with Mr. Klein."

"Nonsense," she said. "Let me talk with him about it and see what he says. No harm in that is there?" I couldn't convince her not to. She saw the man five days a week and the subject surely would come up.

I looked down upon the blank page in front of me. No better time to start.

The Yoder family moved to Ohio from Pennsylvania in 1812. Elijah Yoder, the family leader, bought the property with money he earned as a carpenter. He was married and had nine children, the oldest one was named Jensen.

I didn't know if half of that was true, but it was a start. I decided historical fiction was worthless when the reader knows better. I found my mom outside working in her garden. "Maybe meeting with Mr. Klein is a good idea," I said.

"Of course it is," she said. "He's coming over for dinner tonight. He's thrilled to talk with you."

Ed Klein was larger than life to me. I'd met him a few times when I was at the market with my mom. He was a thin, wiry man, standing less than six feet tall. He had a head of white wavy hair, and a year-round tan face with deep wrinkles showing his age of well over seventy. Strong as an ox, I'd seen him throw boxes around like they were full of nothing but air. And I'd seen for myself that he had the strength to lift a man out of his car and into a wheelchair. He was friendly, but a little scary. Maybe it's because I learned so much about him from my mom. She thought so much of him. It was clear he ruled the neighborhood and his opinion mattered. Everyone shopped at the market. He knew his customers by name, including kids and grandkids. If he didn't have something in his store someone needed, he'd find it at another store. If someone couldn't get to the store, he'd take the store to them. It was no surprise that he began to look after Mr. Cummings after Eliza died.

He earned respect. No teenager would dare buy cigarettes or beer from the market. Or try to sneak a pack of gum into their shorts. It was rumored that he had a full casino in the basement of the market complete with a liquor bar, craps, blackjack, and poker tables. I can recall on several occasions seeing a parking lot full of nice cars with barely anyone inside the store.

He knew all about his customers. If someone had been sick. If someone's kid was struggling in school. He knew a pregnant mother's due date. From all I could figure he had all the answers, but only offered them when asked. He was the one doing most of the asking. He was invited to weddings and attended funerals. He was everybody's brother, uncle, dad, and grandpa.

I didn't know what my mom told him that got him to talk with me, but I sensed I had better be ready. I was sure he had better things to do than give a thirteen-year-old kid a neighborhood history lesson. Maybe he was returning the favor for the help I gave James. If he knew the rest of the story—of the gang's shenanigans—I'd be preparing for a much different conversation.

My mom gave me no clue how things might unfold. "I told him you were going to write a story about Jensen Yoder for Mr. Cummings, and he said he'd be happy to help give you the family's history." Maybe he was considered the Yoder family historian and had a canned speech that he'd given a hundred times at schools, libraries, 4H clubs, and garden clubs. *Thank you for coming; today's speaker is Ed Klein who is going to tell us the history of the Yoder family.* Praying this was the case, but prepared if it wasn't.

The white Caddy pulled into our drive at precisely six o'clock p.m. Out stepped Mr. Klein in the only thing I'd ever seen him wear—khaki slacks and a white, short-sleeved button down. For extra measure he rolled his sleeves up one fold to reveal more of his tanned, muscular arms, sometimes a pack of cigarettes tucked inside the fold.

My nerves were rotten by the time my mom called for me. I grabbed my writing notebook and headed to the dining room.

We'd barely finished saying hello when Mr. Klein began. "So, your mother tells me you've got an idea for a story you'd like to give to Mr. Cummings."

"Yes, sir," I said.

"That sounds like a noble challenge," he said. "How can I help you?"

"Umm, I don't know," was the best I could come up with.

"He wants to write about Jensen Yoder," my mom said coming to my rescue.

"What would you like to know, Jonny?" Mr. Klein said. "I was fortunate to have known the man, not well, but he was a rather legendary character around these parts. And did you know that Mr. Cummings lives in the house he built with his own hands?"

"No, wow! Really?" I said. I was hooked.

"Yes sir, he did. Built it. Lived in it. Died in it. Now if that ain't livin', I don't know what is."

"Yes, sir," I returned.

"He was a carpenter by trade. Never drove a car. Got around in a horse-drawn buggy."

"Yes, sir," I said again.

"Built a one-room schoolhouse for all the Amish children in the area. Built a church, part of which still stands on Yoder's farm way back in the woods. Buried in the family cemetery behind the church. I'm sure you kids have explored that."

"Is it true he is a ghost?" I asked.

"Now we're getting somewhere," he said, looking at my mom with a laugh.

For the next ninety minutes, the more I opened up with questions, the deeper Mr. Klein's answers were. I not only learned about Jensen Yoder, but his wife, and his mother and father. I learned things about the Amish culture. I learned of the business deals, which saw the land change ownership several times over. I learned why his old house still stood and why the Cummings' four acres remained off-limits to developers.

Finally, after our history lesson, he got around to answering my first question. "Oh, and by the way, yes, he *is* a ghost!"

He was funny. He was warm. He was talkative. He would have stayed all night had I not run out of questions. But before he left, I couldn't help but ask him one more. "Is Mr. Cummings a nice man?"

"Yes, Jonny," he responded. "Hank is a wonderful man. He's just a very private individual. That's the way he chooses to live his life, and we all respect that. But I can promise you this. If you want to give him this story after you write it, I'll be sure to get it to him, and he'll be sure to read it."

Hearing this gave me chills. He suddenly said, "Oh my goodness, I almost forgot. Please excuse me, I'll be right back."

He went to his car and returned with a book. "Hank wanted me to give this to you," he said. "It was just published. And if you like ghost stories, you'll be sure to like this one."

The Wrath of the Old Hag, by H. E. Cummings Jr.

CHAPTER
36

I COULDN'T PUT THE BOOK DOWN, nearly completing it before falling asleep with every light in my room on because I was afraid to close my eyes for fear of the Old Hag. When I got too tired to keep my eyes open, the book fell from my hands onto my face, leaving me with a nice little bruise across the bridge of my nose. I needed wonder no more whether Mr. Cummings was the kind of writer who could change lives.

I skipped out on a date with the gang to hang out on the farm for the day. No excuse to ditch them was good enough. We could never say we just didn't want to, or were too tired, or had something better to do. I used the card that always worked; my cousins were coming to visit.

I needed space. I sat at my desk and pieced together the scribbles I'd written from my conversation with Mr. Klein. Whenever I began writing a story, the first sentence was always the hardest. After many starts and stops, I looked over at the book by Mr. Cummings. A ghost story. His first line, *I held my dead mother in my arms.* I made my pen move.

Title: The Ghost of Jensen Yoder

Elijah Yoder was a builder. He built homes. He built a community. He built a legacy. What was once a dirt path equally dividing his 400-acres of land— farm land to the south; unfarmed land to the north—is now a road that divides a neighborhood of hundreds of families to the south from the land to the north on which sits just one house. The road is now called Yoder Road. The unfarmed land, which is overgrown, and largely as nature meant it to be, is ironically now called "The Farm."

The lone house that sits on the farm was built and lived in by Elijah's oldest son, Jensen. He also built the homes for his own community of Amish people, and many of the buildings they depended on, including a one-room schoolhouse and a church, part of which still exists. The other structures have long been ravaged for their valuable lumber and other fine building materials. Jensen and his wife, Anna, both died in the home. Both in the basement. Both of heart attacks. Two years apart almost to the day. Both were buried next to Elijah and his wife in the family cemetery fifty feet from the church's altar. Anna went first and left Jensen with a broken heart and soul that he finally gave into, leading him to the basement to take his own last breath, sitting in the same oak chair that Anna died in. He was found with his head laying on the oak table.

Jensen lived his entire life on the plot of land his father was gifted at the end of the Civil War. He was born on this land. He died on this land. At least his body died. But his ghost? It didn't die. It lives on. In the basement of the house. In the bedroom he shared with Anna. Wading through Yoder's Creek and skipping stones across the pond. Swinging from the tire that hangs from the maple tree.

All of the pews in the church have been torn apart, the good wood stolen. All but one, that is. The first pew not only stands as sturdy as the day Jensen built it but remains clean of dirt and dust. Its shine allows one to see their reflection looking back at them when the light is just right. The steps to the altar still appear new. The cross. The lectern. All remain in their original perfect condition. None of this is an accident.

A path is worn through the tall grass that leads from the grave of Jensen Yoder to what was once the church's front door, then proceeds before stopping abruptly at the shiny seat in the front pew. The path can be found through all seasons. Fine dust swirls in the wind during the dry days of summer. The fallen leaves are batted away to either side during the fall. In winter, outlines of bare footprints can be seen melted in the snow. In the spring the mud from the rains gets trampled in and down the aisle of the church.

Over the years many investors and developers brought forth plans to develop the two hundred acres of the farm. Many deals were signed, but before a shovel ever went in the ground, before a tree was ever cut down, before a mound would ever be leveled, in fact, before even a blade of grass would be disturbed, the deals fell through. The reasons given were never said out loud. Afterall, a grown man would never risk the shame that would come from saying he was scared.

Written by Jonny Smith

The story took ten hours and twelve drafts before I felt it was worthy of sharing with Mr. Cummings. Typing it on our old Olivetti typewriter—with keys that stuck and the bottom part of the G missing—without any mistakes took another four. I slid the pages into a large brown envelope without showing it to anyone.

I added a cover note: *Dear Mr. Cummings, thank you for giving me your book to read. I enjoyed it. I hope you enjoy my story.*

"It's ready," I said as I gave it to my mom.

CHAPTER
37

I WAS IN BED SCRIBBLING when I saw the lights of Mr. Klein's Cadillac pull into our driveway. I looked at the clock on my bedside table. It was a minute past ten o'clock. My mom greeted him at the front door, and he was gone before even stepping a foot inside. Seconds later, she slid an envelope under my door. It was addressed in type, *For Jonathan Smith's eyes only.*

Dear Jonny,

Thank you for sending me your lovely ghost story. I enjoyed it so much I read it three times and it gave me the heebie-jeebies each time. I'm not sure I'll ever be able to go to my cellar again, for fear the ghost of Jensen Yoder might jump out from the canning cupboard! I would like to read more of your writings. You certainly have a talent that I wish I'd had at your age.

I'm glad you liked my book. Although it's a fictional story, it's very much based upon real events, as your story about the ghost of Jensen Yoder surely is. Perhaps our characters have met.

Please enjoy this draft of the first paragraph of my next book. Perhaps we could meet someday and share more ghost stories with each other.

Best wishes,
Hank Cummings

Mr. Cummings' note would lead to another night of restless sleep. Clearly the way to his heart was through storytelling, so I immediately began crafting my next story. When I woke in the morning I felt my open notebook laying across my face. My pen was still gripped between my fingers. I was held captive in the in-between stage—not fully awake—trying to go back to sleep so my dream wouldn't die. I was sitting around a crackling campfire with Mr. Klein and Mr. Cummings. Mr. Klein was wearing his khakis and white short-sleeved shirt, holding a cigar in one hand and a glass of brown liquor in the other. Mr. Cummings wore what he referred to as his "flight gear" uniform—boots, brown slacks, a leather jacket with what looked like lamb fur around the neck and cuffs. He sat motionless telling us stories of the ghosts of soldiers in WWII. A man in a wheelchair sat next to him, but with his back to us. The dream faded away as I woke. I reached for his note from my bedside table and read it again. And again.

"Looks like you have a pen pal," my mom said as I walked into the kitchen. "You and Mr. Cummings are becoming friends?"

"He wrote me," I said. "Even said maybe we could meet. Do you think that's possible?"

"Really?" she asked in astonishment. "Well, if that's what he wrote I'm sure that it is."

I showed the note to her. "Wow," she said. "That must have been some story you wrote! 'Heebie-jeebies?' I would guess that's a mighty high compliment.

Do you think you'd really like to meet him? I can ask Ed what he thinks. Maybe he can arrange something. But I'm not even sure we need Ed to do that. Seems like you and Hank can fend for yourselves."

"Yeah, I mean, I guess," I said. "But it feels kind of scary. You know, everything I've heard about him."

"There is nothing to be scared of," she said. "He's one of the nicest men I've ever met. He's kind. He's considerate. He's friendly. He's a recluse, that's all."

"I mean, he's all scarred and stuff," I said. "It kind of scares me."

"That's just his outside, Jonny," she said. "A man's physical appearance doesn't define him. It's what's inside that counts."

"Does he have any friends?" I asked.

"Of course he has friends," she said. "Don't you have some chores to do this morning? It's allowance day! Now run along."

After I cleaned my room, mowed the lawn, and swept out the garage, I met up with Billy. Hickey found through some snooping around that it was Missy Botkin's birthday, and she and her friends were going to the swimming hole at the farm late afternoon. We all met up in the fort. Luckily, three pairs of binoculars were still ditched in the brush. You couldn't see the hole from the fort. It was a distance away and there were too many trees in the way. We had a few hours to kill so we broke out a game of euchre. Maybe due to some newfound moral compass, I decided I wasn't going to cheat, so Billy and I got swept three straight, only taking a total of six tricks in all. He kept looking at me with a *what gives* expression. We devised our plan for later in the afternoon, when the sun would be hot, and there would be girls in bikinis at the hole. My moral compass abandoned me when it came to girls.

There were some good climbing trees within about a hundred feet of the hole. We'd be spotted if we waited until the party began, so we timed it so we'd get in position early, but not too early. Time moves slowly when you're lying on a branch waiting for something to happen. Billy and I chose a maple we'd climbed before, so we knew the sturdy branches from the rickety ones. Radish and Sully teamed up. Tubs and Hickey stayed together. Each pair in separate trees. Between the six of us, we were stationed in three trees nearly surrounding the hole. Each of us had one pair of binoculars. The pair Billy and I had cost me a dollar of my allowance. 'Rental fee,' Sully said. We perched ourselves and waited. And waited. And waited.

Finally, the hole had some guests we weren't expecting. Three old men, Barney Conklin, the owner of the Sunoco gas and tire station down on Mulberry Street, and a couple of his grease monkeys set up some rickety lawn chairs on the bank of the pond, cast their lures across the water, and pulled the tabs off their cans of Budweiser. A transistor radio blared the Indians game. Even if Missy and her friends were to come at this point, they weren't going to frolic in front of these slugs.

We often fell into the lazy misconception that we ran the farm during the summer and were pissed when we were forced to share it. On this day, Conklin and his cronies weren't our only company. Above the noise of the chirping birds, mating grasshoppers, and static scratching sound of the ball game, we heard the approach of dirt bikes ridden by Jarvis and Gerald. We would have felt little shame being seen climbing down from the trees by the old men, but it was best that we avoid the harassment of Jarvis and Gerald. They tore around the hole a couple times, annoying Conklin who threw a half-filled can of beer in their direction, shouting something at them that couldn't be heard over the whining engines of their bikes. Gerald flipped them the bird before heading out deep into the woods and out of sight. We took that opportunity to get out of the trees and back to the safety of the fort.

"Why'd you ditch us last night, Lightnin'?" Radish asked as he lit a cigarette. "You crushin' on your little cousin? You know what they say 'bout incest don't ya. It's okay as long as ya keep it in the family." He laughed as he smacked my shoulder with a closed fist, which he had a way of doing with the knuckle of his middle finger protruding outward, which felt more like being stabbed by the end of a broomstick, leaving a nasty knot and bruise in its wake.

"The only time Lightning's little wee wee gets to play is when he's rubbing on it," Sully said.

"That reminds me," Hickey said. "We ain't got the new *Playboy*. Thought your brother was gonna git it for us, Tubs."

"We ain't give him the money yet," Tubs said.

"Fuck that," Radish said. "I'll just go down to the Red & White and slide it down my pants."

"You ain't even allowed back in there," Sully said.

"I'll go down there when the old lady's workin'," Radish said.

"No, man," I said. "How much does Jarvis need?"

"Three bucks," Tubs said. "The magazine costs one and a half. He'll keep the rest."

"I'm in for a dollar," I said handing over the rest of my allowance.

"I'll steal a couple from my old man," Billy said. "Gotta wait till he's got a good drunk on first though, so he won't remember how much he had in his wallet."

"Shouldn't have to wait long for that," Hickey said.

"Fuck off, Hick," Billy said.

"Sorry, man," Hickey said. "Didn't mean it."

"Cards?" I asked as I broke out the deck and gave it a shuffle.

We hung out in the fort until we heard the dirt bikes heading our way. We hightailed it down the tree and took off just as Jarvis and Gerald started sliding their bikes around us kicking dirt, weeds, and twigs in our faces. "On your way, little punk asses," Jarvis shouted out. By the time we reached Yoder Road, they had lost interest in us and we all rode back to our houses flipping them the bird as we left.

I'd forgotten that earlier in the week I'd invited Billy to spend the night, and my attempts to uninvite him proved unsuccessful.

"What's up with you, man?" he asked. "You don't want to hang out anymore? Your cousins weren't even here last night. I rode past your house three times. No cars in the drive. You lied to me. Come on man."

He had me dead to rights. Like most kids, I'd learned the angles to be crafty enough to cover my tracks with my mom and dad until something bigger came up or they lost interest. But when your best friend lied to your face at thirteen years old, it was a big deal.

"I'm sorry," was all I could say.

"Sure, you're sorry," he said. "But what's up? What's the big mystery?"

"It's hard to explain," I said. "First, what's going on with the Cummings house? Anything else happen? Anything go on the last couple nights?"

"No, man," he said. "Don't think so. We didn't even talk about it last night. Why?"

I reached under my bed and pulled out the box I keep my writing notebook in. On top was the note that Mr. Cummings wrote me. I handed it to Billy.

"Holy shit," he said before he could even read the first word.

Chapter

38

BILLY HAD TO LEAVE EARLY the following morning to go to swimming lessons. It was a good thing he did. I heard my dad's car pull into the driveway around nine o'clock. He worked the seven a.m. shift so it was unusual for him to come home, but I didn't think too much about it. I heard him talking with my mom in the kitchen. She started crying. I was nervous about walking into whatever was happening. I sat on my bed and tried to hear the conversation. I could only make out short bursts, 'I can't believe it, how could it be, how could this happen? What's going to happen to him? Is he still being held? Where's Ed? What's going to happen now?'

I went into the hall to get closer, but I couldn't hear enough to piece together what was going on. Finally, I walked into the kitchen.

"Jonny, go back to your bedroom, please," my dad said.

"What happened?" I asked.

"Go back to your room, honey," my mom said. "I'll come and talk with you in a minute."

The phone rang. Mrs. Arnold from next door knocked on the door. I saw other neighbors congregate outside in front of their homes. Whatever the news was, it was traveling quickly. The phone rang again. Muffled voices, quieter now. My parents went outside and talked with neighbors from across the street. I went to the kitchen and called Billy. There was no answer. I woke up my brother. He was clueless.

I called Billy's house again. A man's voice I didn't recognize answered the phone. I asked for Billy. The man was abrupt and said he wasn't available to talk at the moment. I called Tubs' house. There was no answer. I looked out the window and watched my mom as she crossed the street to come home and waited for her in the living room.

"Jonny," she said. "Oh, Jonny, dear."

"What happened, Mom?" I asked.

"There's been an incident," she said.

"What?" I asked frantically.

"There was a shooting last night. At Mr. Cummings' house. He fired a shotgun at Gerald Nelson and Jarvis Turley."

"What do you mean he shot at them?" I screeched.

"I guess the boys were outside of Hank's house, rattling the door or looking in the window. I don't know. Trespassing, though. Mr. Cummings shot at them, scared that they were trying to break into his house. Mr. Cummings was arrested. He's in jail now."

"But he was just defending himself, right?"

"Looks that way," she said. "We just don't know enough yet."

My dad came in the house. "Anything else?" my mom asked him.

"Nothing we don't already know," he said. "This is why we begged all you kids to never go near his house, Jonny."

"It's not his fault, Ralph. It was self-defense. You can't blame him."

"It ain't a matter of whether I blame him or not," he said. "That excuse ain't gonna fly. They gonna string him up, I fear."

"What do you mean, string him up?" I asked.

"It just don't look good, pointin' a gun at two boys and shootin' at 'em," my dad said.

"What was he supposed to do, Ralph?" My mom was irritated. "He didn't hurt them. Only wanted to scare them."

"I'm just seein' it the way the prosecutor will, is all," he said.

I reached for the phone to call Billy. "Who are you calling?" my dad asked. "Billy," I said.

"I don't think that's a good idea," my dad said. "I'd stay clear of the Nelsons for now."

"Why?" I asked.

"Just think it best ya stay clear of the mess right now's all," he said.

I went outside and got on my bike. I rode to Billy's. There were cars in the driveway I didn't recognize, and no sign of Billy. I knocked on the door and was greeted by a man with the same voice who answered the phone when I called. "Billy's not home," he said.

I rode to Tubs' house. There were two police cars in the drive. I kept moving, riding on to Hickey's house. His mom answered the door, surprised to see me so early in the morning. Hickey was still sleeping, but I asked her to wake him up. "It's important, Mrs. Hickman," I said.

Hickey came outside still rubbing sleep out of his eyes.

"You haven't heard have you?" I asked him.

"Heard what?" he said.

We got on our bikes and rode to Radish's house. Woke him up. Then rode to Sully's house. Woke him up too. The three of them now knew what I knew. Billy and Tubs knew a lot more. I was worried about Billy. More worried about Mr. Cummings.

"That old fucker's crazy," Radish kept saying.

"It was self-defense," I said. "He was just protecting himself. Gerald and Jarvis shouldn't have been snooping like that."

"Shit, Lightning," Sully said. "Could have been any one of us."

"I doubt he'd have shot at us when we weren't even on his property," I said.

"Bullshit," Radish said. "Just lucky he didn't see us. He'd of seen us, he'd of shot us for sure."

"Exactly why we shouldn't have done it," I said.

I didn't want to be around the guys anymore. They were only pissing me off. I took off for home to the shouts of 'pussy' on my heels. I rode past Billy's house but didn't look like anything had changed so I went home.

My mom went to the market to work. Surely Mr. Klein was with Hank. Deciding he could do nothing to help anyone, my dad returned to his shift. All I could do was wait. And fret. I called Billy's house again. The same man answered the phone. I hung up.

I rode to the market. It was full of people. And gossip. I watched my mom try to manage the conversations the best she could.

"I heard he shot him right in the eye," an old man said.

"Just fired a warning shot's what I heard," another one said. "Didn't even hit him."

"Then why's Cummings in jail?" another asked.

"Attempted murder," one said. "Gonna hang the gimp."

"Enough," my mom shouted. "Everyone out. Off the property. Go on home unless you're going to buy something."

Knowing I needed something to keep me occupied, she put me to work in the back room unloading some boxes. People kept coming and going, trying to find out more, seeing who knew what. When it got to be too much, she'd shoo them away again.

The *Mansfield News Journal* was an afternoon paper. The wire bound stack arrived with a thud near the front door of the market. Without thinking, she sent me to fetch the bunch and rack them for sale.

The headline above the fold in large bold type read: ***Shots Fired, Henry Cummings Jr. Arrested***

The mugshot of Hank Cummings took up nearly half of the top page adjacent to the article. The man who was so determined to stay out of view, so afraid of what people thought of him, so fearful of humiliation, was now on parade for all to see. Everyone would now see that, indeed, Hank Cummings had no ears. No nose. One eye scarred shut. A leathered, rutted face of mismatched skin tones. Crooked lips that looked like they were painted on. No hair. No eyebrows.

No sooner had I brought the bunch in to put them in the rack, cars converged on the market. The papers sold out in five minutes. I stuffed one down my pants. My mom set another aside. People gasped at the picture of Hank Cummings with such curiosity you'd think they'd never witnessed such a sight. Maybe they hadn't.

"Don't read it, Jonny," she said. "Please. Not until I do." It was too late.

Shots Fired, Henry Cummings Jr. Arrested
By George Constable

June 18, 1973

At approximately 12:15 a.m. on June 18, Gerald Nelson, age 15, and Jarvis Turley, age 16, were shot at on or near the property of Henry Cummings Jr. on 430 Yoder Road. It is believed that Cummings was startled by sounds outside his living room window. The boys, who were fired upon, were found several hundred feet from Cummings house. Cummings was arrested and transferred to the Mansfield City Jail. Official charges are expected to be brought at his arraignment scheduled for later this week. No further details were available upon printing.

I tried Billy's house again. There were more cars in the drive and out front. I knocked on the door. Billy answered. We sat in the front yard.

He only knew Gerald's side of the story, which was that Gerald and Jarvis had been hanging out on the farm, riding their dirt bikes, fishing and swimming in the hole, playing truth or dare by the church, and climbing trees, goofing off. They lost track of time. Didn't even know it was past midnight. Some wild turkeys ran by and they ran after them trying to catch one. They weren't paying any attention to where they were running. They were just chasing the wild birds, which led them into the vicinity of Hank Cummings' house. They weren't closer than fifty feet from the house when they heard gunfire. Hank Cummings came out with his shotgun, pointed it at them, and said if they moved, he would blow their brains out. He must have called the cops himself because within minutes police and ambulance sirens blared toward the house. Hank Cummings was handcuffed and arrested.

Billy said that Gerald was at the police station giving his statement.

I didn't know whether to believe Gerald's story. Nor did Billy. We considered our own fate.

Into the drive pulled Billy's mom and dad with Gerald in the backseat. Billy's uncle, aunt, and cousins came out to greet the car.

"Outta the way," Billy's dad said as he opened the car for Gerald. "Give him some room now, will ya. He ain't no spectacle. Move out."

"The fucker's gonna hang for this," Billy's uncle yelled out. "Gonna fuckin' hang!"

CHAPTER

39

STRANGE HOW YOUR SON getting shot at will suddenly turn a mean drunk dad into a protective shield, his only plan being revenge. "That son of a bitch is going to be sorry he ever moved to town," I heard Mr. Nelson say. "The long arm of the law's gonna do us justice. And if it ain't, I'm gittin a lawyer to make sure that monster ain't ever seein' the light of day again. And if that don't work, I'll settle the damn score myself."

I couldn't stay at Billy's. He didn't want to be there either, but he had to play the family game and show Gerald some pity. I didn't want to be with any of the guys. I figured the situation at Tubs' house would be much like the Nelson's.

I considered disbanding the gang until things died down. It wouldn't be possible to keep any sense of normalcy when the brothers of two of our guys had been shot at by a man who lived a couple hundred feet from our hangout and was in jail for attempted murder. I at least decided we needed to take a break. Radish and Sully both called me to try to pull Hickey and me together before nightfall. I told them to go on without me.

My mom and dad wouldn't say much to me and were careful to keep their conversations private. All I knew was that Mr. Cummings was in jail and that Mr. Klein was working on getting the best criminal defense lawyer his money could buy.

The article in the paper the next day made it clear how the community felt.

Boys Claim Innocence: Cummings Expected to be Charged
By George Constable

June 19, 1973

Both Gerald Nelson and Jarvis Turley claim they were innocently chasing wild turkeys when they were ambushed by Henry Cummings Jr. without warning. They had spent the evening on the adjacent land to Cummings' property, riding dirt bikes, fishing, and playing in the woods; doing what many young boys that live near the abandoned land do during the summer.

"We was just running around, goofin' on each other," said Nelson. Jarvis Turley's recount of the incident is much the same. "We wasn't doing nothin' to bother no one. Just got shot at. Don't even know where it came from. Bang. Bang."

The Mansfield Police Department has not released any statements other than saying that the shooting took place on the property of Cummings, which contradicts the boys claim that they were many feet from the property.

Bernie Davis, the attorney retained to represent Cummings, issued a statement: All evidence points to Mr. Cummings acting in self-defense. The individuals who were shot at were trespassing and represented an imminent threat to Mr. Cummings' safety. He gave them a warning to vacate his property before he fired a single shot into the air. The intruders ran into the adjacent woods where the police found them. I am confident he will be cleared of all charges once all the evidence is revealed.

Leonard Nelson, Gerald's father, said, "That man's been a menace to all the boys who play in the farm and everyone around these parts knows it. Was only a matter of time before something like this is going to happen. It's unfortunate, but he ain't going to get away with trying to kill kids for no reason. He stalked them down like they were pheasants. They just boys."

It is expected that formal charges will be brought during Cummings' arraignment scheduled for Friday morning at nine o'clock.

After dinner, Billy came over. "My dad says we're going to get rich. Says we're going to sue Cummings for a lot of money. Lawyers were calling the house all day trying to represent Gerald. He's a punk. He admitted to my mom that they were drinking. My dad started screaming at him to keep his mouth shut. Billy said the cops found a bottle of Mad Dog and took it. Asked them if it was theirs. They were drunk. I'm sure of it. This lawyer that my uncle knows came over and started going over Gerald's story with him. Telling Gerald there were two stories, the one that really happened and the one he was going to tell from now on. He said, 'I want you to forget whatever happened and replace it with this. You never went near the house, not even near the property line. If you could sign here and then we can officially get going.' Then he said, 'Call Jarvis' father and tell him it's important I represent both of the kids. Otherwise we could have conflicting stories and that would hurt us.' He said the key was the first shot was from inside the house through an open window. Cummings came outside and shot at them at close range where they were found. He said detectives will be digging into this really deep. Might even want to talk to other kids to see if they've ever been harassed by Cummings."

"Jesus," I said. "If they do that, someone might snitch that we spied on him."

"How would they know that?"

"Gerald already knows," Billy said. "Or did you forget that little fact?"

"Fuck," I said. "Well, who's going to believe him anyway? He's going to be lying about everything else. We'll just deny it. It'll be our word against his. We've got to do the same thing that lawyer said. Need to get our stories straight. We gotta talk with the guys."

Billy had sweat marks under his arms and was biting his nails. He was bobbing his leg up and down so hard, I could feel the floor shake.

"What about Tubs? Wonder what's going on at his house," I said. "I rode by his house and there were a bunch of cars there. Too scared to go knock on the door. Haven't talked with him yet. Have you?"

"No," Billy said. "In the morning, we gotta get all of us together. I'll work on Tubs. You get the rest of the guys. Fort at ten o'clock, prompt. Cool?"

"Cool," I said.

Mr. Klein came to the house after he closed the market to give my mom and dad the latest update. Among other things, he had a message for me. "Jonny," he began. "Hank says he's sorry that he might not be able to meet you. He said to continue to write. You have a talent that shouldn't be wasted." I was excused to my room. I reread his note to me and started to cry.

The gang met as planned. I was glad to find that Radish and Sully were taking it seriously. We went hands in on the agreement to erase any memory of spying on Mr. Cummings. If we were ever to be asked, we would deny it. Our party line was that we never bothered him and he never bothered us.

Tubs said that Jarvis was playing it up big time. Moaning and groaning about being shot at. Gerald's lawyer came to his house too and had a similar conversation. Weren't near the property. Just chasing turkeys.

Out of curiosity we walked toward the line of pines. There were two police cars on the property and a 'Crime Scene: Do Not Cross' yellow ribbon wrapped through the trees that went all the way around the property. The police were going in and out of the house. We couldn't get close enough to the side of the house where the shots supposedly came from. The ribbon was probably two hundred feet from the house. If that were the true property border, I couldn't imagine the story the lawyer was trying to weave, that Mr. Cummings was able to track them down and shoot them at close range.

I again brought up the idea of the gang taking a break for a while but was voted down 5-1. Billy and Tubs convinced us they needed to hang with us. Neither of them wanted to be home.

The next few days were nerve-racking. I was anxious that any minute a detective was going to show up at the house with questions. The gang only met a couple times and mostly played cards or just rode around the farm, staying clear of the Cummings house. My mom asked me not to come to the market. It was buzzing of gossip, not on Mr. Cummings side. Mr. Klein frequently shooed the crowd away when it would begin to form. He temporarily closed the basement casino bar.

My parents attended the arraignment on Thursday morning, where charges were formally brought against Mr. Cummings. My mom was distraught when she returned home and wouldn't discuss it. I got my info from the afternoon newspaper, which was delayed over an hour to make sure the news could make it in. It was short. Not sweet.

Cummings Formally Charged
By George Constable

June 22, 1973

Henry Earl Cummings Jr. was formally charged with assault with a deadly weapon and attempted murder in connection with the shooting on or near his property at approximately 12:15 a.m. on June 18. Cummings fired upon teenagers Gerald Nelson and Jarvis Turley, neither of whom were injured. Cummings' bond has been set at $100,000. The trial is scheduled to begin in August.

Under the short article were Mr. Cummings' mug shot and Gerald's and Jarvis' high school portraits.

CHAPTER
40

THE SUMMER WAS MARKED by the gloom of the pending trial. The gang pretty much fell apart, held together by formality alone. We rarely met and never achieved the kind of fun we expected when we laid out our summer plans. Our typical shenanigans were replaced by bickering, mostly about the upcoming trial. We started picking on each other over the smallest stuff. It drove home the sad realization that these guys weren't the best friends I'd thought they were. At least not Radish, Sully, and Hickey. I don't know if they were the ones who had changed as the summer progressed, or me. It didn't matter. Things with Billy and Tubs were much more complicated. Tubs withdrew from all of us. Billy and I remained as close as possible despite the atmosphere of his household as they prepared for the trial. The town was equally divided into two camps—those who believed Gerald and Jarvis were hellraisers, bad kids, delinquents who probably asked for it, versus those who believed they were preyed upon by an isolated, disfigured loner who was off his rocker.

My mom said the market lost half its business because of Mr. Klein's support of Mr. Cummings. The only people who shopped at the market anymore were on Cummings' side, whether by choice or convincing through the many heated discussions that took place on the premises. Mr. Klein even held impromptu town halls in the market's basement where people deliberated. As much as Mr. Klein tried to suggest all were welcome, he had disdain for those who prematurely judged the situation, taking the side of the boys.

A lot of innocence was lost that summer. Instead of spending evenings running around with the guys, I spent them in my room, writing and reading. I wrote more about Mr. Cummings, continuing to work on the fictional life I had created for him, but now with a nonfictional finality, or so it seemed.

As the first week of August approached, an aura of doom closed in around me, our house, and, from what I could tell, the entire neighborhood. Mr. Klein visited my mom and dad many times, always being cordial to me, but delivering no more messages from Mr. Cummings.

He refused any offer from Mr. Klein to post the $100,000 that would have freed him until his trial. He said he preferred to remain in the safety of his jail cell. Mr. Klein told my parents that if sent home, he'd certainly be harassed and something even more tragic would likely happen. I imagined him preferring to sit in a jail cell, waiting for his trial when he would be put on display like a freak at the county fair, wondering if he would be going to prison.

I had written down the message that Mr. Klein delivered on behalf of Mr. Cummings and taped it on the wall above my desk. *Hank says he's sorry that he might not be able to meet you. He said to continue to write. You have a talent that shouldn't be wasted.* The words felt like the last wish of a dying man.

Mr. Klein made frequent visits to our house over the summer, often sitting out back for hours into the night. All I was privy to was that the evidence was overwhelming that the boys' account of the incident was very different from the truth. Whether the judge and jury would be impartial and fair was another thing all together. Bernie Davis, the attorney Mr. Klein hired, had a history of representing people who were most likely guilty of the crimes they were on trial for. Murderers, drug dealers, and burglars—clients without the best reputations. But he was a winner, often getting his clients to be found not guilty or, at worst, guilty on considerably lesser charges.

Mr. Klein hired a security guard to protect Mr. Cummings' property. Initially after the arrest, Mildred Perkins stayed in the house to make sure it didn't remain vacant, but the curiosity of people who wanted to see the crime scene brought cars down the drive and noise outside the house that made her feel unsafe.

I rode my bike past the house a few times. People had stuck handmade signs in the ground. *Murderer, Freak, Monster*. It wasn't long before signs of *Faggot, Homo,* and *Cocksucker* were added to the mix.

Everyone wanted to know more about Hank Cummings. The *Mansfield News Journal* answered their call.

The Mystery of Henry Earl Cummings Jr.
By George Constable

August 3, 1973

Henry Earl (Hank) Cummings Jr., the man accused of shooting at two teenagers on June 18, lives at 430 Yoder Road, Mansfield, Ohio. Cummings moved to the house, previously owned by his sister, Eliza Cummings, in the spring of 1972. She passed away of cancer in April of this year, leaving the house to Cummings.

Cummings is a forty-seven-year-old WWII veteran who was badly wounded when the B-29 bomber he was a tail gunner in crash-landed at their base in Guam. He was credited with saving the lives of three soldiers and was awarded the Medal of Honor, Purple Heart, and Silver Star. He was subsequently discharged from the army due to 'undesirable behavior.' It was reported that he had a homosexual relationship with another soldier, an act considered criminal by the United States Army.

Cummings is currently being held without bond pending his trial, which is set to begin next week.

CHAPTER

41

I WOKE UP EARLY on the Monday morning of August 6 to be sure to see my mom and dad before they left for the courthouse on the first day of the trial. It was hot and the air was thick, steam rising from the dew on the grass. They shared that they would be sitting with Mr. Klein and Mildred Perkins, directly behind Mr. Cummings and Davis, in a row reserved for family members of the defendant. This shook me a bit, certain to further fuel the tension between Billy's and Tubs' family and ours. They were nervous, whether apprehensive of their appearance as supporters of Mr. Cummings, the uncertainty of what was to come, or both.

"Good luck," I said as they got in the car.

"Remember, Jonny," my mom shouted out. "Stay home today."

Minors were not permitted in the courtroom, even if they were siblings of the plaintiff or the defendant. I imagined Billy and Tubs were both at home with someone watching over them, an aunt, uncle, or older cousin. I imagined Radish, Sully, and Hickey running around like usual, probably at the fort that they had taken as their own. I was stuck at home with my brother who was told to not take his eyes off me.

I spent the day watching game shows on TV, reading, and writing, anxious for my mom and dad to return. I wrote a short story about a man who lived alone on a mountain who was attacked by three mountain men drifters. Fighting for his life, he slayed them with his hunting knife and buried the bodies under rocks on the mountain.

When the afternoon paper didn't arrive on our doorstep at 3:30, I knew the print deadline must have been delayed again. It landed with a thud against the front door at 4:15.

Opening Statement Shocks the Courtroom
By George Constable

August 6, 1973

The trial of Henry Earl Cummings Jr. began promptly at nine o'clock this morning with an opening statement by Cummings' attorney, Bernie Davis. The packed courtroom sat in shock as Davis revealed his defense strategy, which included surprises no one could have anticipated.

Following are excerpts from the opening statement:

"Ladies and gentlemen of the court, the facts we will present on behalf of my client will prove he is innocent of all charges brought forth by the prosecution.

"We will introduce you to Mr. Henry Earl Cummings Jr., a peaceful, law-abiding, honorable, man, who has never been in trouble with the law, and who has never harassed anyone. A man who only wanted people to respect his privacy. We will introduce you to a highly decorated World

War II veteran. So distinguished, he was awarded the Medal of Honor along with dozens of other medals and ribbons. We will prove that the story being woven by the prosecution is grossly inaccurate. We will prove that Mr. Cummings shouted out numerous warnings to the boys to leave the premises. We will prove that Mr. Cummings fired only one shot, not two as the boys have asserted. We will prove that the boys were just five feet from the western facing window of Mr. Cummings' home, not hundreds of feet from the home and on the other side of the property line, as the boys have asserted. We will show that Mr. Cummings fired high into the air from his front door, nowhere near the trespassers. We will show you that Mr. Cummings is legally blind, with limited sight in his left eye only, and he is impaired to the degree he cannot see in darkness, due to wounds sustained in the war. We will show evidence that the fingerprints of the boys were found on the side of Mr. Cummings' house, as well as on his front door and doorknob.

"Last, we will show that there was a witness to the events of the night. That Mr. Cummings was not alone in his house. We will introduce you to Walter Brunson, a friend of Mr. Cummings, who saw everything that happened that evening, and reveal that it was Mr. Brunson who called the police.

"Our fact-based evidence will prove beyond a shadow of a doubt that Mr. Cummings merely did what any of us would do, protect himself, his friend, and his property, in an act of self-defense.

"Ladies and gentlemen of the jury. We will give you no alternative but to find the defendant, Henry Earl Cummings Jr., not guilty of these charges."

Murmurs could be heard throughout the packed courtroom as Attorney Davis laid out his strategy. Honorable Judge Joseph Peacock instructed the court to take a brief recess before the opening statement from the prosecution.

No further information was available at the time of this paper's print deadline.

I was giddy after reading the article. If half of what the attorney said in the statement was true, I couldn't imagine how a jury could find Mr. Cummings guilty. Then there was the reveal of Mr. Cummings' friend, Walter Brunson.

When my parents returned their mood was upbeat, different from the trepidation that hung over them in the morning. I was holding the paper.

"Tell me what else happened?" I asked them.

With the understanding that everything would be reported for me to read anyway, they finally opened up about what they knew.

"What else happened?" I asked again. "What was the opening statement from the other side like? Come on, it will be in the paper tomorrow. Tell me."

Both of them read the article first so they would know where to begin.

"After the recess," my mom started, "the prosecutor gave his statement, contradicting what Attorney Davis said. But we know what the facts are. They won't be able to prove anything that they claim. He said the boys were shot at from a long distance. They weren't. He said the boys were never on the property. They were. He said the boys had never harassed Hank before. They have. He said that Hank hunted them down and threatened to kill them. He didn't. He said the boys are model citizens. They aren't."

"The witness? Walter Brunson," I said. "Is he in a wheelchair?"

My mom and dad turned to look at each other with an expression of surprise.

"Walter Brunson?" my mom said.

"The witness," I responded.

"What do you know about Walter Brunson"? she asked. "Nobody said anything about a wheelchair."

I was caught. There was nothing in the opening statement about Walter Brunson being disabled. For all I knew, my mom and dad didn't even know as much about Walter Brunson as I did. That is, assuming he *was* the man in the wheelchair we'd seen Mr. Klein deliver and pick up from Mr. Cummings' house.

I had never gotten away with a serious lie in my life. Plenty of white lies went unnoticed, though looking back I realize my parents probably knew the truth but let things slide. But a real lie? With consequences? I'd always been caught. Honesty was a virtue my mom drilled into me from birth. I tried to lie once when I ran my bike into my dad's car scraping the side panel. The evidence was clear as day. The paint scraped off the car was now on my handlebars. I tried to lie when I changed my report card, turning a C into a B. All my mom had to do was call Mrs. Asher to verify the truth. I tried to lie when I stole money from my brother's piggy bank. How could I explain how a six-year-old suddenly had accumulated eight dollars and twenty-five cents? I couldn't.

"Tell us what *you* know about Walter Brunson," my dad said.

My parents never went off the handle during a crisis or difficult situation. Instead, they both always took a deep breath and regrouped to approach a problem in unison. They never panicked. I never saw them overreact.

"Let's go have a seat," my mom said, leading us to the couch.

I let out a few deep sighs. I regrouped.

"I saw him once," I began. I waited for a reaction, but all I got was a look from both of them indicating, 'go on.'

"One time the guys and I were running around the farm and we were kind of close to Mr. Cummings' house, I guess. We saw a car pull down the drive. We stopped and looked to see who it was. I saw Mr. Klein help a man out of the car and put him in a wheelchair and wheel him up to Mr. Cummings' door. That's all I saw."

"Were you snooping? Trying to spy on Hank Cummings?" my dad asked.

Another moment of truth. Spill it all or face the risk of going deeper.

"Well, the guys ... I don't know," I fumbled. "They wanted to see him. See what he looked like. I just ... I guess I just followed along."

"And?" my mom said.

"And, yeah ... I guess we tried to see him on purpose."

"Who were you with?" my dad asked.

Now I was faced with violating my oath to the guys—what happens here stays here; never rat out a fellow member; always have each other's backs. But a good lawyer never asks a question unless they already know the answer.

Without naming names, I said, "The gang."

"And what exactly did you see?" my mom asked.

"I just saw Mr. Klein and the man in the wheelchair."

"That's all?" my mom asked. "And you would swear on your grandma's grave?"

"Swear on grandma's grave, that's all."

I stayed still, looking down at the threads of the shag carpet under my feet. There wasn't much else I could say. Wasn't much more they needed to say. We all knew I disobeyed their order to leave Mr. Cummings alone. They didn't need to rub it in. They also knew they couldn't lie to me—that everything was going to come out in court, and they couldn't stop me from knowing all the details.

"I'm sorry," I said as I started to cry. "I know I shouldn't have. I know it was wrong."

"Alright, Jonny," my mom said. "Why don't you go to your room now. I'll bring you your dinner when it's ready."

I was scared when I walked into the kitchen the next morning as they were finishing their breakfast, preparing to go to the courthouse. There was no mention of the previous evening's revelation. My mom again instructed me as she went out the door, "Stay home today, Jonny."

The trial lasted three days. The opening statement from the prosecution disputed the story Attorney Davis laid out. Detectives and police were called to the stand by the prosecution. Gerald Nelson's grandma was called as a character witness for Gerald. Sister Mary Dunn was called as a character witness for Jarvis Turley. Gerald and Jarvis each testified. They did their best to stick to their story that they couldn't remember anything other than minding their own business and getting shot at with no warning.

Both of their testimonies were twisted in knots by Davis, proving beyond any doubt they were lying and should be charged with contempt.

Davis never called on Mr. Cummings to testify. Instead, he called two witnesses. The first was a private detective who provided overwhelming evidence that substantiated Mr. Cummings' statements made in depositions. There was only one shotgun shell found at the property, inside the front door. Nelson's and Jarvis' fingerprints were discovered on numerous surfaces outside the house. Footprints outside the house were traced to their shoes.

The other witness Davis called was Walter Brunson. The transcript of the testimony was printed in the next day's paper.

"Mr. Brunson," Davis began. "Tell us about yourself."

"I live in Shelby, Ohio. I work for American Greetings in Cleveland. I work from home. I design greeting cards."

"What is the nature of your disability?"

"I have polio. I am unable to walk."

"What is your relationship with the defendant?"

"I met Hank earlier this summer. We are friends who enjoy each other's company."

"How often do you spend time with the defendant at his house?"

"Nearly every evening."

"Have you ever witnessed people on or near the property owned by the defendant?"

"Yes."

"How often, please elaborate."

"At least a dozen times over the summer. We've seen kids outside the house, looking in the windows. We've heard kids banging on the windows and the door. We've yelled at them to go away. That we would call the police."

"But you never called the police, did you? Not until this incident. Why not?"

"Because we didn't want to escalate things. And we didn't want any attention.

We wanted our privacy."

"No further questions."

The prosecutor's cross examination:

"Mr. Brunson, is it true you are a homosexual?"

"Objection! Not appropriate and irrelevant," Davis shouted.

"Sustained," Judge Peacock said. "The jury will ignore the question."

"Mr. Brunson, is it true that the defendant is a homosexual and that the two of you have engaged in sodomy?"

"OBJECTION," Davis shouted.

"Sustained," Judge Peacock said. "The jury will ignore the question. Stop this line of questioning immediately, counselor."

"No further questions," the prosecutor said.

CHAPTER

42

MY MOM RACED TO THE PHONE the second it rang on Friday, around three o'clock. The jury had reached a verdict. It would be read at four o'clock. She asked me to kneel with her. She prayed for the soul of Hank Cummings regardless of the verdict. As soon as my dad pulled in the drive, returning from his shift around three-thirty, she kissed me on the head, fixed her lipstick, grabbed her purse and ran to the car, yelling to me, "Don't leave the house."

I took our transistor radio into my room and tuned the dial to WMAN 1460 to hear the news as soon as it would break. Through the scratchiness of the live broadcast outside the courthouse, the reporter relayed the activity. People were holding signs, everything from *Free Hank* to *Hang Hank*; from *Murderer* to *Protect Your Right to Bear Arms*. The overwhelming sentiment according to the reporter was not in favor of Hank Cummings. In the background I could hear the chants of *Hank must hang, Hank must hang, Hank must hang*. The reporter said it was near mayhem, with fistfights breaking out.

The verdict would be read to a man, holding a megaphone, on the top steps of the courthouse, who would read it to the crowd below. As the clock ticked, minute by minute, past the four o'clock hour, through the radio I could sense the rising tension in the air and in the reporter's voice. Occasionally, over the crowd noise, I could hear commands from the megaphone of, "Stay calm, people, stay calm."

At 4:23, the reporter excitedly said that the man with the megaphone had been given a slip of paper. He held his microphone in the air to hear the verdict, as the crowd noise dimmed.

"Count one, attempted murder. We the jury find the defendant, Henry Earl Cummings Jr., not guilty."

The crowd erupted in a mix of yelps, cries, screams, and hoorays.

"Order, order, order," cried the man with the megaphone. The reporter shouted over the crowd noise to report the chaotic scene.

After the crowd quieted enough for the man with the megaphone to be heard, he continued.

"Count two, assault with a deadly weapon. We the jury find the defendant, Henry Earl Cummings Jr., not guilty."

The radio turned to static due to the crowd noise, the reporter's words drowned out and unrecognizable. A studio reporter intervened to repeat the verdict from the quiet of the station.

I turned the radio off and pumped my arms in the air and screamed out in celebration.

My parents were ecstatic when they returned home. I ran to the car as it pulled in the drive. My mom hugged me. Her mascara had run down her face from tears. "It's all over, Jonny," she said. "The nightmare is over."

But it wasn't over for Hank Cummings. Far from it. He couldn't return to his house for fear of his safety. Many people characterized him as a monster and thought he deserved to be punished. It was widely believed that Gerald Nelson's father was ultimately going to seek revenge during one of his drunken rages.

Among the nasty signs that had been planted near Mr. Cummings' drive was a new one. It read, *For Sale*. Hank Cummings would never return to his property.

On Friday morning, just a week after the trial, my mom poked her head inside my room. "How would you like to meet Hank Cummings?"

"What?" I said. "Are you serious?"

"He's leaving, moving to California tomorrow," she said. "Ed told me that he would like to meet you before he leaves."

"I don't know, Mom," I said. "That sounds kind of scary."

"There's nothing to be scared of," she said. "I think it's an opportunity you'll be sorry to have passed up. It's a pretty special invitation if you ask me."

I knew she was right. I'd regret it for the rest of my life if I didn't meet him. We planned on meeting the following day, a Saturday afternoon.

With my dad behind the wheel, we turned off Millsboro Road a few miles from our house, onto a long, winding drive leading up a hill. At the top stood the biggest house I'd ever seen with my own eyes. It looked like the White House, and as far as I knew, was every bit as big. Ed Klein's white Cadillac was parked in front of a three-car detached garage. Next to it was Mildred Perkins' rusty Buick. My dad pulled our car next to hers.

Without waiting for us to approach the front door, Mildred bounded out and greeted us with a smile.

"Well, if it ain't the Smiths," she exclaimed as she gave my mom a hug. "Hello, hello, hello. And, Jonny Smith, it's mighty good to see you again. James is here. You two ain't seen each other since you saved his hide, have you?"

"No, ma'am," I said.

"Well, come on inside and I'll fix you some iced tea, if you'd like," she said. "Or, Mr. Smith, you know where Ed keeps his liquor. Not that I'm pushin' it, mind you," she howled.

My heart was pounding as my dad put his arm around my shoulder as we walked to the house. Mr. Klein opened the screen door for us to enter and exchanged greetings with my parents.

"Hello, Jonny," he said. "So glad you came. Hank is looking forward to meeting you. Come on inside, will you?"

We entered the foyer that opened up to a large living space. To the right and left were two long halls that led to the wings of the house.

"Hank's in the study reading," Mr. Klein said. "What can I have Mildred get you all?"

I opted for lemonade, my mom an iced tea, my dad and Mr. Klein bourbon. We sat in a sunken seating area surrounded by big, white fluffy pillows. I bit at my nails listening to the adults make small talk, looking up to the foyer for a sight of Hank Cummings. Mr. Klein offered that I go outside and play with James, who was climbing a tree in the backyard, his ankle fully healed. I chose to stay with the adults. I was here on business.

As the small talk wound down, Mr. Klein excused himself and went down one of the halls. When he returned, he said, "Jonny, would you like to meet Mr. Cummings now?"

I nodded.

"Come on, then," he said. My mom smiled, and my dad gave me a wink. I followed Mr. Klein into a dimly lit, wood-paneled room, lined with books on shelves. In the corner, in a big leather chair, sat Mr. Cummings.

"Hello, Jonny," he quietly said. "Come sit with me."

JONATHON

CHAPTER
43

EACH YEAR ON MY BIRTHDAY, I take inventory of my life and reminisce. I turned forty-three in the spring of 2003, thirty years from the summer that forever defined my life. Thinking about the summer of 1973, when I was a thirteen-year-old, has taken on greater meaning as my own son was now the same age. I often wonder how different life might be had I not left the neighborhood that so many felt tethered to.

Not too many boys make it out of Little Kentucky. Most follow their fathers' footsteps into jobs at the mills and factories in town, work at gas stations, tire dealerships, trash hauling, junk dealing, or go into the military. Of the Greasy River Gang, I was the only one to go to college. Tubs and Sully went to work at the General Motors plant. Radish and Hickey both joined the marines. Hickey made the military his career and moved frequently, finally settling in the San Diego area. When Radish came home, he found nothing but trouble, having numerous run-ins with the law—DUIs and domestic violence. Rumor was he moved out of state with a woman and everyone lost touch with him. I don't even know if he's alive. Sully moved to Canada to live with his brother, who never came back to the States after he left to avoid the draft during the Vietnam war.

The summer of 1973 caused a split with Billy and me we never recovered from, ignoring each other all the way through school from that point on. His family moved to Florida before he started high school, and I couldn't tell you where he has ended up. I hope he's in a good place. What happened was the fault of neither of us; we were victims of circumstance. I understand the pressure from his family to support his brother, and I don't think he held any personal grudges against me because of my family's relationship with Hank Cummings. I hope not.

That summer took away our innocence. It should have been the best summer of our lives. I've often wondered how things would have been if Hank Cummings had never moved into that house with his sister. Would the gang have remained tight to this day? Would Billy and I still be best friends? Would I have ever gotten out of Little Kentucky and gone to college? One thing is certain. I would have never met Hank Cummings.

People often talk of those who most influenced their lives. Parents, a teacher, a coach, a spiritual guide. For me, that person has never been in doubt since the time I spent alone with Hank Cummings in Ed Klein's study that August evening. He taught me about love, kindness, and compassion; taught me about forgiveness; about healing; about acceptance. He taught me about the arc of a journey and the role of fate. He was kind. He was gentle. He was engaging. He moved slowly. Breathed deeply. Spoke softly. He listened intently, though I had little to say. This man who at one time I was prohibited from seeing, opened his soul to me. He told me to surround myself with good people. I have. He told me to be a good son. I have. He told me to get my education. I did. He told me to never lose hope in my fellow man. I've tried not to. He told me to never take anything for granted. I've tried not to. He told me to never stop writing. I haven't. And to use my words responsibly and respectfully. I try.

He told me to read Ulysses by James Joyce. I did. He told me to read Tolstoy, Dostoevsky, Melville, Harper Lee, and Saul Bellow. I've tried.

Hemingway, check. Twain, check, Virginia Woolf, check.

He told me to get an education. He told me to be clear about my dreams and to follow them. He told me to have courage. He told me to never lose my passion for life, for it is precious.

He read by heart Rudyard Kipling's poem, *If.*

> *If you can keep your head when all about you*
>   *Are losing theirs and blaming it on you;*
> *If you can trust yourself when all men doubt you,*
>   *But make allowance for their doubting too:*
> *If you can wait and not be tired by waiting,*
>   *Or being lied about, don't deal in lies,*
> *Or, being hated don't give way to hating,*
>   *And yet don't look too good, nor talk too wise;*
>
> *If you can dream—and not make dreams your master;*
>   *If you can think—and not make thoughts your aim,*
> *If you can meet with Triumph and Disaster*
>   *And treat those two impostors just the same:*
> *If you can bear to hear the truth you've spoken*
>   *Twisted by knaves to make a trap for fools,*
> *Or watch the things you gave your life to broken,*
>   *And stoop and build 'em up with worn-out tools;*
>
> *If you can make one heap of all your winnings*
>   *And risk it on one turn of pitch-and-toss,*
> *And lose, and start again at your beginnings*
>   *And never breathe a word about your loss;*
> *If you can force your heart and nerve and sinew*
>   *To serve your turn long after they are gone,*
> *And so hold on when there is nothing in you*

Except the Will which says to them: 'Hold on!';

If you can talk with crowds and keep your virtue,
    Or walk with Kings—nor lose the common touch;
If neither foes nor loving friends can hurt you;
    If all men count with you, but none too much;
If you can fill the unforgiving minute
    With sixty seconds' worth of distance run—
Yours is the Earth and everything that's in it,
    And—which is more—you'll be a Man, my son!

He told me to memorize it. I did.

I spent over an hour with Hank Cummings on that Saturday afternoon in Ed Klein's study. This was no chance meeting. He was prepared for me. He had respectfully crafted a sermon and delivered it with such weight I was rendered in awe and could only revere the man. And of all he told me, I am certain only a fraction of it stuck. But what stuck became my gospel for life as if it were spoken by God himself.

The mystery and the guarded nature of his existence, so protected by those who cared for him that we were prohibited from even sneaking a glance at him, made this meeting monumental. It would have been impossible to anticipate how our relationship might unfold.

Hank Cummings was a noble man. A peaceful man. A good, caring, wholesome person who gave so much of himself for his country. He deserved a better fate. How many people walk into fire, risking their life to save the lives of others? How many people would persevere through the injuries he sustained? How could any man overcome his fate without anger, victimhood, and resentment?

They say God never gives you more than you can handle. That those who bear tragedies so great are the chosen ones. For they will survive and make something good out of themselves.

There were three words he told me as we said goodbye that day that I'll never forget. As I stood in the doorway, ready to rejoin my mom and dad, he said to me, "Jonny, if you remember just one thing from our conversation, remember this. Don't waste it."

The gravity of my meeting with Hank Cummings was not lost on my parents, who remained quiet on the ride home. As if they didn't want to dilute the value of what I was working to process. They could see it in my eyes, in my face. When we got home, my mom just smiled at me. We didn't speak. I went straight to my room and opened up my writing notebook and began to document the lessons learned. I feverishly wrote everything I could remember. At the top of the page, I wrote, *Don't waste it.* The next day, I asked my mom to take me to the bookstore and with money I planned to spend on a model car, I instead bought a book: Poems of Rudyard Kipling. It was $1.99.

All my mom said to me about Hank Cummings after we met was, "I told you."

The next day, he left Ohio and moved to California. Ed Klein drove him out in his Cadillac. He hired a couple of men to follow them in a truck with the few possessions Hank held onto.

In the fall of 1973, his property was purchased by the same developer that owned the rest of the farm. The house was knocked down, flattened by a bulldozer. I don't know how many times the property was sold to various developers, but finally, the fears of the Yoder family ghosts were overcome. Today on that property stands a Home Depot, a Walmart, a Walgreens, an Applebee's, a nail salon, tanning bed franchise, and, ironically, a hobby shop that specializes in model cars. Every time I return home to visit my folks, it pains me to drive down Yoder Road.

Upon graduating from Mansfield High School in 1978, I went to Ohio State with help from academic scholarships and grants for being a first generation student. I majored in English and literature with dreams of becoming a novelist, a pursuit that continues. In the meantime, to put bread on the table, I found a career in the advertising business, writing copy for print, radio, and

TV ads. I've never strayed far from home, working for agencies in Toledo and Cleveland, before settling in Columbus. I wouldn't call my career overly fulfilling, but it has provided me with the means to comfortably support my family. My fulfillment comes from my work late in the evenings and early mornings, when I seclude myself in my home office to write what I want, not what the clients of my day job demand. I've written three manuscripts, none yet published. I've learned to overcome my frustration by writing for myself and finding value in the process. I've gotten better. I've kept the faith.

CHAPTER

44

"IS THIS THE ONE you thought you lost?" Patti asked.

My eyes grew wide and I lost my breath.

On many occasions I would pull an old shoebox from my closet shelf. On the lid, in big block letters, I had written, *HANK*. It contained his two books of the Old Hag, a photocopy of the story I had written for him, his note back to me, the book of poems by Rudyard Kipling, newspaper clippings from the shooting incident, a newspaper article from the *Grayson Gazette* when he returned from WWII a hero, and my writing notebook from the summer of '73.

My family was well aware of the sentiment the box held for me. I had often talked about Hank Cummings to them and frequently referred to the contents of the box. My daughter, Becky, was still a bit too young at eight, but Jon Jr., now thirteen, could clearly feel Hank's presence in our lives. He, himself, had memorized the poem *If*, and relished the opportunities I offered him to read through my writing notebook.

Patti affectionately referred to Hank as "Grandpa Hank," occasionally asking me, "What would Grandpa Hank suggest you do?" whenever I'd get writer's block. I never hesitated to respond, "He'd tell me to keep writing." "Then keep writing and quit complaining," she'd return.

It was the first week of June 1978 when I excitedly drove my car, a 1962 Ford Falcon hand-me-down from my brother, into our drive, hitting a pothole full of water, making a splash clear into our neighbor's yard, causing Mrs. Packer to shout, "Slow down, young man."

"Sorry Mrs. Packer, last day of school," I yelled back as I bounded in the house. I was overjoyed putting high school in my rearview mirror. I was an awkward, gangly teenager, with swooping long hair and glasses that always seemed crooked on my face. Due to an iron deficiency in my vertebrae, I spent my sophomore and junior years confined in a back brace that ran from my hips to my shoulders, causing me to stop playing all sports. Whenever I felt self-pity, which was often, I would snap out of it by reminding myself of Hank Cummings and all he overcame. I would do what he did to move past his deficiencies. Write. What at the time seemed like a curse turned into a blessing.

I went into my house and down the hall to my bedroom. As I started to toss my bookbag on my bed, I stopped when I saw a manilla envelope on my pillow. The first thing I noticed was the name in the upper left-hand corner, *Hank Cummings*. I froze.

The last and only correspondence I'd received from Hank was the note he wrote me five years earlier, after he read my story, *The Ghost of Jensen Yoder*, so this was quite an unexpected surprise.

I carefully sliced the top of the envelope open with a pocketknife, being sure not to damage the return address.

June 1, 1978

Dear Jonny,

I trust this note finds you well. I understand you are graduating from high school soon if you haven't already. This marks an exciting passage into your next adventure, which I hear will be at the university. Well done, my boy, and congrats!

I recently came across the ghost story you wrote for me a few years back and thought you'd like to have a copy of it. You're not getting the original back, for I'm keeping it forever! But, I xeroxed it for you for your own safekeeping, if indeed that would be important to you. I, at least, take great pleasure in reminiscing. I find it a way to keep alive memories that I value.

Ed says you and your parents are doing well. I've not forgotten the nice time we spent together at his place. It's planted fondly in my memory bank and something I lean on for faith when I think back to the awful events of that summer. Whether you know it or not, our get together helped send me off to my own next adventure with a smile on my face and a sense of restoration in the youth of today. I hope that's not too much a burden to share!

You stay well, my friend. Good luck at the university and keep writing.

Your friend,
Hank

I don't know if the value of reminiscing was, yet, another lesson I learned from Hank. But my sense of sentiment and nostalgia was something I often profited from. It couldn't be possible, I thought, that I could have touched Hank in this way. As if I needed another reason to revere this man. I couldn't read his letter enough. I was sure he wrote, "I hope that's not too much of a burden to share," in jest, but the gravity of that sentence weighed heavily on me. Did he mean for me to think that as a thirteen-year-old kid, I had some magical power? I thought of what he told me when we left each other, "Don't waste it." A wonderful burden.

I grew into adulthood with Hank on my shoulder. Often, during moments of self-doubt, for example, I'd think back to what he wrote, and with that, found him guiding me to a better place. A place of self-confidence and self-respect.

It was a good thing that I read his letter so much and could recite it from heart, for I lost it several years earlier, which saddened me to tears whenever I thought about it.

"Oh my God," I remarked as I looked at what Patti held in her hand.

"Is it?" she asked.

"Yes!" I exclaimed. "Where did you find it?"

"On the closet floor behind a bunch of my shoe boxes," she said.

"I can't believe it."

"Read it to me," she said as I took it from her.

"Dear Jonny," I began before breaking into tears and falling to my knees. I felt Hank's presence in the room.

"Oh, hon," Patti said as she knelt next to me and held me. "Grandpa Hank," she said through her smile.

"Yes," I said. "He's back. *Dear Jonny*," I started again.

It had been at least ten years since I lost it, and, ever since, I'd felt as though the shoebox was incomplete. I felt as though I'd lost a piece of Hank. Almost a betrayal.

Jon Jr. walked by and saw Patti and me sitting on the floor. "What's wrong?" he asked.

"It's not what's wrong," I said. "It's what's right." I handed him the letter. He had only heard me talk about it—in fact, recite it—for he was just a toddler when it went missing. After reading the first line he knew what it was.

"Wow!" he exclaimed.

That evening, I treated my family to the many stories about Hank and the summer of '73 that they'd heard way too often. They justly humored me as I went through them with all the emotion and drama I could muster.

CHAPTER

45

"YOU'VE GOT TO GET in touch with him," Patti said.

"I don't even know if he's still alive," I said. "I have no idea where he would even be now."

"Your parents ..." she started.

"They wouldn't remember," I interrupted her.

"Probably not," she said. "Worth a try though."

"Maybe," I said.

The following day, a Sunday, we packed the kids in the car and drove to Mansfield to see them.

My parents corresponded with Hank periodically but would lose track of him on and off throughout the years. I knew that he and Ed Klein stayed in touch through the years, but Ed had died in 1995. Mildred Perkins died a year after Ed.

We tend to think we have all the time in the world. I cursed myself for not making an effort to stay close to Hank. Looking back, I think I wanted to keep my memory of him in the pristine state it remained from 1973. I'd been spellbound and he remained mythical. Maybe I didn't want anything to spoil that. I must have missed out on so much. Now, it felt so selfish. Maybe I'd deprived him as well.

I remembered my mom saying I'd be sorry if I didn't pounce on the opportunity to meet him before he left Ohio, that likely being my only chance. I was grateful to have had the good fortune of having that one chance. I never imagined I'd have another one.

Meeting him shaped me and left an imprint upon my soul. It was like he was a part of me—my DNA. He was a lens through which I evaluated my life, my decisions, and behavior. How I judged myself. What he meant to me was extremely personal, not something I shared with anyone other than my wife. He wasn't a topic of conversation or gossip within my family or for anyone else. Short of just a few, nobody seemed to care what had happened to him.

My parents struggled with significant memory issues as they aged. I was always grateful that my older brother, Tom, had stayed in Mansfield and looked after them. I often made the hour drive north from Columbus to visit on weekends so our trip to the old neighborhood wasn't unusual. At times, my mom became her old self and interacted with Jon Jr. just as she had with me when I was young. My dad seemed to favor Becky. Though their memories were fading, their love for life and family weren't.

There were days when they were both sharp. Some when neither were. This Sunday was one of those days.

"He still lives with Eliza, doesn't he?" my mom said when I asked about Hank.

"No, Mom," I said. "Eliza died a long time ago. He moved to California, remember?"

"Oh, that's right, he did."

"Have you heard from him lately?"

"Who?"

"Hank Cummings," I said.

"Oh, I don't know," she said.

"Mom," Tom interjected. "He's written you, don't you remember?"

"Oh, has he?" she said. "Hank?"

"Yes," Tom said. "He wrote you to tell you he's sick, didn't he?"

"Oh, yes," she said. "He's sick. Cancer, I think. Poor soul."

"Hold on," Tom said to me. He went to my parents' bedroom and came back with a stack of mail. He found a letter Hank had recently sent them.

April 13, 2003

Dear Ralph and Betsy,

I hope my letter finds you in good health and that you are excited for spring. I've always missed Ohio this time of year, when life begins to rise from the gray and gloom of winter. It has been raining in San Francisco for a week straight. I enjoy sitting on my balcony under the awning watching the people below try to dodge the rain drops as they stroll up and down Castro Street. I wish I could join them in their galivanting, but my health won't allow it. I'm afraid I'm rather confined now to my apartment. Nathan provides great care and company, and Tiptoe won't leave my side. Please write back and let me know how you and your boys are doing.

With love,
Hank

The return address:

126 Castro Street, San Francisco, California, 94114

One evening after the kids had gone to bed, I opened my laptop and typed him a letter.

May 29, 2003

Dear Mr. Cummings,

I was visiting my parents, and they shared a recent letter you had written them. I just wanted to reach out to let you know I think of you often. You may not even remember when we met in Ed Klein's study the day before you moved to California, but that meeting has forever shaped my life in unimaginable ways. I am forever grateful. I am keeping you in my thoughts and prayers.

Best regards,
Jonathon (Jonny) Smith

I had no expectations that he would write back, but was hopeful, none-theless. I'd go straight to the mail every day when I got home. About a month later, I received a letter.

I yelled for my wife, Patti, who came running. I handed it to her. "Open it, open it," she said as she handed it back to me. "What are you waiting for?" Patti asked. "If you don't open it I will."

June 23, 2003

To Jonny, my dear,

What a pleasant surprise to hear from you. Of course I remember you and our pleasant conversation at Ed's. I believe it was on a humid and sticky day in August late on a Saturday afternoon. I remember that you were a writer even at your young age. I think your mother shared that you have continued the craft. I hope so. Whatever your passion has become, I trust you have found fulfillment and joy. Will you please let me know?

I am living a peaceful and somewhat quiet life in San Francisco now. I'm not without my worries and challenges, but I still wake up every morning, have my coffee with my purring kitty, Tiptoe, on my lap, and watch the escapades up and down Castro Street from the small balcony outside our living area.

Jonny, it was joyful to hear from you. I hope you write again.

My very best back to you,
Hank

I sat in near disbelief with such a sense of reverence and gratitude for this man with whom I had now reconnected. For so many years—three decades to be precise—I felt compelled to respect his privacy, no different than during the summer of 1973. I'd heard dozens, if not hundreds, of church sermons in my youth. From not one can I remember the message, or who gave it. My parents certainly lectured me on life's virtues, dos and don'ts, rights and wrongs. I can't remember one conversation.

As much as he's been a part of me, I've considered him a distant memory, as one would a favored grandpa who had long since passed.

July 1, 2003

Dear Mr. Cummings,

I am so happy that you wrote back and that we've reconnected. And I'm especially happy to know that you are living a good life in San Francisco. I've often wondered about you and how life has treated you since we met.

I have continued to write and have completed three manuscripts but have had no success getting them published. In the meantime I write advertising jingles and slogans. It pays the bills, so I can't complain. I met my wife, Patti, at Ohio State and we got married in 1982. I have two great children, Jon Jr. and Becky.

I would love to hear from you again. Do you still write? I found your book, The Return of the Old Hag, on Amazon, and of course still have The Wrath of the Old Hag. Certainly you've written more. At least I hope so.

I've been to San Francisco twice on business and thoroughly enjoyed it. What a wonderful city. I understand why it suits you.

I am curious about you and hope I'm not intruding by asking questions. But it means so much to be in touch. I remember well how you value your privacy, and I hope I'm not infringing upon that.

Hope to hear from you again.

My very best,
Jonathon

July 13, 2003

Dear Jonathon,

Hello, sir. I see that Jonathon is your adult name. Well done.

First, you are in no way intruding upon my privacy. You are correct that I was an extremely private person when I lived in Ohio. Things are much different for me here. I don't live the life of recluse that I was tethered to when I was a younger man. I live in a community of acceptance and love, and with the help of many, have become quite comfortable in my own skin.

I stopped writing commercially a few years ago. I published just four books under the name H. E. Cummings. The commercial success I've had has been writing under pseudonyms. I've written under several aliases for a variety of reasons, initially to protect my anonymity. It has suited me well, as I never wrote a word for notoriety, recognition, or fame. I write because I enjoy it.

You may want to check Amazon or Barnes and Noble, under the names of Frederick Ervin and Richard Oakley. If you like the stories, I wrote them. If you don't, those other characters, Ervin and Oakley did. Please don't part with your money. If you'd like some copies, I'll be happy to have the publisher send them to you. I've written several others under a different alias, but I'll save you from that for now.

Your letters make my day—I trust I'll receive another one.

Best to you,
Hank
P.S. Please call me Hank

I was astonished to find no less than twenty-three books written by Hank under the names of Ervin and Oakley, each favorably reviewed. Ervin wrote in the crime genre; Oakley was a mystery writer. I purchased two books from each author and read them cover to cover within days of receiving them. I was intrigued that the styles of each were unique, and both very different from the two *Old Hag* books I'd read. I couldn't comprehend the talent that took.

I wrote back to him immediately. Hank had been responsive to my letters. It was unusual that I didn't hear from him in over three weeks.

Finally a letter came.

August 5, 2003

Dear Jonathon,

I'm sorry it's been a few weeks since I've written. Please don't take it as a lack of interest in our correspondence, which I very much enjoy. I haven't been feeling well of late.

In your next letter (which I trust I can count on), will you please share more about your writing? You mentioned that you had completed some manuscripts? I'd like to read them if you're willing to share. Could I tempt you to send something to me? I would also advise you to please not give up on this if it remains your passion. It takes effort, effort, and more effort. But you must do it because you are fulfilled by the process. Notice I didn't say "enjoy" the process—that's an entirely different proposition. Don't do it for the result, because that is entirely out of your hands and far from the best judge of success. But if you enjoy the process and are doing it for yourself first and foremost, it's not work.

I must go now.

Yours,
Hank

"What do you have to lose?" Patti asked me. "You know it doesn't stink. Just because you haven't found a publisher doesn't mean anything. Maybe Hank can give you some advice."

She was right. I went to Staples and printed 188 pages of my most recent effort. A story called *From the Dust* was about a woman I had worked with who moved two blocks from the World Trade Center only three days before the attacks of 9/11. She kept a detailed diary of what she witnessed and experienced for the year that followed. I knew it was good. It was compelling, well written, and timely. The problem was the market was flooded with books about 9/11 at the time, and I couldn't get any interest.

August 12, 2003

Dear Hank,

I'm sorry to hear that you haven't been feeling well. I hope things are improving.

I've enclosed a draft of my most recent manuscript. Please don't feel obligated to read it. It is a nonfiction story of a woman I used to work with in Columbus who moved to New York City two blocks from the World Trade Center on September 8, 2001. You probably don't need a calendar to know the significance of that date. She kept a diary so well written and with such specificity that there was a lot to work with. I also spent close to one hundred hours interviewing her and some of her neighbors that she came to know, even though she was forced out of her apartment three days after moving in. She and her fellow tenants were moved to a hotel in Jersey City, directly across the Hudson River, for six months before being allowed to return.

I've tried fiction. It was always my dream to be a novelist. I haven't entirely given up on that, but I will admit I enjoy the journalistic nature of writing to the truth. It allows me to tap into my imagination without having to solely depend on it if that makes sense.

I need to share with you that so many aspects of my life have been influenced by the wisdom you shared with me during our time together on that Saturday afternoon in 1973. As soon as I got home that day, I went straight to my writing journal and wrote down everything I could remember from what you said. Such a gift it was. Among so many other things, I don't know if I'd have pursued a writing career. Gone to college? Maybe. Read James Joyce? Never. Maybe someday, someway, I'll find a way to properly express my gratitude.

Perhaps you'll be able to get through at least a couple chapters of my story. And, by the way, I ordered Into the Mist and Under a Gray Sky by Ervin, and Subsequent Fears and Unthinkable Acts by Oakley. I enjoyed them immensely. I appreciated your offer to send them to me, but I'll sleep better at night having paid for them.

Please feel better soon.

Best,
Jonathon

Over three weeks later, a letter arrived from San Francisco.

September 6, 2003

Dearest Jonathon,

I consumed From the Dust. Devoured it. Ate it up with great pleasure. Slurped it up, actually. I do believe you have something special here. Unfortunately the 9/11 genre is saturated, and as a new author, I can understand (not that I endorse, mind you) the hurdles facing you. And I have some thoughts for you if you're interested. But I will refrain from pushing them on you. For publishing is not always a clean and noble game.

That being said, might I see you? I hope that's not a bridge too far to propose. Of course, this would mean you traveling to San Francisco if you are willing and able. Nathan and I can even accommodate you in our apartment if you'd like, but if you'd rather stay in a hotel, I would understand.

My hope is that we could arrange a visit soon, perhaps even in the next several weeks if your schedule would allow it.

What do you say?

Your friend,
Hank

"Go," Patti told me. "Don't waste it!"
I nodded.

Chapter

46

"YOU SHOULD TAKE HIM something," Patti said to me. "Maybe a story."

It was a good thought, but I had a lot of things to finish before leaving in just two days. For starters, it wasn't easy to schedule a week off with little notice in my business. Advertising, for those who do it, feels like life and death. In fact, I kept a framed cartoon in my office of two surgeons peering over a patient on an operating table. One doctor says, "Oops." The other one responds, "Relax, Harry, it's just brain surgery. It's not like we're doing advertising here!"

On Friday morning, I met with Bob Maxwell, my boss, to tell him I needed some time off. "This fellow, Hank," Bob said to me. "He's the one you've told me about."

"Yes," I said.

"Well, you might not get another chance," he said. "Go. We'll figure things out here."

There aren't too many shops where I'd get that response. I'd worked for several agencies, but Stanton & Maxwell was where I belonged. The culture was familial and several of my best friends were associates I'd worked with for nearly fifteen years. I almost walked away from the business before my career even started. The first agency I worked for wanted me to fly to Chicago for a new business presentation at a moment's notice. The timing conflicted with my dad's open-heart surgery and I had promised him I'd be there. When I told my boss I couldn't go, he said, "Welcome to the NFL." I asked, "What's the supposed to mean?" He said, "It means you're going to Chicago." I've regretted not being there for my dad to this day.

I went into the office to wrap up some loose ends on Saturday morning. Before I shut my computer down, I thought about what Patti had said.

I've always struggled with the discipline of writing. I've studied many authors trying to learn how they are able to turn out such a volume of great work, time and time again. Most treat it like a nine-to-five job, writing whether the urge hits them or not. Working through blocks, resistance, and self-doubt. It's work. I've regretted that I've not been able to do that. Having a full-time job and a young family hasn't helped, but there've been times I've taken time off and left my family for a week to do nothing but write. It's always proved difficult. I am hopeful when my life settles without so many commitments, I'll find a way.

I'm not the only aspiring author in the agency. Chad Weber comes in the office every morning at five o'clock and writes for three hours before work obligations take over, and writes again each evening for another three hours. He's been doing it for four years, working on the same book. The working title: *The Autobiography of God*. He recently struck a publishing deal. I asked him how he's stayed so dedicated. "Get divorced and ignore your kids," he said through regret.

That's not a formula for me. If forced to choose between family and trying to make it as a writer, I'll stop writing tomorrow. I figure they'll be plenty of time to write full time when I'm retired and the kids are grown. Until then, I'll keep dabbling and push forward the best I can.

My block has always been that unless I have an idea fleshed out, it's hard to stroke the keys. I stared at the computer wondering what to write to Hank and suddenly felt inept. Why could I not generate a story on command for him now as I had when I was only thirteen? What did I know then that I didn't know now? How was I able to overcome resistance, a feeling that at times now paralyzes me. Why so much self-doubt in adulthood?

There are two types of creative directors. There are those who are blindly arrogant whose shit don't stink, and who bully their ideas through. That's never been my modus operandi. I'm in the other camp. The ones driven by insecurity and the fear of failure. It's likely why I've only made it to associate creative director and not the head creative honcho, or why I've never been recruited by shops in bigger markets. "Too nice a guy for that," people often would tell me. "You're too sensitive. Need to toughen up. Don't let them give you any crap." Sensitivity was a virtue in the home I grew up in. It's one of the traits Patti fell in love with and one she claims she adores. At least until I start to sulk or withdraw over a stupid argument. Then I'm *too* sensitive.

I'll accept it as a strength. It's rejection that is the bane of my existence. My thirteen-year-old self had not yet felt real rejection. I would soon learn its effect of misery, sadness, and self-doubt the following school year when Billy stopped talking to me, compounded when Missy Botkin chose him over me as her date for the eighth-grade dance. Ever since then, I've not handled it well and have also learned that the emotion is not a good bedfellow with sensitivity.

Sadly, that thirteen-year-old boy had more self-confidence when he wrote *The Ghost of Jensen Yoder* than the forty-three-year-old version now frozen over his typewriter. The innocence of youth is impossible to reclaim.

My dad was a kind and gentle man who was quick with the kind of fatherly advice that was always good to hear but seemed simple and obvious. Tom and I affectionately called it "surface stakes." He was good with the basics. He taught me how to use a razor without nicking my chin—or when I did, how to stick a torn piece of tissue on the wound to stop the bleeding. He taught me I should change the oil in my car and rotate the tires every five thousand miles. He taught me how to tie a bowtie. He taught me to open doors for women. He stressed the importance of a firm handshake. He taught me how to throw my knuckleball. He was who I went to when I needed to learn to do something.

When it came to how to feel about something, I went to my mom. My brother and I called her advice, "deep stakes." She had the advice for how to mend a broken heart. For how to soothe a crying baby. For how to keep a stiff upper lip and hold your head high. To listen more than talk. To remember the golden rule. To never let your ego give you advice. That good looks are only skin deep and beauty comes from the soul. To give your best to those who love you, for they'll be there when you need them. To eat your vegetables. To never get smug. To pick your battles. That when you screw up, forget about it, for tomorrow is a new day. To be the hero of your own life. To find a good woman and keep her happy.

I had found a good woman in Patti. She was much like my mom but tougher, which is what I often needed. Each provided me guidance and comfort during moments of insecurity and self-doubt, yet in very different ways.

As my mom's memory issues worsened, and she was no longer capable of providing the wisdom I so often leaned on, I missed her terribly. Neither she nor my dad could comprehend the significance of my trip to see Hank. While Patti could boldly tell me I should write something for him, my mom would've helped connect me to something that would touch him. I felt robbed that my parents couldn't share my excitement and anticipation of seeing him again.

"Oh, that's nice," my mom said when I told her my plans.

"Tell him we said hi," my dad added.

I looked at my keyboard, unable to write. I wanted to call my mom. I shut it down without writing a word.

CHAPTER

47

I PURCHASED A ONE-WAY TICKET on American Airlines, putting me in San Francisco at nine-thirty on the Sunday evening of September 14, 2003. I was not naive to the fact that Hank's neighborhood, the Castro District, was a gay neighborhood, but still it was a bit of a culture shock to find myself to be the only straight male around from when I stepped out of the taxi. I checked into the Parker Guest House, a beautiful Edwardian-style hotel built nearly a century ago, and was greeted with flamboyancy, which I adored.

It was past midnight Ohio time, but my adrenaline was pumping so I decided to explore the neighborhood and find my way to Hank's apartment, which was less than a mile from the hotel. Along the way, I was entranced by the color, the architecture, the sounds, the overall fabric of the area. It was alive with energy. Noise cascaded from the open windows and doors of the packed bars and restaurants. Cable cars sung their way by. I walked by the Castro Theater where the Gay Men's Chorus was performing. A gentleman outside offered me a free ticket to join him, which I politely declined. Men in tiny shorts, midriff tops, some with no shirts showing off their tattoos and nipple rings, many walking dogs—bulldogs seemed the breed of choice, many sporting spiked leather collars. People of all sexes, races, ethnicities holding hands, kissing, groping on every corner uninhibited. Music surrounded me, resonating from clubs and street musicians. I wasn't in Ohio anymore. I was loving it.

I found Hank's apartment building and gazed up at the tiny terrace he had described to me in one of his letters, the spot where he drank his morning coffee with his cat on his lap. There were two chairs with a small table in between. I imagined that spot perhaps being where we would spend our time together, whether it be a single afternoon or several. Directly across the street from his place was a bar with windows open to the street. I sat at a table, ordered a beer, and gazed across, looking at the front door of the building that would lead to his apartment door somewhere within.

I imagined Hank walking these streets, maybe even sitting at this very table having his own beer. It was clear how he found comfort in this neighborhood void of judgment. The contrast from how his life in Ohio might have played out was hard to comprehend. It was comforting to know he had found his home here. His belonging. His sense of place. That soothing helped quell the anxiety I felt in anticipation of meeting him. I wondered if he ever found love. Was Nathan his partner? I could never erase the image of him from 1973, over thirty years ago. He looked like an old man, his face so scarred, his eyes hidden by dark sunglasses, only with two fingers and a thumb on his left hand, a cane resting beside him against the chair. In twelve hours I would see the effects of thirty more years of aging. His only image of me, if he remembered, was of a meek, shy, thirteen-year-old boy. Now, I was nearly the age he was when we first met.

Three beers were enough. Too many actually, but they went down easily. I found the streets on the walk back to the hotel more alive than before, tempting me to grab another beer, but I didn't. I fell asleep quickly but woke up throughout the night. I managed to roll around in bed until nine-thirty.

After a croissant, coffee, and juice in the hotel café, I retraced my steps from the night before to Hank's apartment. I was thirteen years old again, riding to Ed Klein's house in the back of our car. Nervous as hell. The moment was upon me as I pressed the buzzer outside the apartment building's front door and waited for the click of the open door.

Apartments A and B were inside on the ground floor landing. C and D were up the stairs. Hank lived in apartment D. The stairs creaked with each step as I made my way up. I rang the bell on the frame of the door.

"Coming," an unfamiliar voice came through the door. "One second."

The door opened. "Jonathon, I presume," the man said. "I'm Nathan. Please come in."

"Yes, thank you," I said. "Pleased to meet you."

Nathan was in his eighties. He was a short man, and quite thin. He had a scraggly beard, white as cotton, just like his long hair that was tied in a ponytail that strewn down his back. His eyes were blue and warm, as was his smile. I felt instantly welcome.

"Please have a seat," he said, motioning me to the sofa that was positioned with enough room to walk behind it to the French doors that opened up to the balcony. The apartment was immaculate, spacious, filled with paintings, drawings, photography, and sculptures. "Something to drink?"

"Water would be fine," I said. "Thank you."

A cat greeted me, rubbing against my leg before hopping up onto the couch next to me.

"Tiptoe!" Nathan yelled, as he handed me a glass of water and put a coaster on the coffee table in front of me, "Leave our poor Jonathon alone."

"I don't mind," I said. "I happen to love cats."

"That's good, Hank was worried you might be allergic. That would be a deal-breaker," he laughed.

He sat in a chair across from me and began to make small talk. "How was your flight? How's the hotel? Have you ever been to Castro before? Hank tells me you're a writer. Married? Children? What's Ohio like? Never been there myself. Flyover state, right?"

I heard the sound of shuffling footsteps on the hardwood floor from the hall.

"Oh, Hank must have risen from the dead," Nathan said laughing as he rose and walked toward the sound. I stood in anticipation of greeting my friend. Slowly, holding on to Nathan, Hank appeared from the hall and turned to face me.

When I met Hank in the summer of 1973, I perceived him as an old man. He stayed seated in Ed Klein's study, so I never had a true read on how tall he stood. Even so, I remembered his legs and arms appeared long and thin. And when I saw him from the pines that summer, his height filled the entire frame of his front door. Ever since meeting him, his image remained statuesque to me—intellectually, philosophically, emotionally, and physically.

He looked twice as old as I remembered him. And smaller. He was hunched over. He was not wearing sunglasses like before. His right eye was gone, nearly covered by weathered, scarred skin. He squinted at me through his left eye. On his neck and face were lesions of small purple patches. An IV ran from his arm to a stand on wheels, which Nathan guided. He wore baggy jeans and a short-sleeved colorful shirt adorned with parrots. His clothes hung on him like on a store rack. He didn't look well.

He labored to walk with a noticeable limp, favoring his right side. He leaned on his cane, which he held in his left hand. Nathan held his right arm, near the stump, to help steady him, as they made their way to the couch. He couldn't have weighed more than 130 pounds and I sized him up to be well over six feet tall if you could stretch him out flat.

"Hello, Jonathon," he softly said. "Come sit with me."

CHAPTER

48

"SO," HE BEGAN SOFTLY. "How are you, my boy?"

"I'm well," I said. "It's my honor to be here. So good to see you."

"My honor," he said. "We have a lot to catch up on, don't we?"

"Yes, we do," I said. "I don't even know where to start."

"Tell me about Jonathon," he said. "That would be a fine place to begin, would it not?"

His voice was weak and raspy, at times barely audible with an intermittent muffled cough. I sat close to him.

"What would you like to know? Where should I start?"

"First, oh please forgive me," he said. "Have you met Nathan?"

"Yes, he welcomed me in."

"Dandy. Nathan is my good chap. We look out for each other. Would you like something to drink?"

"I've got a glass of water right here," I said motioning to the glass on the coffee table in front of us.

"Of course," he said. "I didn't see it. My eyesight isn't the keenest these days. Nathan, darling, would you please bring me a ginger ale with a twist?"

"Yes, master," Nathan said laughingly. "He's quite bossy today," he directed at me.

"What's that?" Hank asked him.

"I said, you're a sassy boss today," Nathan barked, causing them both to laugh.

"Tiptoe, here kitty kitty, here Tippy" he called out. "Come here sweetie. Are you good with kitties, Jonathon?"

"Yes, love them," I said. "We have two at home, plus a puppy."

"Marvelous, I find a kitty is wonderful company," he said. "Dogs are incredible creatures, not sure man deserves them. But cats? We deserve them, just ask them. Tiptoe has quite an attitude. He knows he'll outlive me, and he rubs it in my face."

Hank laughed and started coughing, placing his handkerchief over his mouth. It had spots of blood on it. He scrunched it in a ball and put it back in the pocket of his shirt. Nathan pulled it out and returned with a fresh one, giving me a look as though he hoped I was prepared for this.

Hank reached down to try to pick Tiptoe up. The IV tube wrapped around his arm causing him to jerk at it, pulling at the tape that held the needle in place near his wrist and almost tipping the stand over.

"This damn thing," he said. "Promise me you won't get old and sick, Jonathon."

"Not sure we have much of a choice in that," I said.

"Well, that's true I suppose. The old part at least," he said. "Not if we're lucky. It's the sick part that we could do without." He paused and sipped on his ginger ale. He took some deep breaths as Tiptoe jumped into his lap. "I should probably stop talking for a while. So, let's start catching up. Where has life taken you since I last saw you, when was that, 1973?"

"Yes, sir," I said. "Saturday, August 18 to be exact."

"Impressive," he said.

"Well, I kind of cheated," I said. "I've got it written down in my journal. I actually brought it with me."

"Even more impressive," he said. "In any event, bring me up to speed."

"Okay, but to do that right, I'll have to start from the day we met. You know I was pretty scared to meet you. I didn't know how that might go, especially with everything that happened that summer. My mom convinced me. She told me I'd be sorry if I didn't take you up on the offer. So, I did. But I was shaking in my shoes."

"Don't make me laugh," he said with a giggle. "It's not good for my lungs."

"Well, it's true. I was only thirteen. I still remember when Ed Klein walked me into his study. It seemed like it took forever just to walk down the hall. You were sitting in a big leather chair. I sat down across from you and you started talking. I don't even know if I muttered a word. They say you should never meet your heroes because they'll always disappoint you. That has usually proven to be true for me. Except once, when I met you …"

"Oh, stop it now …"

"It's true," I continued. "You were this larger-than-life figure to me. My parents drilled in me that you were such a private person and wished to be left alone. All that did was stir up the curiosity of my friends and me. You were this mysterious figure. Kind of famous, actually."

"More like infamous, I think you mean."

"No, I mean everyone knew of you. Wondered about you. Who you were …"

"What I looked like," he said.

"Well, sure, I suppose," I said. "Anyway, back to when we met, I don't know if I even said a word. But I listened and you said so much. Looking back, I don't know how I knew at that young age that I had just been handed a book of life lessons, but somehow I knew. I remember riding in the car on the way home, not even speaking. My mom just smiled as if she knew. As soon as I got to my room, I wrote everything down that I could remember in my journal."

I reached into my bag and pulled it out. I opened it to the flagged page from that day and handed it to Hank. He reached for a pair of reading glasses from the table. He held the journal close to his face and began to read to himself, struggling with my scribbles, occasionally asking me to help him with a word. He smiled as he read and dabbed at his moist eye with his handkerchief.

"I remember," he said. "You were a receiver. I could sense it. Thank you for sharing this. I'm deeply touched."

"I want you to know how much that day has shaped my life, steered me, guided me. See what I wrote in quotes at the top of the first page?"

"Don't waste it," he read.

"That's right. The last thing you said was ..."

"I remember," he interrupted. "I said, 'If you remember nothing else, remember this—don't waste it. Don't waste it.'"

"Right! And I've tried my best not to. It's my life mantra."

"Jonathon, you've filled me with joy."

"I'm glad."

"Continue. You've built a life. Tell me about it."

"I stayed in school. I wanted to go to college so I worked hard, got good grades. I went on to Ohio State where I studied English and literature. I read many of the authors that you told me to as part of my studies. My dream was to be an author. I wrote and wrote and wrote. I married my college sweetheart, Patti, as soon as I graduated. She loved the thought of marrying an author but wasn't too keen on supporting one. Being pragmatic got the best of me and I focused on starting a career instead. I got a job as a copywriter with an advertising agency and that was that. I'm an associate creative director now with a firm in Columbus. It pays well. I write for a living during the day. I write for myself every morning for two hours before the house wakes up and sometimes late at night. And that's about it."

"Sounds like you've built a nice life for yourself."

"So far, so good," I said. "Now, it's your turn. What happened after you moved to California?"

"After the trial, there was no way I could stay in Mansfield. I had a friend, Sam Boswell, who you'll learn more about, who had settled here in San

Francisco. In fact, in this very apartment. He coaxed me out here. He graciously took me in, so to speak.

"I was in a sorry place. The incident, the trial, the threats, just everything. This on top of already being so withdrawn I didn't want to go outside. I wouldn't even get on an airplane. Ed Klein drove me out here himself. With Sam's help, I found my independence. It took baby steps, and I owed him so much. Think about this. I met him in the army and we became intimate. We fell in love. When I shipped off overseas it was dreadfully painful for us both. Then I was wounded. Long recovery. He went in a different direction. Oh, and here's the cherry. I was married at the time. Bet you didn't know that. Anyway, moving out here. This neighborhood welcomed me. Nobody judged me. I found comfort. I stopped being scared of my own shadow. After a couple of months I got my own place, not far from here. It's where I lived until a few years ago when I moved back here to be with Sam when he became sick.

"I need to rest for a second," he said. He rang a small copper bell that was on the table. Nathan came from the hall. "Darling, will you please bring my oxygen?"

I picked up the bell and studied it.

"That bell has been with me since my recovery from the war," he said. "Margaret got it so I could hail her when I needed something. Funny how sentimental things become more valuable over time."

Nathan returned with a portable oxygen tank on wheels and helped wrap the tubes around Hank's head and place the tips in his nostrils, which were really just holes in his face among the scars.

"Thank you, dear," he said. We sat in silence, the only sound coming from the hissing of the tank. I looked at the IV and saw a constant drip from the bag. Nathan returned with a syringe of medicine.

"It's time for your Demerol, dear," Nathan said. He stuck the syringe in the extra port in the rubber tube taped to his wrist and pushed the liquid into it.

"Yes, thank you, darling," he told Nathan, before looking back to me.

"Now it's important that you understand what the Castro District was like in the '70s and '80s. It was a time of freedom of expression in every sense you could imagine. I look back on it now as a time of debauchery. Then I called it fun. I was living a life I could never have dreamed of. Keep in mind, when I moved to Mansfield, I did so with the intent of living out my life in that house with my sister. You can imagine how much my life had changed. My writing became better. I was getting advances on new books and royalties on old ones. I had a growing circle of friends. I had lovers. There was no such thing as safe sex. Didn't even know what it was. But then everything changed."

He leaned his head back and his mouth opened. For a moment he appeared as I imagined death looked. I stayed silent. Nathan gave me that look again, grimaced, and slowly shook his head before Hank lifted his head back up. Nathan whispered at me, "He's going to fall asleep."

"What?" he was startled. "Where was I?"

"Debauchery, my dear," Nathan said.

"Oh, yes, the debauchery. Good times roared. We had some good times, didn't we, dear? Didn't we? Oh, boy. I'm tired. Blanket. Blanket, please." He leaned his head back again. "I moved out here with Ed. No, not Ed. I moved to be with my lover. Samuel. He was my lover, isn't that right, Nathan? My long-lost love. Oh, yes, that boy Steven. He was in my way." He smiled.

Nathan rose and returned with a blanket and placed it over Hank who began to snore.

"The Demerol puts him to sleep," Nathan said to me. "I should have warned you. I'm sorry. It makes him a little cuckoo. Not uncommon for him to break into gibberish talking about the past, talking about things that only happen inside that thick head of his."

"No need to apologize," I said. "I understand. What's going on with him? If I could ask."

"Better he tell you the details," Nathan said. "But he's very, very sick. Cancer. And he's declining quickly."

"I'm so sorry," I said.

"You have no idea how important it is to him that you're here," Nathan said. "He'll be fine when he wakes up. You're welcome to stay, or if you want to come back, whatever you want."

"Thank you," I said. "Do you mind if I ask, how long have the two of you, been, you know ..."

"Oh dear," Nathan interrupted me. "We are not, you know, not partners. We are just friends. Great friends. I moved in to help take care of him. We're too old for those shenanigans anyway. Besides, he's not my type. Too much an introvert for my taste."

"I couldn't help but ask. Just curious."

"Of course," he said. "Of course."

"If it's okay," I said. "I'd like to stay. I have plenty to do, and I'd like to be here when he wakes up."

I pulled my laptop out of my bag and began to catch up on work. Even in sleep, attached to the IV and oxygen, his body shrunken, his mouth agape, he was dignified. All I believed him to be thirty years ago still held true. He had already charmed me, humored me, and welcomed me at his most vulnerable moment.

"Where was I?" he awakened. "I was somewhere. Where was that? I'm still alive, aren't I? A gift or curse? That is the question."

"Risen from the dead once again," Nathan teased. "Good afternoon, Sunshine. I believe you were at debauchery."

"Ah, yes. Debauchery. Is that what I was bragging about? Ah, the debauchery of it all. Yes. What was the last thing I told you?" he asked me.

"You were describing what life in the Castro District was like when you moved here," I said. "And then mentioned something about, there was no such thing as safe sex, and everything changed."

"Ah yes," he continued. "They called it the gay plague. The gay cancer. The HIV virus. AIDS. It ravished the neighborhood. Decimated it. Destroyed our lives, didn't it Nathan? Our friends dying right and left. The amount of loss was incomprehensible. Watching boys die such a horrible death. I didn't escape it. I was struck in 1992. Fortunately survived long enough for treatments to come.

Never went to AIDS. From that point on, safe sex was the rule. For most of us anyway. There were boys who continued to be as careless as ever. Just awful. Remember Elvin, Nathan? That boy was a pest.

"Sam and his partner, Steven, both contracted HIV which turned into full-blown AIDS. Steven died in this very apartment, the bedroom down the hall on the left. Sam and I were with him. Nathan was here. So were some other friends. I loved that man. Not like Sam loved him. I mean Sam adored him. Full commitment. I understood why. Steven was an adorable sort. I wasn't so much jealous as I was envious. Shortly after his Stevie died, Sam asked me to move in with him. He was devastated. We were never lovers again. Too old. We cuddled. We hugged. I helped him regain his footing, as he had helped me regain mine years earlier. You know, I loved that man since 1944. I cherish that time I had with him. Within about two years his health deteriorated to the point he just started to wilt away, didn't he, Nathan? He died in the same room Steven did, down the hall. My room now. It'll be where I die, God willing. He had been in the hospital because we couldn't manage his care anymore. But he wanted to come home. One afternoon, another friend and I were visiting him. The three of us went outside to sit on the bench and catch some fresh air. A cab pulled up in front of us. Sam said, "Let's go home." We unplugged him from his IV and loaded him into the cab and brought him home. He died four days later.

"He was an artist. All the paintings on these walls were his. He had a warehouse full of them. He left them to the International AIDS Society who auctioned them and raised over $3 million dollars. Sam taught me who I am. He set me free, gave me purpose, filled me with courage, and kept my dream alive. We fell in love when I was just nineteen when it was forbidden to be gay in the service. Not to mention that I was married at the time. Did I mention that earlier? I don't believe I did. Margaret. My high school sweetheart. A wonderful woman, God rest her soul.

"When I was so badly wounded, Sam and I lost touch. Over the years, we had a few chance encounters, but he had moved on and found Steven. I stayed married until 1971. Both of us did our best to honor our wedding vows but I was a deplorable recluse, too scared, embarrassed, and humiliated to show my face to the world. She found out about Sam. No small detail there. It was too much for her. She found someone else and we divorced. We remained friends and stayed in touch. That's when I moved to Mansfield to live with Eliza, my sister, may she rest in peace. The rest, I think you know."

"Can I ask a personal question and go back to the shooting?"

"Of course," Hank said. "Nothing to hide."

"Who was Walter Brunson?"

"Ah, Walter. He was my friend, a wonderful man. Crippled from polio. Needed a wheelchair. Ed Klein introduced us, figuring two gay cripples would get along. And we did." He chuckled and smiled.

"What happened to him?"

"Our relationship didn't continue after I moved out here. We stayed in touch at first, but I lost track of him. I learned he passed away quite a while ago."

"He was a witness at your trial, wasn't he?"

"Yes, he was."

"That was crazy," I said. "I listened for the verdict on the radio. I was so happy when you were found not guilty. My parents were in the courtroom."

"Oh, I know they were. Ed Klein and your mom and dad were my rocks. How are they, by the way?"

"They're hanging in there," I said. "Thanks for asking. They are both losing their memories. My brother looks after them. They are so happy I'm out here with you."

"Please give them all my love," Hank said.

"Certainly will," I said.

"Now Jonathon," Hank said. "I didn't ask you to visit me simply to catch up. I'm damned sick. Pretty evident, right?"

"Yes, pretty evident," I said.

"Well," he laughed. "You don't have to be mean about it."

"Sorry," I said with a smile.

"Now you're talking. About four or five months ago I was diagnosed with Kaposi sarcoma, a type of cancer common in HIV patients. I started to go through the chemo, radiation, and all the drugs, but it all made me sicker than the disease itself. Wasn't worth it. I stopped all treatment last month except for pain management, hydration, fluids, this IV thingy, and oxygen. It has metastasized now, in my stomach, intestines, and lungs. Just like the doctors said it would. Why do they have to be so smart? It's happening fast. Faster than I was ready for. It's killing me. I don't know how much time I have left. Could be a few weeks. Could be tomorrow. But, my friend, it's around the corner. Just don't know how far away the corner is."

"I'm so sorry," I said.

"Oh, don't be," he replied. "I've outlived all the odds. I should have been dead at nineteen. Do you know, they gave me my last rights three times? Gave me a 5 percent chance of living. I should have been dead at sixty-five. I'm old now. How much longer do you think I want to be around?" He chuckled, causing him to cough. He held the handkerchief to his mouth. Again it became bloody.

"But I've got unfinished business and now I'm in a hurry. First things first, did you happen to notice what is on the coffee table?"

"The manuscript I sent you," I said. I had noticed earlier but didn't think anything of it.

"No, it's not the one you sent me," he said. "It's a copy. The one you sent me is at HarperCollins."

"Excuse me?" I said.

"I hope you don't mind," he said as he handed me an envelope. "Open it up and read it. It's a letter from Fin Talbot. Fin's my agent."

September 8, 2003

Hank,

From the Dust is an outstanding piece of work. I sent it over to Bill and he thinks it needs some work, just as he says with all of your drafts. And don't get defensive, you know he's always right. Just ask him. But he is willing to work with Jonathon if Jonathon's willing to work with him. He and I both think we can get it to print and on the shelves. It's a good piece!

Have Jonathon call me and we can go from there.

Hope you're feeling better.

Best,
Fin

"How do you like them apples?" Hank asked. "You now have the A-team at your disposal with Fin and Bill. Bill's my editor. I hope you're not upset with me."

"Are you kidding?" I said. "Of course not. But you didn't have to do this."

"I wouldn't have done it if it was garbage," he said. "But you, my friend, *are* a writer. And you should be recognized as such. I was very impressed with your style, how you captured the emotions, your tone, context, everything. It's okay to get a little help. Nearly impossible for a first-time writer to strike a publishing deal these days."

"Well, I'm rather speechless," I said. "Thank you. When should I call him?"

Hank pointed to the phone on the side table. "No time like the present."

Hank punched the numbers on the cordless phone and held it flush to the side of his face.

"Hello sweetheart," he said. "It's your favorite human. Is your boss around by any chance? ... Hello, Fin ... Oh, good days and bad, you know ... I've been blessed to have a visitor this week, all the way from Ohio ... That's right. He's right here ... Do you have time now? ... Here goes, then. I'm turning the two of you over to each other. And with that, I wish you both good luck."

He handed me the phone. If anybody sounded like a New York City agent, it was Fin Talbot. He spoke loudly, quickly, directly, and decisively.

"What do you say we try to get this thing published?" he asked.

"I very much like that idea," I said.

"Good, Bill's taking a look. He'll get back to you. Don't be offended when he tells you it's a piece of garbage. That's his way of telling you that you need him. Take it as a compliment. I'm going to send some paperwork your way. Have a lawyer look at it if you want. It should be self-explanatory but call me with questions."

"Yes, sir. Thank you."

"What about Hank's project? Where are you with that?"

"Hank's project? Not sure what you mean."

"Oh, he hasn't mentioned it? Sorry, jumped the gun. We'll talk again after you two talk through it."

"Yes, sir. Sounds good. Thank you."

Hank smiled at me as I shook my head in astonishment.

"I don't know what to say," I said. "I won't waste the opportunity, I promise. He said something about 'Hank's project.'"

"Ah yes, my project. The real reason you're here. Would you perhaps be interested in another writing assignment? Before you answer, it might behoove you to know what it is."

"I'm intrigued," I said.

"I've got my affairs in order but for one thing. It's an obligation to Fin that I need help with. I've kept a diary since I was in high school. The only lapse when I didn't make any entries was when I was incapacitated during the war. My journals from the army were confiscated for a bit and one was never returned, the most important one to me.

"While I don't have a proper perspective on the life I've lived, others seem to think it's been rather interesting and there is a story somewhere in the crevices of all that journaling that I agree is meant to be told. I've worked on it intermittently over the past few years. One gets lulled into thinking they have forever. But since the cancer took control of my destiny, it has become too much. Fin's been pushing me. 'How are we going to get this goddamn thing done?' he keeps asking me. He said if I can't write it, he'll find someone else and asked me to leave my diaries to him. I was hesitant but felt I might not have much choice, until you showed back up in my life. Here is my proposition. I want to leave my diaries and journals to you for you to write my story. I've already explained this to Fin. He has a broader proposition for you at my request, bigger, no offense, than your current book. Well beyond, potentially.

"As much as I'd like to say you're under no obligation to do this, if you agree, I'll trust you to carry it out. There are other writers Fin and I have discussed, some are friends even. And I'm sure they would do a fine job. But they've all fallen into a mechanical sort of writing for their own genres. Not original. Your draft, *From the Dust*, is original. It's because you haven't become formulaic, which can happen to the best of us. Don't let it happen to you. There's some advice to remember. Anyway, your draft. It is really quite magnificent. There is a rawness to it that resonated with me. With how I want my story told. It might sound far-fetched—it did to Fin—but here's the other thing that draws me to you. You've known me longer than anyone else who's alive, except your folks.

"I always wake between two and four in the morning. Always have. I used to get up and write. During those two hours, my thoughts gel in an absolute truth. I'm most cognizant, most creative. Those thoughts have always proven to be most dependable. It's when I make the best decisions. Anyway, last night, as usual, I woke. I thought about Jonathon Smith. I considered our relationship, how fortunate we reconnected. I wondered how different it might be had we somehow stayed connected over the past thirty years. How different we might both be now. How we might have become comfortable and taken all of this for granted.

"I was so deeply touched reading your journal of the day we met. I have thought of you often over the years. It would be much too presumptuous and arrogant, ignorant actually, to have believed I had touched you in some way. But I sensed that I may have. As I look in your eyes now, I see you that day, as the young lad, wide-eyed, on the edge of your seat, seemingly drawing yourself closer to me as I spoke with you. A receiver. Yes, indeed you were. I wonder, Jonathon, if there isn't some serendipitous magic of fate that has reunited us at this moment, when you can perhaps nurture the seeds that were planted that day. Nothing I told you was scripted. It would not normally be like me to preach from such a high pulpit as you seem to recall. As the saying goes, a teacher can only teach if the student is willing to learn. I surmise that you came to me that day as a student, searching for answers, guidance, direction, a North Star. Serendipity and fate. Aren't they grand jewels? I need someone I can trust. Someone who cares about me. Someone who can write! And I think that person is you. We'll work on it together for as long as I'm around. What do you say? Are you still intrigued? Do you want to be a writer?"

I resisted as long as possible before allowing the tears that gathered in my eyes to run down my cheeks. But when they began to flow, they took off. Hank gave me his bloody handkerchief, reached for my hand, and wrapped his fingers around mine. I felt such love for this man. I was blessed to be with him. Also burdened by the unmitigated responsibility he had levied on me.

"It's okay, my boy," he said. "Tell me, are these tears of sadness or of joy? Of fear?"

I wiped my tears and snot on my arms and took some deep breaths. "It's everything, I believe," I said. "Feeling a little overwhelmed by everything."

"Yes, I suppose so," he said. "You can say no. I'll think nothing less of you."

"No, I mean, yes, I want to be a writer," I said. "I don't think you're leaving me much chance to say no."

"That was the idea," he said.

"Well then," I said. "I am honored. It's a firm yes."

"As I expected," Hank said. "I imagine this could take one, maybe two years," he said. "Do you understand? Full time. Head down."

"But ..."

"You're thinking, what about your job, you've got a family to support. Two cats and a dog."

"Yes, of course I am."

"I will compensate you handsomely. Need not worry."

"I can't accept that," I said. "No way."

"Jonathon, I'm asking you to work. This isn't charity. This is a job. I've made a good life for myself. Plus, Sam left me too much money. I'm leaving enough for Nathan to live out his life comfortably and giving the rest to charity, but there is plenty to go around. I can't take it with me. I've got a number in my head. $400,000. Is that enough? Do you need more? Figure that could tide you over for a couple years?"

"That's ridiculous," I said. "Way too much. Nearly twice what my salary would be for two years."

"I'm not going lower," he said. "Let's do half a mill. That's the deal. Take it or not."

"Jesus," I said. "Can I at least talk it over with my wife?"

"Of course," he said. "But we need to know because we've got work to do."

"I'll call her this evening," I said. "How do you see this working? Are you going to send me home with everything? How do we work together?"

"I'll need you here for some period, at least," he said. "There is a lot to review. I don't think we can do this long distance."

"How long?"

"A couple weeks, perhaps. Or as long as you want."

"This is a lot to think about."

"Yes," he said. "I'm tired now." He rang the bell. "Nathan, I'm ready for my punch." He paused. "Let me ask you one more time. Do you want to be a writer?"

Chapter
49

NATHAN MET ME at the door Tuesday morning.

"Welcome, my lad," he said. "Come, come."

I greeted him and followed him inside.

"Hank hasn't blessed the day with his presence yet," Nathan said. "The chap had a restless night. Let me go check in with him and help get his skinny old butt out of bed."

I stood and surveyed the apartment that could be featured in *Architectural Digest*. The French doors behind the couch were open to the balcony and the street sounds filled the room. I sauntered around, not to be nosey, just curious. Off the main room to the right was a hall that led to several bedrooms, or living quarters as Hank described them. I peeked down the hall to the left that led to a spacious kitchen, a library, and a dining room, which featured a table that could seat twenty. On the table were dozens of three-ring binders and several boxes full of papers.

"Ah, you've found our office," Hank said as Nathan helped him into the room and onto a seat at the head of the table, IV stand and oxygen tank in tow. "Have a seat."

I sat and surveyed the overwhelming amount of content in front of me.

"Did you talk with your wife?" he asked.

"Yes."

"And?"

"She said I was crazy," I said.

"Of course she did," he said.

"Then she said, 'Follow your dream. Sounds like you're going to be a writer.'"

"That's a good woman," Hank said.

Nathan returned to the dining room with a syringe full of Demerol. "It's that time again, darling," he said to Hank. "Last shot was four in the morning. You are long overdue."

Hank continued to talk as Nathan pushed the Demerol into Hank's vein. "These binders contain all my journaling, from 1942 to the present day. In the boxes are random notes, research, other stuff probably not important. Everything is ordered chronologically. I've flagged various topics with these sticky things on the pages. Different colors for different topics. Took me almost a year. I got to relive my life nearly one day at a time. Cathartic, you might ask?"

"Was it?"

"In a way," he said. "I relived my journey. A journey of survival. A journey of love, loss, hope, forgiveness, redemption. Discovery. Reclamation. I wouldn't have wanted any other life. It's been grand."

I picked up the first binder in the stack closest to me. It was labeled *January 1942 – December 1944*. "May I?" I asked Hank as I opened it.

"Of course," he said.

"It's a bit hard to read," I said, noting the messy handwriting.

"Oh, yes," he said. "It gets easier the rest of the way. One of the benefits of losing my right hand is that I had to start typing after the war. Will make your job easier."

We both spent thirty minutes perusing the enormous amount of content in front of us. He began rifling through binders and boxes in no particular order. I picked up the second binder and began to skim through it.

Hank got up from his chair and steadied himself with the stump of his right arm on the table. He dug deeper into one of the boxes, muttering to himself, "I'm sure this is in here. Where is the damn thing? It's got to be here somewhere. I'm sure of it. Oh dread, what am I even looking for? This Demerol is stealing my mind."

He sat back down and began coughing. He rang the bell and called for Nathan. "Yes, darling," Nathan said. "What is it?"

"Where is that thing?" he asked Nathan. "Did you move it?"

"What, dear, are you talking about?" Nathan asked. "What thing?"

"I don't know. It was just here," he said. "Never mind. I'm tired. Help me, chap. To the master."

Nathan gave me his all too familiar look and helped Hank rise from the table and shuffle down the hall.

"The Demerol fog," he said when he returned. "Sorry about the timing. He usually gets the first hit around nine o'clock in the morning so he can recover enough to stay lucid into early afternoon. He was sleeping too soundly this morning. I had to wait. It's a roller coaster."

"I understand," I said. "Maybe I should time my visits better."

"Perhaps," he said. "But I doubt it would matter much. I'm so worried about him. He's in bed most of the time when you aren't here. I don't want to overreact, but sooner or later it will be time to call hospice."

"I don't want to exacerbate things," I said. "Is it too much, what we're trying to do?"

"Oh no, on the contrary. Your visits cause him to rise to the occasion. I can see the life in him when you're here. My advice to you is to go full speed when he's able. And promise you won't weep over him. Remain a ray of sunshine. That's his oxygen."

I turned my attention to the stack in front of me. I counted thirty-seven binders, about one hundred pages each. A total of 3,700 pages—the equivalent of reading James Joyce's *Ulysses* five times—though I hoped the journals wouldn't be as arduous.

I randomly parsed through the binders to try to get an idea of what I was up against. On the bottom right corner of each page, Hank had managed to scribble by hand the page number and the corresponding binder number. The first page of the first journal was marked, P1B1. The second P2B1, and so forth. Sticky Post-it notes of all colors poked out from the paper's sides. Many pages were dog-eared for some significance I hoped to learn.

Rather than become overwhelmed by the seemingly insurmountable task, I decided to wait for Hank to return with some direction. I found Nathan to be wonderful company. He had met Hank and Steven about twenty years earlier. They ran in the same circle of friends. He laughed reminiscing over the stories of Hank's lovers over the years, again admitting that Hank wasn't for him. "Couldn't get over the fact that he had no nose," he roared. He went on to say that once a person got to know Hank, they never saw his scars again.

"Can I ask what is probably an inappropriate question?" I said.

"I don't know," Nathan said. "Can you?"

"Why didn't he ever get more surgery, you know, on his face?"

"Good question," Nathan said. "You know he lost all his military benefits, including health care. 'Cause he's a fag. Do you believe that? I think after he moved out here, he didn't care anymore. He can certainly afford it. I just don't think he gives it a thought. Or maybe it's an act of defiance, kind of like shoving it up the butts of whoever might care."

"I'm actually glad to hear that," I said. "He's such a gem."

"Hank is the kindest person I've ever met," Nathan said. "For someone who has every right to be bitter at the world, he emanates peace and serenity. He was, is, a magnet. People flock to him like bugs to a light. The saddest thing for him, me too, has been to lose nearly all our friends. AIDS, cancer, old age. No one gets out alive. A big piece of him died with Sam. There was a layer of joy that disappeared and never returned. The cancer diagnosis barely phased him, though. He is at peace. But he's not ready yet because of this damn book."

"No pressure," I quipped.

"None whatsoever," Nathan laughed.

"I don't even know what the story is about yet," I said.

"You'll figure it out," he said, pointing to the binders. "It's all in there. Somewhere. The thing is, Hank's not always clear about what he wants. Half the time he makes no sense. I think he and Fin have different expectations. You'll figure that out too."

The bell rang from Hank's room. Nathan went to attend to him. Five minutes later Hank appeared from the hall and joined me at the table. "I'm glad to see you didn't run away," he said. He had spots of blood on his shirt that Nathan dabbed at with a wet cloth.

"Let's get started," he said. "I'm quite proud of my system of organization per topic. Here is the color key. Orange is immediate family. Yellow, my former wife, Margaret. Blue, the army. Green, my writing career. Pink, my loves. Purple, my cause, my mission, my book. The pages that aren't flagged are just a bunch of fluff. That's not to say they don't contribute to the context. So, you'll probably need to read every entry and judge for yourself. Another thing. Don't let Fin push you down a path different than mine. I fear you'll learn what I mean, and it will be too late for me to do anything about it."

"I don't even know what your path is yet," I exclaimed. "When are you going to let me in?"

"Two things," he said, changing the subject. "First, your compensation. Let's get it out of the way. I can either write you a check or wire the money to your account. Second, I'm working on an addendum to my will that will stipulate that you, and you alone, not only have the right, but also the responsibility to carry out my wishes. That'll teach Fin it's not his parade."

"Okay," I started. "You want to give me half a million dollars? All at once? Now?"

"Well, when the hell else am I going to give it to you?"

"I imagined there would be an estate or something."

"The hell with that. They would just tax it. It's a gift. You'll take it."

"But I could take the money and not write the book. You would never know."

"But you wouldn't," he said. "I already know that. Besides, Fin would sue you."

He began to laugh, which led to coughing up more blood. He couldn't catch his breath. Nathan hurried to his side with a cloth to wipe the gunk from his lips and chin and reattach the oxygen tube to his nostrils.

"Ah, fuck!" Hank barked. It was the first time I'd heard him really swear.

"Do we have the addendum typed up yet, Nathan?" he asked. "Gotta get this done now."

"Yes, master darling," Nathan said. "I'm working on it. Give me one more day."

"At this rate, I may not have one more day," he said. "That's a joke," he said looking at me.

"Not funny. Don't strike the fear of God in me like that," I said.

"Ah, the proverbial fear of God," he said. "What exactly is that? I think that's something that only happens to young people. I don't fear God. Rather looking forward to seeing Him. Have a lot of questions for Him."

"Well, *I* fear Him," I said. "*And* I have a lot of questions for Him."

"Don't rush it," he said. "You can read all this stuff later after you're home. I think the best use of our time will be to talk and spend time together."

"Agree," I said. "Waiting with bated breath."

"Bated breath," he said. "Yet another proverbial. Have you ever wondered how these things get started? I heard once they all started in Ireland, with the Irish. A couple of pints of warm beer and they get all philosophical on you. I knew a number of Paddies in the army. Wonderful men. Scrappy, tough. Witty as can be, quick with a limerick, a joke. And passionate. I always believed they made great lovers. Never found out for myself, though."

He lowered his head and gave it a slow shake from side to side, possibly reflecting on days gone by. I laughed at the thought of the proverb—days gone by. Or maybe he was tired. He was starting to come and go, in and out, his thoughts fluid one minute, foggy the next. I didn't know if it was the meds or the cancer, but I could sense when he began to travel to another universe.

"Are you okay?" I asked.

"What? Oh, yes," he said. "I'm right here. I'm sorry. I drifted, didn't I?"

"A little," I said.

"I'm sorry," he said. "They say it's not in my brain, the cancer, but sometimes I'm not too sure of that. I think I'd feel better lying down. Can you lead me to the couch?"

I helped him from his chair and grabbed the IV pole with one hand and his stump of an arm with the other. He couldn't pick up his feet, but slid them across the hardwood floor, the soles of his orthopedic shoes grabbing at the surface, making him unsteady. I supported him as he gently landed on the couch. He was like a feather. I put a pillow under his head and pulled a blanket over his body.

"Do you not love the sounds of Castro?" he asked. "More cars and motorbikes than in the old days, but the music still floats in the air, as lovely as ever. And the trollies. I'm going to miss their rings. Nathan, my dear, a ginger ale with a twist if you will. And fix my friend a scotch and soda."

"No, Nathan," I said. "I don't want a scotch and soda but thank you."

"That's your drink, isn't it?" Hank said.

"No," I said. "It's not. What made you think that?"

"Oh, I thought it was," he said. "Oh, right. That was your father's drink."

"What's your story, Hank?" I asked.

"Ah, yes, my friend. My story. Fin likes to call it the 'Hero's Journey.' I don't like that. I'm no hero. In fact, I've come to despise that term. But I will say ... I will say that ..."

"That what?" I asked as he started to fade.

"Some say I've paid a heavy price. That I've overcome. Been redeemed. That I've reclaimed my identity after having it stripped away."

"You are a war hero," I said. "Ed Klein told me that himself."

"And what exactly is a war hero?" he asked me.

"Someone who risks their life to save others, is willing to make the ultimate sacrifice, who pays an enormous price for their bravery."

"And what price might that be?"

"Don't you agree?" I asked. "Don't you see it that way?"

"Probably not the way you do," he said. "You see my scars. You see that I only have two fingers. A thumb. No toes. A stump for a right hand. No face, so to speak. Is that the price you're referring to? Tell me, Jonathon. Have you ever pitied me?"

His tone was changing. He asked me to help him sit up straight. He called for Nathan to bring him his oxygen. He became more attentive and asked me to sit next to him. He turned to face me and reached for my hand with his fingers.

"You don't need to answer that," he said. "It's not a fair question. Of course you've pitied me. How could you not? The world pities me. And the world has punished me. Herein lies my story, and I need to know that you can write it without pity. Without looking through that lens of, 'that poor man, Hank,' despite how you think I've been punished. And pitied. Do you understand?"

Nathan had joined us, sitting on the other side of Hank, an arm on his shoulder. A heaviness masked the sweet sounds from the street. Hank waited for me to answer.

"I honestly don't know," I said.

"That's fair," he said. "Nathan, will you go get my little charm box?"

"Jonathon, you're going to write a story of the human spirit. I am only the vehicle. Have you thought about your legacy? When you're gone, what remains? Is there a way one can continue to contribute to humankind?"

Nathan returned with a wooden box and set it on the coffee table. "Will you please open it, dear?" he asked. Nathan opened the box to reveal medals, badges, ribbons, more decorations than you'd find on the jacket of a five-star general. Hank reached for the medal surrounded by felt from the middle of the box and handed it to me.

"Can you read to me the word at the top of this medal?" he asked me.

"Valor," I read.

"And what exactly does valor mean?"

"Courage, heroism in the face of danger?"

"Correct," he said. "And what if I told you that, even though I still have these in my possession, they were stripped from me. Taken away as if they were never mine. As though they were a mistake. Whoops, didn't mean to give these to you. Erasing all acts of heroism or sacrifice. That they are only physical things, with no symbolism attached to them. No significance. No more valuable than this copper bell."

"I'd say that would be unjust," I said.

"And would you pity me?"

"Yes," I answered honestly. "I would feel sorrow for you. It wouldn't be fair."

"Ah, fair. What's fair? Is life fair? Does life keep score? I am the same person whether these are mine or not. Whether life is fair or not. In fact, I am a more whole person without these than I ever was with them. If I had remained Medal of Honor recipient Private Henry Earl Cummings Jr., that would have defined me. I would have never found my true self. I would have never found redemption. I would never have been given the chance to climb back up from such a deep recess. The army deemed me worthy until they found out I loved a man. I was no longer worthy in their eyes. They punished me. Stripped me of my existence. For thirty years I was a prisoner of my own war, secluded, embarrassed, humiliated. An outcast. A hero? Defined how? By whom? Fair? You see, Jonathon, the only way one can truly be a hero is to be a hero of your own life. As you define it. Not as others might. Understand?"

"Yes," I said. "I understand."

"I am not afraid of death. What I fear is being forgotten. I fear my life will have been in vain. That it will be as worthless as these medals are, physical things with no significance. That I've come through all of this, and there'll be nothing to show for it. That is my story. It is all there," he said pointing to the binders.

"One may think this is ego driven, wanting my story told. If that's how it's written, it will prove to be. Ego, that is. So, Jonathon, you must promise you're able to write it as egoless. It's nuance. For it is not my story. It's a story of the human spirit. This isn't a story about loss. It's a story about gain. It's not a story about travails, it's a story about the strength to survive. About dreams. About hope. Have you read Viktor Frankl's book, *Man's Search for Meaning*? Frankl is a Holocaust survivor. Does that make him a hero? Do you think he allowed himself to be defined by others? Or did he define himself?"

"Darling," Nathan interjected. "It's time for your shot."

"Not yet," Hank said. "I need to be clear. My mind is working now. I'm on a roll. Sharp now, right? Yes? So I believe at least. Jonathon, do you know that I've had over fifty books published? And not one was credited to Hank Cummings, four to H. E. Cummings, granted. I might be the most prolific pseudonym writer who ever lived. I told you about Frederick Ervin and Richard Oakley. I haven't told you about my others. Terrance Mains. Look him up. He became a leader of the gay rights movement in the '50s and '60s. He wrote about the injustice of gay soldiers being stripped of their identities by being dishonorably discharged from the service in WWII. I haven't told you about Marion Burgess. Look him up. He became a big thorn in the side of the government, exposing the inhumane treatment of gay soldiers who were court-martialed, imprisoned, locked up in stockades, their lives ruined. He had more to do with the 'Don't Ask, Don't Tell' movement than anyone. I played the two authors off each other. Mains and Burgess were the heroes. Not Hank Cummings. What mattered is the military has transformed its ways. What matters is soldiers are no longer court-martialed and imprisoned for being gay. What matters is that a gay man or woman can serve this country and exhibit as much bravery as anyone else. Those are the things that matter. Not that Hank Cummings did squat. It's not about me. It's about the cause."

"But why?" I asked. "Why not be recognized for it? Isn't that the legacy of not being forgotten?"

"Two reasons. First, I wanted to remain a hidden figure. Not only did I not want fame but I also hid from it. Second, because it's not about *my* legacy. It's about *the* legacy. That's the story."

He sighed deeply and leaned his head back. "Nathan, dear, please put me in la la land now. I rather hurt."

Nathan was ready with the syringe. After he injected it, he helped Hank from the couch and to his room.

"I'm trusting you understand now," Hank said to me as he turned toward the hall leading to his bedroom. "Maybe that's enough for today. I'm so tired. Help yourself," he said, pointing to the dining room.

"By the way," he added as he turned back. "How do you like, 'By Jonathon Smith, as shared by Henry Earl Cummings Jr.?'"

I was confused. It seemed he wanted it both ways and that didn't leave an angle or foundation from which to write. Nathan returned after he tucked Hank in.

"Do you get it?" I asked him. "Is it just me?"

"Do I get *it*?" he asked. "Is that what you're asking? Or are you asking if I get *him*? Before you answer, let me tell you I'm not sure I get either."

"Why is he so hell-bent on not being recognized for anything?" I asked.

"Because he spent nearly a lifetime grooming himself to be invisible," Nathan said. "A ghost. I think it's bullshit. So does Fin. You need to talk to him. I think you'll find he has a different idea for the book."

"What's his idea?" I asked.

"Better I not speak for him or get in the middle of this," he said.

"Fair enough," I said as I gathered the first three binders and took them to my hotel. The only way through this was from the beginning.

CHAPTER
50

GOOD NEWS DID NOT await me when I arrived at the apartment Wednesday morning. The previous evening when Nathan was trying to help Hank to the bathroom, he collapsed and could not get up. He relieved himself on the bedroom floor, covering himself with urine and bloody diarrhea. He was in bed when I arrived, a fresh shot of Demerol coursing through his veins.

"I called his doctor. He said it's time to call hospice," Nathan said. "I don't know how to manage this. Blood in the stool. It's one of the symptoms of the sarcoma we were told to watch for. It likely means a perforated bowel. He's bleeding. Oh, Jonathon. I'm sorry. I know you didn't count on this, but I'm glad you're here."

"I agree, calling hospice is the right thing to do," I said. "And I'm glad I'm here too."

"By the way, we finished the addendum to the will," Nathan said, handing it to me. "He signed it and I witnessed that he was of sound mind and body. I have a check for you too. He slightly amended your agreement. Half now. Half when the book goes to print. Will that work?"

"Yes," I said. "Actually much more comfortable with that arrangement. This is still the craziest thing imaginable."

"I've seen crazier with the man," he smiled.

I sat at the table and read the addendum, which covered specific requirements for the book, including a draft outline Hank had prepared. It was convoluted and messy—more confusing than the direction he'd given me, as if that weren't messy enough. There was no doubt there was a treasure trove in the voluminous amount of content I had to work with. How to put it all together was going to require the faith with which Hank had anointed me.

From his addendum:

The story is to be about philosophy, about the richness of the human spirit and the fruits that come with the labors of perseverance. It is a hero's journey without the hero. For the hero is all humankind. My experiences and any accomplishments or accolades one attempts to cast on me is insignificant to the universe. I simply cast the stone in the middle of the lake. The rings that resonate—therein lies the story.

Faith. Faith. I told myself, faith. I opened binder number four and continued reading.

"He wants to see you," Nathan said.

I stepped into his bedroom. It was bright and airy, the walls covered by murals of the same genre as Sam's paintings in the living room. He lay stretched in his king-size, four-poster bed. Traces of blood stained the white sheet, which lay over him. His appearance had changed remarkably from the previous afternoon. He was ashen, his arms laid still across his chest, his breath labored.

"Hello, my friend," he whispered.

"Hello, to you, my friend," I said.

"Sit with Hank," he said.

I pulled a chair close to his bed.

"Well, this wasn't exactly planned," he said. "You must feel like I invited you all the way out here just to watch me die. Even had I planned it, not a bad week together was it?"

"No," I said. "A wonderful week. It's been truly amazing. A gift."

"Nathan showed you the addendum, I trust?"

"Yes, he just did," I said. "You are quite generous."

"You're not upset with the new arrangement?"

He started to cough. I knew to quickly grab for the washcloth on his bedside table and cover his mouth to collect the blood. He struggled to bring up the phlegm from his throat, making squeaking and grating sounds as he coughed. He tried to sit up, reaching out to me for assistance. "Up, up," he tried to call out. I leaned down so he could wrap his arms around my neck and pulled his shoulders to help him become upright. His ribs stuck out from his back against my hands. He laid what was left of his frame against me. I called for Nathan.

"Oh dear," he said as he hurried in. "A bloody mess." I felt him dabbing a cloth against my back. He bunched pillows behind Hank and helped lean him back in an upright position. His coughing subsided.

"I'm good," he forced. "I'm good. I'm good."

"A matter of opinion," said Nathan. "But I'll take your word for it. Don't laugh. That wasn't a joke."

"Oh, Nathan," Hank said. "What to do with you? You're going to paint the walls, aren't you? You're allowed to move in here, just don't ever paint the walls."

"Never," Nathan said. "Promise."

"I promise to come back and haunt you if you do," Hank said. "I'll bring my mother, the Old Hag!"

"Do we need to talk anymore?" he asked me. "Regarding the book?"

"I have some questions," I said. "But they can wait."

"Wait? I don't have time to wait. What is it?"

"A little struggle," I began. "I understand and appreciate the philosophical direction you desire, the professorial nature of it. That is extremely rich, and I am on board. You've been clear that this is a hero's journey. I just don't know how to write it without the hero."

"Ah, I see," he said. "Hero, hero, hero. You and Fin think alike. Goddamn hero's journey. Have you spoken with him yet?"

"Not yet."

"Have you two spoken about this?" he asked Nathan and me.

"Not a word, darling," Nathan said, lying.

"Oh dear," Hank said. "So I appear to be mightily outnumbered."

Nathan went to Hank's dresser, removed the Medal of Honor from the box, and draped the ribbon around Hank's neck without objection. He positioned the medal flush against the middle of Hank's chest.

"You, my dear ..." Nathan said. "*are* a hero. If there is ever a time to properly accept this medal, it's now."

"I'm too tired to fight," Hank said. "You and Fin figure it out."

"Do you trust me with this story?" I asked him.

"Yes," Hank said.

"I promise I'll tell it in a way that would make you proud," I said.

"I'll bet it will make him blush," Nathan directed to me.

"Oh, I promise to make him blush," I said.

Hank smiled. "I think you're blushing," Nathan said to him.

"Tear the addendum up if you choose," Hank said. "I do think it was a bit preachy, trying to make a point. I trust you. I trust Fin. Write it as you see fit. And write it well."

"The first book published by Henry Cummings Jr.," I proudly said.

"It's about time, isn't it?" he said.

"Indeed, it is," I said.

He laid his head back against the pillow and closed his eyes. His mouth opened. I adjusted the oxygen tube under his nostrils.

"You rest, now," I said. He gave me a slight nod in agreement.

The hospice nurse's name was Beth Kearns. She was midsixties, pretty, full-bodied, her silver hair tied fashionably in a ponytail. Her presence proved that she'd been through this many times. She was warm, yet matter-of-fact. "There is no sugar-coating death," she said. "Only leaning into it and accepting it."

She spent over thirty minutes with Nathan and me before she asked to see Hank. She wanted to get to know the man first. I was glad to be able to add my small part, telling her what I knew of his days in Mansfield, the short time I spent with him, and how deeply he touched me. I felt a part of his life. Nathan painted a picture of a character who often held court over groups of people who adored and admired him. Of a man who dedicated his life to the causes of others, to justice, to right the wrongs, and to try to make the world a better place. Neither of us mentioned his physical appearance. It wasn't an intentional omission. I had stopped seeing his deficiencies. When Beth asked Nathan to introduce her to Hank, I stayed alone in the great room.

When Beth joined us after meeting Hank, she explained that the process of dying had begun. His organs were likely shutting down. The blood in his stool indicated internal bleeding in his intestines and maybe stomach. Ulcers, perhaps a rupture. His lungs were raspy, and his oxygen level was below 90 percent. His blood pressure was low. His heart rate irregular.

"When bleeding occurs to this degree," she said, "decline can come quickly. We could give him plasma, a transfusion, but that would just prolong things. I've spoken with Dr. Cattikay. He is not a candidate for surgery or any other treatment. I think we just try to keep him comfortable. Lots of pain management, morphine as needed. I'll get a catheter going, and I suggest lots of diapers. It's messy down there. Let's try to keep him clean and spiffy. He won't need to get out of bed anymore. I trust you're comfortable managing things. If you aren't, we could get him to a hospice house or palliative care."

"Nothing I haven't seen before, sweetheart," Nathan said jokingly. "He ain't going anywhere. We've got it covered."

She spent the rest of the afternoon with us, tending to Hank, as well as to us. Going over detailed instructions for care and being clear about what to expect. She said to call her anytime, day or night, and that she'd be back in the morning.

"I called Fin," Nathan said. "He's flying out this afternoon. He wants to be here."

I ran back to my hotel to retrieve some clothes and personal items. I wasn't going to leave Hank. The apartment had four bedrooms, enough space for me and Fin. Nathan and I took turns tending to Hank. Without resistance I let him take care of the messy parts. He teased me for my squeamishness.

Fin arrived at eleven o'clock p.m. He was short and plump, balding, with a bushy mustache. Quite different than I expected from the picture I'd found on the Internet featuring a much younger man. He greeted me as if we were long-lost partners, with a firm, long handshake, and a fond hello. He embraced Nathan, who kissed him on the cheek.

"Stop it with the smoochy shit," he said. "Where is the patient?" Nathan took him back to Hank's room. It was late and I was tired. After talking with Nathan for a while, I poked my head in to see Hank and say goodnight. He was asleep. I gave him a soft kiss on the forehead. Fin was sitting next to him slumped over, resting his head on the bed sleeping. Nathan and I had arranged to take shifts. I could catch a few hours of sleep before relieving him at four o'clock a.m.

When I woke to take over, I found Nathan in the same position as Fin was a few hours before. "My turn," I said as I woke him with a touch to his shoulder. Hank was deeply asleep. I checked the oxygen mask to make sure it was flush to his face and checked the oxygen reader clamped to his finger. It was dropping. A rattling sound was audible from his chest with each breath. I placed 20 mg of morphine under his tongue with a medicine dropper. I stepped out to let Nathan change his diaper and clean him up.

I stayed awake through my shift, continuing to monitor Hank's breathing and oxygen levels, keeping my eye on the catheter bag, which remained empty, a sign his kidneys were failing. The sun began to peak through the bedroom blinds, casting rays of bright yellow stripes across Hank's face and saturating the painted murals on the walls. He looked at peace. His arms were draped across his chest, just above his medal. As the sun crossed his eye, he stirred and let out a slight moan.

I whispered in his ear, "Good morning, Private." He smiled and reached for my hand. He smacked his lips together and pointed to his face. I held a straw to his mouth so he could sip his ginger ale.

"Thank you," he whispered. "I hurt."

I dropped another dose of liquid under his tongue. "Tastes sweet," he said.

"Breakfast of champions," I said.

"I had a dream that Fin was here," he said.

"Fin *is* here," I said.

"Oh, grand. Please bring him to me."

I knocked on Fin's door to wake him. "Your presence is requested."

Hank continued to decline throughout the day, his mind in and out of fog. At one point he summoned all of us to his bedside. "I'm dying now," he said. "Just wanted to make sure I said goodbye." As night came, he was still with us. None of us wanted to go to sleep. Nathan lay next to him in bed. Fin and I sat on the other side. We were surprised he made it through the night.

I returned to the guest room and lay down for a quick rest, only to be awakened by Nathan thirty minutes later. "He wishes to see you," Nathan said.

I entered the room and walked to Hank's side.

"Jonathon," he whispered. "Come sit with me."

EPILOGUE

New Yorker Magazine

November 2005

<u>*Celestial Valor*</u> *(HarperCollins) is the second book by fledgling author, Jonathon Smith. His bestselling nonfiction work,* <u>*From the Dust*</u> *(HarperCollins), the story of a woman who moved to New York City from Ohio to an apartment just blocks from the World Trade Center two days before 9/11, spent twenty-three weeks on the New York Times Bestseller List and has sold over 400,000 copies.*

His newest work, <u>*Celestial Valor,*</u> *tells the story of Henry Earl Cummings Jr., a distinguished WWII Medal of Honor recipient who was credited with saving the lives of three men when their B-29 crash-landed at their base in Guam. Cummings suffered debilitating burns during the crash and was given less than a 5 percent chance of survival. He was subsequently discharged from the service for undesirable behavior when his gay affair with another soldier was discovered. He was stripped of all military benefits, including his Medal of Honor, and numerous other medals and awards. He was often the subject of ridicule and cruel treatment from others, forcing him into a life of seclusion for three decades. He ultimately moved to San Francisco where he built a new life, no longer encumbered by his fear of the outside world. He became a prolific writer, publishing dozens of articles and books under various aliases. Due to the punishment he received at the hands of the military, he dedicated his life to changing the way the armed services treated gay soldiers. Under two different aliases, he published thirteen books on the subject and has been credited with being an influential voice in the Don't Ask, Don't Tell policy. He remained tirelessly dedicated to helping soldiers who, like him, had their identities stripped due to their sexual orientation. He sought no recognition for his achievements, choosing instead to think of the hero as the cause, not himself. Cummings died peacefully in his San Francisco home on September 26, 2003, with the author and friends by his side.*

Book excerpt from the bestselling novel, *Celestial Valor*, by Jonathon Smith

Celestial Valor
The story of Private Hank Cummings Jr.
By Jonathon Smith, as shared by Henry Earl Cummings Jr.

Chapter five
He would leave a part of himself behind in the Kentucky dirt, which he described as a fertile pasture of hope. When he was a child, his mother would frequently need to rinse the soil out of his mouth, he was so drawn to it. The air was pure. He would miss the fragrance of the bluegrass and manure, the glistening drops of dew that reflected the early morning light. He would never again groom or saddle a horse or walk one slowly around a muddy track.

The town of Grayson, whose people had once cheered for him as he led Grayson High to the basketball state finals for the first time in the school's history, and worshipped him upon his return from the war—Grayson's only Medal of Honor recipient—now assailed him with nasty looks and comments, gossip and innuendos, going so far as to leave signs in his front yard, reading: queer, homo, faggot, gimp, and molester. People would drive by and throw tomatoes at his front door. This, after the nature of his 'undesirable discharge' was revealed. The curse of loving another man.

He withdrew into the shadows of self-imposed confinement, attempting to vanish from the public eye ...

ABOUT THE AUTHOR

PETE McGINTY has seen life through the eyes of a roofer, bartender, bouncer, railroad track laborer, and auto racing photographer. As a writer, speaker, and brand consultant, he has had a vast career in marketing and advertising, observing and influencing how people think and behave. He is now putting his experiences of observation and curiosity to work through storytelling, creating characters beholden to deep flaws and abounding promises, and weaving tales rich with emotion.

Never straying from Ohio, Pete remains a Midwestern kid at heart. A graduate of The Ohio State University and a lifelong suffering Cleveland sports fan, fueled by caffeine and classic rock, he finds escape in love of family, travel, reading, furry creatures, and his home gym.

Pete can be found at www.petemcginty.com